Praise for Gary Gibson

'High-octane action, terrific future tech and a superbly imagined alien civilization help to make this a page-turning belter from one of our best exponents of hardcore SF adventure'   *Daily Mail*

'*Final Days* (A+) has all the characteristics that have made Gary Gibson such a favourite writer of mine: great style, flowing narration that keeps one turning pages, compelling characters and enough twists to keep me guessing'   Fantasy Book Critic

'Balancing flashbacks, sharp characterization and big-scale concepts, Gibson has produced a seriously entertaining sci-fi page-turner not afraid to throw in shocking moments of violence, or to take the plot in unexpected directions'   *SFX*

'With the second novel in the Dakota Merrick trilogy, Gibson stakes his claim to be considered alongside the leading triumvirate of British hard SF writers: Al Reynolds, Peter Hamilton, and Neal Asher. What Gibson does well, he does exceedingly well. He's great at creating convincingly realistic aliens – the fish-like Shoal and the waspish Bandati are brilliant examples of xeno-biological description – and very strong at manipulating genre tropes: here we have sun-destroying weaponry, god-like alien races, conspiracies spanning millennia and lovingly depicted starships . . . *Nova War* is a gripping read and a treat for all fans of intelligent space opera'
Guardian

'A cracking holiday read . . . I liked this a lot, in that it's a plot-driven old-school type of tale with some great new ideas to make it work. I think this is Gary's best to date, and look forward to the next in the series'   sffworld.com

Gary Gibson, who has worked as a graphic designer and magazine editor in his home town of Glasgow, began writing at the age of fourteen. His previous novels include the Shoal Trilogy (*Stealing Light*, *Nova War*, *Empire of Light*) plus the stand-alone books *Angel Stations* and *Against Gravity*.

Gary Gibson

FINAL DAYS

TOR

First published 2011 by Tor

This edition published 2012 by Tor
an imprint of Pan Macmillan, a division of Macmillan Publishers Limited
Pan Macmillan, 20 New Wharf Road, London N1 9RR
Basingstoke and Oxford
Associated companies throughout the world
www.panmacmillan.com

ISBN 978-0-330-51969-4

3 5 7 9 8 6 4

A CIP catalogue record for this book is available from
the British Library.

Typeset by CPI Typesetting
Printed and bound by CPI Group (UK) Ltd, Croydon, CR0 4YY

Visit **www.panmacmillan.com** to read more about all our books
and to buy them. You will also find features, author interviews and
news of any author events, and you can sign up for e-newsletters
so that you're always first to hear about our new releases.

Acknowledgements

Inspiration for this book originally came from two sources. The first is Kip Thorne's 'Black Holes and Time Warps: Einstein's Outrageous Legacy', where he speculates that one end of a wormhole, if accelerated to relativistic speeds, might allow for a form of time travel. The second is a piece written by Ray Kurzweil for edge.org, concerning the idea of transmitting information at greater than light speed.

Considerable thanks are owed to Phil Raines and Jim Campbell for ideas, suggestions and comments while I worked on an earlier draft of this book. Much gratitude is also extended to Ian Sales, whose detailed comments and suggestions helped keep me from falling on my face more often than I might have when it came to many of the finer technical details in the second half of the book. Any errors that remain are the responsibility of the author alone.

I should also say a debt of thanks to the staff at Tor past and present, particularly Julie Crisp and Peter Lavery, whose careful attention to detail and copious notes went a long way to making this book what it is.

ONE

They were making good time along the East Rampart, on their way back to Vault One, when all four life-support indicators for Stone's team suddenly faded to black. Jeff Cairns came to a halt, his pressure suit informing him, in a soft contralto voice, of a sudden spike in his adrenalin and heart rate.

You don't fucking say, Jeff thought sourly. He glanced automatically over the ramparts, his eye following the bright parallel lines of the path markers towards the truncated pyramid of Vault Four in the distance. He waited to see if the indicators would flicker back into life, his mouth suddenly dry and sticky.

Three other life-support indicators – representing Eliza Schlegel, Lou Winston and Farad Maalouf – still glowed on the curved interior of his visor. All three, along with Jeff himself, had been assigned to the first and second vaults for the duration of this particular expedition. Other icons – representing suit pressure, air supply and bio-functions – floated near the bottom edge of the visor, registering clearly against the black and starless sky.

Eliza and Lou, who had been walking a couple of metres ahead of Jeff, both came to a stop at the same time, their helmets also turning towards the fourth vault. Jeff listened, over the shared comms, as Eliza tried to raise Mitchell and the others, the strain becoming evident in the sharply clipped tone of her words.

The comms hissed as they all waited in vain for a response.

The East Rampart was one of four hundred-metre-high walls that connected the vaults together, forming a square when seen from above. For safety, the edges of the rampart were illuminated to either side by rows of softly glowing markers placed at regular intervals. It was a long way down if you somehow managed to wander too close to the edge.

Jeff turned to see Farad standing just behind him, his frightened eyes staring back at him through a smeared visor. The fingers of Farad's gloves were wrapped tightly around the handlebar of a steel containment unit, mounted on four comically bulbous wheels, and his lips were moving silently in what Jeff suspected was a prayer.

'Maybe we should go look,' said Lou, sounding like he was thinking aloud.

'No.' Eliza's voice was sharp, decisive. 'The artefacts are our priority. We have to make our scheduled rendezvous with Hanover's team at the Tau Ceti gate.'

Jeff turned to look back towards her. 'We can't just abandon them,' he heard himself say.

'Nobody's abandoning anyone,' said Eliza. 'If something *has* happened, I don't want to risk any more lives until we know exactly what we're dealing with. Besides, it might just be a temporary communications breakdown.'

'*Might* be,' said Jeff.

Eliza turned and shot a quick, furious look at him. *I'm tired of your insubordination*, she'd warned him more than once.

'Maybe Eliza's right,' said Lou, his tone conciliatory. 'We have to be careful.'

'So just what is it you're saying we should do if we don't hear from them?' Jeff demanded. 'Just *abandon* them?'

'You're not in charge here,' said Eliza, 'and we have our orders from Hanover.'

'I know we're expendable,' said Jeff. 'I'm under no illusions on that count.'

'Nobody's saying anyone is exp—'

'We can get to Vault Four with time to spare if we start out now,' Jeff snapped, his fear flowering into sudden anger; all that adrenalin couldn't go to waste. '*Fuck* the artefacts.'

'Really?' said Eliza. 'Would you like to share that sentiment with Hanover when we get back?'

'That could be *us* stuck in there,' Jeff insisted. 'If they're trapped and still alive, a rescue team won't get here from Tau Ceti for several hours, probably longer. They'd run out of air long before that.'

Eliza's expression suggested she was contemplating murder. *Typical military mindset*, he thought, almost able to see the wheels spinning in her head. It wouldn't be too hard to engineer an accident for him, not with a long, hard drop on either side of them. Unfortunately for her, everything they saw, heard or did was recorded by their suit's A/V systems.

'Dan,' Farad spoke into the sudden silence, 'his life-support indicator. It's back online.'

Jeff glanced down and saw that Dan Rush's icon had indeed flickered back into life, and it was followed a moment later by Lucy Rosenblatt's. Mitchell Stone's icon remained dark, however, as did Vogel's. The suit interfaces felt clumsy and old-fashioned, and again Jeff found himself wishing that a tangle of security precautions didn't prevent them from using UP-linked contact lenses.

'Dan, Lucy, can you hear me?' Eliza shouted into her comms. 'We lost track of you. Can—?'

She was interrupted by a brief burst of static, followed by a voice.

'Hey! Hey, is that you?' Jeff recognized Dan's voice. He sounded panicked, very nearly hysterical. 'Mitch and Erich are gone. It's just Lucy and me. We—'

'Slow down,' urged Eliza, as the rest of them listened in silence. 'Who else is there?'

'Just Lucy. Mitch and Erich, they . . . they just . . .'

Dan paused, and for a moment they listened to the sound of his amplified breathing, sounding loud and urgent and close within the confines of their helmets.

'What happened to them?' asked Eliza.

'We were up on Level 214. It's filled with these deep pits, dozens of them. They were down taking a look inside one, while Lucy and me stayed up above. Then it started to fill up with some kind of liquid.'

'And they didn't get out again in time?'

For a moment, it sounded like Dan was trying to suppress a sob. 'Not exactly . . . no. I'll send a video squirt over, maybe it's best if you just see what happened for yourselves. And . . . get here soon, okay? The tokamaks packed up all of a sudden, and it's pitch black in here.'

Jeff found himself watching Eliza as they listened. She had turned away, to look back towards Vault Four, but from where he stood he could still see her face through her visor, and her lips were pressed together in a thin and bloodless line. She clearly didn't want to have to go into Vault Four, but none of them did, not really, not when there was a chance that whatever had happened to the others might happen to them too. But Jeff knew that didn't matter. He knew, deep in his gut, that they had to make the attempt, regardless.

'We'll be there soon,' Eliza finally replied, glancing towards Farad's cart filled with its precious treasures. 'There's no way you can find your way back out to us?'

'No. It's too dark to avoid the chance of getting lost, and this part of the vault hasn't been secured yet. We can see some way with our suit lights, but not far enough to be sure exactly where we are. Don't want to wind up like Rodriguez, right?'

No, thought Jeff with a shiver, nobody wanted to end up like Rodriguez.

Dan's voice faded for a moment, and then came back. Jeff glanced down and saw the man's life-support icon flicker in that same moment.

'Lucy,' continued Eliza, 'how about you? Can you hear me?'

'Yeah.' Lucy's voice sounded tense with pain. 'I'm good.'

'You don't sound it.'

'Hurt my leg,' she replied. 'Had a bad fall.'

'Hang on and we'll be there soon enough. But send that video squirt over so we can get some idea what we're dealing with first.'

They watched the A/V from Dan's suit in silence, projected on to the curved surface of each of their visors.

Standard operating procedure specified that, even once a chamber had been declared safe by the reconnaissance probes, and pressurized prior to a thorough eyeball examination by the artefact recovery teams, pressure suits must be kept on until a team leader was certain there was no danger of contamination or some other, less predictable risk. Mitchell Stone's team had been tasked with just such an assessment.

The A/V showed two suited figures, as seen from Dan's point of view, kneeling at the bottom of a pit that looked about five metres deep, with a series of wide steps cut into the sides. The two men's helmets almost touched as one pointed at hundreds of indentations drilled into the lower steps, and arranged in stylized, looping patterns. One turned to glance towards Dan, and Jeff saw Mitchell Stone's face behind the visor.

The video blurred as Dan looked up suddenly at the shallow, copper-coloured dome of the chamber's ceiling high overhead. Jeff noticed a fourth suited figure waiting up above, and Lucy's face was visible through the visor: small and imp-like, loose wisps of her blonde hair pressing against the clear polycarbonate.

As Dan clambered up the wide steps, Jeff saw that half a dozen carbon arc lights had been mounted on tripods close to the chamber entrance. They cast incandescent light across dozens of pits, each one only narrowly separated from the next.

Dan then turned to look back down at the suited figures of Mitchell Stone and Erich Vogel, still crouching at the bottom of the pit. Without any warning, a viscous, oil-like substance began to gush out of the indentations, flooding the pit with astonishing speed. Jeff heard Lucy yell a strangled warning, and Stone and Vogel both jerked upright as if they'd been scalded. The liquid was already covering the top of their boots.

It was Rodriguez, all over again.

From the subsequent sudden blurring of the video, it was obvious that Dan had descended into the pit once more, in order to try and reach the two men. Stone and Vogel were already making their way towards the steps but, even as Jeff watched, he saw their movements become slower, as if the oil were congealing around them. By now it was up to their knees.

The oil appeared to defy gravity, racing up the sides of their suits and soon swallowing them both up in a black tide. Stone was the first to collapse, followed by Vogel a moment later. Jeff watched in mounting horror as their suits began to disintegrate, the metal and plastic dissolving and falling away from their bodies with astonishing speed. Jeff had one last glimpse of Stone's eyes rolling up into the back of his head, before they were both swallowed up by the still-rising tide.

The oil had behaved purposefully, like something alive, which made Jeff think of childhood monsters, of yawning black shadows filled with imaginary horrors. Tears pricked his eyes but he couldn't bring himself to stop watching.

The video jerked once more as Dan hurried back up and out of the pit, with understandable haste. Jeff saw Lucy step back, her face aghast, then, with a terrified cry, stumble backwards over the lip of an adjacent pit.

Dan said 'Oh shit' very softly, and Jeff watched with numb despair as he hurled himself down the steps of the neighbouring pit.

It was clear from the way one of Lucy's legs was bent under her, as she lay on the floor of the second pit, that she was badly hurt. Dan grabbed her up in a fireman's lift and rapidly made his way back to safety. And, even though Jeff could see nothing but the chamber ceiling through Dan's A/V, he felt an appalling certainty the second pit was already filling with the same deadly black oil.

And then, just as Dan reached the top, the lights went out.

They followed the rampart to where it merged into a tunnel leading deep inside Vault One. They moved on past branching corridors and ramps to either side, each leading up or down to other levels and chambers. The beams projected from their suits flashed reflections off hastily epoxied signs printed with luminescent inks, which were mounted near junctions that had not yet been fully explored. All carried explicit warnings never to leave the already lit paths.

Catching sight of these warnings, Jeff found himself thinking once more about Rodriguez.

David Rodriguez had been an engineer recruited to the ASI's retrieval-and-research branch several years before to help run the remote reconnaissance probes, but instead had quickly become the stuff of legend for all the wrong reasons. He was the one recruits got told about during their training and orientation, as an example of how *not* to conduct oneself when exploring the Founder Network.

He had been part of a standard reconnaissance into a then unexplored level of Vault Two, and had ignored the warnings about sticking to the approved paths. Instead, he had wandered into a side chamber, trying to find a probe that had failed to report back.

He had found the probe and, some hours later, his team-mates found him.

Time, it turned out, worked differently in the side chambers of that particular level. It became slower, the farther inside them you got. Rodriguez had discovered this when he stepped up next to the probe, probably thinking it had simply broken down.

He was still there, to this day: right foot raised and looking towards the far wall, his face turned away from the chamber entrance as he headed forward, still clearly oblivious to his fate. That alone was what really sent the shivers down people's spines; the fact that no one could see his face got their imaginations working overtime.

Rodriguez's team-mates, when they finally found him, had been a lot more cautious. One had thrown a spanner just to one side of Rodriguez's frozen figure, from the safety of the chamber entrance. It still hung there now, motionless, caught in the course of its long trajectory through the air, on its way to eventually landing in some future century. The reconnaissance probe – a wheeled platform mounted with cameras and a range of sensitive instrumentation – stood equally immobile nearby.

David Rodriguez, as new recruits to the most secretive department of the UW's retrieval and assessment bureau were told, had been a fucking idiot. The vaults were filled with unpredictable dangers, which was why they had to stick to the paths already pioneered by the probes. You wandered away from them at your own risk.

The current popular theory was that these slow-time chambers were stasis devices designed for long-term storage. Time-lapse cameras had been set up at the entrance, to try to estimate how long it would take Rodriguez to set his right foot down, turn around and walk back out of the chamber. The best estimates suggested anything up to a thousand years.

Sometimes Jeff woke from nightmares of Rodriguez still standing there, his face turned away, as the years turned into centuries. Sometimes he *was* Rodriguez, waking to find himself lost in the darkness of some future age, all alone on the wrong side of a wormhole gate that bored its way through time and space very nearly to the end of everything – a hundred trillion years into a future where most stars had turned to ashes, and the skies were filled with the corpses of galaxies.

They re-emerged from Vault One and followed the North Rampart until they reached Vault Four, half an hour after receiving Dan's distress call.

Beyond the vaults lay nothing but the blasted, airless landscape of a world that had been dead for immeasurable eons. The planet on which the vaults stood orbited a black dwarf: the shrunken, frozen remnant of a once bright and burning star whose furious death had long since stripped away any vestiges of atmosphere.

Dan, who was an expert in such things, had once told Jeff the vaults themselves were tens of billions of years old, meaning they had stood for longer than the entire lifespan of the universe as it had been measured back in their own time. They were constructed, too, from a material that resisted all attempts at analysis. Despite a near-eternity of bombardment by micrometeorites and other debris drawn into the planet's gravity well, the exterior of the vaults appeared as smooth and pristine as if their construction had just been finished.

Jeff glanced up at the towering slope of Vault Four, at the moment before they passed into its interior. He could hear Eliza talking to Dan and Lucy over the general comms circuit, trying to keep them calm, assuring them that help was almost at hand. He found himself wondering what they'd have to say once they discovered Eliza had been all for abandoning them.

Farad came abreast of him and tapped the side of his helmet: a request for a private link. At least Eliza had let him leave his cart of goodies back at Vault One, rather than wheel them all this distance.

'I have come to believe,' Farad told him, his eyes wide and fervent, 'that God must have abandoned the universe long before this time-period.'

Jeff regarded him in silence, but with a sinking feeling.

'Do you know what occurred to me when we heard about Stone and Vogel?' Farad continued, an edge of desperation in his voice. 'I could not help but wonder what, in the absence of God, happens to their souls.'

This wasn't a conversation Jeff wanted to be having right now. His feet ached, and the interior of his suit stank from the long hours he'd spent inside it. Stress knotted his muscles into thick ropes of fatigue.

'Their souls?'

'This far beyond our own time, the universe is dark; no new stars are being created. Most of the galactic clusters have retreated so far from each other that they are no longer visible to one another, and most of the galaxies themselves have been swallowed up by the black holes at their centre—'

'I know all this, Farad. They covered it in the orientations.'

'Yes but, if God is no longer here, what happens if you *die* here?' he demanded, his voice full of anguish. 'Where do you go? There is only one conclusion.'

'Farad—'

'Hell is, by its very nature, the absence of God, is it not?' the other man persisted.

Jeff stopped and put one hand on Farad's shoulder, finally bringing him to a halt. Farad stared back at him, his nostrils flaring.

'Listen, you need to calm down a little, okay?' Jeff told him. 'You're letting your imagination run away with you.'

Jeff glanced to one side. Eliza and Lou had moved ahead, apparently unaware that the pair had stopped. Up ahead lay a wide atrium, containing electric carts they could use for zipping about the 'designated safe' parts of the vaults.

Farad was a large, bluff man with a thick dark moustache, and he sometimes compared his attempts at picking apart the self-adjusting routines controlling the Vaults to a pygmy poking at electronic circuitry with a spear. He was intelligent and sharp, an excellent poker player – as some back at the Tau Ceti station had discovered to their cost – and also in possession of a keen sense of humour. But something about the black, unforgiving void that hung over the vaults, like a funeral shroud, could get to even the best of people.

It seemed to Jeff that the more intelligent people were, the harder it was for them to deal with witnessing a darkened universe far advanced in its long, slow senescence. Self-declared atheists began sporting prayer beads, while the moderately religious either discovered a new fervour for their faith or, more frequently, abandoned it altogether.

Farad refocused on him after a moment, and Jeff could see that his face was slick and damp behind the visor.

'I'm sorry,' said Farad after a moment. 'Sometimes . . .'

'I know,' Jeff replied, with as much sympathy as he could muster. 'But we'll be home in a few days. Remember, we've got a plan.'

'Yes.' Farad nodded, his upper lip moist. 'A plan. Of course.'

'You just need to hold it together for a little while longer. Okay?'

'Yes,' Farad said again, and Jeff could sense he was a little calmer. 'You're right. I'm sorry.'

Jeff gave him his best winning smile. 'You already said that.' He nodded, indicating somewhere further up the corridor. 'I think we'd better catch up.'

Eliza had glanced back once, but chose to say nothing as the two of them caught up.

They pulled a spare tokamak fusion unit from a pre-fab warehouse established in Vault Four's primary atrium and loaded it on to the rear of an electric cart, before letting it zip them up a steep incline that switched back and forth the higher they rose. When they reached Level 214, they found the passageways and chambers shrouded in darkness, so had to rely on their suit lights while they swapped the new fusion unit for the failed one. There was no telling why it had shut down, but inexplicable power-outs were far from unusual.

The lights strung along the ceiling flickered back into life, revealing closely-cramped walls on either side. An airlock seal had been placed across the passageway, and they stepped through it one by one, emerging into the pressurized area beyond.

Jeff wanted nothing more than to crack open his helmet and breathe air that didn't taste like his own armpits, but Eliza would have none of it. He understood the reasons for her justifiable caution, but still felt resentful.

When they entered the chamber that Stone's team had been studying, they found Dan had now managed to drag Lucy on to a narrow strip of ground located between four adjacent pits. The pit that had swallowed up Stone and Vogel was now full to the brim with black oil, its calm stillness looking to Jeff like a black mirror laid flat on the ground. It seemed strange that none of the reconnaissance probes first sent into this chamber had triggered a similar reaction.

The furthest walls of the chamber faded into darkness beyond the pools of light cast by the carbon arc lights. There were hundreds more of the pits, Jeff could see, stretching far out of sight. He watched from the chamber entrance as Eliza guided a limping Lucy back to safety, Dan following close behind. They had to shuffle along sideways, one at a time, wherever the edges of the pits came closest together.

He found himself wondering what purpose these pits might have served for the vault's architects. A garbage-disposal system, perhaps, the black oil being some universal solvent for breaking down unwanted items? Or perhaps they represented something more inexplicable, a puzzle that could never be solved – like so many of the artefacts that had already been recovered and brought back to their own time . . .

Something suddenly moved just beyond the illuminated part of the chamber, snapping him out of his reverie. Jeff stared hard into the shadows, then stepped forward. Lou and Farad were too busy arguing to have noticed anything, as they discussed how to recover a sample of the black oil, should it prove equally adept at dissolving any type of container they might attempt to collect some in.

'Did you see that?' asked Jeff urgently, turning back to look at the two men.

'See what?' asked Eliza over the comms, audibly puffing with exertion.

Jeff stared into the shadows once more. 'I'm not sure. Maybe it's . . .'

Maybe it's nothing, he thought. The vaults lent themselves effortlessly to the imagination, after all.

But he saw it again; a slight movement almost on the edge of his perception. Lou must have seen it, too, for he stepped up next to Jeff, unclipping a torch from his belt and shining its powerful beam across the chamber.

The torch revealed Mitchell Stone, naked and shivering, kneeling between two empty pits and blinking up into the light.

It's not possible, thought Jeff, in the shocked silence that followed. But a moment's reflection suggested otherwise. After all, the lights had failed almost immediately, so Stone might have managed to crawl out of the oil-filled pit, unseen by either Lucy or Dan, and then got lost. But why hadn't he called out for help?

'Jesus!' he heard Eliza exclaim, followed by a muttered prayer from Farad.

Stone raised one hand towards them, and then slumped forward soundlessly.

Without thinking, Jeff stepped forward and began to navigate his way towards him.

TWO

A few hours after emerging from the Copernicus–Kepler gate, moving lightly in the .85 gravity, Saul Dumont stepped out from the lobby of the Heping Plaza Hotel and soon found himself in the heart of one of New Kaiohsung's busy night markets. He navigated his way through dense crowds of shoppers, the air thick with the smell of barbecuing meat and *cho dou fu*. Their breath frosted where it emerged from ten thousand throats, while the street vendors were stained with orange light wherever they clustered under the tall municipal heating units rising above their heads.

Saul tilted his head back to catch a glimpse of Kepler's moon, its fractured outline floating cool and serene far above clustered high-rises and jerkily kinetic video advertisements. He brought his gaze back down, ignoring the occasional stares of passers-by, most of whom were immigrants from China, Korea and other Pan-Asian Congress nations. Saul's clothes and ebony skin, by contrast, screamed Western Coalition.

It wasn't long before he found his way to a quiet alleyway where he spotted Jacob Maks sitting in the window of a *shui-jiao dian*, forking steamed dumplings into his mouth with a pair of chopsticks. A TriView screen, bolted at an angle between the ceiling and rear wall of the eatery, ran news items piped through the local Array from back home.

14

Jacob looked up, in the middle of chewing a mouthful of pep-pered meat and cabbage, and started when he saw Saul enter. The new arrival pulled down the hood of his parka, and placed his brief-case on the floor next to Jacob's table.

Jacob gestured with his chopsticks to the empty seat across from him, the motion quick and birdlike. 'You want something? I'll buy.'

'First,' Saul replied, his tone even and careful, 'tell me why we aren't meeting at the hotel like we were supposed to, *Jacob*, or I might not be able to resist the urge to break both of your arms.'

Jacob's hands never remained still, constantly twirling the chop-sticks between his fingers or fiddling with the edge of his paper plate. 'I can always tell when you're pissed at me, Saul,' he replied, with a nervous twitch of the mouth.

Saul took the seat opposite, slow and easy as always. Jacob watched him cautiously, as if trying to assess whether he might follow through on his threat.

'You left me sitting there waiting in the lobby of the Heping for over an hour before you got in contact,' Saul persisted. 'I had no idea what was going on. You're *supposed* to keep me informed of any last-minute changes, so what the hell happened?'

Jacob cleared his throat. 'Look,' he said, putting the chopsticks down, 'this was a *very* last-minute change of plan. I couldn't call you without compromising myself. But, now you're here, you should know that we aren't meeting Hsiu-Chuan at the warehouse any more.'

'No?' Saul cocked his head, the movement typically slow and deliberate. 'Why not?'

'Apparently his security people didn't think it was secure enough, so they picked another location. Not a damn thing I could do about it. We're just lucky he didn't pull out altogether.' He leaned to one side and looked down at Saul's briefcase. 'Is that the bait?'

Saul nodded fractionally. 'What about Hsingyun? Do you trust him?'

Jacob had the courtesy to look offended. 'Of course I don't, but he's a street soldier looking for a fast promotion, and he's got too much to gain from helping us to want to screw us over. And remember, he's still the only real link we have connecting Hsiu-Chuan with the Tian Di Hui.' The Tian Di Hui, of which Hsingyun was a member, were a loose network of separatist groups that railed against the Western Coalition's monopoly on the wormhole gates.

'A pretty tenuous link at that, don't you think? One seven-second segment of footage showing Hsingyun and Hsiu-Chuan talking together, and that's it.'

Jacob smiled. 'Still more than enough to merit us being here, right?'

'I guess,' Saul sighed, leaning back. 'It looks like most of what he's been telling you checks out anyway.'

'Who did you talk to? Narendra?'

Saul nodded. 'I got back from Sophia just this morning. Narendra put out some feelers and, from what he's heard, the Tian Di Hui are moving on something. Could be big.' He shrugged. 'Hard to say just what. But according to Narendra, Hsiu-Chuan is involved, whatever it is.'

Jacob shook his head and chuckled. 'And you just asked me if I trust Hsingyun? I could ask you the same about Narendra.'

'And I'd give you the same answer.'

Jacob sighed and sat back. 'All right, *touché*. Look, as far as Hsingyun goes, as long as I pour enough booze down his throat, he's been happy to tell me pretty much anything I want to know. Which, if you'll remember, is how I managed to set this all up in the first place.'

'How worried should we be about the last-minute change of venue?'

Jacob shrugged. 'My gut tells me they're just being cautious. It took a lot to get someone like Hsiu-Chuan to even entertain the idea of doing business with a couple of strangers.' He drummed his fingers on the table top and gestured at the unfinished plate of dumplings, a plastic bowl full of chopsticks next to it. 'Eat something,' he said. 'It's going to be a long night.'

Saul shook his head. 'Not hungry.'

Jacob sighed. 'Try not to look so worried.'

'We really need,' warned Saul, 'to not screw this up.'

'Yes, I *know* that,' Jacob snapped, failing to hide his irritation.

Saul nodded, far from mollified. There had been talk about pulling Jacob out of the investigation once it seemed to be going nowhere. Then all of a sudden, like a magician pulling a rabbit out of a hat, he'd come up with Hsingyun: someone who could finally get them close to Hsiu-Chuan.

The details, long since memorized, span through Saul's mind like an endless loop. Shih Hsiu-Chuan was a rising star in the Pan-Asian Congress of Pacific Sphere States, popular for his aggressive stance in favour of full independence for the colonies administrated by the Sphere Congress and also the establishment of their own, dedicated network of wormhole gates. There had never been any solid evidence of a direct link between member-nations of the Sphere and the Tian Di Hui – nothing good enough to stand up in the international courts, at any rate – but showing that Hsiu-Chuan had been present at a Tian Di Hui-moderated meeting could change the whole distribution of influence between the power blocs for ever.

'I want to make sure we've got everything straight,' Saul said, as Jacob finished his meal and pushed his plate to one side. 'As far as Hsingyun or anyone else is concerned, I'm—'

'Donald Lassen,' Jacob interrupted, wiping his mouth with a tissue. 'You're an Earth-side broker for a private financial concern with a hefty reputation in the Western Coalition's underground economy. Your employers moved into the lucrative realm of biotech fencing after the global financial situation took a turn for the worse a few years back. You're ambitious, and you're willing to trade an illegally cloned black-box arbitration device, with a solid-gold record in market speculation, in return for becoming the Tian Di Hui's newest bulk distributor of illicit off-world materials. Have I got it all?'

Saul nodded.

'And, of course,' Jacob continued, 'I'm Victor Cowles, a small-time operator who runs an import-export company based in South-east Asia, as a cover for his real business, and who has formed a partnership with Mr Lassen, whom he regards as his ticket to the big time.'

'Sounds about right, but no more surprises, Jacob, understand? If there's anything else I need to know, now's the time. Starting with, *where* the fuck is the meeting taking place?'

'At sea,' Jacob replied, standing up. 'Offshore.'

Saul stared at him. 'You're shitting me.'

Jacob shrugged. 'Official Sphere jurisdiction stops thirty kilometres off the coast. Beyond that, it's effectively lawless.'

'So we're heading to one of the islands?' Saul asked, standing as well.

'Not exactly.' Jacob pursed his lips in thought for a moment. 'Well, more like an iceberg, really.'

'The meeting is on an ice-pharm?'

'A big one,' Jacob nodded, 'with a whole town carved into it.'

They found Lee Hsingyun in a dive bar near the docks, where the stars were far more easily visible than they were in the middle of New Kaiohsung. Saul had read through the names of some of the local constellations in a magazine article back at the hotel, but found he couldn't recall a single one. Nonetheless, one of those far away speckles of light, hanging over the snow-sprinkled concrete like frozen diamonds, was Sol, all of fifty-five light-years distant.

Hsingyun was small and wiry, with fashionably streaked hair and calculating eyes, and something about his manner made Saul take an instant dislike to him. Hsingyun and Jacob clasped hands like old friends as soon as they arrived there, but Saul still couldn't shake the feeling of unease that had been plaguing him since he'd first realized Jacob wasn't going to show up at the hotel.

Hsingyun led them to a private booth at the rear of the bar. From where Saul now sat, he could see another TriView running what might be the same news feed. The sound was inaudible in the noisy bar, but the closed captions running underneath, in both Mandarin and English, followed a story about Galileo. A series of rapidly cut shots, taken more than a decade before, showed separatist graffiti decorating various Galilean settlements, followed by footage of attacks on the ASI forces that had been sent in to quell the unrest.

The captions gave a voice to the images: 'Nearly a decade after separatist groups affiliated with the Tian Di Hui claimed responsibility for the destruction of Galileo's CTC gate, Sphere representatives are meeting with leading Coalition member nations in advance of the link's re-establishment.'

The scene changed to the UN building in Strasbourg. More than half the men and women mingling on a platform before an audience of journalists were from Pan-Asian Sphere nations, and of those the majority were probably representatives of the Chinese Confederacy. The rest came from affiliated nations like Malaysia and Indonesia, along with a smattering of black and brown faces drawn from Africa and the Indian subcontinent.

The commentary switched to cover an interview with a protester whose skin was even darker than Saul's. 'All we ask is for the same right to choose our destiny as enjoyed by citizens of the Western Coalition states, and that means full access to the wormhole tech-nology. We should be able to set up our own network of wormhole gates, so that the colonies can link to one another directly, instead of forcing people to pass through the Lunar Array every single time they want to move from colony to colony.'

'The Coalition States all say the Lunar Array is the only adequate means of providing support and protection to the colonies,' replied an unseen interviewer.

The protester shook his head. 'That's a lie,' he said angrily. 'This way, they control access to the colonies, and make them dependent on the Coalition. Everyone knows that what happened to Galileo happened because they tried to push for independence.'

'But separatist groups are believed to have been responsible for the collapse of the Galileo wormhole,' suggested the interviewer.

This time the protester laughed out loud. 'Well, I think it was a cover-up. The ASI did that deliberately, to stop the revolution spreading to the other colonies.'

'Saul?'

He dropped his gaze back down, to meet Jacob's. 'What?'

'Ignore that bullshit.' Jacob's hands tap-tapped on the edge of the table before him. 'Did you hear what Lee was just telling us about?' He gave Saul a meaningful look: *play along*. 'His new gun fires ice bullets.'

Saul shook his head. 'It's pykrete, not ice.' He had to shout it over the pounding music filling the otherwise empty bar.

'What the hell is pykrete?' demanded Jacob.

Saul looked at him with an expression of infinite patience. 'Ice water mixed with cellulose fibre,' he replied. 'The same stuff the ice-pharms are made from.'

Jacob looked surprised. 'It's just ice, isn't it?'

'Nope.' Lee shook his head. 'Pykrete's hard as steel, makes the pharms extremely resistant to a direct assault. Now, the guns have cooled chambers that—'

Just then a waitress deposited a tall green bottle and three glasses on the table between them. Hsingyun quickly poured them each a shot.

'A celebration,' he said, pushing a glass each in front of Saul and Jacob. 'Tonight we sleep as rich men.'

Saul recognized the brand as one containing a variety of power-ful synthetic psycho-actives native to Kepler. He caught Jacob's eye and nodded at him to come closer.

Jacob leaned over the table towards him and, for once, Saul was glad of the pounding music. 'Why are we drinking this shit?' he demanded.

'It's not that strong,' Jacob yelled in his ear. 'Read the label; it's a mild derivative at best. You'll get a bigger hit from the alcohol, I swear.'

'Mr Lassen,' Hsingyun raised his glass towards Saul with a smile that sent shivers down his back, 'if you will.'

Saul picked up his glass, unable to resist a certain fascination at the way the sudden movement made the gene-engineered biolu-minescent bacteria within the liquid glow more brightly. He knew the consequences if he failed to drink it.

He shot a quick, angry look at Jacob, when he was sure Hsing-yun wouldn't notice, and swallowed the contents in one go.

'So this ice-pharm we're going to,' Saul asked a little while later, 'what does it research?'

'They collect samples of sea-life, mostly microbial,' said Hsing-yun. 'As I'm sure you're aware,' he tapped the rim of his glass with a fingernail, 'the rewards for finding commercially exploitable gene-sequences are enormous.'

'And how many of the pharms are doing actual legitimate re-search, as opposed to just synthesizing illicit drugs?' asked Saul.

Hsingyun smiled enigmatically. 'We all need to make a profit to survive, Mr Lassen, whatever rules the Coalition may impose on us.'

Playing his part, Saul patted the briefcase next to his knee and grinned. 'Couldn't agree more.'

Hsingyun nodded. 'Money is the only thing that matters, what-ever world you're on. If you don't know that, you're just one of the sheep. Which reminds me.'

He dipped one hand into a pocket.

Saul tensed, but Hsingyun withdrew only a slim roll of pale yellow paper, pulling it open to reveal several tiny powder-blue balls individually wrapped in cellophane, each one stamped with a minuscule portrait of a wolf howling under a full moon. Hsingyun next reached into another pocket and withdrew an inhaler-like device, loading three of the balls of loup-garou into its chamber.

Saul felt as if a yawning chasm had opened up inside his gut.

'A little confidence boost always helps, yes?' Hsingyun enquired, glancing between his two companions.

Saul watched dry-mouthed as Jacob took the first hit. The stuff was favoured by street gangs back home, and by Mexical hijacking crews in particular. There were stories that it had achieved near-religious significance amongst the death squads roaming the Russian wastelands. Loup-garou wildly boosted aggressiveness, while reducing the controlling influence of the super ego. It didn't exactly make you grow fur or sprout fangs, but the feeling it gave you was close enough.

Jacob's head jerked back as he fired the sweet-smelling smoke down his throat, then laughed as the drug punched its way through the soft tissues of his lungs and into his bloodstream. A thin wisp of smoke curled out of one nostril.

Hsingyun was next, inhaling sharply. Saul knew that, when his own turn came, he had a perfectly good excuse for not indulging. He could tell Hsingyun he wanted to keep his head clear, particularly if they were expecting to engage in serious business. But, as Jacob's new friend passed him the inhaler, Saul found that all he could really think about was just how good it had felt the last time he'd taken a hit, and wasn't it a damn shame he'd left it for so long.

He pressed the inhaler against his lips and clicked the igniter button. The acrid smell of burning plastic filled his nostrils, and a moment later smoke tasting faintly of peppermint and ash plunged its way through his lungs.

Saul breathed in deeply. Already he felt sharper, more alert, more in control. His tongue and the back of his throat tingled as he passed the inhaler back over, feeling now like he could handle anything the night could throw at him. He watched with detached amusement as Jacob tipped his head back and howled at the ceiling. Hsingyun laughed in response.

*

An indeterminate number of drinks later, they stumbled out of the bar and into a taxi that sported an actual human driver. Ten minutes later they found themselves standing on the edge of a bleak-looking airstrip running parallel to a long stretch of shore. A single unmanned drone-copter waited for them on the flat concrete, its blades already slowly rotating in anticipation of their arrival.

While Hsingyun and Jacob argued over who got to pay for their flight, Saul stepped over to the edge of the airstrip nearest the ocean and stared out at the slate-grey sea. His wife and daughter came, unbidden, to mind as a frozen wind pulled at the hood of his heavy parka, and he found himself remembering Deanna and Gwen the way they'd been before they'd left for Galileo, almost a decade before. A feeling of bottomless despair fought its way past the haze of alcohol and narcotics, and gripped his heart in a vice.

A lot could happen in ten years, and Galileo had been caught up in the middle of an uprising when the wormhole gate had collapsed. A starship carrying a new wormhole link was now only months away from achieving orbit around Galileo, but instead of feeling elated, all Saul felt was a numb apprehension. He hoped and prayed they were still alive, but beneath that lay the guilt. If it hadn't been for him, Deanna would never have taken up that administrative post on Galileo, and never taken their daughter there with her.

He sighted several dark shapes moving against the tide, sinuous, writhing things swimming in parallel. But by the time Jacob yelled over to him to hurry the fuck up and get on board, the black-skinned creatures had slipped back beneath the waves.

The three of them fell into silence once they climbed inside the aircraft's cramped fuselage. The pitch of its blades rose to a whine as it lifted into the air and headed out over the ocean, dipping occasionally to fight its way past a strong headwind.

Hsingyun dug out his inhaler once more, and offered them another hit. Saul very nearly put his hand out to restrain Jacob as he pressed the device to his lips but, instead, waited until his own turn came, before accepting the device with gratitude.

We're fucking this up, he thought, pressing the inhaler to his lips. The smoke tasted sweet and sharp in his lungs, and immediately he felt like he'd grown taller and stronger.

Barely twenty minutes after setting out, the 'copter began to drop lower once more. Saul leaned his head against the window, and found himself staring down at a flat white plain that appeared to extend to the horizon on all sides. For a moment he thought they must be back over land, until he caught sight of a line of black water foaming against the expanse of ice.

He knew how big some of the pharms could get, but this had to be one of the largest. He could make out a few dozen pre-fab buildings clustered below, off-white domes and warehouses that nearly merged into the ice itself, distinguishable only by the corporate logos on their roofs and the faint shadows they cast under the moonlight.

Once they had landed, they disembarked into a bitingly cold wind. There was no sense of motion, however, no way to tell that they were standing on a chunk of floating pykrete rather than on solid ground. Saul peered into the distance, but was unable to discern where the ice ended and the water began.

'What's to stop the Sphere authorities or anyone else just landing here and storming the place?' Saul yelled over the sound of the wind.

'You mean if we weren't already paying them not to?' Hsingyun yelled back, withdrawing a small antenna-like device and holding it out in the direction of the nearest dome. 'Well, since you ask, there are mines buried in the ice all around us. I can find the safe path through the minefield, so just follow behind me and stay close, unless you want to blow yourselves the fuck up.'

The pre-fab buildings proved to be much larger than they had appeared from the air. Many were several storeys in height, and he

spotted a few automated vehicles traversing the narrow roads linking buildings and warehouses.

'Nobody here to greet us?' Saul asked.

'Trust me, they know we're here,' Hsingyun replied, over his
shoulder, before stepping forward cautiously. The antennae device
he clutched in his gloved hand gave a beep, and he began to walk
more quickly.

As he and Jacob fell in behind him, Saul was not entirely un-
familiar with the technology Hsingyun was using. He knew they
were, in fact, stepping directly on top of mines as they approached
the dome. The mines communicated with each other by radio
frequency, activating or deactivating according to pre-set patterns,
meaning that the 'safe' path through them could change as often
as you programmed it to. You therefore needed something hooked
into the same encrypted network in order to find your way through
the minefield without getting killed.

Saul caught Jacob's eye and flashed him a dark look. If this
turned out to be a trap and they needed to get out, it was going
to be almost impossible to negotiate the minefield without Hsingyun's device.

We should have said the warehouse, or no deal, Saul wanted to yell.

THREE

Kepler Colony, Sphere Administered Development Zone,
15 January 2235

Hsingyun paused and suddenly changed direction a couple of times as they moved towards the dome, stopping and walking off briefly to the side before moving forward again. Saul and Jacob took care to follow very closely in his footsteps.

The snow crunched beneath Saul's boots, the cold quickly finding its way through the soles and numbing his toes. His testicles appeared intent on crawling back inside his body every time he saw a dark shape lodged in the ice directly underfoot, and he shuddered with relief when they finally passed through a door leading into the dome's interior. The air inside felt so warm and thick by comparison that, for a moment, Saul almost couldn't breathe.

A railing in the centre of the otherwise empty dome surrounded a spiral staircase leading down through a wide shaft cut into the ice. Saul took a firm grip on his briefcase and followed the other two downwards, the steel treads clanging noisily underfoot as they descended.

The interior of the ice-pharm proved to be almost as enormous as the exterior. Saul saw room after room filled with industrial machinery, tended by workers wearing masks and protective gear. The air was filled with the constant thunder of production. To one side, thick sheets of semi-translucent plastic hung to the floor from ceiling-mounted railings, shielding the dim silhouettes of laboratory equipment. This, then, Saul guessed, was where the analysis and gene-splicing took place. Enormous vats, concealed behind a tangle of pipework, were used for the mass synthesis of the pharm's products, prior to shipping to markets in the Sphere and Coalition territories back home.

Not for the first time, Saul felt the weight of knowing just how staggeringly inadequate the ASI was in the face of such mass industry. This was just one single black pharm, but it was filled with more contraband than Array Security and Immigration might hope to seize in any single year. And there were hundreds of pharms just like it, spread out across Kepler's vast oceans.

Two heavily armed Tian Di Hui street soldiers, identifiable by their nondescript baggy street clothes – perfect for concealing weapons – were waiting for them at the bottom of the stairs.

'Your contact lenses,' one of them said to Saul in Mandarin. 'Take them out.'

Saul glanced at Jacob. 'I won't be able to understand one damn word they're saying if I don't have my contacts,' he complained.

'Just do what they say,' Jacob muttered under his breath, already pinching his own contacts out. 'They're obviously not taking any chances on us recording anything. I can translate for you if I have to; my Mandarin's pretty good.'

Saul muttered under his breath, then tipped his head back and carefully pinched both of his own contacts out. Their embedded circuitry sparkled silver and gold as he placed them into a silver-plated case he kept for the purpose, tucking it into a pocket. Hsingyun did the same, then the second soldier swiped each of them in turn with a wand before finally patting them down.

As Hsingyun addressed the two soldiers in rapid Mandarin, Saul listened to the up-and-down cadences of their dialogue, unable to understand a word without the benefit of auto-translation. He noticed that the walls were sprayed with some kind of insulating plastic presumably intended to keep the pykrete from melting.

Indeed, the factory floor was swelteringly hot, and Saul was already starting to sweat by the time he'd pulled his heavy parka off and clasped it under one arm.

'They want to see inside your briefcase as well,' Jacob told him.

One of the soldiers waved Saul towards a series of low trestle tables arranged next to a shoulder-high partition that stood to one side of the metal staircase. Saul kept his expression carefully blank as he placed the briefcase flat on a table and lifted the lid, spinning it around so the soldier could see it contained thick bundles of crisp new black-market currency. A small wooden box, painted matte black, sat on top of these bundles.

The street soldier placed the box to one side and riffled through the notes, bundle by bundle, pushing his hands deep inside the case before pointing at the little box and barking something at Saul.

'He wants to see inside the box,' explained Jacob.

Saul nodded and opened it up to show the soldier the arbitration unit nestling within, on a bed of foam plastic. Tiny, silver and featureless, it might easily have been mistaken for a cigarette lighter. The soldier nodded, and Saul placed the box back inside his briefcase, snapping it shut.

Apparently satisfied, the two street soldiers led the way. Hsingyun chatted with them as they proceeded, their words echoing throughout the station's interior.

They didn't have far to go. One of the street soldiers opened a door to one side, and Hsingyun led them through. Saul found himself standing just inside a conference room such as one might find in any of New Kaiohsung's commercial skyscrapers, except that it had no windows. The walls were panelled with strips of accelerated-growth wood, probably grown in another of the ice-pharms.

The two soldiers followed the three of them inside. The room was long and narrow, and had a table, surrounded by several chairs, standing immediately to the right and dominating the nearer half of the room. Further in, two men – one white, one Asian – sat on a couch facing a TriView screen in the far left-hand corner. Beer and wine bottles, in varying stages of emptiness, were piled on a small coffee table to one side of the couch. The room reeked of loup-garou and other substances.

Saul glanced over at the TriView, and saw images of a man in a leather mask torturing a half-naked woman who was chained to a concrete post. She screamed and begged for mercy as her assailant grabbed her by the hair and yanked her head backwards, bringing a live power drill close to her throat. Even from across the room, Saul could see that her movements were a little too stiff to be real. He guessed she was a Japanese torture doll, one of the high-end models marketed to jaded business executives wherever they weren't banned.

A third man stood immediately to the right of the couch, watching the TriView with a look of weary indifference, his hands pushed into the pockets of a very expensive-looking suit: Shih Hsiu-Chuan himself.

Saul felt a thrill of anticipation. Hsiu-Chuan glanced slowly in his direction, then back at the screen.

Meanwhile, Saul's pulse rate began to build, riding on a tide of loup-garou as he followed Jacob and Hsingyun further into the room. The insouciant way in which Hsiu-Chuan held himself, together with that distant, mildly bored expression, suggested that their own presence here was a burden he only barely tolerated.

'Hey!' said the white man, leaping up from the couch and step-ping around behind it to face them. He wore a long woollen jacket over a stained shirt and overalls, a cloth cap pulled down over his ears. 'I see we have company.'

Hsingyun moved towards him and they exchanged a few words in Mandarin. 'This is Ben Tanner,' Hsingyun explained, looking back towards Saul and Jacob. 'He runs this station.'

Tanner's oriental TriView buddy now stood up and eyed Saul critically. 'Nobody told me he was a *hei-gui-zi*,' he remarked in guttural English, also stepping away from the couch.

Even though Saul spoke next to no Mandarin, he knew just enough to recognize the insult.

'Is that a problem?' he asked mildly.

'No problem,' said Tanner, waving an irritated hand at his companion. Judging by his accent he hailed from the East Coast Republic, maybe New York. He glanced at Saul's briefcase, still gripped tightly in one hand. 'And that's the goods?'

Saul nodded and stepped closer, shaking Tanner's hand. Hsiu-Chuan gave every impression of ignoring them all, his attention apparently still fixed on the TriView, but Saul wasn't fooled.

Tanner snapped his fingers at the man who'd been sitting with him on the couch. 'Kwan here would like to apologize for his racial slur,' said Tanner, a broad grin on his face. 'If it makes you feel any better, he calls his dick worse names, when he can find it. Isn't that right, Kwan?'

Kwan just laughed, and nodded them towards the conference table, before addressing Saul in rapid-fire Mandarin and gesturing at his briefcase.

'I already opened it,' said Saul.

'That was to check for weapons or surveillance devices,' Tanner replied. 'This time is for business.'

Saul glanced towards Jacob, who favoured him with an encouraging nod. Feeling the rush of confidence from the loup-garou beginning to slip, he became acutely aware that the two street soldiers who had escorted them were now standing between him and the only exit.

Saul nodded tightly and placed the briefcase on one end of the conference table, clicked it open and turned it around so all the others could see what was inside. He lifted out a couple of bundles of cash, as well as the box containing the arbitration unit. Kwan pushed him to one side, none too gently, and began expertly riffling the notes between his fingers, peering at them closely.

Hsiu-Chuan finally stepped away from the TriView and picked up the box containing the arbitration unit. Nothing else, Saul knew, would have been sufficient to make him risk showing up here.

'This is a clone, correct?' Hsiu-Chuan asked, finally acknowledging Saul's existence. His English was only lightly accented.

'Of one of the most successful predictive AIs currently operating in the Coalition share markets, yes,' Saul agreed. 'It was . . . difficult to obtain.'

'And you understand,' Hsiu-Chuan continued, his manner still offhand, 'what will happen to you personally if it's a fake or if it fails to live up to expectations?'

'I do,' Saul replied levelly.

Hsiu-Chuan nodded, pocketing the unit, then snapped his fingers at Kwan. Kwan responded by tossing a single bundle of cash underhand to one of the two street soldiers. Without another word to Saul or anyone else, Hsiu-Chuan departed the room, followed by the same street soldier.

'Where have they gone?' Saul demanded, turning to glare at Tanner.

'Just making sure everything's legitimate,' Tanner replied with an easy shrug. 'They'll run some tests, won't take more than a minute or two. Have a drink while we wait.'

Tanner stepped back over to the couch and fetched a half-bottle of whisky and four glasses. He placed the glasses on the conference table and poured a hefty measure into each. He then put the bottle down and withdrew a pykrete gun from inside his voluminous coat, placing it next to the bottle.

'What the fuck is that for?' asked Saul, staring at the gun.

'That?' Tanner pretended to be surprised by the question. '*That* is in case your sample of money or your arbitration unit aren't up to scratch.' Tanner picked up his whisky, full to the brim, and drank it in one swallow, before slamming down the empty glass. 'I hope that's not a problem for you,' he added, with a thin smile.

'Not at all,' Saul muttered, picking up his own glass to try and hide his agitation. He noticed that neither Jacob nor Hsingyun had made any move yet towards their own drinks.

There was just enough loup-garou still left circulating through Saul's bloodstream to ratchet up his fight-or-flight responses, but he felt his nerves settle a bit as the whisky slithered down his throat. It had a pleasant, slightly honeyed texture.

'Sometimes,' said Tanner, refilling his own glass before raising it, as if in salute, 'I wonder how it ever got to the point where good honest criminals were forced to print their own money.'

'At least it's real money,' muttered Hsingyun, finally picking up his glass and taking a sip. 'And not just numbers encoded on some fucking computer's memory.'

'Ah,' Tanner nodded, 'that's why I came here, to Kepler.'

'For black-market cash?' asked Saul.

'That and freedom, too. Back there,' he said, waving one hand towards the opposite wall, as if the entire planet Earth were lurking just on the other side of it, 'there's none. Back there it's all invisible credit. But that,' he gestured with his glass at Saul's briefcase, 'that's real, tangible. You can hold it in your hands. Walk around the street stalls back in the city, you'll see that stuff getting used. People here trust it more than they ever did UP-linked credit.'

Saul nodded. The cash in the briefcase had been printed on black-market presses that had been impounded long ago by the ASI. They had been obliged to print their own or they'd never have been able to pay the network of informants they maintained throughout a dozen worlds. Tanner was right, of course: back on Earth and Luna, where the only legal currency had a purely virtual existence, you couldn't do anything without leaving a trail of information behind you. The underground economy had no choice but to develop its own secret banking and credit system, replete with its very own currency.

Tanner paused, as if about to say something, then withdrew a slim device, placing it against his ear and nodding after a few moments. A telephone, Saul realized with a shock; the kind normally relegated to museums. Tanner really was serious, it seemed, about leaving the old world behind.

'Verdict's in,' said Tanner, returning the device to his pocket. 'Your arbitration unit is good, and your money is real.'

Saul nodded, fingering the lid of his briefcase as if to close it again. 'Then we can get started on working out schedules and delivery dates. That means—'

'Not quite.' Tanner nudged the gun closer to Saul. 'Pick it up,' he said.

Saul stood absolutely stock-still. He could see Hsingyun and Jacob to his left, around the other side of the table, while the remaining street soldier had moved to stand by the wall directly behind Tanner. Kwan stood to Saul's right, and nobody was paying any attention to the TriView.

'Why the hell should I?' asked Saul.

Tanner glanced over his shoulder at the street soldier, and said something to him in rapid Mandarin. The man stepped up behind Jacob, grabbing him by both arms just above the elbow, while Kwan crossed the room in a couple of steps, and pulled one arm right back before punching Jacob hard in the stomach.

Jacob crumpled, wheezing. The street soldier and Kwan took a shoulder each and quickly manoeuvred him into one of the chairs by the table. Saul watched, rooted to the spot, as Kwan pulled plastic restraints from a pocket before expertly securing Jacob's hands and feet to the chair.

'Ben,' Jacob's voice was cracking, 'I don't know why you're—'

'Shut up,' snarled Tanner.

Jacob tried to say something else, but Kwan punched him in the jaw before he could get it out. Jacob's head snapped back, and he fell silent, although Saul could see he was still just about conscious. A thin trickle of blood emerged from one corner of his mouth.

The seconds seemed to trickle by at an infinitely slow pace. Hsingyun appeared unperturbed by the sudden violence. His eyes met Saul's, who realized in that moment that they had been compromised since long before he had even arrived on Kepler.

A second weapon had appeared in Tanner's hand, a Koch flechette pistol. He levelled it at Saul's chest, and waggled its barrel towards the table.

'Now pick up the gun, Mr Lassen,' he said, using Saul's false identity.

Saul took a deep breath and slowly laid one hand across the pykrete gun's bulbous coolant chamber, without picking it up. He realized, with a sinking feeling, that the wooden panels on the far wall were rippling gently. That meant the psycho-actives were starting to kick in, and were clearly much more powerful than Jacob had claimed. Everything felt slightly unreal, as if at one remove.

'Why,' he asked Tanner, 'are you doing this?'

'You *say* your name is Lassen,' Tanner replied, then nodded towards Jacob, 'but I have it on good authority that Mr Cowles here is in fact employed by the ASI. And if he's ASI, that means you probably are, too. In fact, everything we know about you comes through Cowles, or whatever his fucking name is. That means, if you want to prove yourself, by which I mean, show me you're legitimate and serious about doing business with the Tian Di Hui, and not just some undercover cocksucker, then you're going to have to walk the extra mile. Kill Cowles and I'll believe you really are who you say you are.'

'If that's what you think, why not just kill me instead?' asked Saul, struggling to keep his tone even. 'Why hand me a gun?'

'The Tian Di Hui have rules when it comes to dealing with new clients,' explained Tanner, the barrel of his Koch dipping until it pointed at Saul's crotch. Saul did his best to ignore the unpleasant tingling suddenly radiating through his loins. 'We like to know if they're genuinely committed to a working relationship with us. Now – let's suppose my information *isn't* correct, and you really are who you say you are. Even if that's the case, the Tian Di Hui will only deal with one person at a time. That means either we deal with Cowles here,' Tanner nodded over his shoulder towards Jacob, 'or we deal with you.' He shook his head slowly. 'But not both.'

'So you want me to kill him?' said Saul. The gun felt solid and heavy beneath his fingers as it rested on the polished wood.

'If you don't,' said Tanner, 'we very definitely will kill *you*.'

Saul stared down at the weapon with the fascination of a rabbit confronted by a hungry lion. 'Is it loaded?'

Tanner shrugged. 'One way to find out.'

Saul glanced back at Hsingyun, and wondered just how long he had known. It wasn't too hard to picture Jacob, stoned out of his mind while crammed into a bar much like the one they'd left barely more than half an hour before, letting slip some clue that he was something other than what he seemed. Maybe the answer really was that simple.

Moving slowly, Saul picked up the pykrete gun, feeling the balanced weight of it in his hands. He then considered his options. Terror and fury waged a war inside his head and heart, while sparks of light like fireflies swam at the edges of his vision, leaving phosphorescent blue trails.

Or maybe, he thought, the whole thing was really a kind of carefully staged test. The gun in his hand might, in fact, not be loaded at all. Maybe neither Tanner nor Hsingyun nor anyone else had any idea that he and Jacob were anything other than who they claimed to be. But the surest way to reveal they *were* ASI would be to refuse to play along.

The knife-edge sharpness from the loup-garou reasserted itself, through the fug of alcohol and hallucinogens. He felt suddenly, supremely confident that everything was going to be just fine; Tanner would never have given him a loaded gun if he really believed he was a cop. Wasn't that how it always played out in the TriView dramas? The gun was never loaded. *Never.*

Saul aimed the gun at Jacob's chest, deliberately fumbling with it to create the impression this was the first time he'd ever held such a weapon.

Jacob tried to struggle out of his chair, and Saul noticed a curious look on Tanner's face. The street soldier moved to one side of Jacob, while keeping one meaty hand firmly clamped over his mouth.

'It's cool,' Saul said to Jacob, the wood panelling on the walls writhing furiously, like wheat in an autumn gale. 'They're just testing us.'

Saul pulled the trigger. The gun made a loud popping sound

and a lozenge-sized chunk of pykrete punched a hole through Jacob's chest. It sounded, thought Saul, not unlike a cork being pulled from a champagne bottle. Jacob jerked back with sufficient violence to tip his chair sideways on to the floor, dead before his cheek touched the carpet.

The sound of the gunshot seemed to resonate through every cell in Saul's body, startling him into something more closely resembling sobriety.

After a few moments' prolonged silence, Tanner turned to Kwan with a delighted grin. 'Well, fuck me, you won that fair and square.' He turned back to Saul. 'I'm seriously fucking taken aback. I really, *really* didn't think you were going to do it.'

'Why not?' Saul managed to croak, his tongue suddenly thick and heavy. He stared down at Jacob's slumped form in horrified fascination, then noticed, as he brought his gaze back up, that Tanner had momentarily lowered his own weapon until it pointed at the floor.

'Because we already knew the both of you were fucking cops,' Tanner replied, levelling his Koch at Saul once more.

Saul reached down with his free hand and grabbed one corner of the open briefcase beside him, whipping it around and up with as much force as he could muster. The briefcase struck Tanner on the side of the head. He dodged back with a yell, arms raised in defence, nearly stumbling over Jacob's body as loose banknotes went scattering through the air.

Already moving forward, Saul grabbed Tanner by the shoulder, pulling him close and twisting him around before the street soldier, who had been standing directly behind the pharm manager, could get a clear shot at him. He reached down and clasped his hand around Tanner's fist, where it held the pykrete gun, aiming the weapon at the street soldier and squeezing. As if by magic, a line of fine red dots appeared across the soldier's neck and chest, and he dropped to his knees with a gurgling sound.

Saul tore the flechette pistol from Tanner's grasp, then ducked beneath the table before Kwan had a chance to fix him in his sights. He could hear the sound of chunks of compacted cellulose and ice water thudding into the wood a second later.

Kwan dropped on to all fours, to try and take aim a second time. His head flowered red as Saul fired, the flechettes tearing into his vulnerable flesh. Kwan collapsed, his legs and arms twitching spastically.

Tanner stumbled away to hide behind the couch. Saul looked around and saw Hsingyun fumbling desperately with the door, cursing in his panic to get out. Saul fired a stream of flechettes towards his ankles. Two intervening chairs spun away from the side of the table, as if shoved aside by invisible hands, and Hsingyun went down screaming.

Saul darted back out from under the table, and meanwhile glanced towards the couch. Several bottles previously standing on the table next to the TriView rolled noisily across the tiled floor.

'Tanner,' Saul shouted hoarsely, 'if you so much as twitch from where you are, I swear I'll blow your fucking head off. Do you understand me?'

There was a muffled reply, just audible over the sound of the chainsaw and the combined shrieks of both the torture-doll and Hsingyun.

Saul backed towards the door, and Hsingyun, and a moment later Tanner's head popped back up over the top of the couch. Saul fired without thinking, the flechettes ripping gouts of foam out of the couch. Tanner made a strangled sound and fell backwards, crashing into the TriView, its sounds of carnage cutting off instantly.

He turned back to Hsingyun and found him slumped half-conscious against the door in an ever-widening pool of blood, his lower legs now a mess of pulverized meat. Saul kept a tight grip on the Koch, and used his free hand to rifle through Hsingyun's pockets until he located the device that could get him past the minefield.

Now all he needed to do was get to the surface alive – and pray the 'copter was still parked where they'd left it.

And if it wasn't, he was totally, irretrievably, fucked.

He dragged Hsingyun out of the way and cautiously pulled the door open. When he leaned out, he could see no one bar the distant figures of white-suited workers going about their business.

There was so much noise out there that no one had even heard the fighting.

Saul had got most of the way back to the spiral staircase before someone finally raised the alarm.

A high-pitched whine filled the air, followed by a muffled shout from somewhere nearby. Saul started to run, and heard shots echoing through the cavernous space behind him. In that moment he remembered that his parka was still back there in the conference room. That was going to be a problem once he got outside.

He reached the stairs and clanged his way up them as fast as he could go: three, four, five steps at a time. There came more shots, one ricocheting off a step ahead of him as he climbed higher. He glanced back to see the street soldier who had departed with Hsiu-Chuan, waving his hands as he yelled at two other men in white worker gear, both with pykrete rifles gripped in their hands.

Saul reached the dome and burst through the outer door and on to the ice. The cold came as a brute physical shock that brought him to a sudden halt, gasping as he filled his lungs with freezing air. Saul was wearing nothing more than a light business suit, barely sufficient to keep him warm on a January afternoon in New York or London, let alone amid Kepler's half-frozen oceans.

Hands shaking and teeth chattering, he fumbled Hsingyun's mine detector out of a pocket. Peering across the ice, he felt a surge of overwhelming relief when he saw the 'copter was still exactly where they had left it. He tried to estimate how long it would take him to work his way past the minefield, and how long it would take the men chasing him to catch up. Then he decided to think of something else.

Hsingyun, he remembered, had pressed a red button . . . here.

Ah, thought Saul, as a screen blinked into life on the device, accompanied by a beep. He saw a grid of dots appear on the screen, a blinking zigzag line superimposed over it. A circle at the centre of the grid clearly represented the dome.

He walked a few metres forward, and the zigzag line began to blink faster, finally changing colour as he found himself standing almost directly on top of a buried mine, its dark shape visible just millimetres beneath the ice.

Still grasping the Koch in his other hand, he stepped forward, half convinced he was about to get blown to bits – but nothing happened. He walked faster, then began to run, stopping only when the screen began to blink again.

Hearing shouts from behind, he turned and fired in the direction of the dome, but wide of the mark. Two figures that had just emerged from the dome's entrance ducked back inside.

It occurred to Saul that if one of his pursuers thought to shoot at the mines to either side of him, that it might just set them off. He crouched low as he ran, filled with an overwhelming sense of urgency, keenly aware of just how good a target his dark suit made him against the ice.

More shots came, and Saul stumbled forward, landing on his knees. For a moment he thought he'd only slipped on the ice, then realized with numb shock that he had been hit in the shoulder. He twisted around, raised the pistol and once again fired towards the dome, but his hands were shaking too badly for him to be able to take proper aim.

Get to the 'copter, you fucking idiot.

The worst thing – the *nasty* thing – about pykrete bullets was that they melted, leaving a mass of difficult-to-extract and potentially poisonous cellulose fibres buried deep in the tissue of your body. You didn't need a fatal wound to be in serious trouble.

He pushed himself back upright, ignoring a sudden spell of dizziness that threatened to overcome him. He checked the screen on Hsingyun's gadget: all he had to do was move three mines to the right, and then it was a straight run all the way to the 'copter.

He glanced back once again, as he loped towards the aircraft, and heard something whine past his ear. He could just make out one of the white-suited men, his head appearing to float above the ice like a ghost, kneeling as he readied for another shot. Saul stopped and took a two-handed grip on the pistol, holding it steady just long enough to empty the rest of its chamber in the direction of his assailant.

He was rewarded by the sight of ice and snow kicking up a flurry directly in front of his target. It wasn't a direct hit, but his assailant leaped up and darted to one side.

Which turned out to be a bad move. The ice erupted beneath him, and the sound of the accompanying detonation echoed across the flat expanse of the ice-pharm like a peal of thunder, before staining the ice red.

Saul knew it was now or never. He tried to change his grip on the Koch but realized the sheer cold had welded it to the skin of one hand. He turned and ran as fast and as hard as he could, praying he was far away enough now from the dome that the lone remaining gunman would have a hard time taking proper aim. One bullet pinged off the carapace of the aircraft as Saul pulled himself inside it.

'Police emergency override 256,' he gasped, collapsing back across the seat as the door automatically slid shut. 'Officer Dumont, department code six nine zero slash alpha. Take off now.'

'Please be aware that any attempts to gain control of this craft by the use of illegally acquired overrides may be punishable in a court of law by a fine or a possible jail sentence,' the 'copter replied, in a smooth tone. 'If you wish to confirm, please—'

'Confirmed!' Saul screamed, realizing that the slick dampness beneath him was his own blood, pouring out of his shoulder wound. 'Just fucking do it!' he screamed.

The rotors quickly built up to a high-pitched whine and, as it lifted, the 'copter angled to one side, showing him the flat landscape of the station beneath. One or two faint sparks of light from the direction of the dome told him somebody was still trying to shoot him down.

'My systems suggest you may be injured,' the 'copter continued, its tone blandly untroubled. 'Are you in need of any medical assistance?'

'Yes, I am,' Saul replied weakly, aware that dawn was already spreading pale fingers across the sky. 'I need to get to a hospital.'

He could still feel the Koch cold and hard against his fingers and palm. The 'copter dipped again as it angled across the sky, and Saul felt like he was falling into a grey blank eternity that swallowed up the last of his thoughts, as he finally slipped into unconsciousness.

FOUR

Florida Array Exclusion Zone, East Coast Republic, 18 January 2235

The road stretched ahead, a black asphalt line dividing the world in two, with the APC carrying the rest of the squadron just a couple of dozen metres ahead of him. Monk leaned forward to peer up, past the curve of the truck's windshield, at black clouds incipient with rain.

He sat back, shifted his grip on the steering wheel and glanced to his side. Naz had placed his taser attachment and extra magazines of ammo on the upper part of the dashboard while he checked and rechecked his Cobra, snapping open the feed assembly and pushing two fingers inside.

Monk studied him with a growing sense of irritation, before turning back to the road. Small drops of moisture landed on the glass, while a sudden wind stirred the tops of the trees lining the ditches on either side of the road.

'Eyes on the road, Sergeant,' Naz muttered without looking up.

Insubordinate son of a bitch, thought Monk.

The clouds finally broke and gusts of rain billowed across the expressway. Monk caught a glimpse of a sign telling him that Orlando was fifty kilometres away.

'How many times have you already checked that damn thing?' Monk demanded, but Naz only grinned as he snapped the feed assembly shut once more and started to reattach the taser just under the Cobra's barrel. The Faraday mesh, wrapped around the weapon's targeting systems, glittered softly.

'Not enough times, Sergeant,' Naz replied. 'Knew a guy back in the day got blown to shit when his gun jammed. Ain't gonna let the same thing happen to me.' He slid a magazine into place, studying the weapon with the kind of fascinated admiration that most men Monk knew saved for Orlando's strip clubs.

'Islamabad?' asked Monk.

Another sign, so badly rusted that he could barely make out the words, told him they were coming up on what had been a marsh conservation area. Not that anybody bothered with that kind of thing any more; he checked the local network through his contacts and saw nothing about anything getting conserved. The bushes and cypresses lining the road looked wild and unkempt. The traffic was light: most vehicles on the road this close to the Florida Array were either army or supplies, although they had also passed a few private cars belonging to Array staff.

'Wasn't the war, Sergeant,' Naz replied, settling back to scan the horizon. 'Was back in LA. Dumb shithead I knew got caught with a house full of pharm goods, and thought he could shoot his way out when the cops turned up on his doorstep. His gun had a systems failure 'cause he didn't take proper care of it. Had a white coffin at his funeral. Priest in white, wife in white, all three girl-friends and his favourite whore in white. Tackiest shit I've seen in my whole life.'

Monk sighed. Naz had wound up working for Array Security and Immigration after spending a year riding shotgun on convoys passing through Pakistan and Mexical, and that only because the alternative had been jail. He wasn't the kind of guy Monk liked having on his team but, then, Monk didn't get a say in the matter. So he kept an eye on Naz, waiting for him to make a slip, do or say the wrong thing, anything that might give Monk an excuse to file a report or have the son of a bitch reassigned. But Naz never did give Monk the excuse he needed. He was, to Monk's boundless irritation, what the military TriView feeds liked to call an 'exemplary soldier.'

They reached the turn-off to the airfield, a private stretch of road owned by the ASI, and stopped for a couple of moments to let an automated checkpoint remotely query their Ubiquitous Profiles. The truck's wheels kicked up mud as it pulled off the expressway. A sparkle of light several kilometres ahead betrayed the location of the airfield's conning tower.

The armoured personnel carrier carrying the rest of the squad had already negotiated the turn-off. Monk knew that in the back of the truck he was driving was a sealed containment unit, newly arrived via the Array from some exotic off-world location. Monk had no idea what might be contained within it, and couldn't care less. More lichen or mineral samples, probably. Scientist shit, at least. All he'd seen was a steel box with fat wheels and a push-handle, with vacuum seals and hazard warnings printed on all sides. It had been wheeled into the back of the truck by two technicians in hazmat suits.

An icon appeared, floating in the air to Monk's right, indicating a bright-red alert. He touched it with a finger and information appeared, rendered in chrome letters floating in the air.

'My UP says there's been an accident up ahead,' he muttered, glancing forward. Beyond the APC, the road to the airfield looked empty, but it was hard to be sure with all the rain. 'About two kilometres up ahead. An automated transport.'

Naz pushed himself up in his seat and peered through the windscreen, his weapon clanking against the glossy black of the dashboard. He cleared his throat noisily, wound the passenger window down and spat out into the rain. 'I can see all the way to the airfield, Sergeant,' he replied, 'and, with all due respect, I don't see shit.'

'Maybe there's a glitch in the monitoring systems,' Monk muttered, turning the wheel to pull in at the roadside. 'Call the tower for confirmation. We can wait here till we get the go-ahead.'

'Confirmation?' Naz's expression was incredulous. 'With all due respect, Sergeant, there's *nothing* on the road and I also know you ain't blind. We need to keep going.'

That was the problem right there, thought Monk; Naz didn't

understand the necessity of sticking to the rules. 'If the systems says there's an accident up ahead, then the regulations say we don't move until told otherwise.'

'Then the regulations are fucked, Sergeant.'

'We stay here,' Monk snapped. 'Whatever's up there could be carrying hazardous materials or some other poisonous shit. Search and rescue'll be here in another couple of minutes, anyway.'

Naz twisted around in his seat to look at him more directly. 'Look out that window, up ahead of the APC. I know it's raining, but it ain't raining that heavily. Between here and the airfield, do you see anything?'

Monk had to admit the road ahead looked empty all the way. He glared at Naz, then reluctantly opened the mike to Rosewood, in the APC, and ordered him to drive up ahead. He watched as the carrier pulled back out into the road and accelerated away.

Despite what he'd said about a glitch, Monk knew the ASI's mapping satellites were near as damn infallible. If they said there was something blocking the road up ahead, then there was something definitely blocking the road. No surprise if an ex-jailbird grunt like Naz was too dumb to understand that, and yet, as he watched the APC retreat into the distance, Monk couldn't ignore a growing sense of unease.

It wasn't like the Mexical 'jacking crews worked this far east, after all. In fact the ASI extended their security envelope far beyond the CTC mass-transit facility, and their present convoy was well within the hundred-kilometre exclusion zone. There were only two tightly controlled air corridors, along with aerial spotter drones programmed to hunt out anyone hiding in the swamps and bayous who shouldn't be there. Monk himself spent three days a week in charge of a manned ground patrol.

He assuaged his nervousness by checking his armour, layers of Kevlar alternating with artificial spider-silk that could absorb the impact from any number of high-calibre rounds.

Naz muttered something under his breath, clicked his Cobra's safety off and cracked open the passenger-side door.

'Hey,' said Monk, outraged. 'I didn't tell you that you could—'

'This doesn't feel right,' Naz snapped back, jumping down to the roadside and taking a two-handed grip on his weapon. 'I think we should at least rec—'

Monk saw Naz's eyes widen, and glanced forward just in time to see the APC, a hundred metres up ahead, come crashing back down on to its roof, bodies tumbling out of its rear like broken dolls. The sound of the detonation arrived a moment later, a flat bass thump deadened by the rain, branches and dirt pattering down all around their own truck.

He turned back to speak to Naz, but the man wasn't there anymore.

It occurred to Monk, in that same moment, that their truck might very well be next. He kicked open the door next to him and threw himself out of the cabin, hitting the ground with his shoulder and rolling away, before picking himself up and making straight for the cover of the trees on the same side of the road Naz had been on.

He slid down an embankment until he came to a stop against a tree, then yanked the safety off his own gun, wishing with a mixture of regret and aggravation that he'd checked it as thoroughly as Naz had his own. He tried to uplink to Command, but the security channels were all blocked.

It looked like they were on their own. He sent a signal to the truck, activating its defence protocols. He heard it shift and rumble as it reconfigured itself accordingly.

Monk waited long, tense seconds, the chirping of cicadas intermingling with the sound of the APC burning. The air meanwhile smelled of mud and burning plastic.

It was starting to look like whoever or whatever had hit the APC wasn't going to try and blow up the truck, too, which meant they were almost certainly after the containment unit in the rear.

He heard rustling in the bushes, then spotted Naz's back about twenty metres ahead, moving cautiously through the undergrowth towards the thin trail of greasy black smoke that betrayed the

APC's whereabouts. He was, Monk noted with disgust, intent on being a goddamn hero.

Just as Monk opened his mouth to yell, he heard a low, throbbing buzz like a chainsaw. Something flashed overhead in the same moment that Naz glanced back in Monk's direction, after presumably hearing the same sound.

Monk instantly dropped down into the long grass and saw an aerial drone flashing through the treetops, heading towards Naz's location. He raised his Cobra, squinting down the sight, but, before he could fire, the ground beneath Naz erupted and he disappeared in an uprush of dirt and leaves.

Chunks of wood, soil and Naz himself pattered down all around Monk, and he suddenly felt his bowels threaten to loosen.

Keep it together, Monk told himself, once again trying his best to make himself as small a target as possible. But the drone was now moving further away from his location.

Monk let out a silent sigh of relief. If the drone was anything like the ones used by ASI, it would be equipped with IR sensors, and no way was he going to be able to hide from shit like that.

Monk crouched down low, considering his options, then heard a sound he at first took for another car or truck pulling up at the roadside. The sound grew deafeningly loud, and a dark triangular shape dropped down beneath the treetops, rapidly descending towards the road. A VTOL pond-hopper, by the looks of it.

He doubled back the way he'd come, retreating along the ditch and pulling himself up the embankment once more, panting and swearing all the way. The drone had by now passed over to the other side of the road, its rotors buzzing increasingly far away as it hunted for survivors. He'd been lucky, *very* lucky, not to end up the same way as Naz.

Monk kept himself flat in the long grass bordering the verge of the road, his Cobra in front of him as he looked around. The truck was sitting right where he'd left it, but it had closed its doors and adopted a rounder shape by curling itself up like an armadillo, and then surrounding itself with sheafs of armour plating. He watched as the VTOL – a sleek-bodied machine with the black hawklike appearance of a military unit – sent a furious blast of air rippling across the road and through the surrounding trees, as it dropped down alongside the truck.

Monk batted leaves and grit away from him and waited, as the VTOL's engines died down to a low hum. Before long a door cranked open in the side of the craft and two men in jumpsuits climbed down. From what he could see out of his vantage point in the long grass, they wore standard ASI air-patrol patches on their shoulders. One headed for the truck, while the other moved towards the rear of the jet.

No way are they ASI, thought Monk, watching them for a moment. The uniforms didn't look quite right, like they'd been imperfectly faked.

Monk heard the chainsaw buzz of the drone as it circled round towards him, then saw it pass back across the road in his direction. He figured he had maybe thirty seconds before it passed over him a second time, and he was pretty sure that this time it wouldn't fail to pick out his heat signature.

He scrambled backwards down the embankment, and pushed himself in as far as he could get between the wide, blade-like roots of a banyan tree. With any luck those thick, damp roots would block out his heat signature.

His heart thudding, he watched the drone pass overhead but, instead of blowing him to pieces like it had Naz, it kept going. Monk let his head fall back against the gnarled trunk behind him and groaned with relief. He had two, maybe two and a half minutes tops, before it came back his way a third time.

He quickly crawled back up the embankment and peered through the long grass in time to see one of the two hijackers wheeling the containment unit back over towards the VTOL. The VTOL's nose section had meanwhile opened up to reveal a ramp, looking like some winged monster with its jaws wide open and its tongue lolling across the road.

Monk glanced beyond the ruined APC, now struggling to push

itself the right way up, like some mortally wounded animal, and saw the drone once more pass across the road and into the treetops on the far side. Before he could change his mind, he leaped up and ran, crouching low in order to present as small a target as possible, before dropping to one knee and preparing to open fire.

One of the hijackers spotted him and shouted a warning. Monk instantly let loose a rapid blast of fire from his Cobra, and saw the man collapse with a scream. The second hijacker ran for the cover of the containment unit, and began to return fire.

Monk flattened himself on the road and glanced towards his truck. He had maybe sixty seconds before the drone passed back over the road and spotted him. If he could take out the remaining hijacker before then, he could hide under the truck bed, where the drone's IR sensors wouldn't be able to distinguish his heat signal from that of the engine.

Monk heard the surviving hijacker reload his weapon, and took it as his cue to again dart forward. A second later, he heard a buzz-saw whine coming from entirely the wrong direction.

He gazed up in stupefaction at a second drone hovering almost directly over the roof of his truck, the downdraft from its rotors scuffing up dirt and leaves from the tarmac as it moved closer. At the same time, he heard the buzz-saw rattle of the first drone returning through the trees.

There's two of them, Monk realized, with a sudden lurch of terror. Maybe the second one had stayed invisible on the far side of the truck, or maybe he'd activated a motion detector of some kind . . .

The last thing he saw was the flash from an exhaust port as the drone launched a grenade at him.

FIVE

Saul had been gazing out at the distant cliff walls of Copernicus Crater, when he heard someone enter the observation room from behind him. The Earth hung low above the horizon, the lights of the city blotting out all but the brightest of stars, so that the planet seemed to float in a lightless void.

He reached down and gripped the right-hand wheel of his wheelchair, pushing back on it so that he turned just in time to see one of two men he didn't recognize close the door, shutting out the constant bustle of the hospital corridor beyond.

Saul cleared his throat. 'Can I help you?'

The shorter of the two had unkempt, sandy hair, while his companion was thin as a rail, his expression morose. The shorter one stepped up next to Saul and peered out through the window, while his companion eased one buttock on to a side table next to the door, and folded his arms. Both wore dark, conservative suits, while their UPs merely identified them as employees of the ASI.

The shorter man turned back from the window and glanced down at Saul with a smile. 'Alec Donohue,' he said, introducing himself. 'And my friend here is Joshua Sanders,' he added, nodding towards his companion.

'Let me guess,' Saul grunted. 'Internal Affairs?'

'We prefer 'Public Standards Unit,' Donohue corrected.

After four days in the hospital, Saul had begun to hope against the odds that Public Standards had somehow forgotten about him. He should have known better.

'So,' he asked with forced levity, 'exactly how much trouble am I in?'

'That depends,' Donohue replied, and nodded towards Saul's hands, folded in his lap. 'How're the grafts working out?'

'Fine.' Saul glanced down at the thick swathes of bandage covering his hands. 'Had some cosmetic work, but they should be back to normal in the next couple of days.'

'And the shoulder wound?'

Saul shrugged, and felt a sympathetic twinge in the upper part of his back. 'Didn't hit anything vital.'

'Nice.' Donohue nodded. 'And, in response to your question, you're in a shitload of trouble, my friend. One colleague of yours dead, a major undercover operation seriously compromised, not to mention a running gun battle in an economic development zone under foreign jurisdiction. That's not even to mention the pharmaceutical horn of plenty we found in both yours and Jacob Maks' bloodstreams. The pair of you practically had the contents of a fucking pharmacy chugging through your veins.' Donohue leaned back against the window and shook his head, as if in sorrow. 'All in all, one royal humdinger of a fuck-up.'

Saul stared at him with a venomous expression. 'How about I throw you a stick, you run and fetch it?'

'Easy,' said Sanders from over by the door.

'First up,' said Saul, 'the ice-pharm was out in the middle of a fucking *ocean*, well outside of anybody's official jurisdiction.' He realized with a mounting sense of doom that they must have found some way to recover Jacob's body from the pharm, otherwise how could they possibly have known so much?

Donohue regarded him with an amused expression. 'The standard rules of jurisdiction cease to apply when enough people start shooting at each other, at which point the corporations and government interests controlling the legal pharms seek to protect their interests. Coalition peacekeepers were called in to help keep the peace.'

'I'm sure they were,' Saul muttered.

'There's something I want you to take a look at,' said Dono-hue, gesturing to the other agent. Sanders stood up and pulled a folder from inside his jacket, before stepping over. He handed it to Saul, who found it contained nothing more than a single sheet of charged paper.

'What is this?' Saul took the sheet out of the folder and regarded it with suspicion.

Sanders leaned down and tapped one corner of the sheet. Dense lines of single-spaced text materialized on its crisp white surface, and Saul recognized it as the incident report he had filed the day after waking up in a Copernican hospital ward.

'Skip to the end,' Donohue advised, as Sanders stepped back and out of the way. 'There's some additional material you might find of interest.'

Saul found a detailed analysis was tagged on to the end of his own report. It described a covert raid on the ice-pharm, follow-ing his escape. There were orbital satellite photos showing it as a misshapen white lump standing stark against the black of Kepler's largest ocean. Video footage, recorded at extreme magnification, replayed his dash to the helicopter.

'You were tailing me the whole way,' Saul muttered, dropping the sheet back into his lap.

'There were questions about Jacob Maks,' said Sanders, from beside him, 'and about the nature of his relationship with Lee Hsingyun. We had reckoned for a while that he might be on the take. Kepler's black pharms are enormously lucrative, after all, and the Tian Di Hui finances a significant portion of their activities from the proceeds of the pharms they control. Maks wouldn't be the first to decide that working for them was a better bet than holding out for an ASI pension.'

'So you think he cut a deal with Hsingyun?' Saul asked.

Donohue shrugged. 'That's what we thought at first. He was spending a lot more money than any field agent might be expected to have, so naturally that raised an immediate flag. You know how the ASI can't afford to take chances when it comes to compromising our investigations.'

'So you put him under surveillance.'

'Both him and you, as a matter of fact. It wasn't the first time you'd worked together.'

Saul glared at him. 'And that was reason enough to spy on me, too?'

'The whole thing was a debacle, Saul. It was a five-year investigation with Shih Hsiu-Chuan as the prize, except you let him get away. At the very least, that makes an internal investigation near-as-damn inevitable. And once that investigation shows how you went into the field with a fair proportion of the narcotics coming out of the ice-pharms stuffed back up your nose, it's going to be the easiest thing in the world to make you a scapegoat for everything that's gone wrong. If you're very, *very* lucky, you'll only lose your job.'

'And it's not like you've had an exemplary record before, either,' Sanders cut in. 'At least, not after Galileo. You were nearly kicked out.'

'I had a breakdown. That's hardly a secret,' Saul replied through gritted teeth. 'I pulled myself together.'

'Except you haven't been promoted since,' Donohue pointed out. 'You're still stuck doing the same kind of shitty undercover work, ten years on. However, what the peacekeeper task force found when they got to the ice-pharm raises other, more serious questions.'

Saul caught sight of his own reflection superimposed over the lifeless lunar landscape, and realized how scared he looked. 'Like?'

'Jacob Maks was killed by a single shot from a pykrete gun,' said Sanders, his grin bright and feral. 'We took prints from that pistol, Saul. *Your* prints. Your DNA.'

Saul licked suddenly dry lips. 'It's more complicated than you think it is.'

'I'll bet,' said Donohue. 'Did you kill him, Saul?'

Saul felt a sudden flush of rage and waited until it passed. He fantasized about slamming Donohue's head repeatedly against the floor, but he was so full of painkillers that his body felt like a sack of cotton hanging off his skeleton, leaving him far from capable of giving anyone a beating.

'I had a gun to my head,' he replied instead, his voice rasping. 'They told me if I wanted to prove I really was who I said I was, I was going to have to kill him to prove it.'

'You killed him to save yourself?' asked Donohue.

'No!' Saul slammed the side of his wheelchair with one hand. 'They were *on to us*. It was obvious Tanner wasn't going to let either of us walk out alive. And Hsingyun . . . something about him bothered me from the moment I met him. He and Jacob acted like they were old friends, but I think Hsingyun had been on to him from the start.'

'Go on,' said Donohue.

'The arbitration unit was bait for Hsiu-Chuan, but it was highly lucrative bait. There's plenty of motivation, right there, for Hsingyun to string Jacob along until I turned up with the goods. That way he doesn't just get hold of the arbitration unit, he gets himself closer to Hsiu-Chuan and the financiers behind the pharms. Maybe he thought he could get his own pharming operation out of it.'

'Nice theory,' said Sanders, 'but you still haven't answered the question. Did you kill Jacob?'

Saul let out a groan. 'I was convinced the gun wasn't loaded. I took a gamble they were trying to test us, that there weren't any bullets in the damn thing. But they already knew exactly who we both were.'

Donohue shook his head. 'The fact remains, all the evidence says you pulled the trigger, and that's all any internal investigation would care about. In fact,' he added, barely repressing a smirk, 'it might actually have been a lot better for your career if you'd refused, and let them shoot *you*. No dishonourable discharge, and no possibility of a long jail sentence – and a funeral paid for by the ASI.'

Saul fought back tears of frustration. 'Fuck you. If you're going to hang me out to dry, then damn well get on with it.'

'That isn't why we're here,' said Donohue. 'And that' – he waved at the charged sheet still sitting on Saul's lap – 'is the only copy of your field report still in existence. All other copies have been deleted.'

Saul stared at him. 'What exactly is going on?'

Donohue brushed invisible lint off his jacket. '*Normally*, as I say, there'd be an internal tribunal. A proper hearing. There might still be – but not if you don't want it to.'

Saul thought hard. 'Are you telling me you want to cover this up?'

Donohue's smug expression once again made Saul want to drive a fist into his face. Public Standards seemed to attract individuals of such a reptilian nature that it was easier to imagine them lying on sun-baked stones, catching flies with their tongues, than engaging in any kind of normal human interaction.

'If we open this up to a tribunal, the whole case goes on official records,' said Donohue. 'But if we make it look like none of it ever happened, we'll want you to do something in return.'

Saul imagined Donohue's mouth opening wide to reveal long rows of glistening fangs. 'Go on.'

'Your fuck-up gave us an excuse to send in that task force, and naturally we took an interest in any records we happened to come across.'

'You found something?'

'Something even better than Hsiu-Chuan,' interrupted Sanders, picking up the thread. 'We said earlier that we were watching Maks because we thought he might be selling information to the Tian Di Hui. Well, it looks like maybe he wasn't the only one. So, in return for making this whole mess disappear, we want you to accept a temporary reassignment to another ASI task force.'

Saul settled back in his seat. 'Why?'

'Because someone in that task force is playing the same game. Public Standards can't infiltrate the task force, because someone there will recognize who we are, and that means we need someone else who they're much more likely to know and trust.'

Saul regarded them both with undisguised loathing. 'So you want me to spy on them? And if I refuse?'

Donohue regarded him unpleasantly. 'Think about how much you have to lose, Saul. The Galileo link will be re-established in just a couple of month's time. Do you really want to be stuck inside a cell on charges, just when you have the chance to finally find out if your wife and kid are still alive?'

The man was right, of course, but it didn't make Saul hate him any less.

'All right,' Saul slowly forced the words out, 'what exactly is it you want me to do?'

'The task force is run by a man named Constantin Hanover. You know him?'

'Of course.' Saul nodded. 'He ran the investigation into the collapse of the Copernicus–Galileo gate.'

Donohue's eyes gleamed in the dim light of the observation room. 'There's a lot we can't tell you, but you need to be aware that you're on your own if the mole in Hanover's team figures out you're looking for him. There's only so far we can protect you.'

Saul's eyes drifted back towards the lunar landscape outside. 'You're asking me to make a hard choice, whatever the consequences.'

'There's something else you should know,' said Donohue. 'We found evidence that could link Hsiu-Chuan not only to the Tian Di Hui, but to the people directly responsible for sabotaging the Galileo gate. And if Hsiu-Chuan is involved, then you can bet the Sphere governments are in deep, as well.'

Saul glanced back at him, startled. 'We can prove that?'

'Not quite,' said Donohue. 'We need to talk to whoever it is on Hanover's team that's been dealing with Hsiu-Chuan, in order to make a solid case, but the point is this could be your chance to find out who's responsible for Galileo. That's what you've always wanted, isn't it?'

Saul nodded slowly. 'What exactly did you find there on the pharm?'

'A couple of days ago, a shipment came through the Florida Array from off-world, and got hijacked in broad daylight on its way to an airfield,' said Sanders. 'The hijackers managed to get so deep inside the Array's security zone that they could only have done it with the help of someone on the inside. What we found suggests that the whole operation was planned by Hsiu-Chuan's people, and that means the whole operation was done with Sphere backing.'

'What kind of shipment?'

'Does it matter?' said Sanders. 'Take a look at these.'

Saul's contacts flashed him an alert that Sanders had sent him information. He reached out and touched an icon visible only to himself, then watched as the air rippled, a series of half a dozen photographs materializing around him.

'It doesn't look like much,' he said, after studying them for a moment. 'Just a big metal box with wheels. How did you swing my secondment with Hanover?'

'One of his task force's members got killed in the line of duty,' Sanders replied. 'A man named Mitchell Stone, to be exact.'

Saul opened and closed his mouth. 'You're shitting me. Mitchell?'

'I know he was a friend of yours,' said the agent. 'I'm sorry to have to be the one to tell you.'

Saul had a sudden mental flash of the last time he'd seen Mitchell, years before. They'd been in a bar far up north, near Inuvik, close by the Jupiter platform's CTC gate. They'd both moved on since then – Saul to police work, Mitchell to off-world security – but they had a shared history that bonded them. He remembered Mitchell, sober and drawn, at his brother's funeral; then, months later, grinning in a field under a brilliant Arizona sun, tugging off his wing-suit and laughing as Saul clung to the soil as if it were a lover.

'He was killed serving under Hanover?'

Sanders glanced at Donohue, who replied. 'He was just coming to the end of a long-term secondment to a high-security research programme when he died, so, strictly speaking, no. He was due to rejoin Hanover's task force in a couple of weeks. His death makes it easy enough to put you in his place as a temporary replacement. Frankly, the timing couldn't be better. Hanover's going to be taking his task force out to follow up the hijack, and we're going to make sure you go with them. We're betting that if someone on his team was involved in the snatch, they're going to show themselves.'

'Show themselves how?'

'Put yourself in their shoes, what would you do?'

Saul thought about it. 'Find any evidence of my involvement and do what I could to destroy it.'

Sanders stepped up close to him. 'Find our mole, then, Saul,' he said, 'and there's a chance we can figure out who's responsible for losing Galileo.'

SIX

Thomas Fowler checked his reflection in the elevator's mirrored side walls and saw the face of a man who hadn't enjoyed a decent night's sleep in weeks. A course of amphetamines from an understanding physician was helping with that, but he'd been warned more than once there was only so much abuse his body could take. But, then again, a solid night's sleep was out of the question when you happened to know the world was going to end.

The doors slid open to reveal a busy operations room. While he waited for a guard stationed by the elevator to clear his ID, he counted at least a dozen uniformed ASI staff and a smattering of civilian analysts manning workstations. Dr Amanda Boruzov came towards him, weaving her way through staff and between workstations. The director of research for the Founder Project had skin like porcelain, while small folds around her eyes hinted at an Asiatic inheritance worn smooth over several generations. On this occasion, however, her eyes were rimmed with red, her exhaustion also showing in the way she carried herself.

The problem with women who had skin like porcelain, thought Fowler, was that they always looked like they might easily break.

'Thomas,' she said, as the guard gave him the all-clear, 'I must have just beaten you here. I wasn't sure I'd even be able to make it, at such short notice.'

Fowler stepped forward, once again struck by the unaccustomed buoyancy of his body. No matter how often he made the trip to Copernicus, he never quite adapted to the sudden drop in gravity once he had passed through the Florida Array. The first-aid clinics that served the tens of thousand of people flowing back and forth through the CTC gates worked twenty-four-seven repairing broken bones and fractured skulls. They'd wound up padding the ceilings of the lunar-transit systems, once they realized most people coming through from Earth kept smacking their heads into them.

Their hands touched as they spoke, the touch lingering. If anyone had been paying attention at that moment, they might have guessed at their relationship.

'I guess we should get started,' he said.

He followed her across the busy room, passing wall-mounted TriView panels displaying real-time video of the mass-transit systems connecting Copernicus City to the nearby Lunar Array. They arrived at a second bank of elevators, where another guard checked their UPs for clearance, before allowing them passage.

They both relaxed as soon as the elevator doors closed. Amanda stepped in close to him, her hands taking hold of his lapels and tugging him down towards her, so that he had to bend over, in order to kiss. Fowler reached out and touched a button that halted the elevator between floors.

She pulled back and looked up at him. 'I think it's long past the time we started making plans, don't you?'

He lifted her hands away from his jacket and faked his best smile. 'Yes, I know. I've been thinking about it a lot.'

'And Marcie?'

'I already told her lawyer that Marcie's welcome to the house in New England, if she wants it. She can enjoy it while she has the chance.'

He cleared his throat, suddenly business like once more. 'Listen, there's something I need to tell you before we go into this meeting. There's been a major breakdown in security. We're working to plug it right now, before it has a chance to go public.'

He saw her eyes widen. 'What happened?'

He started the elevator moving again, and it jerked slightly before continuing on its way. 'One of your shipments of Founder artefacts has gone AWOL, grabbed off the road well inside the security perimeter, back in Florida,' he explained, sending a copy of the latest report to her contacts. 'We're still trying to figure out how they managed to fly in a VTOL without us even knowing. That means a very high level of technical access to the perimeter systems.'

She nodded, her eyes becoming unfocused for a moment as she received the report. 'Inez is in charge of local security there,' she said. 'Has he got an explanation?'

Fowler cleared his throat. 'He realizes his neck is on the line over this, but it's starting to look very much like an inside job, which takes a little of the pressure off him personally. And even if he *has* been negligent in some way, we're still going to need him to protect the Arrays as soon as things start to turn bad. Right now we're following up some possible leads, but it's going to take time.'

She nodded, and he could see how the weight of what they were doing oppressed her. They would, after all, be abandoning billions to die; a large enough number to be little more than a comfortable abstraction for some, but not perhaps for Amanda.

She shook her head wearily. 'It just doesn't get any better, does it?'

Fowler shook his head. 'I'm afraid not. But we've managed to track down most of your remaining civilian staff.'

He watched her throat bob as she swallowed. 'And the ones you haven't found yet?'

He smiled grimly. 'They'll be taken care of soon enough.'

'Please tell me that's all the bad news you have.'

'It's not, I'm sorry to say.'

She sighed and nodded. 'Can it wait until after the meeting? I'm not sure how much I can take right now.'

She glanced at her own reflection in the elevator's mirrored wall, reaching up to touch one perfectly shaped eyebrow as if it were somehow out of alignment. He was forced to recall how Amanda had herself been deemed too great a potential security risk to be allowed to seek refuge in the colonies, and that knowledge still left him desolate. It was only meant to be a brief affair, following his divorce, and instead he had developed such complicated feelings for her – feelings that had already compromised his own chances of survival, given one single devastating discovery he had yet to share with her.

But, as she had said herself, there would be time for all that later.

The elevator doors slid open with a faint hiss, and Amanda flashed him a quick, tight smile before stepping out.

Every time he kissed her or felt her smooth milky skin moving against his own, a part of him wanted to shout out his confession to her, and that she knew too much for their masters to ever allow her to live.

And yet, whenever he summoned up the courage to tell her the truth, his tongue turned to lead and the words refused to emerge from his throat.

Tonight, he thought, *after the meeting*. It had to be then.

'All right, first of all, let me bring you up to date on the current state of affairs,' Fowler began, leaning back in his chair and regarding the various faces arranged around the table. 'I'd like you all to make sure your contacts are live.'

The only visible decoration in the room was a framed photograph of the Copernicus CTC Array, taken from the vantage of a nearby ridge. It showed a sprawling complex that extended for kilometres around part of the crater wall.

Dana Paxton represented the Coalition Space Command Authority, while Hendrik Lagerlöf fulfilled the same role for the Board of Extraterrestrial Affairs. The current border situation with Mexical meant that Jimenez couldn't be present. Coalition Navy Captain Anton Inez was also there, of course, taking time out from organizing the evacuation of essential personnel via the Florida Array.

Across the table from Amanda, and the two field investigators reporting directly to Fowler, were Mahindra Kaur and Marcus Fairhurst, representing the European Office of Security and the Three Republics Intelligence Office respectively. Fowler had met these last two only briefly in his capacity as the ASI's Director of Operations, but they were also the reason this meeting was taking place.

A map of the local and interstellar wormhole networks appeared, floating above the table. A single wormhole gate connected the Florida and Lunar Arrays to each other, but the latter facility housed many further wormhole links connecting Earth's moon to a dozen other star systems, some up to a hundred light-years distant. Galileo's collapsed and soon-to-be-re-established gate was represented simply by a dotted line.

'Part of the reason we're here today,' continued Fowler, 'is to do with the consequences of the unique physics existing within the wormholes, and you're going to have to forgive me if I go over some points you may already be very familiar with. Mr Kaur, Mr Fairhurst, this being your first time here, would you say you're reasonably *au fait* with wormhole physics?'

'In the very broadest details,' Kaur replied.

Fairhurst laughed and shrugged his shoulders. 'If I'd known there'd be a test, I'd have done some homework.'

Fowler nodded. 'I'll try and keep it simple, then. As you know,' he glanced quickly around the table, 'the colonies were founded by starships travelling at close to the speed of light, each carrying inside it one end of a wormhole linking it back here to the Moon. However, the way time flows within the wormholes means we can step through to a new star system within months of launching a starship – even though, within our own time-frame back here at home, that starship hasn't yet arrived at its destination.'

'I'll have to admit I've never exactly been clear on just how that works,' said Fairhurst, leaning forward.

'The clue is in the name we use to describe the wormholes,' said Amanda. 'CTC means "closed timelike curve", right?'

Fairhurst nodded.

'Well,' Amanda continued, 'CTC is just a fancy word for time travel. When we send one end of a wormhole to another star, time on board the ship carrying it moves extremely slowly, relative to the outside universe. But, because of the wormhole link on board, we can walk through the wormhole and on to the deck of that ship any time we like, throughout the journey, since the flow of time within the wormhole remains contiguous with its point of origin.'

She tapped a finger on the table in front of her. 'It essentially allows you to step decades into the future, since the time-frame on board the starship is such that anyone who remains on board throughout its journey is going to experience a transit time of only a few months. So long as the far end of the wormhole is moving at relativistic speeds, it's a time machine as well as a shortcut across the universe.'

Fairhurst nodded uncertainly. 'I never understood why we can't see the wormholes from the outside. I mean, if they go all that way across space, we should be able to see them, shouldn't we?'

Fowler barely managed to suppress a grin at the look on Amanda's face.

'That's because the wormholes don't pass through the intervening space at all,' she explained patiently. 'They tunnel through hyperspace instead, outside of the physical constraints of our universe.'

Fairhurst looked none the wiser. 'Please tell me all of this has something to do with why we're here.'

Fowler nodded to Inez. 'If you would, Anton.'

Inez cleared his throat and leaned forward. They'd already decided the bad news was best coming from him.

'What I'm about to tell you,' he began, addressing Kaur and Fairhurst in particular, 'was known to only a very select group until a few days ago. About fifteen years ago, a standard unmanned reconnaissance of the outer Kepler system stumbled across the first evidence of advanced alien intelligence.'

Fowler watched for any signs betraying that either man might know more than he should. Fairhurst simply looked stunned, but Kaur, before reacting, hesitated just a moment too long to be quite convincing.

The CTC network map was replaced by an image of an irregularly shaped lump of rock, the swirling atmosphere of a gas giant visible behind it. The only thing that suggested it was anything other than a typical fragment of stellar detritus was the gleam of burnished metal dotted about its cratered surface.

'Specifically, we found an abandoned space station,' Inez continued. 'Inside was a wormhole gate connecting to a network of thousands of *other* wormhole gates that may have been in existence for . . . well, billions of years. The network also appears to extend across what might be billions of light-years. We've been exploring it for some time, and we've made some interesting discoveries.'

Understatement of the century, reckoned Fowler.

'We've had research and exploration teams investigating the network ever since,' continued Inez. 'We call the hypothetical aliens who built the network "Founders", for want of a better name. We don't know what they looked like, where they came from, or whether they even constituted a single species or more than one. If they left any written records – or records of any kind – we haven't found them yet. All we have are the wormhole gates they left behind and a few recovered artefacts.'

Fairhurst uttered a strangled sound, glancing between Inez and Fowler. 'Captain Inez,' he finally managed to say, 'with all due respect, assuming any of this is true – and I'm not convinced you aren't pulling my leg – I'm struggling to understand why something like this wasn't already known to me.'

Inez started to reply, but Fowler cut in, instead.

'Marcus, we both report to the same people, but not to each other. We've managed to keep a very tight lid on this for a long time, and we did it by not sharing information unless it was absolutely necessary. It's not like there haven't been rumours for years.'

Fairhurst pursed his lips, clearly unsatisfied. 'Crackpot rumours, you mean. Are you suggesting that, with our involvement, this information would have been less secure?' he demanded, his tone noticeably sharp.

'That decision wasn't made lightly,' Fowler replied, 'nor was it made in isolation. It was deemed strictly need-to-know, all the way to the top.'

'You mentioned artefacts,' said Kaur. 'Are these samples of alien technology?'

'Yes,' said Inez. 'In fact, based on our analyses of some artefacts, we managed to develop a form of faster-than-light quantum-communications device.'

'I'm not sure I quite understand,' said Kaur.

Inez spread his hands. 'Communications instantaneously, without limitations – even across light-years.'

'So you've tested this technology,' Kaur asked.

'We did.' Inez nodded. 'In fact, we attempted to contact our future selves.'

'Excuse me?' said Fairhurst, his expression transforming into outright incredulity.

Fowler realized he had been right to pick Inez for the job. He had an air of authority that made it hard for others to challenge even the most lunatic-sounding ideas, when they came from him.

'Specifically,' Inez continued, his face set like granite, 'we transported a prototype quantum transceiver to Ptolemy, fifty-five light-years from here. The intention was to communicate with identical transceivers located both here on Luna and on Earth.'

He spread his hands, then clasped them again. 'Keep in mind that time dilation means Ptolemy, as accessed through the CTC gates, is about sixty years in our future. So when that message was sent from Ptolemy to here, *without* passing through the gate, it arrived – or, rather, it will arrive – sixty years from now. That means any reply from back here can't be sent until then.'

'And?' asked Kaur, his skin taking on a grey tinge.

'The only reply we got from our future selves was a montage of video fragments,' Inez explained. 'What it showed made us very worried indeed. Once you've seen it, it'll be clear why we need your help.'

Fairhurst made a sound of disgust and leaned back, arms folded, but Inez continued unfazed. 'Based solely on these video fragments, we made the decision to send a starship carrying a secret wormhole gate *back* to Earth, from a star system much closer to our own, in order to try and understand what happened.'

'And this gate arrived back here . . . when?' asked Kaur.

'A little over a decade in our future.' Inez brought up a new set of images that segued from one to the other every few seconds. 'Before we get to that, you'd better take a look at the video sequence.'

The image of the mottled grey rock changed abruptly to a view from the deck of a ship somewhere on Earth, sailing close to the base of a clearly alien structure rising out of the deep ocean. It looked, at first glance, like some abstract sculpture of a flower rendered in sheet metal and plastic, and painted in gold and silver. Compensation software, built into the contacts of whoever had recorded the footage, reduced natural eyeball jitter.

They watched as the view panned first across and then upwards, thus giving a sense of the staggering scale of the thing. Clouds drifted around its uppermost petals. The view suddenly blurred as whoever was recording it shifted himself to cope with the ship's rolling motion.

Fowler found his attention drawn to clouds of dark steam shrouding the structure at the point where it rose out of the waters. From what his analysts had been able to tell him, its apparent rate of growth was so great that it might have attained this enormous size within days. There was even reason to believe it had spread roots deep into the Earth's crust, which might account for the overwhelmingly violent seismic activity that would shortly be contributing to the near-extinction of the human race.

'There's nothing like that thing in the oceans anywhere on Earth,' said Fairhurst, his voice rising.

'Not yet, no,' Fowler agreed. 'Here's more, recorded by our

own sci-eval teams, after they'd passed through the CTC gate leading back to our near future.'

Images now appeared of the airless ruins of Copernicus City, and these were followed by high-definition orbital images of the Earth's scarred and lifeless surface. Photographs, taken under high magnification from orbit, showed dozens more flower-like structures pushing through the cloud cover over land and sea. Much of the land was wreathed in smoke like ash, and what little remained visible had clearly been scorched empty of life. All in all, it looked like a vision of hell.

'I still don't understand,' said Fairhurst, squinting as if in pain. 'You're saying this has *already* happened?'

'Is *going* to happen,' Inez corrected. The images continued to cycle through, like the holiday snapshots of a dark and vengeful god.

Inez sat back then, and Fowler picked up where he'd left off. 'Once we'd established the wormhole link back to our own near future, we found no signs of life anywhere on Luna or Earth. Whoever uploaded that montage to the transceivers did it as a warning.'

'But . . . what could possibly have caused this?' Fairhurst blurted.

'To be frank,' Fowler replied, 'we have no idea. It seems obvious the growths and the devastation are linked, although we can't say for certain one caused the other. But it does seem likely.'

'But how?' Fairhurst demanded. 'Was it a meteor, something like that?'

Fowler shook his head. 'There's no impact crater, so no. There's no trace of radioactivity in the near-future atmosphere that might suggest some kind of nuclear bombardment; nothing but the growths, and a lot of ash. Apart from those few slivers of information, we're as much in the dark as you are. All we know is that the end is coming, far, far sooner than anyone realizes.'

Kaur stared at him, his face pale. 'So just how long do we have?' he finally managed to ask.

'Less than three weeks, possibly only two. Ever since we made these discoveries, we've been working on an emergency evacuation programme for essential personnel. If you can help us with certain matters, I can guarantee safe passage for yourselves and your immediate families, at the very least.'

'I know this is hard for you to take in,' Dana Paxton spoke up for the first time, 'but I've been through the CTC gate to our future, myself. So has Mr Lagerlöf. There were hundreds of these flower-like growths scattered all across the globe. We dropped a number of winged drones into the atmosphere from orbit, but they always slipped out of contact after just a few minutes.'

'So whatever did this,' mumbled Kaur, 'whatever force brought this about, it's still down there?'

'That's the only reasonable assumption,' Paxton agreed. 'We had some of the same problems when it came to exploring the near-future Moon, but we were at least able to investigate the remains of Copernicus City with remote probes. Given the circumstances, you can understand how we were ready to shut down the gate leading back to Tau Ceti the instant we came under attack. Luckily, we never had to. But if you *do* decide you want to see all this for yourselves first-hand, I'll be responsible for your safety.'

'We're facing an extinction event,' added Fowler, 'and if it wasn't for the existence of the interstellar colonies, the human race would be finished. We can save some of the people back home, and here on the Moon, but not all. Our responsibility from here on is to make sure the colonies survive.'

'Three weeks?' echoed Fairhurst, sounding like he was having trouble getting the words out.

Kaur's skin had taken on a waxen quality. 'And we'll be allowed to bring our families through the Array – *if* we help you in some way?'

Fowler nodded.

'Surely there must be some way to prevent this,' Fairhurst protested.

'Possibly,' Fowler replied. 'Or, at least, it would be monstrous of us not to try. Which brings me to my next point: we need your help in locating a missing shipment.'

Fowler held the whisky at the back of his mouth, rolling it around his tongue before finally swallowing it down. Amanda had collapsed into the chair opposite, settling slowly into the cushions under the lunar gravity. Behind her, a window of Fowler's apartment looked towards the tall peaks rising at the centre of the Copernicus Crater. Much of the city was buried deep beneath the regolith, but a significant number of buildings, whose financiers could afford the extra shielding, rose to a considerable height.

'I spoke with Anderson at the Coalition Security Council,' he said, staring out the window. 'You'll be thrilled to know he still thinks we can pull a rabbit out of a hat and save the day.'

'He really thinks we can change what's already happened?'

He finally glanced over at her. 'Can you blame him? Look at Fairhurst – he's probably already convinced himself our meeting never even happened, and both of them are cut from the same cloth.' He studied the glass in his hand. 'Even so, the heads of all three Republics have agreed to making some kind of joint public announcement.'

'When?'

Fowler shrugged. 'That's the question, isn't it? My guess is they'll wait until it's obvious to everyone else that something terrible is happening.' He thought of some of the atmospheric phenomena recorded by the probes studying the devastated future Earth: bright twists of light that some interpreted as distortions of space and time, and others considered as evidence of some non-material intelligence.

He noticed her shiver. 'Maybe there's a chance it *isn't* too late,' she said. 'Maybe we can still stop this from ever happening. Maybe that's why someone left us that warning, because they knew there was still a way.'

'How?' Fowler shook his head. 'By going back into the past and changing things? Can't be done. Remember your Novikov.'

'Yes, I know.' She sounded irritated. 'If an event can bring about a paradox—'

'Then the probability of that event taking place is zero,' he finished for her. 'Or were you thinking about alternate timelines? They're a fiction, and there's nothing we can do to change the inevitable.'

He quickly drained the last of his whisky; no telling when he'd next get the opportunity for another. To his irritation, the glow of the alcohol failed to chase away the clamminess of his skin.

'Now for some of that news I've been saving,' he said. 'We've identified your survivor – the one your people brought back from the near future.'

She gripped her glass in both hands, the knuckles turning pale. 'And?'

'His name is Mitchell Stone. He used to be under Hanover's command.'

They'd found him preserved inside an experimental cryogenics unit on Luna, ten years in the future. He'd been the only living thing left alive, and there were many, many questions they wanted to ask him.

'But he's—'

'The same Mitchell Stone who suffered what *should* have been a fatal accident at Site 17 just a few weeks ago,' he agreed. 'And now,' he arched an eyebrow, 'thanks to the vagaries of time travel, we have *two* Mitchell Stones in existence at once, both recovering from separate incidents.'

'Oh, for . . .' Amanda put her glass down on a small side table next to her chair, and covered her face with two carefully manicured hands before letting them slide down to cover only her mouth and nose. She peered over her fingertips to regard him with a mixture of horror and awe. 'The one you brought back here from the near future? The one who was frozen? Is he awake yet?'

'Yes, and has been awake for a couple of days now. It was touch and go for a while, when it came to reviving him, but we've already begun an interrogation. Hopefully he can tell us something about just what it is we're dealing with now.'

'And the other one? The one who got swallowed up in that pit?'

'Still under heavy sedation. Obviously it's the near-future Mitchell we really need answers from. He must have witnessed everything that's going to happen.'

He gave her a moment to try and absorb everything he'd told her.

'Listen,' she said after a moment. 'About . . . us.'

He raised both eyebrows.

'I know we've been avoiding discussing any plans about the future,' she said. 'It's not like there was ever a right time to talk about it. I wasn't sure until now, but . . . I'm not going off to the colonies with the rest of you.' She cleared her throat. 'I'm staying here.'

He stared at her wordlessly for a moment, before he could summon a response. 'I don't understand.'

She took a deep breath, her shoulders rising and then falling. 'I don't know if I want to survive what's coming, knowing I had a part to play in all . . . all of this.'

In the end of the world, he guessed she meant to say, but couldn't bring herself to speak the words.

'You're serious?'

'Think of it like the captain going down with the sinking ship after she's steered it straight into an iceberg, Thomas. I should have listened more to my staff when they warned me not to let those artefacts be brought to Earth until we knew exactly what we were dealing with.'

'We don't know that the artefacts are responsible. And you can't blame yourself for—'

'Then who do I blame?' she snapped.

He cleared his throat. 'There's no point worrying about what can't be undone.'

'If we do follow the rest of them to the colonies, we'll be cut off from everything we've ever known. All of it . . . gone.' She shuddered. 'I'd say I can't even imagine it, but I don't need to. I've *seen* it.'

She stood up then, smoothing her skirt down over her thighs, her movements slow and fluid in the lower gravity. He had a sudden flash of memory from several nights back, of her laughing and then sighing as he kissed her thighs, pulling himself up and on top of her.

'Wait,' he said. 'Don't . . .'

She walked over to the door. 'Don't even bother trying to convince me, Thomas. I want to see how it ends.'

'There's something you need to know,' he said.

'What?'

'About the video message – the warning. You haven't seen all of it.'

She frowned and let go of the door handle. 'I haven't?'

'I had part of it redacted.'

She regarded him uncertainly. 'What's in the bits you took out?'

He got up to fetch himself another drink. He was going to need it to get through this.

'You are,' he replied.

SEVEN

Flathead Lake, Montana, 25 January 2235

It took Jeff Cairns nearly six hours to navigate the hire car to his cabin in the Rockies. Early spring rains, bringing the last of the meltwater down from the peaks, had flooded out a bridge and also wiped out a section of road, meaning long detours and one eye kept constantly on the weather feed, throughout his long drive north from Missoula.

As soon as he had left the city limits and the hopper port behind, Jeff took manual control, ignoring the dashboard's warning that his insurance was void if he didn't stick to automatic so long as the weather bureau warned of adverse conditions. He took pleasure in the feel of the steering wheel under his hands, despite the periodic squalls of rain that lashed at his windscreen, but after a while the rain faded to a light drizzle and the car altered its configuration, becoming lower and more aerodynamic, and even changing colour according to some pre-programmed algorithm. After a couple of hours, a break in the clouds suddenly appeared, and Jeff soon found himself driving through sunlight of such glorious intensity that it seemed to bore through his eyes to touch against the back of his skull.

He took the off-ramp when the car instructed him to, the roads thereafter becoming gradually steeper, higher and narrower, until finally he followed a series of switchbacks, up the side of a hill above Flathead Lake, to a gravelled driveway fronting a gable-roofed log house.

Jeff climbed out and walked around, stretching his legs after such a long drive, while his car sidled over to the grassy slope, there sucking up leaves and twigs and any other available biomass. He tucked his hands into the pockets of his down jacket, and gazed down the slope of the wooded hill to where the waters of the lake shimmered gold and silver. The evening was drawing in as the sun dipped down towards the peaks on the far side of the lake, the last of the rain clouds evaporating even as their fading shadows drifted across hills dense with larch and aspen.

When he felt ready, he walked around to the rear of the cabin and checked the mini-tokamak that supplied it with power. He next headed over to a tool shed standing below some trees that grew up the slope behind the cabin, where he stepped inside and cleared away a tarpaulin laid across the floor. Beneath was a metal door with a combination lock. He rotated it in different directions a couple of times until the lid clicked open, then withdrew a foil blister-pack from inside his jacket and placed it inside the safe, before locking it once more.

As he returned to the car to collect his luggage, Jeff accessed his UP and saw there were new messages waiting for him, all left by Olivia. He left them unopened, afraid that, if he did read them, he might make the mistake of calling her back and telling her all the things he'd struggled to keep hidden from her.

He woke with a start not long after dawn. He had been dreaming of Site 17, of walking through the abyssal dark with lights strung along on either side. Farad had been standing in front of him, his face full of alarm, shouting at him silently through his visor.

Jeff got up, his body stiff and sore, and ate a sparse breakfast before driving the rental downhill to where a trail met the road close by the lake. He still retained vivid memories of hiking along this same trail in what now felt like another lifetime. He'd been working on his graduate thesis the first time he'd come here and, although he'd hiked across other parks and trails in the years since,

Flathead Lake still held a special place in his heart. The girl he'd brought with him all those years ago was long gone, but he'd come back almost every year since. The bonuses he and Olivia had received for their work on the Jupiter platform had gone towards the down-payment on the cabin, and they had spent several summers there together, before things had soured.

Later hiking trips, whether with other people or on his own, had taught him that particularly intractable problems – whether related to his work in the University of California's exobiology department or to his intermittent love life – could often be best solved during his traversing of the trails scattered around the lake. On such occasions, the mountains and sky became a great blank canvas for his thoughts, a cosmic whiteboard that left him feeling he understood the way the world worked just a little bit better than before.

But this time was different. This time he didn't want to think at all. He wanted to become lost in the scent of budding wildflowers, the sight of whitetail deer or the occasional elk picking their way down forest slopes, or amidst the meltwater cascading down those same slopes in the first weeks of spring.

He pushed himself hard for the first half-dozen kilometres, sweating beneath his down jacket, despite the freezing temperatures, his feet chafing painfully inside stiff new hiking boots. And, for a while, it worked; but the first time he stopped to eat a granola bar and take in the view, looking out across a world he could almost imagine was devoid of people, all he could really see was a great pyramidal mass under a starless sky, squatting on an airless plain in a future he would have found unimaginable if he hadn't already visited it.

He felt, to his bitter annoyance, lonely. So when an unexpected visitor appeared as if out of nowhere, a few days later, he felt pathetically grateful even while he knew the only reason they could possibly be here was to bring him very bad news.

Jeff squinted into the brilliant morning light, beyond the porch, to see the lean figure of Dan Rush, his long, sallow features and weather-beaten skin somehow more appropriate to an ageing cow-boy than a materials analyst.

'Dan?' Jeff peered at him groggily, his dressing gown clutched around his shoulders, as he'd slept well past midday. 'What the fuck are you doing out here?'

Dan rocked from foot to foot on the narrow porch, looking at him expectantly, dressed only in a light sports jacket more suited to visiting a bar than the great outdoors. A second hire car was parked near Jeff's own, where it shuffled closer to the verge and began tearing up the same patch of grass, sucking the biomass deep into its guts prior to converting it to ethanol.

Jeff glanced down and saw that Dan was wearing dress shoes, even less appropriate to the Rockies, at the tail end of winter.

'Will you just let me in?' Dan demanded, shoving his hands into his pockets and shivering. 'It's cold as hell out here.'

Jeff pressed the fingers of one hand into the corners of his eyes before stepping to one side, waving for Dan to come in.

Dan headed straight for the fire that Jeff had left smouldering overnight in the hearth. He leaned over it with his collar pulled up, still shivering, rubbing his hands vigorously before the naked heat. He glanced briefly at the dozen beer bottles piled up on a table next to the couch, but elected to say nothing.

'I've got coffee on the go,' Jeff mumbled, head still throbbing from his night of drinking and channel-surfing. 'You want some?'

Dan glanced at him and nodded, before returning his attention to the hearth.

Jeff checked the filter had finished dripping the last of the Arabica into a pot, and nuked a packet of frozen waffles while he was at it. Given the long drive to the cabin, he guessed Dan probably hadn't eaten any breakfast. He then grabbed a couple of mugs and put them on a tray, along with the coffee and waffles. By the time he returned to the living room, Dan had pulled a chair up next to the hearth, and sat there staring contemplatively into the flames.

They ate in silence at first, Jeff watching Dan plough his way through most of the waffles. He seemed twitchy as a bird, tension visible in the set of his jaw and the way he kept massaging his hands in the rare moments they weren't holding either food or coffee.

'How did you find me out here?' Jeff finally asked. 'I don't remember telling anyone where I'd be.'

'We did agree to stay in touch, right?' said Dan.

'Yes, but that's not the same as telling each other where we'd be. Why didn't you just get in touch the way we agreed, rather than actually hauling your ass all the way out here?'

'Your ex-wife in Vermont told me where to find you,' Dan replied. 'She told me she thought you'd been acting strangely and that, if you'd gone anywhere at all, it was probably here.'

Jeff groaned and leaned back, closing his eyes for a moment. 'How did you find her?'

'I met her one time when she came down to Orlando to meet you, remember?' Dan replied. 'Right after you got back together with her, and you'd already mentioned she lived in Jacksonville. There's only one Olivia Jury there. I told her I badly needed to get hold of you.' He looked around the room. 'So why did you decide to come all the way out here?'

'I've been hiding in case someone figured out we'd hacked the Tau Ceti databases. I got tired of sleeping in motels and thought I might as well hole up here as anywhere else, at least until I heard from Farad.'

'And you didn't bring Olivia with you?'

'I thought I'd be putting her in danger if I did.'

'You haven't told her anything?'

'No.' Jeff shook his head. 'You still haven't told me why you're here.'

Dan chewed his food for several long seconds, as he gazed into the flames. 'I came to tell you Lucy's dead.'

Jeff stared at him, his hangover suddenly forgotten. He remembered the sight of her crouching by the pit next to Dan, in the moments before they found Mitchell.

'Police found her in her car in a motel parking lot.' Dan finally looked back up. 'She'd been on her way to Miami.' He took a sip of his coffee and finally met Jeff's eye. 'Officially it was a heart attack, but she'd called me the day before and told me she was certain she was being followed. She wanted to know if I'd noticed anything like that myself.'

'That's . . . that's dreadful.'

'Terrible,' Dan agreed. 'And particularly worrying since Lou Winston also appears to have vanished. First thing I did after hearing about Lucy was try to get hold of him. Turns out he has a place on one of those floating platforms just offshore from New Orleans, but his family reported him missing more than a day ago.'

Jeff felt like a cavity had been hollowed out inside his chest. 'They know about the files, right? And now they're coming after us.'

Dan shook his head, his expression bleak. 'Don't be so certain that's the reason. I tried to get hold of people from the other sci-eval teams, people who're supposed to be back home by now, and nobody knows where they are. My guess is Hanover or somebody higher up the food chain – Fowler, maybe, or Borusov – figured the civilian staff were too much of a security risk to be allowed to live.'

Jeff gaped at him. 'You don't seriously think they're *all* dead?'

Dan shrugged. 'As far as I'm concerned, we're all that's left of the sci-eval teams. If we're lucky, they don't even know about the files, but either way they're still going to come looking for both of us.'

'How can you be so sure?'

Dan took a sip of his coffee before replying. 'Where I live in Orlando is right across the street from a hotel. After I heard about Lou, I hired a room there with a good view of the inside of my own apartment. I wasn't there more than a couple of hours before I saw someone sneaking around inside my place. I grabbed my rucksack and left town as fast as I could.'

'Maybe we should talk to the police.'

'What could we tell them? The only thing that connects us to each other is our work on the Founder Network, and officially that doesn't even exist. They'd have laughed us out of the station as soon as we started saying anything about Founders or ancient alien artefacts.'

Jeff nodded, feeling his heart sink. Everyone on the sci-eval teams based out at Tau Ceti knew that the catastrophe that would wipe out life on Earth was due some time during the next thirty years. They had lodged protests regarding the restriction on their access to the data recovered from the near-future, and it hadn't helped that the time-stamps had been carefully removed from the few images and scraps of information they were granted access to. *Something* was being deliberately kept from them and, being scientists, it was only a matter of time before one of them took matters into their own hands.

Stealing a copy of the entire database had been Farad's idea, and he'd first approached Lucy, since she was the one with the in-depth knowledge of the Tau Ceti station's security protocols. With her help, and with Jeff and Dan's more than willing support, they had found a way to hack into the station's networks and copy the unaltered records recovered from the near future. Unfortunately, the files they had recovered proved to be protected by a particularly impenetrable form of encryption, one that Farad had assured them would take time and considerable skill to break.

The four of them had agreed to return to their respective homes at roughly the same time, Farad volunteering to try and find some way to reverse-engineer the protected files in the meantime. And then, once they had acquired the proof they needed, they would go public.

A sick chill wrapped itself around Jeff's bones as he poured himself another coffee. He noticed his hands were shaking. 'Then I guess we're lucky we managed to stay alive this long.'

Dan shot him an exasperated look and pointed at the cabin's wall-screen. 'Don't count your chickens just yet. Haven't you seen the news?'

'I didn't come here to watch the news. The whole point of a place like this is to avoid the outside world.'

'Right.' Dan stood and gestured towards the screen. It came to life and he quickly navigated to one of the main news-feeds, in which Jeff saw an aerial view of the ocean. The water was foaming for kilometres around, while a headline caption suggested they might be witnessing an undersea volcano. An inlaid satellite image revealed that the disturbance was taking place a few hundred kilometres north of the Mariana Islands, nearly halfway around the world.

'It's already started,' said Jeff, that sick feeling getting worse.

'I figure we've got no more than a couple of weeks before it's all over,' said Dan. 'You've seen the way the ASI and military have been building up reinforcements all around the Florida Array. Training exercise, my ass. They're trying to tell us the increased security is because of some hijack, but I figure our glorious leaders are going to evacuate themselves to the colonies before things turn really nasty. The last thing they need is us finding proof that they were the ones responsible for all this before they have a chance to make their getaway.'

Jeff swallowed. 'I guess it's too late to talk to the press.'

Dan nodded. 'Even if we did, we'd only be making ourselves easy targets. And we'd have no way of proving what we know – not unless we can find some way inside those encrypted files. You still have your copy of them, right?'

Jeff gave an involuntary glance towards the rear of the cabin. 'It's somewhere safe.'

'Uh-huh. I hope so.'

Jeff rotated his coffee mug between both hands. 'You really think they're going to try and take over the colonies by force?'

'What else are they going to do? Ask them for refugee status?' Dan barked. 'Fat chance of that. They're going to want to run things themselves, and their job'll be that much easier if they can find a way to convince the people out there they had nothing to do with the end of life on Earth.' Dan stabbed at his chest with a finger. 'But we're the ones who can tell them all what really happened. We're witnesses to the greatest crime in history. So we'll make our own escape, and stop these bastards in their tracks.'

'Escape where?'

'To the colonies.'

Jeff sighed and put his mug down. 'You're not thinking logi-cally. How could you possibly get inside the Array, and past the ASI's own cops if they're out looking for us?'

'I know people in the Florida Array, and up at Copernicus,' said Dan, his expression fervent. 'People I trust. They can help us get through safely.' His hands tightened into fists, his expres-sion intent. Jeff was reminded of a deer standing poised in the long savannah grass, ready to take flight at the first sign of danger.

'You didn't say whether anything's happened to Farad. The files are useless unless he managed to find some way to crack them.'

Dan shook his head. 'I tried getting hold of him, but he seems to be completely offline. Even if he's okay, I couldn't begin to tell you for sure where he is.'

Jeff wondered if that didn't make him the most sensible out of all of them. 'He's on Newton, visiting family – or that's his cover story, anyway. What if we can't warn him before the ASI locate him?'

Dan regarded him bleakly. 'Then we're screwed, unless we can find a way to hack the database files ourselves. That's not to men-tion the risk we'd be taking if we actively went looking for him. We could wind up making it easier for them to catch us, as well as him.'

'There must be someone else we could send the files to, who could help us?'

Dan sighed and shook his head. 'Remember, the files are stored in an intelligent format.'

'Lucy mentioned something about that, but I didn't quite follow it all.'

'It's a compression technology that automatically transmits an alert back to its point of origin whenever it's sent through any kind of network. And if it doesn't have explicit permission to be transferred on that network, it tells the ASI exactly where it's been and where it's headed, making it even easier to track us down. And assuming we just went ahead and forwarded the information to a news agency or anyone else, there's a chance the whole package might erase itself if they didn't use the correct decryption method. That's why we're keeping our copies strictly offline.'

Jeff nodded, embarrassed now that he hadn't paid more attention at the time.

Dan's expression grew more contemplative. 'But that doesn't mean we couldn't maybe still find a way to break that encryption, if there was someone we know much closer to hand, someone we could trust. I was thinking about Olivia, as a matter of fact. She's a network-security consultant, isn't she? Would she be able to do it?'

Jeff felt himself stiffen. 'I don't want Olivia involved in any of this.'

'We're *all* involved in this,' said Dan. 'Everyone on the whole goddamn planet is involved. Or would you rather just wait a couple of days and let her figure out what's going on along with the rest of the human race?'

Jeff felt a sudden, desperate need to be with her. 'It's not that simple. We were supposed to spend time together after I got home. Instead I barely stopped by long enough to tell her I was going to disappear for a while, but I couldn't tell her the reason why. I mean, the less she knows, the better, right?' He had tried to assure Olivia that he would explain everything once the time was right, but even as he'd spoken the words, the look on her face had told him how very inadequate they were. 'Maybe we could just wait and see if Farad tries to get in touch before—'

'No.' Dan shook his head firmly. 'The longer we wait, the more chance that whoever caught up with Lucy and Lou will find us as well.' He gazed pointedly at Jeff. 'I had an easy enough time finding you, so how hard do you think the ASI would find it?'

Jeff stared at him, mute with shock.

'Exactly.' Dan nodded, half to himself. 'Your UP can be traced with a court order. Every time you buy something, or rent a car or anything else, your contacts know where you are and when you were there. Same goes for me. All the ASI have to do is prove sufficient cause.'

Jeff swallowed. 'We could get ourselves new contacts.'

Dan shook his head, 'Purchasing them legally leaves us right back where we started. No, we need black-market contacts preloaded with fake UPs, the whole works.'

'I have no idea where to get hold of something like that.'

'I do, though,' Dan replied, picking up his rucksack and dropping it on a table standing near the couch. He dug out a slim black rod and then a smaller, metal oblong the size and shape of a credit chip, dumping them next to each other on the table.

He picked up the black rod. 'I used this to fry every locator node in my hire car and clothing. You'll need to swipe it down over all your own clothes, as well.' He put the rod down and picked up the metal oblong. 'This is what car-jacking crews use to override a vehicle's locking system.'

'Where did you get hold of this stuff?'

'I didn't,' Dan said simply. 'I built it myself. There's hardly an electronic lock or locator in the world that can stand up to even crude hacks like this one.'

Jeff glanced towards the door. 'So your car . . . ?'

'Is stolen,' Dan confirmed. 'I also made some enquiries on the way here and found out about a guy in Missoula who can get us untraceable UPs. Nobody will know who we are.'

'Why not just use unregistered UPs? They're good enough in an emergency.'

'But they won't help us get through Array security, will they? We need complete false identities for that.'

'Okay.' Jeff nodded. 'Do you want me to come to Missoula with you?'

Dan squinted at him. 'Do the people around here know you?'

'Some of them, yes.'

'Did you go into town on your way here?'

'Nope.'

Dan thought for a moment. 'I need to head down to Lakeside just now, and try and find another car. I can ditch the one I brought while I'm at it, but I think it's best I do that on my own.'

'Why?'

'Nobody there knows who I am, whereas you need to stay out of sight in case someone's been making enquiries about you. It shouldn't take me more than a half day, at the most, to track this guy down. If it takes longer, I can sleep in the back of the car and be back here by tomorrow morning. What supplies do you have?'

'You mean like food, that kind of thing?' Jeff glanced at the beer bottles piled on the table. 'That was pretty much it. I meant to pick more supplies up today.'

Dan sighed. 'Okay, if I've got enough time, I'll grab us something for the trip, but I'd rather not use any rest stops on the way if I can avoid it. You get yourself ready and I'll be back as soon as I can. Sound like a plan?'

'Sounds like a plan,' Jeff agreed. 'Assuming I still believe we even had this conversation after I have some more coffee.'

Dan nodded towards the wand-like device. 'Remember to use that on all your clothes as well as your car,' he advised. 'Just hold down the button, swipe it over your stuff, and the readout'll warn you if you missed anything.'

'And the car-jacker?'

'Just press it against any car's ID panel, and you'll be in after a couple of seconds.'

'That's it?'

Dan grinned. 'I know. Scandalous, isn't it?'

He walked over to the door, hesitating as he put his hand on the handle. 'We're not to blame for all of this, Jeff. We even warned the ones who are. I really don't know how much more we could have done.'

'I wish I could feel that sure.'

Dan pulled the door open, letting in a blast of freezing mountain air. 'I'll be back as soon as I can.'

'Okay.' Jeff pulled his crumpled bathrobe closer around him. 'If anything happens, should I call you?'

'If anything happens, it'll probably be too late.'

'Right.' Jeff felt far from reassured. 'Okay. I'll be waiting for you.'

EIGHT

Mitchell Stone awoke to pale-green light filtering through a barred window, high up, the shadows of branches flickering against the wall opposite. He stared up at a ceiling painted yellow, faint lines scarring the plaster, before smoothing both hands across his face and close-cropped scalp. The air smelled of detergent.

The memories slowly trickled back. He remembered being revived in a lunar cryogenics facility, then being transported to a ship carrying a wormhole gate that led back to a time when grey ashen clouds hadn't yet swept the world clean.

He tested his fingers, wiggling them slightly before raising one arm and bringing it close to his face. He studied the delicate whorls of his fingertips as if he had never seen them before, more memories slowly dripping back into his conscious mind like sticky molasses. With every day that passed, they came back to him a little more quickly – an inevitable side effect, Albright had assured him, of the cryogenics revival process.

Mitchell sat up on the thin mattress, clad only in disposable medical blues, and swung his arm from side to side, slowly at first, then with increasing rapidity, until it moved in a blur of speed. He finally stopped and pressed it close to his chest, gasping at the sudden pain lancing through his muscles.

He looked over at the far wall of his cell, four metres away. He imagined himself there, and—

—he *was* there, his face pressed to the opposite wall, pinpricks of sweat standing out on his forehead. He groaned as cramp took hold of both his legs, pinpricks of fire spreading simultaneously through his chest and belly. He let himself slide down the wall to rest on his haunches, once more waiting for the pain to diminish. But, with every day that passed, the agony was just that little bit less.

After that, he stood up again, on unsteady legs, and stepped over to the wall immediately beneath the window.

The barred window was tiny, much too small to even contemplate squeezing through. It had also been placed far enough above head height to make it almost impossible to see more than a thin sliver of sky. Mitchell jumped up, and managed to grab hold of two bars, before pulling himself up with a grunt.

On his first day here, he'd been as weak as a fish flopping on a fisherman's deck, but now his upper-body strength was coming back to him fast. He caught a glimpse of sycamores planted in a line beyond the window, and an airstrip further off. Low one- and two-storey buildings with whitewashed exteriors stood beyond it. He dropped back down, entranced by that vision of blue skies and flourishing grass. Just then, he heard the sound of footsteps approaching his cell door.

The guards were coming for him yet again.

'All right, interview five,' began Albright, tapping at the desk between them.

Mitchell guessed his interrogator was in his mid-forties, with hair greying at the temples. He wore the uniform of the Second Republic's military.

'Subject is Mitchell Stone. All right, Mitchell,' said Albright, looking back up. 'Let's start from the beginning again. Tell me how you wound up in that cryogenics lab.'

Mitchell shifted in the folding metal chair, to which he was handcuffed on either side, and glanced up at the bouquet of omnidirectional lenses mounted in the ceiling directly overhead. 'You've asked me that same question every single day since I woke up,' he said, dropping his gaze again. 'And every single day I give you exactly the same answer.'

Albright's expression remained stony. 'Things are going to be a little different this time, Mitchell, so just humour me.'

'I was trying to reach the colonies,' Mitchell replied, spreading his hands as far as the handcuffs would allow. 'By that time the growths were spreading fast back on Earth. I couldn't get to any of the colony gates in all the panic, so I figured I had at least an out-side chance of staying alive in the cryo lab.' He lowered his hands again. 'And that's where you found me, ten years later.'

Albright glanced down and scratched a note into the reflective surface of his desk with a plastic stylus.

Books lined a plywood bookcase set against one wall, next to which stood a hospital gurney equipped with leather restraints and a small medical-supplies cabinet. A window beyond the desk of-fered a better view of what was undoubtedly one of Array Security and Immigration's regional admin centres, and Mitchell gazed past Albright's shoulder and out at the sunlit landscape with longing.

'Why were you trying to reach the colonies?' asked Albright.

Mitchell sighed. 'I didn't want to die, any more than anyone else did.'

Albright frowned. 'Are you sure that's the only reason?'

Mitchell shrugged. 'I can't think of any other.'

Albright touched the desk once more, and Mitchell saw icons blink and shift across its surface. Contacts would have made his life much easier, but clearly they weren't going to trust him with anything like that.

A small TriView screen came to life on the wall behind Al-bright's desk. It showed a still image of a man lying in a hospital bed, surrounded by a tangle of machinery and tubes. A figure dressed in a protective suit, face hidden behind a visor, stood by his bedside, taking notes.

This, thought Mitchell, was something new.

'Do you recognize the man in the bed?' asked Albright.

Mitchell found he couldn't drag his eyes away from the image. Intellectually, he'd realized that his younger self was, at that very moment, still recovering from his recent experiences at Site 17, but actually seeing the evidence here was another matter.

'It's me,' he replied. 'Where are you keeping him?'

Albright smiled. 'Don't you remember?'

He did, of course, although the memory only returned to him at that very moment. Mitchell found he couldn't tear his gaze from his younger self, his features soft and relaxed under the influence of powerful sedatives.

'Do you actually understand *why* there are two of you?' asked Albright.

'Because when you brought me back here from that cryo lab ten years in the future, you brought me into my own past,' Mitchell replied, finally looking away from the screen.

He could barely remember the ward they'd put him after Site 17; they'd kept him unconscious almost around the clock. Someone had rescued him – no, *would* rescue him – by breaking into the ward and half carrying him to safety, but for the moment that rescuer's face remained an unidentifiable blur. After that Mitchell had woken up in a motel, alongside everything he needed to get himself to Copernicus.

'You were delirious when they recovered you from the chamber of pits, but Eliza Schlegel made sure everything you said was properly recorded and transcribed.' Albright glanced again at his desk. 'Now, apparently you made reference several times to being 'sent back' to carry out some task.' Albright leaned forward. 'What kind of task?'

Mitchell licked suddenly dry lips. 'I don't remember ever saying that.'

'Really? I can play it back for you right now.'

The picture on the screen changed to show the interior of a medvac unit. He now lay on a palette with an oxygen mask over his mouth, while Lou Winston passed a diagnostics wand over his body. Mitchell watched his younger self suddenly jerk awake on the pallet, ripping the mask from his face in a panic. A rush of words came spilling out, ones he even now couldn't remember uttering, and his voice was filled with a terrible urgency. He had a sudden vivid recollection of grabbing Dan Rush's arm, as they lifted him into the unit, but that was all.

Mitchell gripped the arms of his chair tightly, and waited for Albright to switch the recording off. 'I don't remember any of that.'

Albright shook his head. 'We know you're lying, Mitchell. The effects of long-term cryogenic storage are well known, and full recovery of memory takes a week at best. You've been here longer than that, and perhaps you don't remember everything, but you'll still remember enough to answer most of our questions.'

'Why does it matter to you?'

Albright laughed, shaking his head. 'Now you're just being obstructive. We have recordings of you claiming this task was given to you by the Founders. How is that possible?'

'I don't know.'

'Why don't you tell me the truth?'

Mitchell leaned back, staring once more up at the small constellation of lenses overhead. 'How about I answer a question, but only if you answer one of mine. Is that a deal?'

'We don't do "deals", Mitchell.'

Mitchell stared at him and waited.

'Fine,' Albright sighed, after more than half a minute had passed. 'But I'm not making any promises.'

'I know you sent unmanned probes into the ruins of the near-future Copernicus City, right?'

'The same probes that recovered you from the lab, yes.'

Mitchell licked his lips, suddenly full of a nervous anxiety. 'Did you send them into the Lunar Array itself? Did they tell you if the CTC gates to the colonies were still open?'

Albright regarded him steadily. 'There hasn't been the time to make a detailed enough investigation. Certainly the Array *looks* half ruined but, as to the integrity of the gates, I don't have enough clearance to know one way or the other. Now it's my turn,' he said, pointing a finger towards the screen. 'How the hell did you get out of that secure ward and find your way to the Moon, in the first place?'

The corner of Mitchell's mouth twitched. 'You mean, how am I *going* to get out of there? That's what you want to know, isn't it?'

Albright stood up from behind his desk and walked forward to stand in front of Mitchell, his face red with anger. 'Stop fucking around. There's too much at stake, and the people who put me in charge of getting answers from you are starting to get *very* impatient.'

'Whatever I tell you doesn't matter a damn,' Mitchell rasped. 'You know why? Because, from my perspective, everything you're trying to stop has already happened more than ten years in my past. The only reason you're here, asking me these questions, is because the people you work for are too mentally limited to understand that one simple fact.'

Albright was breathing hard through his nose and, for a moment, Mitchell thought he might strike him. But, after a second or two, his interrogator took a step back, wiping his hand across his mouth.

'You were in charge of interrogations at the Lunar Array, a few years back, weren't you?' asked Albright.

'Sure. Right after the Galileo gate was sabotaged.'

Albright nodded. 'And how did *you* know if detainees were telling the truth or not?'

'We used infra-red cameras to pick up increases in subcutaneous blood flow, and voltage scanners that could remotely map brain wave functions in three dimensions and tell us whether or not they were lying. That the kind of thing you mean?'

'You've already noticed we have the same devices here?' Albright nodded towards the lenses suspended above Mitchell's head. 'You've also worked in the ASI long enough to know just what's going to happen to you if you don't start telling us the truth.'

Mitchell closed his eyes for a moment, remembering how, after waking in the motel, he'd managed to make his way through the

Florida–Copernicus gate, only to be spotted by ASI agents on the lookout for him inside the Lunar Array. He'd found an airlock equipped with pressure suits, and made his escape across the silent lunar landscape, the great crescent shape of the Array rising to one side as he headed for the cryo labs situated further along the crater wall.

'You want to know the truth?' he said, opening his eyes again. 'The learning pools remade me. They pulled me apart and put me together again, better than before.'

Albright frowned. 'Learning pools?'

'The pits me and Vogel got caught in.'

He remembered the sense of stark terror as the black, tar-like liquid had started to fill the pit all around them, and then that sense of floating in a timeless void. 'When Jeff Cairns found me, I was still trying to understand what had happened to me. But one thing above all had changed: I wasn't afraid of anything any more, not even death.' He locked eyes with Albright. 'Or anything you could possibly threaten me with.'

Albright stared at him for several seconds, then stepped back to his desk and swept his hand across it in a practised gesture. The desk's surface dulled to an inanimate grey.

'The next time we meet isn't going to be nearly as civilized,' said Albright. 'Because there's too much at stake. But I want you to think about one thing that's been puzzling me, before we meet again tomorrow morning.'

'What?'

'You were the only thing still alive anywhere on the Moon or Earth, when we found you,' said Albright. 'Why *you*? Why would whatever wiped out every last trace of life everywhere else leave *you* untouched?'

Mitchell looked towards the window, and said nothing.

NINE

'Tell me, you ever jump out of a plane? Go parachuting, or any-thing like that?'

Saul glanced at the man opposite: lean and sharp-faced with deep-set eyes, his head jerking slightly from side to side as the sub-orbital slammed through the stratosphere. Saul's UP floated a tag next to him, identifying the man as Sefu Nazawi.

'Once,' Saul replied. His knuckles shone white where they gripped the padded restraints confining his chest and shoulders.

Up until now, the conversation had been distinctly muted, ever since taking off from an airfield in Germany. Saul didn't need a degree in psychology to know that he was the reason.

He glanced up front towards Hanover, who was leaning over the pilot's shoulder. The two men were conferring quietly as the craft angled its nose downwards at a terrifyingly steep angle. They were approaching the endpoint of a sharply curving trajectory that had boosted them to the edge of space, before hurtling them back down towards the South China Seas, and nearly ten thousand kilo-metres to the east.

Sefu looked sceptical. 'For real?'

'Why do you ask?' Saul replied, doing his best to maintain eye contact while the sub-orbital bucked and shuddered with profound violence.

'Just in case we have to evacuate.' Sefu barely suppressed a grin.

'I mean, we're a long way up and, with all those storms scattered around, we could get ripped to shreds before we reach the ground. It happens.'

'Shit, yes,' said the man next to Sefu. Saul registered that his name was Charlie Foster. 'Did you ever see the UP footage from that guy who fell out of a sub-orbital? The one that came apart just fifteen minutes after take-off?'

'I did,' Sefu replied, turning to Foster with a snap of his fingers. 'His 'chute failed, right? And his contacts kept recording, the whole way down.'

'Bullshit,' said Saul.

Foster nodded enthusiastically, gazing at Saul with an innocent expression. 'No lie. Bastard screamed like a banshee right up until the end.'

Sefu noisily sucked air through his teeth.

'Hit the ground so hard his skull wound up lodged in his ass,' Foster added, shaking his head sadly.

Saul considered a variety of responses, most of them anatomically impossible.

The sub-orbital hit a fresh patch of turbulence, lurching like a truck dropping one of its wheels into a deep pothole. Saul drew in a sharp breath and wished he had something to cling on to, as the turbojets grumbled and whined in preparation for the last stage of their descent.

'And there's a reason you're sharing this with me?' Saul managed to say.

'Well,' Sefu replied, 'I got the impression you weren't enjoying the flight, for some reason.'

'Me, I love turbulence,' said Foster, his eyes wide and happy. 'It's like being rocked to sleep by Mother Nature.'

Text, rendered in silver, floated on the lower right of Saul's vision, telling him that the sub-orbital was now only seven kilometres above the ground, having already dropped nearly fifteen kilometres in the last few minutes. The external temperature was minus seventy, and the air still thin enough to qualify as vacuum.

'Now Mitchell,' Sefu continued, twisting around in his restraints to catch the attention of the rest of Hanover's task force, 'that son of a bitch was in fucking *love* with jumping out of things.'

'Fuck yeah,' confirmed a woman further down the two rows of seats facing each other on either side the craft's interior. Her tag read Helena Bryant. 'I trained with him this one time, when we had to jump from about twelve kilometres up. He got to within maybe a half-klick of the ground before he even *started* to pull back up. Scared the shit out of me then, but the man was fucking fearless.'

'Wing-suit, right?' Saul guessed.

'Yeah, that's right,' she replied. 'You know what I'm talking about?'

'Sure,' Saul replied, assuming an air of false bravado. 'I even went on a jump with him once, years ago. He'd been daring me for months.'

'You knew him?' interrupted another voice over to his right.

'We worked together way back when,' Saul replied. 'Somehow he . . . talked me into it.'

'Why'd he have to talk you into it?' asked Sefu. He was still grinning, but there was a shade more respect in his tone. 'Because you were too chickenshit?'

'Too sane, I think,' Saul replied. 'The dive was made from low orbit.'

That shut them up.

'Real orbit, or sub-orbital?' asked Helena.

Saul grinned. 'Sub-orbital. I'm not *that* crazy.'

'That's pretty dangerous shit nonetheless,' someone else said.

'Sure.' Saul made a point of shrugging, as if to say no big deal. 'Maybe one in a thousand orbital divers wind up dead, but Mitch and me did it together, from more than twenty kilometres up. We used foam and Kevlar heat shields for the first five kilometres down, then wing-suits the rest of the way.'

Saul recalled the wide wings embellishing the one-piece flying suit. Rigid stabilizers built into each suit kept them from going into a deadly spin as they dropped down through the thickening atmosphere. At the time, he'd thought the experience might cure him of what had then been nothing more than a mild fear of flying, but instead it had made it much, much worse. He'd never even have agreed to it if Mitchell hadn't been having such a hard time back then, coping with the death of his brother Danny.

Sefu waved a hand in mock dismissal, and several of the task force laughed. Saul felt himself grinning back.

'So why the fuck do you look like you're about to crap yourself?' prodded Sefu.

'When you jump, you're in control,' Saul explained. 'Being on a plane isn't the same, though, since your life's in someone else's hands. And anyway, it's been a long while since I rode in a sub-orbital.'

'Told you,' said Sefu, looking around at the rest of them. 'Chickenshit.' They all laughed, but when Sefu gave him a grin, Saul could see it was much more friendly than before.

Confirmation of Saul's temporary transfer had come through a few days after his interrogation by Donohue and Sanders.

Almost a week after his meeting with Donohue and Sanders, he'd made his way back through the Copernicus–Florida gate, re-acquainting himself with the tug of full gravity and working at rebuilding his muscle strength in a government gym close by his apartment in Orlando. He scored himself some Bad Puppy – a milder derivative of loup-garou – and used it to steady his nerves and kill some of the pain still seeping through despite the medication he'd been given for his injuries. After that, he had hitched a ride aboard a military cargo hopper to an ASI facility near Berlin, where he'd then undergone a brief interview with Hanover in his office.

'I realize that you knew Mitchell,' Hanover had said, an operations room clearly visible through a glass pane behind him. 'It's too bad what happened to him. You should remember, however, that there's a reason this is just a temporary assignment for you. Men like Stone are not easily replaced.'

'I appreciate how that would be the case, sir,' Saul had replied. 'Can I ask just what happened to him? All I was told was that he'd been under some kind of secondment when he—'

'No, you may not,' Hanover interrupted. 'You don't have the requisite clearance.'

Saul nodded perfunctorily. There was something distinctly glacial about Hanover's manner.

'Now, I don't want you to take this the wrong way,' Hanover continued, 'but you weren't actually the first name I had in mind. In fact, why my original request was turned down remains something of a mystery to me.'

'I can only do my best, sir.'

'It's more complicated than that. The members of this task force have a level of clearance that you don't. They're often engaged in highly classified work which you don't need to know the details of.'

Saul guessed Hanover was digging for something. 'It wasn't my idea, sir. I was reassigned, and that's all I can tell you.'

Hanover regarded him in silence for a moment before standing up and pulling open the door leading to the outer office. 'You should know it's my intention to file a complaint with your superiors. Not because of anything you've done, but because I'm concerned at the lack of explanation.'

'Sir,' Saul replied, standing too.

'You'll report for a final briefing at 0800 tomorrow morning,' said Hanover. 'I believe you've already been briefed on the essential details of our mission. We're to recover ASI cargo hijacked from Florida.'

'I was briefed, sir. Thank you.'

Hanover nodded, but his eyes glinted with suspicion. 'Good. For as long as you're with us, I don't think you'll need to worry about a lack of action.'

The sub-orbital started to level out just as an alert sounded. Saul pushed his head back, relying on the padded restraints around his shoulders, neck and waist to keep him from being thrown around the cabin like a rag doll. The back of his mouth felt sticky and hot still, with the memory of the Bad Puppy, and he found himself wondering if anyone else in Hanover's squad was holding. Before long the engines kicked in, sending powerful vibrations rattling through his bones in the moments just before they made their final approach.

'Everybody get ready to move out!' Hanover yelled, pulling himself out of his own restraints before heading for the rear hatch. Saul glanced in the direction of the cockpit and caught sight of jungle silhouetted against star-speckled blackness, as they scrambled to disembark.

They dropped down one by one into humid darkness, milling around the small forest clearing in which the sub-orbital had landed on its powerful VTOL jets. The subtropical heat seeped in through Saul's suit, enveloping his skin like a warm blanket and carrying with it unidentifiable scents. The black outline of a mountain rose to one side; the gentle rush of a river was audible somewhere close by.

The briefing earlier that morning had involved detailed orbital maps of a region in the central mountains of Taiwan, an island nation south of the coast of mainland China. Dozens of villages lay dotted around the slopes and lowlands, most of them accessible only by narrow, winding roads. Industrial compounds and mining operations, mostly abandoned and half swallowed up by the jungle, stood along the banks of every river. A few had been reclaimed by paramilitary groups left over from the days of the Hong Kong blockades, the majority of which continued to enjoy a profitable business partnership with the Tian Di Hui. Given that they were operating deep inside a Sphere-aligned nation, their mission was by necessity a covert one.

Saul first checked his Cobra's fire parameters, then adjusted the temperature control of his suit until he felt more comfortable. He wasn't quite the outright object of suspicion he had been when they set out, but he didn't let himself forget that whoever had tipped off the hijackers was almost certainly standing just a few feet away.

Hanover called for everyone's attention. 'Check your UPs now for an updated overlay of the area with the latest intel.' Saul watched as a shimmering grid of data positioned itself over the surrounding landscape. He pulled the focus back for a moment, until he could see the surrounding region displayed before him in its entirety, all the peaks and valleys painted in false colours.

'Our destination,' Hanover continued, 'is less than a half kilometre along a footpath running beside the river,' he told them, pointing beyond the sub-orbital. 'Make sure you're all properly networked, or I will be *very* unhappy if anyone gets lost because they didn't maintain their uplink.'

Computer systems woven into Saul's suit kept him in constant touch with the rest of the task force, while his mil-grade contacts could switch easily between active IR and thermal-imaging video feeds that were particularly useful in the middle of a darkened jungle.

He took a moment to test his night vision. The jungle flashed green for a second until his contacts again painted the ground and foliage in a variety of false colours. He glanced at the others around him, their eyes showing up as ghostly black dots floating amid pale and featureless faces.

'I'm having a problem with my A/V uplink,' said Saul. His contacts were refusing to connect with the task force's network.

'Anyone else?' asked Hanover.

The rest muttered negatives or shook their heads.

'Then it's just you,' Hanover replied. 'Could be a software issue. Give it a couple minutes to see if it sorts itself out.'

They moved out, following the river downstream and making their way along a narrow path that had once been asphalt but had long degenerated into loose black grit mixed with thick tufts of wide-bladed grass. The failure of his uplink set Saul's nerves on edge. He couldn't rule out the possibility someone had sabotaged the connection deliberately.

Saul caught sight of a snake slipping off towards the river once it scented their approach. Its scales looked as if they had been painted in hallucinatory colours.

Before long they caught sight of a cooling tower and several low buildings constituting part of an abandoned chemical-processing plant. Hanover called a halt and they gathered around him.

'Tovey, the path splits just before we reach the fence. Take your men around past the first gate, and you'll find a second gate round on the far side of the compound.' Bright neon lines appeared on Saul's map overlay, winding out of sight through the dense jungle. 'Wait there until we have some idea what we're up against, then move in the moment you get the signal. The rest of you follow me – we'll cut through the fence on this side, and enter that way. The main admin building will be closer to our position, and that's where the sats tell us the trucks and cars are parked.' He looked slowly around at them all. 'Remember, we want them alive if possible. Now move out.'

Tovey muttered a quick *yessir*, and Saul watched as he and his assigned half of the task force hurried away, hunkering low through tall grass that rustled with their passage. Hanover led the rest of them up to a two-metre-high wire fence surrounding the compound, where Saul watched as Sefu and another soldier, using the pale-blue flame of a plasma torch, sliced their way through the thick mesh steel in just seconds.

There were no lights visible inside the compound. The roofs of several of the buildings had collapsed, while bushes and saplings pushed their way out of windows gaping under a half-moon. Tall weeds had fought their way through the cracked concrete base on which the chemical-processing plant itself stood.

Keeping to the shadows, they spread out. The only vehicles Saul could see had clearly been abandoned for as long as the compound itself.

His contacts dropped icons over every building, including the one housing the administration offices, which constituted their primary target. Hanover continued to lead the way, Saul staying to the rear, as he'd been instructed. They turned a corner and, sitting next to the admin building, saw a flatbed with a portable tokamak mounted on the back with cables leading inside. It appeared just as dark and silent as the rest of the compound.

Saul checked for body-heat with his IR, but got nothing more than a few tiny blips of light that probably indicated rats fleeing from their scent. There came a rustling sound from another building, and moments later a flock of birds spiralled into the night sky, flapping furiously and calling to each other as they rose.

The men entered the admin building via three different entrances. There were five floors in all, and two of them were assigned to each floor. Saul followed a Filipino named Geradz Zurc as he searched the ground floor, poking the barrel of his Cobra into room after darkened room, but there was no one to be found.

The building had, however, clearly been occupied recently. When someone turned on the generator, the rooms were suddenly flooded with light. Zurc swore, and Saul closed his eyes until he could shut down his night-vision. He heard someone muttering an apology over their shared comms.

When he opened his eyes again, he saw loose papers scattered all about, while empty desks had been pushed up against the walls. Saul tapped at the surface of one and a manufacturer's logo appeared, slowly spinning above the desktop, glowing faintly under the crackling strip lights. A moment's exploration showed that all its data had been wiped.

Someone had obviously known they were coming.

'All clear,' Zurc called over his link.

Saul followed him back to the central foyer, where other members of the task force soon joined them. Hanover was the last to arrive.

'This place is empty,' he confirmed, glancing around. 'At first sight, anyway. But I don't think they could have cleared out more than a few hours ago.'

'What about the others, sir?' asked Sefu. 'Tovey and the rest are still sitting out there in the jungle, waiting.'

'No, I just called them in,' Hanover replied. 'They'll scour the rest of the buildings, see if they can turn anything up. In the meantime, I want the rest of you outside.' He jerked a thumb towards the stairwell. 'I'm going to take another quick look around myself, to see if I can find anything before we head home.'

Sefu shrugged in assent, and the rest followed him back out into the hot night air, grumbling amongst themselves. After a couple of hours of being trapped in a sub-orbital with nothing to do but look at each other, Saul could sympathize. He settled against a wall, while the others found places to sit or just squatted on the ground.

Saul recalled what Donohue had told him: whoever on Hanover's team was responsible for supplying the information that led to the hijacking might also be linked to the terrorist action that had stranded Saul himself eighty light-years away from his family.

He thought of the way Hanover had looked at him during their first meeting. Maybe this was just a very tight-knit squad that didn't take to strangers.

Or maybe it was something else.

Saul came to a decision. Damned if he was going to figure anything out by squatting here in the dark.

'Hey, where you going?' asked Helena as Saul stood up, looking around him.

'Gotta pee,' Saul replied.

'There are bushes out front,' Sefu advised from nearby. 'Try not to get caught with your pants down, will you?'

Someone laughed and Saul made himself smile in response before heading around one side of the building. Once he was out of sight, he found his way back inside through a side entrance, then made his way past a row of defunct elevators to the stairwell.

He stared up the central shaft towards the ceiling, the staircase spiralling above him. After a few seconds he caught the flicker of a shadow through an open door somewhere on the top floor, followed by the distinct click of a door being closed. It had to be Hanover.

Saul slung his Cobra over his shoulder and started to climb, his gaze fixed upwards in case Hanover reversed direction and started to make his way down again. Saul wasn't sure what excuse he might give if that happened, but it was a chance he just had to take.

He rested for a few seconds on reaching the top floor, then gently pulled open the door to reveal a corridor beyond. He glanced back the way he had come and found he had a good view of the rest of the compound through a wide window on the other side of the stairwell. He activated his IR filter and saw flickers of red and yellow in the darkness: presumably Tovey's team searching the rest of the compound.

Saul stepped into the corridor, closing the door gently behind him, unslinging his Cobra once more before moving forward cautiously.

He found Hanover in the last room on the right, his back facing the doorway. Several steel cabinets stood along one wall, and Hanover was busy pulling thick sheafs of paper out of the drawers of one of them, and dumping them in an untidy pile on the floor. Opposite a window overlooking another part of the compound were a series of security screens, all clearly of much more recent manufacture than anything else contained in the room.

One displayed a live video feed of the stairwell. Hanover had known he was coming.

Hanover paused, a bundle of documents grasped loosely in both arms, and turned to glance backwards at Saul. He shook his head with irritation and turned away again, dumping the documents on top of the rest, before opening another drawer and extracting its contents as well.

'What are you doing?' asked Saul.

'What does it look like I'm doing?' Hanover replied over his shoulder. 'I'm destroying evidence.' He scattered more documents on the floor.

'I want you to stop,' Saul replied, taking a firmer grip on the

Cobra. Targeting overlays appeared in front of him, flashing red because he was aiming at a friendly target. 'Right now, sir.'

Hanover paused, then his shoulders rose and fell in a sigh before he turned to face Saul fully. 'I knew why they sent you the moment I heard you were coming,' he said, his tone bitter. 'Do you like playing the part of a spy, Mr Dumont? Is it everything you hoped it would be?'

'Why are you destroying evidence?'

'Mitch is a good man,' Hanover replied. 'A thousand times better than you could ever hope to be. Poor bastard was just in the wrong place at the wrong time. But, I guess, if it wasn't you coming after me, it would be someone else. I actually let myself think it might not happen, but here we are.'

He held one hand up to Saul, palm facing outwards, while slowly reaching into a breast pocket with his other hand, and with-drawing a slim black oblong.

'What is that?' Saul demanded, training his rifle on Hanover's chest.

'Fast-acting incendiary,' Hanover replied. 'It'll turn this office into an inferno in seconds. You won't want to be here when that happens, believe me.'

'I want you to put it back in your pocket, sir. You won't be needing it.'

Hanover smiled and flipped the black object into the air, catch-ing it again on its way down a moment later.

Saul's heart leaped into his mouth, and he took a step back to-wards the door.

'You know why you were sent after me?' Hanover asked, kneel-ing to place the incendiary on top of the untidy mound of paper. 'Because the ASI is looking for someone to blame for this whole fucking mess. But I'm not going to be anybody's scapegoat, when the end comes.'

Saul's hands felt warm and damp where they gripped the Cobra. 'If I have to, sir, I *will* shoot.'

'I want you to take a message back to whoever's paying you,

and it's this: as long as they let me and my family go through to the colonies, I won't tell the Sphere anything about what's been really going on. Otherwise, I tell them everything I know: about Tau Ceti, the Founders, the Pacific growth . . . *everything*. They can't blame me for whatever happened to that shipment, when it should never have been brought to Earth in the first place. Do you understand me?'

Saul frowned. He had no idea what Hanover was talking about.

Hanover held the incendiary delicately at both ends. 'See this strip of red paper here, on the side?' he asked, eyeing Saul. 'Ten-second timer.' He took hold of one end of the red strip. 'You just pull it back, then run like hell.'

'Let go of it and stand up slowly, or I'll blow your head off your fucking shoulders, sir. That's a promise.'

Brilliant light flooded in through the window. Saul saw a flare descending from above the treetops, illuminating the compound in lurid orange.

He turned back to Hanover just in time to see him yank at the strip of paper before hurling the incendiary at him.

Saul ducked back and fired his Cobra at the same time, but the shot went wide, digging chunks of plaster out of the ceiling. The incendiary bounced off his chest and fell to the floor.

Suddenly he was face to face with Hanover, and they struggled for a few moments as Saul tried to stop him reaching the entrance. Hanover kicked him in the knee, sending him sprawling on to the dust and scattered paper before ducking out of the office.

Saul heard the rattle of automatic gunfire somewhere close by.

He stumbled upright and followed Hanover back out of the office, just as it exploded with flames behind him, blowing out the window glass. He felt a wave of heat slam into the back of his neck and threw himself to one side of the doorway with a yell, desperate to put distance between himself and the inferno. When he next looked up, he found himself staring along the barrel of a snub-nosed Agnessa pistol.

'Easy,' said Saul, spreading his hands wide, and licking his lips.

His Cobra lay just out of reach. 'You're the reason my uplink isn't working, right?'

'Some things are better without witnesses,' Hanover replied, his nostrils dilating. He stepped slightly to the side and kicked Saul's rifle back inside the blazing office. Shouts and more gunfire echoed through the compound outside.

'Maybe you should tell me just what's going on,' Saul replied, keeping his voice even.

'I already explained myself.'

'And I don't know what you were talking about. You said you were a scapegoat, but a scapegoat for what?'

Hanover regarded him with obvious disbelief. 'You really don't have any idea what's going on, do you?'

'I'm guessing you're the reason that whoever we came looking for had enough advance warning to clear out before we arrived. If that hijacked shipment was ever here, it's long gone by now, am I right?'

'Let me give you some idea of how things really stand, Mr Dumont,' said Hanover, the muscles in his neck rigid with anger. 'We're all dead men now. I've seen the world covered in ashes and, sometime very soon, the colonies – Kepler, Newton, all of them – are going to be on their own. They're going to need strong leadership if they're going to have any chance of surviving.'

Even from a few metres away, the heat was appalling. Smoke billowed along the ceiling of the corridor, until Hanover ducked in order to avoid it.

'You're talking about the separatists, right?' Saul guessed.

Hanover laughed again, louder. 'No.' He swallowed, and for a moment Saul thought the man was about to start crying. He watched the barrel of the Agnessa wobble just centimetres away from his face.

'No,' Hanover repeated, regaining some of his composure. 'Now listen to me carefully. Local government forces are storming this compound. They're going to take us into custody. *Your* job is to go back home with your tail between your legs, and deliver my message. Is that clear?'

He's crazy, thought Saul, realizing in that moment that he might very well be about to die. He watched with numb fascination as Hanover took a firmer, two-handed grip on his weapon.

'Sir?'

Hanover twisted around sharply to see Helena Bryant standing at the far end of the corridor, her face smudged and dirty, one hand clutching a wound in her shoulder. From the expression on her face, Saul guessed she'd been standing there long enough to hear most of what Hanover had said.

Hanover brought his pistol around and fired; the bullet caught her in the jaw, ripping bone and flesh away and exiting through the back of her skull. Helena staggered back against the side of the corridor, her body jerking once before slumping lifeless to the floor, like a discarded rag doll.

Hanover quickly brought the Agnessa round to bear on Saul again, motioning him to move back towards the stairwell. Saul complied, crouching to keep his face beneath the billowing smoke and almost stumbling over Helena's corpse.

'What's going to happen to the rest of your people?' asked Saul, as they entered the stairwell.

'They'll die honourably,' said Hanover. 'And if you don't keep moving, you'll be joining them.'

Saul looked through the window across the stairwell, and spotted yet more flares tumbling down, staining the buildings and surrounding jungle orange. He heard voices calling to each other in Mandarin, then realized the gunfire had ceased.

'Go on,' said Hanover, waggling his pistol towards the stairs. 'Head on down.'

Saul didn't move.

'Didn't you hear me? Get the hell down there,' Hanover snapped. 'And when – *if* – you get back home, take my advice: pack a bag, head for Florida, pick a colony and go there. Any damn one.'

'I can't leave until I get some real answers,' Saul replied.

'Don't try me, son,' Hanover grated. 'I'll shoot you, too, if I have to.'

'But then who'll deliver your message for you?' Saul asked, noting there was now barely a metre separating him from the other man. 'And what exactly is it that you think is going to happen?'

'I said don't try my—'

Saul pushed off with his right foot, slamming the heel of one hand into Hanover's jaw. He saw the other man's knuckles whiten as they squeezed the trigger, and he twisted his body out of the way as the bullets slammed into the floor and the walls.

Hanover grunted and fought back, but Saul had the advantage now. He hit Hanover hard in the belly, and the Agnessa spun out of his hand. Saul dived for it, landing on the floor and twisting around to aim it up at Hanover – only to find him staring back down at him with an expression of infinite contempt.

In that same moment, Saul heard the sound of the safety being taken off several rifles.

He twisted around to see half a dozen Taiwanese soldiers in fatigues, their weapons levelled at him, the red dots from their laser sights dancing across his chest.

'If I were you,' Hanover wheezed from behind him, 'I'd think really hard before moving so much as a fucking muscle.'

TEN

'When I said I didn't have the time to fuck around any more,' said Albright, his voice flat and emotionless, 'I meant I *really* didn't have the time to fuck around any more.'

Mitchell spat out a mouthful of blood and used his tongue to feel for the gap where one of his teeth had been until a few moments ago. He leaned forward, grunting as he tested the leather straps securing him to the chair, but there was very little give.

Albright paced in front of him, taking short drags on a cigarette. The stink of the tobacco made Mitchell want to sneeze. The third man in the room – Albright had called him Scott – stepped back, massaging the knuckles of one bruised fist while studying Mitchell with a malevolent expression.

They had come for him that morning, using a gun loaded with tranquillizer darts to knock him out before dragging him down to the garage located in the building's basement. A truck sat on a raised platform towards the rear of the space, tools mounted on racks lining the nearby walls. Mitchell had also noted a work desk littered with drills and hand-held plasma torches, and fervently hoped Albright wasn't intending to use any of those on him.

The concrete drain in the centre of the floor was still dark from the freezing water they'd hosed him down with after strapping him into the chair. Not that they'd been able to get him into it without a struggle, given that Mitchell had come to just as they'd hustled him down the steps leading to the garage. He had managed to wriggle out of the grasp of the two guards escorting him, but Scott had slammed him face-first on to a workbench, before delivering a roundhouse kick that dropped him to the ground. The guards had then strapped him in while he was still dazed and half-conscious.

'There has to be some reason why you survived,' said Albright, his voice thick with impatience. 'What kept you alive while the rest of the human race died en masse?'

'I don't know.'

Scott glanced over his shoulder at Albright, but Albright merely shook his head. The glowing tip of his cigarette painted patterns of light in the dimly lit space, as he took a draw.

'You want one?' Albright asked, raising the cigarette when he noticed Mitchell was looking at it. 'It's the healthy kind. Lots of antioxidants and anti-cancer agents. My doctor swears by it.'

'No thanks,' Mitchell swallowed, tasting his own blood.

Albright came closer, kneeling before Mitchell and regarding him from just a few centimetres away. 'Here's what I don't get,' he said. 'Why aren't you rushing to help us find some way to try and stop this whole terrible tragedy from ever happening?'

Mitchell looked away, his mouth fixed in a tight line, breathing hard in expectation of the next blow. Albright stared at him, waiting for an answer, then straightened up, shaking his head with disgust.

'There's something wrong with you – on the inside,' Albright told him. 'Did you know that?'

Mitchell looked back at him warily. 'What are you talking about?'

'We took you out of your cell, night before last, and ran some deep-tissue scans on you: fMRI, X-ray, the works.'

'No, you didn't. I'd have known.'

'Your evening meal was stuffed with sedatives. Anyway, the results were pretty remarkable. We ran the same tests on the *other* you, but the physiological changes in *your* body are significantly more advanced. We also ran a DNA analysis, and found it didn't quite match the original sample taken when you first started working for the ASI. Not only that, there are structures in your brain we can't make sense of. Your body temperature is a degree and a half cooler than it should be, and that's not even mentioning the more extreme physiological changes. I've seen surveillance footage of you moving around your cell at a speed no normal human being should be capable of. There's no conceivable way that even a couple of years in some cryogenics facility could produce changes like that.'

With a sour expression, Albright ground out his cigarette under the heel of one boot. 'Now, we've analysed, frame by frame, the A/V footage from when you and Vogel disappeared into that pit,' he continued. 'Both of your suits dissolved and, the instant the black oil touched your flesh, you both lost consciousness and collapsed. Those suits are made from extremely tough materials designed to withstand an enormous range of lethal environments, and yet they came apart like wet tissue paper in a hurricane.'

Albright lit another cigarette and drew on it, stepping away to lean against a nearby workbench. 'The liquid in those pits clearly acts like a universal solvent. Some of your colleagues tried to bring back samples, but it dissolved everything they tried to put it in. Which all rather begs the question: are you, in fact, the real Mitchell Stone, or are you something else altogether?'

Mitchell shook his head and laughed. 'You're out of your fucking mind.'

'Okay, here's what we've been thinking. Maybe the answer we need is *inside* you, in some way we can't decipher just by running non-invasive scans or occasionally bouncing you off the walls. Maybe,' Albright took another draw, 'we're going to have to go a little deeper.'

'What are you talking about?' asked Mitchell.

'Dissection,' said Albright. 'Peel back your skin and see what it is that makes you tick. Put your organs in steel trays and pick them apart to see if you're really human.'

Mitchell felt his insides twist in horror. 'How the hell is doing that going to tell you anything?'

'We won't know until we look, will we?' said Albright, an unpleasant glint in his eyes. 'We've tried persuasion and reasoning, and look where it got us. But now we're staring a holocaust in the face and, in the absence of any willing response on your part, do you really think we'd hesitate one Goddamn moment to get the answers we need, by any means necessary?'

No, thought Mitchell, *not for one second*. 'There's nothing you can do to stop what's coming,' he insisted, regardless. 'Don't you understand that? From where I'm standing, you've all been dead for years. You're a ghost, Albright.'

Albright's jaw worked like he'd just swallowed something nasty. 'Let's be clear on one thing: I'm not interested in this predetermination shit. The future isn't fixed.'

'You brought this on yourselves. I saw how the science teams at Tau Ceti were forced to take chances. They were bringing technologies that nobody understood back to Earth without any idea what the consequences might be. The sci-eval staff all filed protests, but nobody listened.' Mitchell cleared his throat. 'But I *did* listen, and I saw how anything that looked like it could turn a profit or win a war was packed into a crate and hauled straight back home.'

Albright stared at him, the cigarette burned down almost to his knuckles.

'What you don't seem to understand is that the future is indeterminate, yes,' Mitchell continued, '*unless* you find your way into it through a wormhole, and then all time between now and then becomes fixed like a fly in amber. It's like the observer effect: once you see it or touch it, it's locked in one state for ever. That's why the Founders disappeared so far into the future, to a point beyond the reach even of the wormholes. It was the only way they could *escape* predetermination.'

Albright wiped at his mouth with one hand, a frightened look in his eyes. 'How do you know all this?'

Mitchell let his head fall back, suddenly exhausted. They would be recording this interrogation, the same as all the others, of course. He wondered what his unseen audience were making of it all.

'I asked you how you could know any of this,' Albright repeated.

Mitchell brought his head back up. 'I already told you yesterday, because of the learning pools. When I woke up, I *knew* things.'

'What kinds of things?'

Mitchell struggled to find words to describe the vast repository of knowledge now resting inside his brain. He had begun to suspect that this repository somehow existed independently of him – a library inscribed deep in the microscopic foam of reality, at the most minute level, something the black pools had somehow given him the means to tap into.

He shook his head helplessly. 'Everything,' he finally replied.

Albright let his cigarette fall to the ground and formed his hands into fists. 'You're making this shit up, Goddamn you.'

'I can tell you what's going to happen in a thousand years, or a hundred thousand, or ten million – the broad details, anyway. Sometimes . . .' He closed his eyes tightly for a moment and sensed the repository there, hovering always in the back of his mind, vast and nebulous. 'Sometimes I *try* to ignore it, to not *always* be aware of it, but I can't. I know so much, from now until so far in the future, you can't even begin to imagine.'

Albright didn't say anything else for a moment, and Mitchell could hear the sound of a plane droning somewhere overhead, as well as distant voices, muffled through thick walls, passing by and then fading.

'Assuming any of this is true, why didn't you tell me before?' asked Albright.

'Because I knew it wouldn't make any difference,' Mitchell replied. 'I'd still wind up here in this garage having the shit beaten out of me, whatever I said.'

Albright nodded. 'You're right, I'm afraid.' He gestured to Scott. 'Hold him.'

Scott moved behind the chair, Mitchell twisting his head round to try and see him. Albright meanwhile stepped over to a workbench and began to rummage through a bag. As he turned back, he held a syringe in one hand, and a small plastic bottle filled with a clear liquid in the other.

'What are you doing?' Mitchell demanded.

'Something new,' said Albright. 'A development from the Kepler pharms. Apparently highly effective.'

Mitchell shook his head, now terrified. 'You don't need to do this.'

'Oh, but we do,' Albright replied. 'We were worried about damaging you before, but that's not such a priority now.' He came closer, an expression of what looked like genuine sorrow on his face as he approached. 'I won't lie to you, Mitchell. This is going to hurt. A lot.'

Mitchell twisted against his restraints, furious and terrified, and filled with a horrid certainty about what was coming next.

Scott came up behind him, wrapping one forearm around his neck and planting the other hand over the top of Mitchell's head, effectively rendering him immobile. Mitchell struggled as Albright stepped around behind him, and out of sight, but any effort was useless.

'Please don't struggle,' advised Albright. 'I don't want to wind up disabling you when I put the needle in.'

The back of the chair was partly open, making it easy for Albright to pull up part of Mitchell's paper uniform and feel for his spine. A second later Mitchell felt something slide deep inside the thick musculature there.

The pain was like nothing he had ever experienced. Fire spread through his muscles and, as he struggled to escape, he felt as if his bones might snap. Bile surged up the back of his throat and he vomited over Scott's arm.

After a little while the pain faded. He drifted on a black tide under a starless sky, his skull seeming full of soft cotton wool that scratched against the back of his eyeballs.

Well, he's still alive, Albright said from somewhere far, far away. *Tell me more about the learning pools, Mitchell. Tell me what they told you about the Founders.*

Mitchell woke to the dawn light spreading across the upper wall of his cell. He lay there for some minutes without moving, thinking about what it might be like to be strapped to a table and cut apart with scalpels. Albright and the men he worked for were little better than primitive sorcerers, desperate to divine their own fate from his still-warm entrails.

He brought his right hand up close to his face and opened it, keeping it cupped around the thin strip of serrated metal he'd grabbed from the workbench when Scott had taken him down. He could recall only vague snatches of what he had told Albright under the influence of whatever drugs they had pumped into his body, but he was fairly certain he had gone into detail about the Repository, elaborating on the few details he'd already given them.

Mitchell twisted around on his narrow cot until he lay facing the door. If he didn't escape, he would die – and soon.

Mitchell unfolded himself slowly, grimacing with pain while keeping his fist tight around the blade. *Do it now.*

He kneeled by the door, pressing one temple against its cool metal, as if momentarily resting his head there. He used one end of the blade like a screwdriver, slowly working out one of the screws securing a thin metal plate to the door frame.

His palm started bleeding where it clutched the serrated length of the blade. He put the strip down and clenched his bleeding hand for several seconds, swearing under his breath until the worst of the pain had passed.

He started working again. It was funny how things turned out, because the locks were cheap and shoddy crap, the result of some budget-cutting exercise. Fortunately for him.

He took a fresh grip on the blade and started working at the screws once more. After fifteen or twenty minutes of labour, he had removed four of them, but the plate wrapped its way around to the other side of the door frame, where it was presumably held in place by more screws.

Mitchell dropped the blade and took a grip on the loosened plate with the fingertips of both hands and started to pull, grunting with the effort. The metal was thin and malleable but even so it took a considerable effort to bend the plate back aside and expose the delicate electronics beneath. He fell back and massaged his injured hand for a minute, before pulling himself up close to the task once more.

He studied the exposed electronics with a practised eye, then, working carefully, used the tip of the blade to tease a single wire loose, the thumping of his heartbeat increasing to a roar between his ears. He meanwhile took extreme care not to touch any of the circuitry connected to the alarm system.

The door clicked loudly, and swung inwards. Mitchell let out his breath in a rush. He hadn't even realized he was holding it in. He stepped out into the corridor and listened carefully, but there was no sound of anyone approaching. He began to walk, slowly at first, then more quickly, the tiles cold and hard under his bare feet. His injured hand throbbed against his side, the blade held in the other.

Halfway along the corridor, he came to the stairwell leading down to the garage. At the bottom he found a door with a security keypad, where he tapped in a standard override code, then watched with relief as it clicked open.

Mitchell continued down the rest of the stairwell below, noticing the lights were on and the van had been lowered to the ground. A tool bag had been dropped next to one wheel, and the door on the driver's side stood open. He stopped and listened for a moment, but heard and saw no one. Even so, he ducked down to take a look under the vehicle, in case someone was standing on the far side. Seeing nothing but the other side of the garage, he quickly heaved himself up and climbed inside the van, pulling the door shut.

He barely had time to think any further, when the door was suddenly ripped from his grasp. He heard a muttered curse, in the same instant that a fist struck him on the side of the head. Mitchell raised a hand to try and defend himself, moving with the same inexplicable speed as before. Bright pain flared through his body, leaving him helpless, but out of the corner of his eye he saw that his assailant was Albright's assistant.

Scott dragged him roughly out of the seat, and Mitchell landed hard on the garage's concrete floor. His assailant leaned down and took hold of Mitchell's head, apparently preparing to smash his skull against the concrete.

It was a sign of how badly the cryogenic process had affected his thought processes that he only now remembered the hacksaw blade still gripped in one hand. He drew it straight across the bridge of Scott's nose, then watched as the other man screamed and leaped back, his hands clasped to his face.

Mitchell managed to stagger upright and then over to a workbench. Taking hold of a heavy wrench, he gasped as Scott wrapped one arm around his neck from behind. Mitchell swung the wrench wildly around behind him, hearing a wet thud as it buried itself in the side of Scott's head.

It was Scott's turn to stagger, collapsing against one side of the van. Mitchell leaned over him, his breath rasping, and struck him a second, then a third time. He was lost in a black fury, and blood and hair spattered across the grey concrete before he finally let go of the wrench. He wiped one trembling hand across his mouth, then forced himself to look away from the devastation that was the remains of Scott's face.

He headed over to the garage doors and pushed them open, still gasping hoarsely. Brilliant sunlight spilled across the concrete as he gazed out at the same buildings and the airstrip he'd viewed from his cell. The Rockies stood blue and hazy on the horizon beyond the airstrip. He'd never seen anything more beautiful.

The anger had felt good, even cleansing. Mitchell worked at regaining some semblance of calm, all too aware of how lucky he was that nobody had yet noticed his escape from the cell and sounded the alarm.

He stepped back to the van, and rummaged around in the rear until he found a set of overalls. He pulled them on quickly. They were baggy and loose, but a lot better than the paper blues he'd been wearing before.

Mitchell got back in the cabin and touched the dashboard, listening with satisfaction as the van's engine vibrated with latent power. He tapped a softly glowing panel and the wheel unfolded from its slot, the vehicle reconfiguring itself slightly in order to accommodate his smaller frame. He took a grip on the wheel and steered it, slowly, on to the narrow road that ran beyond the garage.

The other Mitchell, the one who'd been kept under sedation ever since he'd been brought back from Site 17, was still locked away in another facility near Omaha. And the only one who could possibly have got him out of there, he realized at last, was himself.

But first he was going to need some help.

ELEVEN

By the time late afternoon of the next day rolled in, there was still no sign of Dan returning. Missoula wasn't much more than a couple of hour's drive away, and the spring floods had abated, leaving the roads clear. When the sky began to darken, Jeff had already started to assume the worst.

He had packed only those items he considered essential into a light backpack he normally used for making short treks. Anything else, he abandoned in the cabin's bedroom. He passed Dan's wand over the contents of the backpack several times, listening carefully with satisfaction to the device's monotone beep every time it fried another locator chip. After that he pulled on his hiking boots and stepped outside to stare across the lake, which was spread out below him like a great dark mirror, bringing back unpleasant memories of Site 17. The sun had finally slipped below the horizon, staining the upper slopes of the mountains across the valley a fiery red. It occurred to him that this might be the last time he would ever set eyes on Flathead Lake.

Whatever might happen next, he wanted to fix this memory in his mind.

Jeff listened to the sound of birds calling to each other across the waters and wondered what he should do next. Besides the crude car-jacker gear Dan had left him with, he had a spare pack of contacts he hadn't yet registered. He could get by with those for a while, but Dan was right in one regard: they'd never be enough to get him past Array security.

He realized, with a start, that the lights of a car were now moving along a highway running parallel to the far shore of the lake. He watched for a few moments, then activated his UP for maybe the hundredth time, to see if Dan had left any kind of message.

Bright lines of text floated before him, suspended in the night air. There was a message all right, but it wasn't from Dan. It was, he realized with a shock, from Mitchell Stone.

Jeff swallowed hard. He hadn't seen or heard from him since Mitchell had been medevaced back to Tau Ceti, disappearing into the ASI's maw as mysteriously as he'd reappeared in that chamber of pits.

He opened the message and read it: *Need to speak with you and any other members of TC sci-eval teams urgently. Am in North Dakota. Where are you?*

Indecision flooded over Jeff. Mitchell Stone had been . . . if not exactly a friend, at least someone who had sided so strongly with the sci-eval teams that he'd run the risk of court martial. But he was also part of ASI Security, the same people Dan was sure were trying to kill them. So who to trust?

Jeff hesitated a few moments more, then made a decision.

Near Flathead Lake in Montana, he sent back. Then added, *I'm here with Dan Rush*.

He waited, but an immediate reply clearly wasn't forthcoming.

He glanced back down at the lake below, and saw the car had now taken the turn-off from the highway and on to the narrow road that circled the lake, coming his way. Maybe, just maybe, this was Dan.

Jeff tried to follow the progress of the car's lights as it appeared and disappeared between the tree trunks crowding the slope of the hill beneath him. He could just make out parts of the sharply winding road that switched back and forth up the steep incline towards his cabin. He watched with mounting tension as the headlights approached the nearest switch back turn.

Hope finally gave way to a desperate paranoia. After all this time, the chances were good that this was anyone but Dan.

Jeff pointed his index finger towards the car, thumb cocked, and quickly drew a circle in the air with the moving car roughly at its centre. His contacts responded by projecting a bright pastel circle against the dark outline of the mountain slope, moving along with the headlights despite the intervening trees, while retrieving whatever public information might be available about the vehicle's occupant or its registration. Nothing came back, but he hadn't really expected it to.

The best thing to do was not to take any chances, so he hurried back inside the cabin and grabbed hold of the backpack. He could always hide out somewhere nearby until he saw who got out of the car. He hoisted the rucksack over his shoulders, remembering to pick up the car-jacker chip only at the last moment.

The fireplace still glowed fitfully in one corner. He'd added wood to it in just the last hour. If there was anyone inside that car looking to hurt him, they weren't going to have too hard a time figuring out he'd only just departed. There wasn't much he could do about that, so he quickly pulled on his gloves and ordered the cabin to turn its lights off, before stepping back out into the frigid evening air.

Jeff jogged along the gravel path fronting the cabin until he reached a flight of steps leading towards the summit of the hill. After ascending the first few dozen steps, he stopped and looked back in time to see the vehicle pull into the driveway.

As two figures got out of the car, Jeff felt a tension at the base of his spine. He reached out again, drawing a circle with them both at its centre. This time he enlarged a single frame of the two men at maximum magnification, until he could see their faces more clearly.

It took a second for his contacts to process the data, and he studied the faces of the two men, who were now approaching his cabin. He recognized neither. One had sandy hair that flew about his forehead when the wind caught it, while his taller companion, thin as a rake, clutched a lightweight suit jacket around his shoulders. Neither of them was dressed for the freezing weather.

Jeff's teeth chattered, not entirely from the cold. He watched them confer for a moment, before they stepped up to the door of his cabin. The shorter one held in one hand what might be a weapon of some kind.

Jeff continued watching as they stepped inside, light flooding on to the gravel a moment later. With a sudden terrible lurch, he remembered that the contacts containing the stolen database were still hidden in the tool shed behind the cabin.

He gripped the wooden hand railing running alongside the steps, and swore quietly. *How* could he have been so stupid?

He saw the cabin door swing open once more. After a moment, the bright beam of a torch flicked first across the driveway, then up towards the path on which he stood watching.

Suddenly galvanized, Jeff hurried further up the steps, taking them two or three at a time. After ascending a short way, he came to another trail encircling the summit of the hill. He jogged along this second path until he found another clear view down through the trees, to where he could see a tiny wharf jutting out into the waters of the lake, where some of the local residents kept their boats moored.

He pulled himself up and over the low wooden railing, whose purpose was to keep summer hikers from tumbling down the hillside, and started to make his way down the steep slope, navigating between dense clumps of pine and fir. He could make out the dark masses of granite outcrops to either side, while far below him lay a relatively smooth grassy slope extending most of the way down to the shoreline. Assuming he didn't take a tumble, he could make it to the wharf in about ten minutes, or fifteen at the outside.

Voices called out to each other from above and behind. Jeff started to move more quickly, grabbing hold of tufts of grass or branches to keep from skidding too fast down the steep gradient. The air smelled of barbecue smoke drifting across the lake from cabins on the far side, as he slid down occasional stretches of snow on his butt.

The clouds passed away from the face of the moon, illuminating the slope beneath him and making the going easier. The ground began to level out, and Jeff started to run. Suddenly a point of red light was visible on a patch of snow a few metres ahead of him. A second later, a thin plume of snow erupted from the same spot, followed by the sound of a gunshot echoing across the valley.

Jeff threw himself towards the relative cover of some bull pine, in his terror almost colliding with a granite boulder. Manoeuvring his way past the boulder, he caught sight of the lakeside road, maybe only forty or fifty metres away. His shoulder blades tingled as he imagined that red dot alighting between them next.

He stumbled over a root, just as the trees began to thin out, and hit the ground hard. He staggered upright, despite the pain, and forced himself to keep moving, pushing through a tangle of brush until he reached the edge of a steep incline overlooking the road. He came to a stop briefly, then darted along the upper edge of the slope until he came across another flight of stone steps leading steeply downwards.

Shit. Jeff stared across the roadway towards the wharf, and suddenly realized there was nothing moored there – nothing he could use to try and get away to safety across the lake. A derelict hut, once home to a diving outfit, stood right next to the wharf, the side of it facing the road adorned with a crude illustration of several divers swimming amidst cartoon bubbles.

As clouds passed across the moon, Jeff grabbed the opportunity and ran across the road, desperate to avoid becoming target to another sniper shot. Glancing to one side, he nearly cried out in relief when he spotted a dinghy pulled up on the shore, quite close to the wharf but just far away enough for him not to have noticed it from the top of the incline. He hurried towards it, the gravelly sand crunching underfoot, and also saw that the dinghy was equipped with a small outboard motor.

He pushed the craft out into the freezing water, getting his ankles thoroughly soaked before he pulled himself inside and settled on the single narrow wooden bench. Jeff touched the engine's interface, and a menu rendered in softly glowing panels superimposed itself against the night sky. The dinghy was fully juiced up, enough power stored in its battery reserves to keep it going for several days.

At the sound of someone splashing through the water towards him, he reached out in a panic to activate the motor. Just as he began to pull away from the shore, a dark shape threw itself halfway inside the dinghy, making it rock wildly.

Jeff didn't even have time to feel scared, but he grabbed hold of the bench on either side of him, and used it for leverage as he kicked out with both feet. He heard an *oof*, and kicked again, as the dinghy began to turn in tight circles. His assailant staggered upright, and Jeff fell backwards against the outboard motor as a fist connected with the side of his head.

His assailant, the tall thin one, had a gun trained on him. Without thinking, Jeff grabbed hold of the tiller and twisted it frantically. The dinghy slewed wildly to one side, and the thin man staggered. Light and sound exploded from the gun, and Jeff felt something hot sear past his cheek. There was a yell, then a splash, as the other man lost his balance and fell back into the freezing water.

Jeff heard another shot, then another, from the direction of the shore. Crouching low, he twisted the tiller back again. Clouds were passing back in front of the moon and, in the pitch darkness, he was unsure where the far side of the lake now lay.

The dinghy jerked, and spun half around, as it smacked violently into something. For one heart-freezing moment, Jeff wondered if he'd somehow run himself aground somewhere alongside the wharf.

Instead, the dinghy continued on its way, its prow cutting cleanly through the water. He saw a dark shape slip past, arms spread out and motionless, and guessed it was the same man who had attacked him.

As the clouds cleared from the face of the moon, he caught sight of another wharf on the far shore, now only a few kilometres away. Shots rang out again, splashing water up on either side of the dinghy. Hoping to make himself a more difficult target, Jeff twisted the tiller frantically from side to side.

He glanced down to see water trickling through a hole just below the waterline, which he was sure hadn't been there only seconds before. There were further shots behind him, but then no more. Assessing the trickle of water pooling around his boots, he decided it wasn't likely to become a serious issue before he reached the opposite shore.

Jeff shivered as the wind cut through his soaking-wet clothes. It froze him to the marrow, and he wondered how long he had before hypothermia set in.

He was going to have to find some kind of transport soon. If he tried to hide in the woods or make it to Lakeside on foot, he'd only wind up dead of exposure.

As he sailed on, the dinghy's motor emitting a barely audible hum, lights became increasingly visible through the trees above the far shore, and music drifted across the still waters. Several minutes later, he finally ran the dinghy up on to the shore, alongside a luxurious-looking motorboat moored to the wharf. He looked back across the lake and saw some headlights suddenly come on close by his cabin. Jeff watched for a few seconds as the same lights headed back down the long switchback road, and he realized he was far from being home and free.

Crossing the road, he soon found himself at the foot of another steep switchback track leading to a cluster of cabins he vaguely recalled were owned by some rental agency in Missoula. He jogged a short way up the road until he came to a cul-de-sac, where he found several private vehicles parked together, some of them busy chewing on bales of leafy biomass. The rear hatch of one car had been left open, revealing the shrink-wrapped cartons of beer stacked inside. Judging by the music, a party was currently in full swing.

Jeff glanced through the trees, and back across the lake, in time to see the headlights descend the final switchback bend in the road. He had five, maybe ten minutes at most, before it circled the lake.

He stepped forward, lifting the cartons of beer out of the rear of the car and dumping them on the grass verge, before crawling inside and pulling the hatch shut behind him. He manoeuvred himself into one of the front seats and tugged his backpack off, dropping it on to the adjacent seat before reaching out to touch the expanse of black glass that constituted the dashboard. He was far from surprised when nothing happened.

He fumbled around inside the backpack until he found Dan's car-jacker, and pressed it against the dashboard. After a few moments the glass flickered, random lines of code scrolling by at speed. For one awful moment Jeff wondered if he'd managed to fry the car's brain, but before very long a standard set of options appeared in place of the gibberish.

He closed his eyes in silent relief and let his head tip forward, as if in prayer, before reaching out and tapping the dashboard to select manual drive. The wheel unfolded before him, optional virtual menus materializing to either side.

He heard someone yell and glanced through the rear windscreen to see a figure running down the road leading from the cabins. Clearly, the car's owner had returned for the rest of his beer.

Jeff gripped the wheel and put the car into reverse. A rear tyre hit a tree root, and one side of the vehicle slammed upwards as he turned it in a tight circle. Fists beat against the door next to him and he found himself staring at an angry face. Jeff hastily engaged the locks before the man could yank the door open, then hit the accelerator hard. The car shot forward, sending its owner tumbling away.

It bounced as it came off the switchback and hit the main road. The wheels spun as Jeff floored the accelerator, the lake sliding past at an ever increasing speed.

With luck he could reach Lakeside in just another twenty minutes.

He turned up the heating as far as it would go, then put the car back on automatic. The wheel folded itself away again while he stripped off his sodden clothes, throwing them on to the rear seats.

He'd stowed a spare change of clothes in the rucksack, but unfortunately it wasn't waterproof, so he climbed into the back and dug around until he came across an oil-stained T-shirt that at least had the virtue of being dry, even if maybe three sizes too big.

Jeff glanced behind, but couldn't see any sign of his pursuer's headlights. The only thing left now, he realized, was to try and find Mitchell. So he accessed his UP and placed a call.

TWELVE

Hong Kong, 30 January 2235

Following his arraignment before a Taiwanese military judge, Saul spent the better part of forty-eight hours in a secure penal facility on the outskirts of Tainan, close to the island's south coast. On his second morning there, a guard woke him by poking a baton into his ribs, before informing him in broken English that a diplomatic intervention had set him free.

His gaolers had taken his gear and contacts away and, Saul felt sure, were already working hard to extract from them whatever data they could. In exchange he was given a pair of powder-blue trousers that flapped around his ankles, and a short-sleeved maroon shirt with a dark stain on the collar, which he suspected was the original owner's blood.

They led him out of the prison in handcuffs, and shoved him in the back of a police car. Saul spent the next hour watching the traffic slip by in either direction, before finally they arrived at an airport on the city outskirts, where he was placed directly on to a commercial hopper bound for Hong Kong.

On his arrival there, he was escorted through a restricted part of the main terminal building, still in handcuffs, to a room displaying the universal attributes of every interrogation room he had ever set foot in: a single table with a chipped plastic surface, unforgivably bright strip-lighting, ceiling-mounted scanning gear and a mirror that was almost certainly two-way.

Donohue was waiting for him there, seated on a plastic chair by the table, clutching a paper cup filled with black coffee in one hand. He watched as the two guards removed Saul's cuffs before they departed.

'You got here fast,' said Saul, his voice cracking slightly.

'You look fucking terrible,' remarked Donohue, then wrinkled his nose. 'And you smell worse. Didn't they give you a shower?'

Saul rubbed his wrists carefully, squinting under the harsh light. 'I just spent most of two days in a prison cell with twelve other men, and a trough in the floor for a toilet,' he said. 'They were out of toilet paper.'

'There's a pay-shower somewhere in the terminal,' Donohue replied. 'But I'm afraid there probably won't be time for you to use it before you leave.'

'Leave?' Saul echoed.

'You're going home,' Donohue explained. 'You have a flight to catch in less than an hour. I'm sure you're glad to hear that.'

Saul nodded, and lowered himself on to a second chair with infinite weariness. 'Where's Sanders?'

'He couldn't make it,' Donohue replied, his expression suddenly sour. He sighed and got up, stepping over to a cabinet, where he poured the dregs from a cafetière into another paper cup before placing it in front of Saul. A faint wisp of steam rose up from its tarry black contents, as Saul curled one hand around the cup, feeling the heat work its way through his skin.

Donohue sat down again. 'I've just spent a considerable amount of time and energy trying to find ways to extricate you before the Taiwanese decided you were trying to overthrow their government, and locked you up for the next hundred years. Care to tell me your side of things?'

Saul lifted the coffee to his lips and took a tentative sip. It tasted better than he'd expected.

'Hanover's your man,' he said. 'He was on to you from the start. Have you got him back yet?'

Donohue shook his head. 'No, we haven't, but that little excursion is costing us dearly. There are videos and photos of dead ASI troopers all over the nets.'

'I found him destroying hard copies – evidence of some kind, I'm guessing. He didn't even try to hide what he was up to, because he knew he was going to get caught, and made plans to save himself. He did, however, tell me he wanted me to deliver a message.'

'Go on.'

'He said that if you don't guarantee his family safe passage to the colonies, he'll tell the Sphere everything he knows.' Saul shrugged. 'I can't make any sense of what he told me, but I assume *you* can.'

'That's all he said?'

'He mentioned some other stuff that didn't make any more sense to me either. Tau Ceti, and something called a Pacific growth?' Saul shook his head in puzzlement. 'I had no idea what he was talking about.'

'You didn't ask him to explain?'

Saul gulped more coffee, and winced as it burned its way down his throat. 'He had a gun to my head, after nearly burning me to death. It didn't feel like a priority under the circumstances.'

'I'll need a full and detailed report.'

Saul shrugged. 'There's not much more to tell, except that Hanover sacrificed his entire squad rather than give himself up to me. Whoever was using that compound must have cleared out just before we arrived, so they'd obviously received plenty of advance warning. It doesn't take a major leap of intuition to guess that Hanover's the one who tipped them off.'

He watched Donohue withdraw a narrow, rectangular slip of paper from inside his jacket, then lay it on the table between them. Donohue drew the tip of one finger across it, and, in response, the logo of a major airline appeared on the sheet of paper, as if by magic, along with lines of text rendered in a fine-serif font.

He scooted the live-sheet towards Saul, who stopped it with his fingertips.

'Diplomatic clearance and your ticket home,' explained Donohue. 'All appearances to the contrary, you've done good, Saul.'

'That's funny, because I could have sworn it was a total fuck-up.'

'It was,' Donohue replied. 'But we already had a pretty good idea that Hanover was our man. We couldn't prove it, however, unless we found some way to draw him out and catch him in the act.'

'So I was just bait,' said Saul, glowering.

Donohue merely smiled, without humour.

'He sabotaged my A/V uplink,' Saul continued, leaning forward. 'That means there's no proof any of this actually happened. You must know that?'

'Corporal Helena Bryant's A/V systems were working just fine,' Donohue replied. 'You'll remember she interrupted your conversation at a particularly crucial juncture. Her contacts had a heavily encrypted satellite uplink, so we've got more than enough solid evidence of what took place.'

'The man is a piece of shit,' Saul observed. 'You're not seriously going to give him what he wants, are you?'

'That decision's not up to anyone in this room,' Donohue replied, standing.

'You have to give me some idea what's going on here.' Saul stared up at him. 'What the hell was all that stuff he mentioned about the colonies being on their own?'

Donohue gazed down at him with an expression halfway between scorn and pity. 'I've no idea what you mean, Saul. Maybe you need to cut back on some of that loup-garou you love so much.'

'What about the hijacked shipment? What's in it that everyone wants so badly?'

Donohue shook his head without answering that, then stepped over to the door and pulled it open. The distant tones of an automated announcement echoed along the corridor. 'You've got just over half an hour to catch your flight,' he said.

'Wait.' Saul could hear the blood pounding in his head. 'What did Hanover mean when he said the colonies were going to be all on their own? And what the hell about finding out who destroyed the Galileo wormhole?' he yelled, anger welling up inside him. 'Does Hanover know something about it, or was that just some bullshit you concocted?'

Donohue shook his head as if in pity. Saul watched as he stepped towards him, pulling a plastic inhaler out of a pocket and dropping it on the table.

Saul stared down at it. 'What the hell's that for?' he asked.

'A little pick-me-up,' Donohue sneered. 'Had the feeling you might need it.'

'Fuck you,' Saul snapped, sweeping the inhaler on to the floor with one hand.

'You used to be a good agent, Saul,' said Donohue, stepping back to the door. 'Maybe you should take Hanover's advice and have a vacation somewhere off-world. And, when you get there, I'd strongly advise you to stay there.'

Saul stared at the closed door, once Donohue had departed, a hundred more questions remaining stillborn in the back of his throat.

THIRTEEN

Lakeside, Montana, 30 January 2235

Jeff woke up in the back of the car he'd stolen, now parked behind a bar and grill in Lakeside with his down jacket pulled up over his shoulders. He sneezed loudly, though he'd left the heating turned up full all night. The recycled air tasted stale, humid and disgusting.

Pushing himself upright, he found to his relief that the clothes he'd left draped over the backs of the two front seats had mostly dried out. Wincing at the smell, he dragged on his shirt and trousers, then fumbled to open a door before dragging himself out into painfully bright morning sunlight. The car had expanded to allow him the room he needed to sleep, but upon sensing his exit it hummed and creaked as it reassumed its default configuration. A room in a local motel would have been a lot more comfortable, but it had occurred to Jeff that it might well be the first place the surviving assassin would think of looking for him.

He stepped around to the front of the bar, and glanced up and down the single highway running through the small town. He could see two- and three-storey buildings stretching off in either direction, while bull pines spread up the steep slopes rising immediately beyond the rooftops, reaching towards the wisps of cloud streaking an azure sky. Jeff activated his contacts, and a breakfast menu appeared next to the bar's entrance.

Jeff listened to his stomach grumble, then noted with some misery that the bar wouldn't open for another couple of hours.

Something flashed in the corner of his vision and he saw that he'd finally got a reply from Mitchell Stone. He'd tried to get hold of him a dozen times as he fled in the stolen car, before finally giving up, so he opened the message without hesitation. Through his contacts, Stone's words were projected as thick black letters floating against the brilliant sky.

Need to talk with you urgently, the message read. *Bring Dan to these coordinates, and meet me there.*

The coordinates were tagged on to the end of the message, which turned out to be someplace in Sioux Falls, the better part of two thousand kilometres to the east.

Sioux Falls, wondered Jeff. What the hell was in Sioux Falls?

He swallowed, his throat dry, and wondered again if looking to Mitchell for help was the right decision. But there were so many questions Jeff wanted to ask him – so many! How on Earth could he have survived, where Vogel hadn't? And where had Eliza actually had him taken after he was rushed back home?

In that same moment, Jeff became aware of someone watching him from across the road. It was a middle-aged man, in scuffed trousers and work-shirt, leaning against the wall alongside a fabricator kiosk.

Jeff shut down his UP and focused his gaze on the window of the restaurant, as if still consulting its vanished menu. When he turned back to view the street half a minute later, he saw the man was gone, but a light had come on inside the store adjoining the kiosk.

Glancing down the highway to the east, he felt his heart skip a beat when a police car emerged, low and black and shark-like, from a side road and turned in his direction. Jeff ducked back into the alleyway and pulled open his car door, grabbing up his rucksack before hightailing it around the far end of the building that stood across the alley from the bar. After a minute he heard the sound of wheels crunching over gravel as the police car entered the alley.

Jeff peered cautiously around the corner, in time to see the police car pull up next to his own. A uniformed officer stepped out and walked once around the stolen car, before glancing all about. Jeff ducked back out of sight, praying that he hadn't been spotted.

Long seconds passed, then he heard the sound of a car door opening and closing, followed again by the sound of tyres rolling over gravel. Jeff stepped back out from hiding in time to see his stolen vehicle, now slaved to the police car, following it back out on to the highway, like a new-born calf trailing its mother.

Jeff let out a long groan and wondered what the hell he was going to do next.

He waited another minute before venturing back out on to the highway, glancing warily in both directions. The shops still seemed mostly deserted, though he could hear tinny music from behind one window as he headed a couple of blocks west, keeping an eye out for the cop car. He recollected seeing a bus station a little further along, and before long found himself standing before a parking area containing a half-dozen unmanned buses gathered around a towering stack of biomass bales.

Jeff glanced back towards the highway, wondering about using the car-jacker to steal himself another car, but that carried its own risks. If a cop could track down a stolen ride that easily, they'd have no trouble catching him driving on the interstate once the theft had been reported. Carjacking might seem a viable option down Mexical way, but the roads were much better protected this far north.

Really, he knew that the best thing for him to do would be to ditch his current pair of contacts. Except almost anything he might need to do – make a purchase, call Mitchell, anything that might require money – couldn't be achieved without access to the funds stored in his Ubiquitous Profile, stored in his contacts; his UP was his bank, ID and means of communication all rolled into one. And even if he did buy and register a new pair, he'd still have to transfer his UP to them before he could use them, and then he'd be right back where he started. Dan's notion of bootleg contacts, complete with their own fake Ubiquitous Profiles, was starting to make a great deal of sense.

Right now, he either risked using his UP or he walked all the way to Sioux Falls.

Sighing heavily, Jeff stepped towards the nearest bus. Its door rattled open at his approach, the hydraulics wheezing slightly. He sat near the back, hunching himself down low in the seat, and purchased a one-way ticket that would take him all the way. He pictured alarms already strobing red in some secret government facility populated by sober-looking men and women dedicated to his immediate demise.

The vehicle was freezing cold, and he wrapped himself tighter in his down jacket. He entertained a brief fantasy of jumping back off, then making his way back to the cabin and the tool-shed to retrieve the contacts containing the stolen database, but a saner part of him knew it would be the best way to wind up dead. And, besides, they'd almost certainly have discovered the safe where he'd hidden them by now.

He pulled the hood of his jacket over his face and rested his head against the cold glass. He then only realized he'd fallen asleep when the bus rumbled into life, bouncing gently as it pulled out on to the highway to follow its pre-programmed route. He coughed and sneezed, and looked around, noticing that he was still the only passenger.

Jeff rode the same bus all the way back to Missoula, passing through several small towns along the way. By now it was picking up and dropping off an endless succession of passengers. A couple of hours later, he disembarked and grabbed a seat on an interstate hopper that flew him over lakes, hills and towns before depositing him on a landing pad just outside the Sioux Falls city limits. It was now nearly seven hours since he'd woken up in the back of the stolen car, and he felt tired, scared and dirty. However, at least he had managed to grab some breakfast from an autocafé during a scheduled stopover.

Jeff let his contacts guide him towards Mitchell's coordinates, which ominously enough indicated somewhere inside a huge cemetery sprawling across the grassy lower slopes on the far side of town. As he walked along neatly mown paths laid out between the rows of headstones, his contacts identified the coordinates by means of a giant cartoon arrow hovering straight ahead and pointing downwards. Before long Jeff came to a small fountain, ringed by wooden benches. The arrow remained directly overhead, but there was no sign of anyone else around.

Nearly twenty minutes had passed before he spotted a lone figure making straight towards him down an alternative path, the newcomer's face largely obscured under the broad hood of a hunting jacket. As he came closer, one grizzled hand reached up to pull the hood back, and Jeff saw that it was Mitchell – looking just as bruised and battered as he himself felt. He swallowed hard, more relieved to recognize the man than he was prepared to admit even to himself.

'I've got to be honest,' Jeff began, 'there's a part of me that's not sure if you've really come here to help me or . . . or to kill me.'

Mitchell regarded him with unwavering pale-blue eyes. 'Why would I do that?'

'I've learned to become paranoid over the past couple of days.' Jeff glanced around. 'Why here? Why a cemetery, for God's sake?'

Mitchell shrugged. 'There's good all-round visibility, and not much in the way of public surveillance. If anyone comes looking for us, we'll easily see them first.' He looked around. 'Where's Dan?'

'He . . . Dan's dead.'

'Dead?' Mitchell's gaze became suspicious. 'How?'

'There were people trying to kill us.'

The frown on Mitchell's face deepened. 'I don't understand.'

Jeff quickly explained the events of the last few days. When he got to Lucy's death, Mitchell closed his eyes and inhaled loudly.

'And all of this made you think I might want to kill you?' he asked, opening his eyes again.

'You're still part of ASI. And we stole those files.'

'*Jesus!*' Mitchell clasped his head in a gesture of despair. 'Who the hell do you think got Lucy access to the security deck in the first place?'

'I don't know. I guess I assumed she and Farad found some way of hacking it remotely.'

'We had a thing together,' Mitchell replied. 'Me and Lucy. I guess you didn't know.'

At first, Jeff couldn't think what to say. 'I . . . didn't,' he finally stammered.

'She knew I was sympathetic, and I helped her out. She took a big chance through confiding in me, but I knew how badly things were being run. So I gave her my access privileges – it seemed the right thing to do.'

'I'm sorry,' said Jeff, his face flushing with embarrassment. 'You didn't say anything when I told you Lucy had . . .' He paused as he remembered the look on Mitchell's face when he had told him.

'It's not the first time I've lost someone close to me.' Mitchell put a hand on Jeff's shoulder. 'Look, you're not the only one on the run. They were planning to take me apart just so they could figure out what happened to me in that pit, and they were very clear about me not being expected to survive the experience. That's why I contacted you. I badly need your help.'

'Of course. But you still haven't told me what exactly happened to you.'

'When was the last time we spoke to each other, Jeff?'

'You mean before I met you here?' Mitchell nodded. 'I guess . . . back at Tau Ceti, just before we set off for Site 17.'

'And when was that?'

'Several weeks ago now.'

'What would you say if I told you it's been a lot longer than that for me? More like the better part of a decade?'

Jeff stared at him, clearly perplexed. 'I have no idea what you're talking about.'

'I've got a lot to explain once we have the chance.' Mitchell glanced around. 'But first we have to do something about your contacts.' He pulled a foil blister-pack out of a pocket. 'These are fresh ones, registered with false UPs.'

Jeff stared at the blister-pack. 'How did you get hold of them?'

'I worked in security for fifteen years, Jeff, so I know a lot of things you don't. Now take out your own contacts, before your friends with the guns catch up with us.'

Jeff hesitated, then reached up and delicately pinched the contact out of one eye, dropping it into the palm of his right hand before repeating the operation with his other eye. He then fished out a plastic case with his other hand, and carefully placed the devices inside.

'You did remember to deactivate your UP before you took them out, right?'

Jeff nodded.

'Hold on to them,' advised Mitchell. 'You might need them later.'

Jeff accepted the blister-pack from Mitchell and popped one of the bubbles open, dipping one finger in to lift out a contact. He leaned his head back and dropped it on to one eye.

'I'm surprised they haven't caught up with us already,' Jeff remarked as he opened the second blister.

'Trust me, they won't be far behind. But as long as we don't use our own UPs for now, it should be a lot easier to stay out of sight.'

Jeff dropped the second contact into position, and blinked a couple of times. A manufacturer's logo appeared briefly in the lower right of his vision, before fading to nothing.

Instead of asking him to register his current UP, the new contacts informed him that his name was Eric Waites, and he was a native of Connecticut. As info-bubbles popped up here and there, he discovered that Eric possessed a big enough bank balance to keep himself comfortable for at least a couple of weeks.

'Okay,' said Mitchell, 'let's start walking. The sooner we get out of here, the better. How did you find your way here, exactly?'

'I had to pay for a bus ticket.' As they rounded a hedge, Jeff glanced ahead and spotted another exit from the cemetery, not too far ahead.

Mitchell eyed him sharply. 'Didn't you tell me you stole a car?'

'Yeah, to get away from the cabin. But it was just sheer dumb luck I didn't get caught once they managed to track it down.'

'Buying a bus ticket made you just as easy to find,' Mitchell said reproachfully.

'To hell with that,' said Jeff, feeling irritated. 'I'm here now, so the most important thing to worry about is getting back to Montana and retrieving that database.'

'You're kidding.' Mitchell raised an eyebrow. 'Unless I heard you wrong, you went to hide out in a cabin that you owned under your own name. Could you have made it any easier for them to find you?'

Jeff felt his face burning. 'I guess I hadn't thought of it that way.'

Mitchell gestured dismissively. 'Well, you can forget about going back there. My guess is they'll have the whole area well covered, in case you try to do exactly that.'

They were almost at the cemetery gates now, Jeff noticed. 'Then what the hell do we do? What's the point in even meeting like this if we're just going to do nothing?'

'You at least want to stay alive, don't you? What's the point of charging back up that mountain, the two of us against the whole ASI? How do you think that would pan out, seeing they're already hunting you?'

He was right, Jeff realized; but even worse was admitting to himself that Lucy and Dan's hard work stealing the Tau Ceti databases might well have been for nothing. He stood there, feeling utterly impotent, and for a moment saw himself as Mitchell must see him: idealistic, naive and foolhardy.

'The best thing we can do right now,' Mitchell continued, 'is just keep ourselves alive. Doesn't anyone else have a copy of that database?'

Of course. It was something he'd actually forgotten for a moment. 'Farad . . . Farad has a copy, but none of us had heard from him. I guess I've been assuming he was dead too.'

'But you don't know for sure?'

Jeff merely shook his head.

'Then don't make too many assumptions, okay? You'll not prove anything if you wind up dead yourself.'

'So what now?'

'Now we get ourselves to the Moon, preferably before the first of the growths makes an appearance here. Are you with me on that?'

'Yes, I . . . guess.'

'Good.' Mitchell turned to him just by the gate. 'But, before we do that, there's something I need you to do for me. You used to work for Arcorex, didn't you? Down Omaha way?'

'Sure.' Jeff nodded. 'That's where they always take the Founder artefacts, after they arrive. Why?'

'Do you still have clearance? Can you still get inside there?'

Jeff shrugged, looking bewildered. 'I don't know, maybe . . . unless it's been revoked. I wouldn't know until I tried, but I haven't been there in a couple of years.'

'Good.' Mitchell chewed his lower lip for a moment, then nodded as if coming to a decision. 'That's where we're going next.'

'Arcorex? What in God's name could you need from Arcorex?' Jeff demanded. 'First you won't help me recover those files, then you tell me you want us to go to the Moon, and now you want to take a detour via *Omaha*?'

Mitchell let out a heavy sigh. 'I swear I'll explain everything to you on the way. Until then, I just need you to trust me. It'll all become clear by the time we get there, I promise you.'

Jeff gave a strangled laugh. 'Maybe you should just tell me now. Why Arcorex?'

'You sound like you don't trust me.'

Jeff let his hands flap against his sides, in a gesture of helplessness. 'I don't know *who* to trust, Mitch. I never thought I'd . . .'

'Screw up this badly?'

Jeff glared at him, his fists bunching.

'Look,' said Mitchell, 'I swear, we'll talk on the way.'

'It's going to have to be a really good explanation.'

'It is.'

'All right.' Jeff managed to push his anger and frustration back down into the same place he'd been keeping them bottled up for the past few days. 'But I've got a condition of my own.'

'What?'

'Olivia.'

'Your ex-wife?' Mitchell shook his head, clearly confused. 'What about her?'

'When we head to the Moon, she's coming with us.'

Mitchell gaped at him, his mouth hanging open. 'Jeff—'

'No.' The muscles in Jeff's jaw tightened. 'That's not up for negotiation – not if you want me to get you inside Arcorex.'

Mitchell sighed again. 'It's going to complicate things, a *lot*.'

'Even so.'

Mitchell shook his head wearily. 'Fine.' He led Jeff out on to the street. 'We'll fetch Olivia, but right now I've got a ride waiting for us.' He pointed to a van with a silver finish parked on the kerb.

'Tell me what's in Arcorex,' Jeff demanded.

'Somebody we need to rescue.'

'It's not a prison, Mitch. They don't keep people locked up there.'

Mitchell grinned, as if at a private joke. 'You're wrong. Somebody's been held there ever since the incident at Site 17, and we're going to bust him out.' Mitchell stepped up to the van, slapping one hand on its ID plate as Jeff stared after him. The door made a clunking sound as it unlocked.

Mitchell looked over at him. 'Get in the van, will you?'

'What happened to you in that pit, Mitch?'

Mitchell climbed inside and touched the dashboard, a pre-programmed route springing up in response. Jeff shook his head, and went to get in on the other side.

'I'll tell you,' Mitchell replied, as the van pulled away from the kerb. 'But I'm warning you, it's going to take a lot of explaining.'

FOURTEEN

Fowler felt a slight vibration as the rail-mounted shuttle-car transported him across a hundred light-years in an instant.

The roof of the shuttle-car was attached to an overhead track that ran directly through the centre of the wormhole. One mouth of the wormhole was located on Luna, the other on board a starship already decelerating on its approach to the Galileo system. It was considerably smaller than the mass-transit models that carried thousands of passengers daily between Luna and the colonies, and existed primarily to transport the engineers and physicists whose job was to maintain the equipment that prevented either mouth of the wormhole from collapsing. Each of the mouths was capped by a vast steel torus containing trace quantities of highly unstable exotic matter, held at bay by enormously powerful magnetic fields, while the surface of the wormhole itself was hidden from sight behind dense layers of machinery and shielding.

Fowler had the sensation of falling for a few moments before he felt his weight return; the starship's near-1g deceleration allowed him to walk around its interior in relative comfort.

His UP was already active, and he now used it to navigate his way to the observation suite, most often the first stop for documentary makers or politicians wanting to see where all the taxpayer's money was going. He arrived to find Donohue already there, gazing up at the broad, curving bowl of the main display screen with tired eyes;

Fowler guessed he'd only just got back from his trip to the Far East. When Donohue lowered his head, Fowler allowed himself a momentary satisfaction at the look of apprehension on the agent's face.

'I've read your summary report,' he began, taking a seat opposite Donohue. 'Your partner is dead, and you still haven't found Jeff Cairns. If you're deliberately trying to display unprecedented levels of incompetence, you're doing an excellent job.'

Donohue regarded him levelly. 'Mr Sanders did his best to follow your orders, sir. Maybe if we'd been told we were dealing with quite such *resourceful* targets, we could have—'

'Or maybe you're just not competent enough to do your job,' Fowler snapped. 'Please don't waste my time with excuses. Have you even found Maalouf?'

Donohue cleared his throat. 'We've found him, and he's still on Newton. However, he's escorted by armed guards wherever he goes.'

'In other words, he's considerably more than just a civilian scientist.'

Donohue nodded. 'We've carried out extensive analysis of his movements prior to being posted to the Founder Project, and we found evidence that he's had at least some contact with one of the local separatist groups.'

Fowler waved a hand dismissively. 'We'll have time to mop up the separatists after the evacuation is over. In the meantime, terminating Maalouf remains a priority. Got that?'

'Sir.'

'All right.' Fowler nodded, still far from mollified. 'What's the latest with Hanover?'

'We're still in negotiation with the Taiwanese authorities, but we've confirmed that he allowed himself to be caught. One of our people managed to get a private interview with him, and he's still threatening to tell Sphere representatives everything, if we don't give him what he wants.'

Fowler grunted. 'Hell of a gamble for him to take.'

'But one that paid off, at least at first.' Donohue leaned forward and clasped his hands. 'We've made progress, however. Network forensics show that Hanover opened more than a dozen anonymous accounts over the past several weeks, all with firms specializing in secure data-storage. He's set the accounts up so that any data held in them will be released and disseminated automatically *unless* he intervenes at specified times.'

'In other words, killing him would just make things worse.'

Donohue nodded. 'And it also puts a time limit on how long we can risk leaving him in foreign custody. However, we've put pressure on the owners of the businesses concerned. Several are in non-Coalition treaty territories, which means we don't have any influence over them directly, but *all* of them do business within Coalition territories – and it's business they can't afford to lose.'

Fowler grunted approval. 'Go on.'

'To cut a long story short, we've already secured access to most of his accounts, and it won't take more than another day or so to shut down the rest.'

Fowler nodded. 'Excellent. Any idea who Hanover's main Sphere contact is?'

'Yes, a member of the Beijing diplomatic service, based in New York. We picked him up a few hours ago, along with a couple of other embassy workers we're pretty sure were involved. That leaves Hanover with no evidence to show, and we've already arranged a diplomatic exchange.' He rubbed his hands on his thighs. 'Regarding him, do you want me to—?'

'No.' Fowler shook his head. 'No termination. I'm going to let him live – for now, anyway.'

Donohue frowned. 'I don't understand.'

'Trust me, he's going to suffer more than you could imagine. What about the shipment?'

'We know the hijackers landed at an airfield outside Tegucigalpa, and the shipment was then transferred to a cargo drone belonging to a shell company registered in the Philippines.' Donohue paused, as if for effect. 'Which turns out to be owned by a subsidiary of Shang-Gu Tech.'

Fowler could feel all the pieces drop into place. Shih Hsiu-Chuan was the original founder of Shang-Gu Tech, and still maintained a controlling interest in the company.

'And after that?'

Donohue sat back with a sigh. 'It's confirmed that the cargo drone went down north of the Mariana Islands, and took the shipment to the bottom of the Pacific with it. We already knew the exact latitude and longitude of where the first of the growths would appear; by the looks of it, the drone crashed at the precise same coordinates.'

Icy tendrils creeping through his belly, Fowler recalled the recovered footage of the Pacific growth, dipping in and out of sight as the ship rose and fell on the turbulent waters. It had been wrapped in clouds of smoke and steam, big enough already it was almost certainly visible from orbit.

It was one thing, he thought, to have foreknowledge of future events. It was another matter entirely to see them so clearly confirmed.

Following the meeting on Luna, he had shown Amanda the full and unexpurgated video, noticing the way her lips had compressed into a thin white line as she watched it.

The view had swung away from the growth to show Amanda standing by a railing, with the Pacific blue and deep and restless behind her. Her eyes suddenly darted to one side, as if she saw something there that frightened her. After that, the video blurred and jerked rapidly before fading to darkness.

'It's going to be hard, you know,' he remarked, almost to himself.

'Sir?'

'The colonial administrations,' he explained, glancing directly at Donohue. 'Most of them aren't going to give up what little power they have without a fight. It might be all over in days, or it might take years – long, hard years.'

'I understand that, sir.'

Fowler made a sound of irritation, aware that he sounded

maudlin. He reminded himself that Donohue was nothing more than a weapon, and almost incapable – if his personnel file was anything to judge by – of anything resembling introspection.

'Any news on Mitchell Stone?' asked Fowler. 'The one we brought back from the future,' he added, by way of clarification.

'I'm afraid not, so far. But the instant he shows himself anywhere near the Array, we've got him.'

Fowler nodded, and wondered how he had managed to underestimate Stone's resourcefulness quite so badly. His mistake, he saw now, had been in allowing a military intelligence unit to run the interrogation. His own people, even Donohue, surely couldn't have made as big a mess.

'Fine. Let him come to us, then,' he said, regarding Donohue with a level stare. 'And let me be perfectly clear on this: screw up again, and I'm going to wonder if you're really competent of taking care of the tasks I assign you.'

'Sir,' said Donohue, standing up.

Once Donohue had left, Fowler leaned back and stared up at the stars displayed across the overhead screen. One of those points of light, he knew, was Galileo, only a few months' journey away within the frame of reference of the ship and of Earth. Just another couple of weeks of deceleration, and radio communication with it would become possible. By then, however, the Earth would have been reduced to a lifeless wasteland.

And where will I be? Fowler wondered. He was supposed to help rebuild the Coalition, under the light of some other star, but he was all too aware of how much of a liability he already represented to that nascent civilization: useful for facilitating the transition of power, but possessing too much knowledge to comfortably be allowed to live.

And if anyone were to be given the orders to terminate him, it would almost certainly be Donohue.

No, Fowler had already come to his decision: neither Donohue nor anyone else would get the chance to kill him. He would fulfil his duty in the meantime, and give whatever orders proved necessary in order to ensure preparations for the transition went as smoothly as possible. But any lingering doubts about staying behind had vanished in the wake of Amanda's decision not to seek escape.

After all, as she herself had quickly pointed out, *someone* had recorded those images of her on that storm-tossed ship, with that incomprehensibly alien structure rising from the deep ocean behind her. And, in his heart, Fowler knew that person could only be himself.

FIFTEEN

Orlando, Florida, 2 February 2235

Not too many hours after Donohue had walked out on him in Hong Kong, Saul woke up in the back seat of a taxi, outside the four-storey walk-up in Orlando he'd called home for the past six years, to the sound of a recorded voice asking him to please get out.

He stumbled out into the night air, feeling bone-crushingly weary, and looked down at the stained shirt and ill-fitting trousers he'd been forced to wear the whole way back from Hong Kong. A woman walking her dog gave him a quick once-over and quickly crossed over to the far side of the street.

Saul tugged the collar of his shirt close to his nose, sniffed and winced, remembering the look on the face of the man forced to sit next to him during the sub-orb flight.

Closing his front door behind him, he activated his UP just long enough to check his mail, and found a message waiting from someone he hadn't heard from in a very long time. Saul came to an abrupt halt in the narrow hallway, and stared at the name floating next to the message icon.

He resisted the impulse to open and read it immediately. Whatever Olivia had to say, it almost certainly wasn't anything he wanted to hear.

At least, not right now.

He instructed the house to run him a bath and meanwhile

waited in the kitchen, dumping the clothes he'd been provided in the waste-disposal unit and pulling on a bathrobe. He ate half a tin of ravioli straight from the fridge, his gaze lingering on an old picture of Deanna and their daughter Gwen, until the house informed him ten minutes later that the bath was ready. He ordered a suit from a local fab-shop before easing himself into the warm water, some of the weight of the past few days sloughing away as he submerged.

He lay staring up at the bathroom ceiling, Olivia's message occupying his thoughts far more than he wanted it to.

I could just delete it, he thought. Reading it had every chance of making his life a lot more complicated than it already was.

When he finally emerged from the bathroom half an hour later, the house informed him that a shrink-wrapped package was waiting by the front door. He opened it, pulling out a jacket and a pair of trousers cut from soft dark cloth, and also a grey silk shirt. They hadn't been cheap but, after what he'd been through the last few days, Saul really wasn't inclined to give a damn.

He got dressed and checked himself out in the bedroom mirror, but something still didn't feel right. Saul felt twitchy and on edge. *Maybe a little loup-garou*, he thought, remembering that he had some stuffed in a coffee jar at the back of one of the kitchen cupboards . . .

No. He remembered the look of contempt on Donohue's face, Jacob's body slumped in a chair. He turned away from the mirror, suddenly feeling ashamed, and left the house.

As he bought himself a steak dinner at a local eatery, thoughts of Olivia continued to nag at him, making him feel lonely even at the one time he felt he needed most of all to be on his own. By the time he'd finished eating and was on his way to Christy's to get good and drunk, he'd noticed a second message had arrived.

Saul abruptly came to a halt, realizing he was only delaying the inevitable. After reading both messages, he changed direction and headed for another bar, one he hadn't stepped inside for several years.

Some of the tension he'd worked so hard at shedding was

starting to creep back. By the time he arrived at Harry's Bar and Diner, Olivia was already sitting waiting for him by the bar.

It was early enough for the place to still be fairly quiet, no more than a half dozen people scattered around the tables. Pebbled-glass windows splashed diffused streetlight across leather couches and dark varnished wood.

Saul climbed on to the stool next to Olivia's. 'This was my plan for tonight,' he said, resting his arms on the counter. 'I was going to get drunk and maybe make up some bullshit about the hard week I've just had, for the benefit of anyone who would listen, then let them call me a ride home when I couldn't stand up any longer. A simple, yet effective strategy, and now you've gone and messed it all up.'

Olivia set her drink down – it came in a tall narrow glass and struck him as an unhealthy shade of pink – and glanced at him sideways in amusement. She had wide dark eyes and black hair that fell across her shoulders, and her features revealed a complex ethnic heritage that included a Seminole father and Korean grandmother.

'As soon as I sat down here, it brought back a whole lot of memories, Saul. Not all bad ones, either, but, if it makes you feel any better, that's not why I'm here.'

Saul ordered himself a drink. 'So why *are* you here?'

'Actually, it has to do with Jeff.'

'Your ex-husband?'

'Do you know any other Jeffs?'

'I guess not.'

The barman deposited a Drambuie on the rocks in front of Saul. Even after so many years, the details of their past affair remained fresh in his mind. Olivia and Jeff Cairns had already been separated by the time she'd started sleeping with Saul – not that this had offered any great reassurance to his wife at the time. However, he'd been well on the road to patching things up with Deanna when the Galileo gate had collapsed.

'Hey, look at you.' She leaned forward to examine him under the overhead lights, and he could tell, from the way her eyes moved, that she was studying the bruises on his face. 'What the hell happened to you?'

He took a sip of the Drambuie. 'All in the line of duty, ma'am.'

Her expression by now was a mixture of pity and horror. 'Still trying to get yourself killed?'

'Still playing amateur psychologist?'

'Only a couple more months, and you'll know if Deanna and your daughter are still alive, Saul.'

'And if they're not?'

She sighed, and shot a glance at her reflection in the mirror behind the bar. 'It doesn't take a shrink to figure you out, Saul. First you let Mitchell talk you into that insane orbital jump, then you started drinking too much, like you were deliberately trying to kill yourself.'

He glared at her. 'I was *not* trying to get myself killed,' he snapped, a little too loudly. Seeing the barman glance their way, he lowered his voice. 'It's just . . .'

'Just what?'

He fingered his drink and, noticing the way she looked at it, gulped it down as if in defiance. It coated his tongue with a sticky numb fieriness.

'There was more to the jump we made than that,' he said firmly. 'You remember Mitch's brother?'

She nodded. 'Danny? I only met him once.'

'You know he died?'

She nodded.

'Mitchell blamed himself for it,' Saul continued. 'Felt he hadn't been there for him. Do you know the actual details?'

She hesitated. 'In the sketchiest sense, yes. But all of that happened after . . . after us. After you'd moved on from the Jupiter station.'

Saul had first met Olivia on being assigned, along with Mitchell, to security on the Jupiter orbital platform. The station had been huge even then, constantly growing as pre-assembled units were shipped there via the Inuvik gate back on Earth. Her husband, Jeff, had worked on experimental helium-dredges dropped into the Jovian atmosphere, while Olivia herself had served as the platform's communications specialist. The sheer scale of the station made it easy for the couple to avoid each other once they'd decided to separate.

'Mitchell and Danny both grew up near the DMZ in post-partition Chicago,' Saul went on, and Olivia nodded to signify that this much she knew. 'It was still a pretty rough place, even a couple of decades after the war. Mitch joined the ASI just to get away from the gangs, but . . .'

'Danny didn't?'

'No.' Saul could feel a sour taste building in the back of his throat. 'Danny disappeared, and Mitchell was frantic. He asked me to help try and find him. I was already doing undercover work, so had an idea how to track him down. To cut a long story short, I was the one who found him.'

Olivia had that faraway look that told Saul she was accessing public records on the incident. 'He got himself involved with traffickers,' she said, glancing back at Saul a moment later. It was a statement, not a question.

'I eventually found him in an illegal gene-lab that had been set up in an abandoned apartment building. The traffickers Danny had been working for were all long gone when I discovered him.'

'They killed him?'

'That's what the coroner's report said.' He could clearly picture Danny's lifeless face, still twisted up in anger. 'The lab had been developing customized embryos for unregulated off-world labour markets. Slaves, essentially.'

'Jesus. And you've no idea why they killed him?'

Saul shook his head. 'Let's just say it was all pretty rough on Mitchell, so when he said he wanted me to go along on that jump, six months later, I didn't really feel up to saying no.'

'I had no idea.'

'Yeah, well, it's like you said. We were all moving in different circles by then.'

Saul stood up and gazed down at her. 'Look, I'm sorry about the way things worked out for us both, but talking to you this way brings back too many bad memories. Deanna would never have gone to live on Galileo if it hadn't been for us two.'

'Saul—'

'Please,' he insisted, 'just hurry the hell up and tell me whatever it is you came here to say, otherwise I'm gone.'

She crumpled slightly, and he could see lines around her eyes showing how much older she'd become since he'd last set eyes on her.

'Just give me one minute.' She patted his vacated stool.

He slid back down on to the seat with evident reluctance, keeping one foot planted on the floor. 'Make it quick.'

'Like I said, I'm here because of Jeff. We had a reconciliation, just in the last year or two.'

Saul couldn't hide his surprise. 'Seriously?'

'I know.' She smiled wryly. 'Took both of us by surprise, too. Most of that time he's been involved in some kind of off-world research that takes him away for weeks or even months at a stretch, so it's not like we really get to see that much of each other.' She licked her lips and took a deep breath. 'The thing is, now he's disappeared.'

'Disappeared?'

'More than a week ago. I knew for a good long while that there was something on his mind, something to do with his work, but he wouldn't talk about it.'

'Maybe he *couldn't* talk about it? The ASI had him working on a lot of high-security research projects, didn't they?'

She shrugged. 'I guess so. Thing is, we'd planned on spending some time together when he got back from his last trip out. Instead he cancelled everything and told me he was heading off somewhere on his own. He wouldn't tell me why, but I could tell that something bad had happened.'

Saul finally lifted his foot off the floor, and shifted himself into a more comfortable position. He was curious, despite himself. 'And you haven't heard from him since?'

'No.' She shook her head. 'Here's the thing, though. Two different people contacted me since he vanished, both desperate to find him. The way they talked made me sure he was in some kind of trouble.'

'Olivia,' he spread his hands in a gesture of helplessness, 'I don't mean to sound callous, but I'm not sure what any of this has to do with me.'

She gave him an angry look. 'Jesus, Saul, he's your friend.'

'*Was* my friend, until I started sleeping with his ex-wife.'

She stared back at him in silence.

'All right,' he raised his hands, 'I'm sorry. Don't you have any idea where he might have gone?'

Olivia shook her head. 'Before I tell you anything else, there's something you need to see.'

Saul's UP informed him that she had just sent him a video file.

'What is it?' he asked.

'Just take a look.' She rolled her eyes.

Saul pushed his glass to one side, then tapped the four corners of an imaginary square on the bar counter with one finger. His contacts responded by projecting the clip she had sent within the confines of the same square.

It turned out to be something snatched from one of the main news feeds. He saw men in diving suits falling backwards off a boat into the waters of a lake, snow-capped hills dense with pine visible beyond the shore.

He glanced at Olivia, as the video clip remained locked to the counter. 'What is this?' he asked.

'They dredged Jeff's body out of that lake yesterday morning. We have a cabin up in Montana, where we used to spend our summers. There was a local news report saying it was suicide.'

Saul swallowed. 'Shit, Olivia, I'm so sorry.'

'No, don't be. I don't believe it.'

'Don't believe what?'

'That it was suicide.'

He gave her an appraising stare.

'I'm not out of my head, all right?' she snapped. 'It just . . . not something he would do.'

'You can't possibly know that, Olivia.'

Tendons stood out on her neck as she replied. 'I *know* him, Saul, and I know he wouldn't drown himself deliberately. I think somebody killed him.'

'Does this have anything to do with the people that were looking for him? Who exactly were they?'

'One was a guy called Dan Rush who'd worked with Jeff. The other was Mitch.'

Saul shook his head. 'Mitch?'

'Mitchell Stone.' She peered at him like he'd lost his mind. 'We were just talking about him, remember?'

Saul froze, with one hand clasped around his second Drambuie. He nodded slowly, his expression impassive.

'He called you during the last couple of days? What day was it exactly?'

She thought for a moment. 'It would have been the 29th.'

'Of January?'

She nodded. 'The other man, Rush, called me a few days before that.'

Four days ago, Saul realized. 'I need you to be sure about that.'

She gave him a reproachful glare. 'Jesus, Saul, of course I'm sure.'

He picked up his drink and took his time with it in order to give himself some more room to think. Donohue and Sanders had told him about Mitchell's supposed death on the 20th – which was more than a week ago.

'This guy, Rush, you ever met him?'

'Just once, not long after I and Jeff got back together. So I already knew they were colleagues. When he called, he told me Jeff was in some kind of trouble.' She pushed her hair back from her face. 'I had a feeling Jeff might have gone up to the cabin, but he never replied to my messages. I was going to drive up there to try and see if I could find him for myself, but then I heard about him on the news.'

'About Mitchell,' said Saul, 'I don't want to sound like I'm doubting you, but are you sure it was really him?'

She looked at him. 'Why wouldn't I be? Besides, I know his voice. Why?'

Saul thought for a moment. 'Okay, let me ask you this. Is there a reason you're talking to me, and not the police?'

'I already spoke to them, soon as I heard about Jeff being dredged out of the lake. They said there was no evidence of foul play and they didn't even sound very interested in what I had to say. In fact, they treated me,' she said, with a touch of venom, 'like they thought I was crazy.'

'But did you explain to them that you thought he might have been in some kind of trouble?'

'Sure, except as soon as I mentioned that he worked for ASI's research wing, they said I had to talk to the ASI instead.'

'And?'

She shrugged. 'So I talked to them as well, and they gave me exactly the same kind of brush-off.' She smiled uncertainly. 'After that, I figured that if anyone was in a position to look into things, it would be you.'

Saul nodded and smiled to hide the tension gripping him like steel. If what Olivia was telling him was true, then not only had Hanover lied about Mitch being dead, but Donohue and Sanders had done so also.

He guessed Olivia must have misinterpreted his sudden silence as reluctance, as she reached out and laid a hand over his. 'I know you think I'm out of my mind, Saul, but I've never been more sane. I know I can't ask this of you lightly.' She smiled again, and he realized her confidence in him was genuine.

If only you knew the mess I've been making of things, he thought.

His mind whirred with possible connections. Mitchell had

originally been a member of Hanover's team, and Saul could see no direct connection between his reported death and the shipment hijack, but if he could be lied to about Mitchell's death, what else might have been kept from him?

He thought back on the failures of the past several days – Jacob's death, Hsiu-Chuan, Hanover – and felt the same anger that had been simmering inside him all throughout the long flight home start to rise up again like a hot tide. Donohue had used Galileo to bait him into volunteering for a risky mission, then discarded him without explanation as soon as he'd ceased to be of any use.

He'd find out why – whatever it took.

Saul reached out, touching two fingers to Olivia's elbow. 'I'll check it out,' he said, struggling to keep his voice level. 'It's the least I can do.'

SIXTEEN

Lakeside, Montana, 3 February 2235

Early the next morning, Saul caught a red-eye hopper to Montana, then fell asleep in the back of a hire car as it carried him towards Flathead Lake. By the time he woke again, cramped and hungry, mountains that had been a distant blue at the start of his journey now rose all around him, their grassy slopes dense with forest and spotted with clumps of snow.

He pulled in at an autocafé, less than fifty kilometres from his destination. Breakfast consisted of paste sandwiches and coffee with a faintly metallic taste, and he sat by the window, browsing local news feeds in case he could discover anything more about Jeff's supposed suicide. Once he'd finished his coffee, he placed a call to the police station in Lakeside. He soon found himself talking with the sheriff there, a man by the name of Waldo Gibbs, who agreed to meet him when he arrived.

Just over an hour later, Saul pulled up outside the police station in Lakeside, a two-storey brick building with an open garage next door, crammed with trucks and cars built for the mountainous terrain. Gibbs stood waiting for him on the steps. Saul guessed he was in his mid-fifties, with a weather-beaten face beneath a fur-lined hat, and he looked like the type who preferred a life outdoors. Saul made sure to activate his UP so the sheriff could confirm his identity, as they shook hands.

'Mr Dumont. I'm a little unclear why the ASI has been showing so much interest in Cairns. Did your boys forget something before they left?'

Saul kept his face impassive. He'd had no idea ASI agents had been involved in the investigation. 'When exactly were they here?'

Gibbs squinted at him in the early afternoon sun. 'Just this morning, but I'm afraid you've missed them. I'm sorry if that means you've had a wasted journey.'

'I'm here to follow up on some things,' Saul improvised. 'Were you present when they pulled his body out of the lake?'

Gibbs nodded. 'I was there all right, and I told your boys they had the wrong man, but they didn't seem interested in listening to me. Now they've gone and put it out that Cairns is dead, when I know for a fact he ain't.'

'I don't understand.'

'What I'm saying is, the man we dredged out of that lake was not Jeff Cairns. But, the way you guys act, it's like you don't give a damn.'

'Then . . . in that case, who was it?'

Gibbs led him round one side of the station to a one-storey extension at the rear. 'This is our morgue,' he explained. 'You wouldn't think we'd need one this big for a town this small, but our catchment area covers a good chunk of the Rockies. If somebody's got a body needs putting on ice, they either fly 'em in or drive 'em here.' Gibbs pushed his way through a swing-door, and Saul followed him inside. 'If a pathologist needs to see them, then they go on to Miles City.'

Saul noticed a lab assistant sitting at a live-desk. 'How did you know for sure it wasn't Jeff Cairns?'

'We didn't know who the hell he was, when we pulled him out,' said Gibbs. 'He was wearing contacts, but they've got some kind of heavy-duty encryption on them that we can't break.'

'You still have them?'

'Nope.' Gibbs shook his head. 'ASI took them. You're lucky you got here when you did. They told us to cremate the body straight away. As it happens, it's still waiting to be picked up.'

Gibbs stepped over to a wall of metal drawers and pulled one open. Saul stepped up alongside him and watched as the policeman pulled the sheet back off the corpse contained within.

Saul found himself staring down at Sanders, Donohue's partner. One side of his skull had been caved in.

'His head—?'

'He got run over by a motorboat,' said Gibbs, 'which we later found abandoned and half sunk on the far side of the lake. With bullet holes in it, I should add. Now, Jeff Cairns has been coming up to Lakeside for some years, Mr Dumont,' Gibbs continued, 'and I'm sure you've noticed this isn't a very big town.' Saul stepped back from the drawer as Gibbs slid it shut. 'I knew we had the wrong guy, soon as I set eyes on him,' Gibbs continued, 'and I told your people that. Except next time I watch the news they're claiming it's Cairns that's dead.' Gibbs made a helpless gesture. 'Whoever that is, we can't even trace him through the tags in his clothes.'

'Why not?'

'There just aren't any. Looks like he didn't want anyone being able to track him.'

Saul nodded slowly. 'So any idea what happened to the real Cairns?'

'None,' said Gibbs, 'and I already asked your people that same question. Now, you have to understand that whenever shit like this happens in my own backyard, I take a considerable interest in it – *not* that your people were exactly forthcoming when it came to sharing information. When you told me you were on your way, I hoped you might be a little more open with us than that other guy.'

That other guy. 'Was his name Donohue?' asked Saul, taking a chance.

'Yeah, that's the one.' Gibbs' face screwed up like he'd eaten something sour. 'Is there anything else you need from me?'

'If you don't mind,' said Saul, 'I'd like to take a quick look at Cairns' cabin.'

Gibbs guided the truck around the first of several switchbacks ascending a hill dense with forest. The sheriff clearly had a taste for driving on manual, and had complained, before setting out, that the auto-drive function in most vehicles wasn't up to the mountainous terrain surrounding the lake.

Saul caught flickering glimpses of the lake itself through a tangle of trees and brush, while he thought about everything Gibbs had told him during their drive here to the lake.

'So whoever stole the motorboat also stole the car?'

Gibbs glanced at him and shrugged. 'Makes sense to me. I figure it must have been Cairns. He drove down to the lakeside, grabbed the boat, made his way to the far shore and stole a car, making mincemeat out of our friend there in the morgue on the way. Seems to me that whatever kind of trouble he was running from had caught up with him.'

'Did he seem to you the kind of guy to get himself mixed up in something like this?'

Gibbs thought for a moment before replying. 'Depends on what you mean by "this". But, y'know, not really. Not if you're talking organized crime or whatever.'

'Right.'

'But sometimes people get out of their depth, without even knowing it. Next thing you know, there's bodies everywhere.'

'I guess.'

'Why ask me anyway?' said Gibbs. 'You wouldn't be here unless you were looking for something. Maybe you should be telling me what Cairns was involved in?'

Saul smiled. 'That's not something I can talk about, sorry.'

'Fuckin' ASI.' Gibbs shook his head. 'Ever thought about cooperating once in a while?'

Saul shrugged, as if to say, *What can you do?*

The sheriff sighed heavily. 'Do you need to see the incident report?'

Saul nodded. 'I'd appreciate that.'

A moment later, a copy of the report appeared within Saul's vision. He focused on the dashboard, thus projecting the report's contents on to it. He quickly shuffled through several UP-generated video-files of Sanders' bedraggled form being pulled from the water, along with several still shots of the motorboat and the bullet-holes drilled through its hull. He next skimmed the text, trying to build a picture in his mind of events as Gibbs had already described them.

Glancing away from the dashboard, Saul saw they had almost reached the cabin.

'I figure the dead guy and one other chased your man Cairns down to the lake, meaning to kill him,' said Gibbs. 'Maybe they meant to shoot him out in the middle of the lake, where it'd be easier for them to dump the body. Except Cairns got away and took the boat for himself – which would at least explain the bullet holes.'

'Two men chased him? Do you have any evidence for that?'

'It's as clear as daylight if you take a good look at the hillside up there. You'll find a shitload of skidding footprints and broken branches. There were two of them all right.'

Saul nodded. 'And you reckon your dead guy shot at him from the shore, then waded out into the water, and got hit on the head by the motorboat?'

Gibbs took one hand off the wheel and waved it in the air. 'Something like that. I don't have any better ideas at any rate.'

Maybe Sanders had been in the boat along with Jeff, thought Saul, while the third man was waiting on the shore. Sanders had fallen out, and got himself rammed in the head, then the third man had tried to shoot Jeff before he could get away. And if Sanders had been present, did that make Donohue the third man?

'Look, I'm dying of fucking curiosity here,' said Gibbs, 'but I know I shouldn't stick my nose in where it doesn't belong. The important thing is that you make sure ASI understands the victim's body has been misidentified. Cairns is still out there somewhere.'

And somebody doesn't want me, or anyone else, to know that either Jeff or Mitchell are still alive, thought Saul. Both of them worked for the ASI . . . and now Donohue or someone else was trying their damnedest to cover something up.

As the truck lurched around a corner, Saul saw the cabin itself for the first time. Gibbs parked close to the edge of the wooded slope out front, and they climbed out. Mountains rose beyond the far side of the lake, and the air was startlingly cold as Saul drew it into his lungs. He walked over to the edge of the driveway and peered down through the trees towards the lakeshore, to where he could just make out a wharf and a boarded-up hut.

'Let's take a look inside,' he suggested.

Gibbs led him over to the cabin, and Saul followed him inside, wondering what the hell benefit anyone got from sitting halfway up the side of a mountain with no one to talk to and the nearest bar a half hour's drive away.

Gibbs closed the door behind them and Saul gazed around. The place seemed comfortable enough, and less primitive than he'd expected. There was even a TriView that responded to his contacts. All in all, it looked quite cosy. There were ashes in the hearth, and the bedroom was visible through a half-open door. The way things were scattered about made it clear that either Jeff Cairns had left in a great hurry or someone had recently turned the place over.

Gibbs waited by the fireplace while Saul stepped through into the bedroom. He glanced under the bed and behind some mementoes gathering dust on a single shelf alongside the window. After that, he proceeded to check out the bathroom and the kitchen.

'Forensics boys already been over the whole place,' said Gibbs when Saul rejoined him a few minutes later.

'I guess,' said Saul, checking the time: almost four. Maybe it was time to give Olivia a call. He made an excuse to Gibbs and stepped out on to the veranda, pulling his jacket close around him as he walked on across the driveway towards the trees.

Olivia answered after just a few seconds. 'You were more than right,' he said. 'I'm at the cabin right now, and they pulled someone out of the lake, but it wasn't Jeff.'

She made a small sound in the back of her throat, followed by a stifled sob. From background noise, it sounded like she was somewhere in town. After a moment the traffic noise faded, and he guessed she'd found somewhere quieter.

'Then Jeff's still alive?' she asked.

'Well, all I can say for sure is that you were right about him being in some kind of trouble. I'm still not sure just what kind.'

'Do you think you can find him?'

'That depends.'

'On what?'

He headed closer to the trees. 'I need you to be absolutely straight with me, Olivia. If you've been holding anything back, now's the time to tell me.'

'Saul, I swear I haven't, and I wish I could tell you more. I tried so many times to get him to tell me whatever the hell was bothering him, but he just wouldn't open up. And if he is still alive, there's a part of me wants to wring his neck for not being straight with me.'

Saul chuckled. 'I wouldn't want to be in his shoes, in that case. Look, from what I can tell, the police have already been over the whole place thoroughly. If there was ever anything here that might tell us where Jeff's gone, it's not here any more.'

'Did you check the tool shed?' she asked suddenly.

'Tool shed?'

'It's around the back of the cabin, just where the trees start. There's a safe embedded in the floor.'

Saul glanced back towards the cabin and saw Gibbs peering out of the window towards him. Saul smiled and raised a hand. Gibbs nodded grudgingly, then moved back out of sight.

Saul ran a quick search of the report Gibbs had given him earlier, for any mention of a tool shed, but found nothing. 'Hang on while I take a look myself,' he muttered, then headed around behind the cabin, where the trees resumed four or five metres to the rear.

He looked around. 'I'm here,' he told her quietly, wary of Gibbs overhearing him. 'I don't see anything.'

'It's quite well hidden,' she explained. 'Look to your left, away from the cabin . . . there's a boulder and some bushes. See them?'

Saul glanced to his left. 'I see them.'

Then he spotted the shed, almost out of sight beyond the boulder. It was painted green, so nearly invisible among the tangled undergrowth.

The structure was in a semi-derelict state, leaning slightly to one side, and he pulled the door open only with some difficulty. Various tools hung from hooks, and the disassembled parts of a chainsaw lay scattered on a tarpaulin spread across the floor, so that he had barely enough room to squeeze inside and close the door behind him.

'What am I looking for?' he asked next.

'All I know is that he kept some stuff in a floor-safe there. Maybe there'll be something there to tell you where he's gone.'

Saul bent down and quickly moved some of the chainsaw parts aside, then hauled away the tarpaulin to reveal a flat steel panel embedded in the concrete floor. 'I've got it,' he told her, 'but there's no external lock.' Doubtless it needed a UP-coded password before it would open up. 'Short of digging it out of the concrete, I can't see any way to get inside.'

'Maybe you won't need to,' she replied.

'How so?'

'Because if he was going to store anything in there, it would probably be a set of contacts, or the like.'

'Yes, but if I can't open the safe, I can't get to them.'

'Remember how there are back doors built into a lot of the commercial contacts. Maybe I can get you in through one of those. Are you physically close to the safe?'

'I'm kneeling right over it, Olivia.'

'Okay, I've got a data key that should do the trick, and I'm sending it to you now.'

An icon suddenly materialized, looking bright and cheery against the drab browns and greys inside the shed.

'Got it. What next?' he asked.

'All you need to do is run it. If there are any contacts, or anything UP-compatible, in there, then they should open right up.'

Saul did as instructed, and a bright blue bubble popped into existence, hovering just above the floor-safe door.

'I see something.' He was suddenly excited. 'Looks like you were right on the money.'

He touched the bubble and it expanded into a three-dimensional image of a filing cabinet. The wall of the shed cut through one side of it, shattering any illusion of solidity.

Saul pushed the shed door back open and peered in the direction of the cabin. Gibbs must be wondering where he'd got to by now.

He touched one finger to a drawer marked ALL, and it took mere moments to copy the complete contents of whatever data device was hidden in the safe over to his own contacts. Once he'd disengaged, the filing cabinet abruptly vanished in a cloud of animated smoke.

'Thanks,' he said, as he exited the shed.

'Did you get anything?' she asked.

'I copied some data across, but I can't check it out just yet. I'll let you know what I've got later.'

He walked back around the front of the cabin and almost ran into Sheriff Gibbs, who had evidently come outside looking for him.

'Find anything useful?' the sheriff asked.

Saul gave him a sheepish grin. 'Not a damn thing.'

Gibbs squinted at him, then scanned the line of trees amongst which the tool shed was hidden. 'Are you sure you don't want to tell me just exactly what it is you're looking for?'

'If I already knew that,' Saul replied, 'I wouldn't need to be here at all.'

Gibbs gave him a frank stare, his whole demeanour radiating suspicion. 'Yeah,' he replied, 'I guess not.'

That evening Saul checked into a Lakeside motel with a fine view of the mountains. He closed the blinds with a single spoken command, before summoning up the same filing cabinet he'd discovered in the tool shed. Some of its drawers refused to open, so he guessed they had been provided with extra security to guard whatever they might contain. Other, more easily accessible drawers contained merely junk: copies of scientific papers and back issues of journals, along with the random bureaucratic detritus of a lifetime.

Saul sat down on the edge of his bed, unable to fight a sense of disappointment. It wasn't hard to guess that if there was anything that might help him find Jeff, it was hidden in one of the restricted drawers. He called Olivia and explained the problem.

'Maybe you could forward the files to me?' she eventually suggested.

Having sent them over, and now feeling obliged to wait for her to get back to him, he pulled on his shoes, thinking maybe it wouldn't be a bad idea to try and walk off some of his pent-up frustration.

The air outside was chill and sharp but, to his surprise, Saul found himself enjoying it. His mind felt clearer, more focused as he breathed in the fresh mountain air. He walked a few blocks until he came to the start of a nature trail, little info-bubbles popping up along its length as he approached. A faint white line joined the bubbles together, snaking upwards and over the crest of a hill.

He had supper later that evening in the hotel's restaurant, where a TriView provided him with a selection of UP-compatible news feeds. Most were focused on volcanic activity near the Mariana Islands out in the Far East.

Olivia got back to him before he could watch any more. 'I'm stumped,' she told him, as he made his way back up to his room. 'Whoever set up the encryption, they did a scarily good job. This is military-level work.'

'You sound hurt.'

'I *am* hurt,' she replied. 'It makes me feel like he didn't trust me.'

Or maybe, thought Saul, *he was trying to protect you*. 'Don't you have any more keys or whatever that you can use?'

'The tools I'd need to get past encryption that strong could only come from the ASI, and everything I can access from the work servers is tracked and tagged. My own security protocols would flag an unauthorized action and sound an alert.'

'It's funny how you're suddenly worried about attracting the ASI's attention, but just a little while ago you were feeling frustrated because you couldn't get them involved.'

'Yeah, well . . .' She paused. 'It's different now. Now that I'm sure he's alive.'

Her breathing had turned coarse and ragged as she made this last statement, and Saul guessed she was weeping.

'Olivia?'

'I'm sorry, Saul.' She cleared her throat and, when she spoke again, she sounded a little calmer. 'Looking at what you sent me reminded me of a detail I'd almost forgotten. I'm sorry I didn't mention it before.'

'Go on.'

'There's a man called Farad Maalouf,' she explained. 'When Jeff wouldn't tell me where he was going, before he disappeared, he told me he'd make up for it. He said that, once he'd done whatever it is he had to do, he was going to take me to Newton, to see Farad. He said Farad had family there – and that we'd both be safe.'

'Safe from what?'

'I don't know, Saul. I'm not really sure I even want to know.'

'This Farad guy, do you know who he is?'

'I met him about the same time I met Dan Rush, back at the

Florida Array. He was another of Jeff's colleagues.' She paused. 'The thing that made me remember Maalouf just now is that he's an encryption specialist. He's well known in certain specialized technical fields. I couldn't think at first why Jeff would need to hide something with military-grade locks on it, but then I remembered him talking about Maalouf and Newton and, with everything else going on, I wondered if maybe there was some connection with the files. It seemed strange he'd bring up Maalouf, of all people. And, even if there isn't a connection, if there's anyone that could break the encryption on those files, my guess is it would be Maalouf.'

'And that's everything you know? Are you absolutely sure there isn't anything else you need to remember?'

'Nothing, I swear.'

Saul found it hard to hide his irritation. 'Jesus, Olivia, *military*-grade encryption? What exactly is it you think Jeff's got himself involved in?'

'I already told you I don't know,' she said, her voice taking on a ragged edge once more. 'I just want to know he's safe.'

Saul was surprised at how much her last words cut him. He'd thought he'd left his feelings for her far behind him, but it looked like he'd been wrong.

He sighed and fell back on the bed, staring up at the ceiling. 'What makes you so sure this Maalouf guy could get inside those files?'

'He's got a fearsome reputation. He's published a few articles, most of it pretty arcane stuff. If you want to build an encryption system, he's the man you call up.'

'Too arcane even for a dedicated systems specialist like yourself?'

She laughed. 'Even for me.'

'Say I managed to get hold of him, how do we know we can trust him?'

'Well, he did work with Jeff,' she said tentatively, 'and I had the definite sense they were friends – maybe even close friends. That must count for something.'

'D'you think *he* might know where Jeff is?'

'It's possible. Maybe I should try and get in touch with Maalouf myself. I know I've asked too much of you already.'

'No,' he said, sitting up, 'I don't want you getting any more involved than you already are.' He had a mental image of dark figures struggling by a moonlit shore, shots ringing out. 'I can start by taking a look in the ASI's personnel databases – see what I can find about him from there.'

She let out a sigh that was comprised in equal parts of relief and worry. 'Thank you, Saul, from the bottom of my heart. Really.'

'There's a lot more going on here than just one missing scientist,' he said. 'I assume you realize that by now.'

'I do.'

'If nothing else, I can go to Newton and track Maalouf down in person – or at least try to find out where he might be.'

And maybe he can tell me just what the hell is going on, he thought.

Once she had signed off, Saul found himself reliving his memories of her body, the way she had whispered his name over and over as he moved inside her, all those many years ago. It had been hard sitting next to her the day before in the bar, wanting to reach out and touch her but keeping his distance nonetheless.

He sighed and pulled himself off the bed, striding across the darkened room. Sleep clearly wasn't coming any time soon. He dropped himself into an armchair by the window and linked into the ASI's security databases, and from there to its personnel files.

He paused before bringing up Farad Maalouf's data. What he was doing now had gone beyond just helping a friend, and he knew as well as Olivia that he'd be leaving a data trail that might trigger an alert, should someone else have already linked Maalouf's ASI files to Jeff's. But his anger at the way Donohue had treated him drove him on, regardless.

What little information he found on Farad Maalouf proved to be out of date. The most recent records were more than a year old, at which point Maalouf had presumably ceased to be employed by the ASI. Then Saul found something that puzzled him. He should have been able to find information on where Maalouf had gone after departing the ASI, but instead there was nothing. It was as if he'd simply vanished for the better part of a year.

Saul felt a prickling sensation throughout his body when he found the situation was much the same with Jeff Cairn's own personnel records. The curious gaps in the data trail for both men might be explained by their working off-world but, if so, there was no official record showing their time of departure. And hadn't Olivia told him that Jeff had returned from his work only a few days ago? Again, there was no evidence, either way, that he had passed through the Array.

Of course, Olivia had pointed out that Jeff was working on some secret project for the ASI, therefore it was entirely conceivable it had been secret enough for the security services to want to conceal both men's movements.

He next checked Dan Rush's files, and felt little surprise when it turned out to be the same story all over again. He subsequently ran a side-by-side comparison, and found they had all ceased to be in the official employ of the ASI on the exact same date, two years previously.

He lastly checked Mitchell's records. His death was recorded as having taken place a month earlier, but when Saul tried to pull up the post-mortem report, he quickly discovered even his own security clearance wasn't high enough to let him see it.

He woke several hours later, still sprawled in the armchair, to find another call alert waiting for him.

'Saul,' Olivia sounded breathless, when he returned her call, 'have you seen the news?'

Saul pulled his rumpled form upright, the muscles in the back of his neck protesting at the awkward angle they'd been forced into for much of the night. It was still dark outside.

He glanced at the wall-mounted TriView at the other end of the room. 'Why?' he mumbled.

'Just turn it on, Saul. Turn it on *right now*. Then get back to me.'

He disconnected and watched the news, while he waited for the room to make him some coffee. By the time it was ready, the first glimmer of dawn had started to push its way above the mountains.

Everything else in the news – even the border incidents down Mexical way – had been pushed to one side by the appearance of what some people described as an artificial island, and a few others were even calling an alien invasion.

Endless aerial shots paraded across the screen, one after the other, of a vast flower-like growth rising out of the Pacific Ocean near the Mariana Islands. There were reports of loud booms being heard and seismic activity within the vicinity, which some claimed were both connected to the rash of earthquakes that had already claimed thousands of lives throughout the Asian Pacific region in just the last few days. Saul struggled to take any of it seriously, deciding it was too much like some overwrought science-fiction drama to be remotely believable.

He pulled up other news feeds, expecting to find nothing but the usual sober mix about politicians and murder hunts. Instead he saw those very same politicians being forced to admit they had no idea what was happening out in the Pacific.

It dawned on him gradually that what he was seeing was *real* – and now, it seemed, there were more of them pushing up from the deep rock-bed of the ocean floor, scattered at distances from the first growth of up to a few thousand kilometres.

Badly shaken, Saul kept a news feed running as his car pulled back out on to the road an hour later, heading south-west. A tsunami had just hit the south-west coast of Japan, and news of further quakes was coming in from other parts of the world. Two talking heads argued over whether or not those things were powering their massive growth with thermal energy drawn from the Earth's deep crust, which just might explain the unprecedented build-up in seismic activity. By the time the interview ended, the two of them were nearly coming to blows.

He switched to another feed, and listened to a Harvard bio-technology specialist suggesting that the booming sounds were the result of that same furious rate of growth. At the rate the first 'growth' was expanding, it would reach more than a kilometre in height within a few days.

Saul shut down the feed, his skin coated in a cold sweat, and thought of weeds infesting a garden. He leaned back, the seat adjusting to his new position, and watched the mountains slide past under a dawn sky, as the hire car sped him towards a regional hopper port.

Something above and beyond the sheer preposterousness of that thing growing in the Pacific niggled at him, until he realized, with a cold clenching in his gut, that it wasn't located so very far from the shores of Taiwan.

SEVENTEEN

The Arcorex facility was located in a business park just outside the Omaha city limits, and consisted of half a dozen three- and four-storey buildings gathered around manicured lawns and picnic areas, their pale walls now gleaming dully in the moonlight.

'Their tags claim they're a toy manufacturer,' muttered Mitchell, frowning, as he peered through the forward windscreen. They were parked on the opposite side of the road, only a short distance from the main gate.

Jeff shook his head. 'Trust me when I say they aren't.' He removed the fake contacts Mitchell had given him, the corporate logos floating above the buildings vanishing from sight for a few moments while he swapped them for his own. He would need to have access to his own Ubiquitous Profile if he was going to have any chance at all of getting past building security.

'You ready?' asked Mitchell, as Jeff blinked his contacts into place.

Jeff shrugged and gave him a look that said *ready as I'll ever be*.

Mitchell touched the dashboard, which lit up beneath his fingers, and the van started to move back out on to the road. They drove straight on past the Arcorex lot before turning off into a car park adjacent to it.

Jeff stared out at his old workplace as they came to a halt once more. 'I'm still struggling to get my head around everything you've told me,' he said, 'but I guess you know that.'

'I do.' Mitchell nodded towards Arcorex. 'By the way, I didn't get a chance to thank you for helping me.'

'For what – listening to your insane plan? Remind me again why you're so sure it's even going to work.'

'It already *did* work, or I wouldn't be sitting here with you right now. And you're the one who got me out of there.'

Jeff gave a laugh, but it came out half-strangled. 'You mean *will* get you out of there.'

'I swear, it's going to be fine.' Mitchell gave him a look that was undoubtedly meant to be reassuring, then pushed the van's door open and jumped down. 'We'll drop him off at the motel, and he'll make his own way to the Moon,' he said, looking back up at Jeff. 'And then we—'

'Stop.' Jeff put out a hand. *Two Mitchells?* It was almost more than his mind could deal with. 'No more. I'm doing it.' His skin felt slick with sweat, despite the cool February air.

'Okay.' Mitchell stepped back and glanced around. 'Time to find a new ride out of here. Maybe that one.' He gestured towards a four-door sedan quietly grazing on some bales of biomass towards the far end of the car park.

'Good luck,' said Jeff.

Mitchell silently nodded, then slammed the passenger door shut. Shuffling sideways into the driver's seat, Jeff took manual control, guiding the van back out of the car park. He glanced in the rear-view mirror, to see Mitchell making his way over to the sedan.

Jeff parked alongside the gates, just next to the short driveway leading up to Arcorex's main entrance. He got out and walked the rest of the way, trying not to think about the gasoline canisters Mitchell had wired up in the back of the van. Floating in the air before him, a message appeared as he approached the entrance, warning him to comply at all times or risk facing unspecified countermeasures. His contacts chose the same moment to let him know he was being remotely scanned. Jeff tried hard to relax, to avoid looking as scared as he felt, but in truth he was rigid with fear.

Another message appeared, telling him he was clear to go forward. He felt his shoulders sag with relief, and he walked on at a brisker pace. He really hadn't believed until that moment that he would still be listed as an active member of staff.

Just then he saw a beam of light flicker between two buildings as Arcorex's armed security made their regular patrol. He wondered if anyone from the neighbouring businesses had ever paused to wonder just why a toy manufacturer needed countermeasure warnings and guards armed with Cobras.

He thrust his hands deep in his pockets and pushed on through the entrance. At least it was the kind of operation where people often put in very irregular hours, which meant being here so late at night did not, in itself, imply suspicious activity.

Jeff had spent much of the last four days helping Mitchell prepare his elaborate plan. Whatever time hadn't been spent sleeping or hiding in the back of whichever van, car or truck they'd stolen that day had been spent driving around Omaha, trying to locate supplies and looking for what Mitchell called the 'right' motel.

'That's it, right there,' Mitchell had gestured through the windscreen towards a nondescript two-storey building set back on the other side of a wide lawn.

'You're sure that's where we took you?'

'Yeah,' Mitchell nodded, still staring out at the motel. After a moment, his shoulders lifted and he let out a heavy sigh. 'That's the place, all right. I remember it distinctly.'

'Has it occurred to you,' asked Jeff, 'that you're caught up in a temporal loop?'

'How do you mean?' Mitchell had asked, as he guided them to a stop.

'We're about to help the other you escape from Arcorex, so he can make his way to the Moon, where he'll get caught. Except – if

I've got this right – he'll escape, and wind up putting himself in cryogenic suspension, until a team from Tau Ceti arrives through a wormhole link sometime in the near-future. Yes?'

Mitchell had nodded. 'Right so far.'

'That team brought him – and by him, I mean *you* – back through the gates, back through time to the present, and now there's two of you. And now you're trying to make sure the Mitch *I* knew from Site 17 makes it to the Moon, so he can escape to that same cryogenics lab and become you. It's just . . . mind-boggling.'

Mitchell nodded, his expression distracted, as he walked around to the rear of the van. He had opened it and lifted out a couple of shopping bags full of clothes that had been stowed in next to the cans of gasoline they'd purchased at such exorbitant cost.

'Shouldn't you book the room first?' Jeff had enquired.

'Did it right there, while you were talking,' Mitchell replied, slamming the doors shut again.

The motel was self-service, and had therefore scanned their UPs before allowing them access to the vestibule. Directions appeared in the air; they followed them up a stairwell and along a cramped corridor. The door of the room Mitchell had booked swung open at their approach.

A TriView opposite the single tiny bed came alive as they entered. It was tuned to a news feed revealing how more growths had been detected, in the Antarctic and North Atlantic respectively, a long, long way from where the first of their kind had appeared.

They two men had glanced at each other wordlessly, then Jeff fell into a chair to watch the rest of the report, while Mitchell ripped open several vacuum-wrapped packs of freshly fabbed clothing, before dumping them on top of a cheap dresser.

'I already kept an eye on the news while you were sleeping on the way here,' Mitchell had explained, after glancing briefly up at the screen. 'There've been a lot more bad quakes occurring in the Asian Pacific.'

'Are those growths the reason?' asked Jeff.

'Not exactly,' Mitchell replied. 'More of a side-effect.'

'Side-effect of what, exactly?'

'They need a lot of power to be able to grow the way they are. What they can't get from the sun, they get by tapping into geothermal energy in the very deep crust.'

Jeff had frowned at that. 'Are they really capable of digging that deep? They look just like big flowers. Terrifying, alien, monstrously huge flowers, but still . . .'

Mitchell had smiled thinly. 'You really don't want to know how much they're capable of.'

After that, they had left the motel and headed for an autocafé, where Mitchell told him more of what had happened to him following his return from Site 17.

'No,' Mitchell had concurred, shaking his head. 'I can barely remember anything from those first couple of hours after you pulled me out of the pit chamber. The first thing I can remember clearly is being taken off heavy sedation, days later.'

'You said they kept you under sedation at Arcorex, too?'

Mitchell had nodded. 'After that, they kept me deliberately unconscious a lot of the time. I have vague recollections of being prodded by lots of people in biohazard suits.'

'They were worried you might be carrying something, right?'

'I suppose. Some kind of future-tech plague, or whatever they thought I might be carrying inside me.'

'And you say you woke up with all this . . . this alien information in your head?'

Mitchell nodded. 'What you have to understand is, those pits were *helping* me and Vogel, and not killing us. They actually remade us: no more diseases or ill-health. I might even live for ever. And I learned so much from them . . .' His voice grew distant for a moment. 'It's hard to even know where to start.'

Jeff's coffee had rested untouched and forgotten in his hands as he listened.

'The Founders weren't a single race,' Mitchell had explained.

'There were many of them, machine as well as biological intelligences, and a kind of hybrid of the two that's difficult to explain.' He paused and cracked a smile. 'Jesus, I could tell you about things that haven't happened yet, that won't happen until our own sun's cold and dark and black.'

Jeff had licked his lips. 'Try me.'

'There's a war being fought, right now. It's been going on for countless aeons and it'll continue for countless more.' He took a sip at his own coffee. 'Really, it's more like thousands of individual conflicts, all through this galaxy and a myriad others. But they're all being fought over the same thing.'

'The Founder Network?'

Mitchell nodded and grinned, almost shyly. 'It sounds like bullshit, right? Like I made this all up. But you've been there too, under that night with no stars, a hundred trillion years in the future. You've been to Site 17, so you know I'm telling the truth.'

'Yeah, I guess I do.' Jeff's voice had cracked slightly. He remembered the coffee and gulped it, to wash a dry stickiness out of his mouth. 'But it's going to take time to get my head around all of this.'

'Not too much time,' Mitchell had replied, nodding at a screen mounted at an angle over in one corner.

It seemed like every channel and feed was running the same footage of the Pacific growth. Wreathed in steam, it had already reached hundreds of metres in height, and was still rising out of the ocean at an accelerating rate. Warships could be seen in its shadow, each of them utterly dwarfed by its broadening petals. Helicopters buzzed around it like so many mosquitoes, while various talking heads debated whether or not the Sphere or the Western Coalition were going to try to nuke it, or any of the others now sprouting all around the globe.

'I feel like I want to get up and yell at everyone we meet,' Jeff had declared. 'Just to warn them to get away.' He had glanced around the autocafé at the lone drivers or tight family groups, all of them undoubtedly talking about nothing but the growths. 'When I think about what's going to happen, I feel . . . paralysed.'

Mitchell's response had been to shake his head. 'There's nothing you can do for any of them. Your best strategy is to just focus on what *we* have to do.'

'I understand that. I just don't know . . .' He paused and glanced down at his half-finished coffee, struggling to control the sudden upwelling of emotion deep within his chest 'I don't know that I deserve to survive what's coming. You understand that, right?' His tone had been plaintive, almost childlike.

'Jeff, listen. I could tell you to try and hold it together, but I already know that you will. I was there in Arcorex – *am* there in Arcorex – and one thing I do remember is when you turned up and got me out of there.'

Jeff had felt a chill running down his spine. 'But what if this time I decide not to? What if I just walked out of here right now and—'

'No, Jeff.' Mitchell shook his head, speaking slowly, as if to a child. 'You're talking about a paradox, but time paradoxes are impossible. Look . . . think of it this way. You won't walk away without helping me, because history already *shows* that you didn't. If you had, I wouldn't be here; but I am here; *ergo* you *did* help me.'

'You're saying we don't possess free will. That our actions are predetermined.'

Mitchell had given him a strange look. 'That's true, but it's not the way it has to be.'

Jeff couldn't hide his confusion. 'What do you mean?'

Mitchell had a look on his face like he was making his mind up whether or not to tell him something. 'If I tried to explain it right now, it would complicate things more than they really need to be. All you need to remember is that, from my perspective, you've already gone into Arcorex and pulled me out.'

Jeff had shaken his head in irritation. 'Okay, okay. I get it. It's just hard to remember sometimes that all of this has already happened for you.'

'Once we've got him out, you and me are going to take him back to the motel, and leave him everything he'll be needing to get himself to Copernicus.'

Jeff had finished the last of his coffee and realized his hands were shaking. The whole thing sounded absurd beyond words, yet one glance at the TriView was all he needed to know otherwise. He looked back at Mitchell, and felt as if the whole universe had somehow shrunk to encompass only the Formica-topped table at which they sat, while the rest of the world had been reduced to a blurred video loop running almost forgotten in the background.

'That simple?' said Jeff, with a slight twist of his lips.

'I remember waking up in that motel room,' Mitchell had continued, clearly not appreciating the joke. 'I headed straight for Florida, because I could see from the news feeds what was coming. I spent – *will* spend – a couple of days setting up a false ID, so I could get past Copernicus's security. That's one reason I was able to get fake UPs for both of us as quickly as I did.'

'You said something went wrong,' Jeff queried.

'Getting to the Florida Array was more difficult than you can imagine,' said Mitchell. 'By that time vast crowds were already gathering there, but I managed to make it through them. I faked my way past the security cordons, and all the way through to the Lunar Array, except ASI agents arrested me soon after I got there. But I managed to escape, stole a spacesuit and made my way out on to the surface. By then things were starting to change fast. The face of the Earth was becoming blanketed beneath dense grey clouds. I managed to get to one of the R&D labs in the middle of all the panic, and sealed myself inside one of the cryogenic units.'

Jeff had shivered at the look on Mitchell's face. Even though he was describing the end of the world, his expression remained soft, almost dreamy.

'And that's what saved your life, while every other living thing on the Moon and Earth was wiped out?'

'Maybe.' Mitchell shrugged. 'At least I can't think of any other explanation. The next thing I remember is being revived, and I couldn't believe it when I learned I'd been brought back into my own past. I remember staring through the window at things I was sure I'd never see again – things like trees, birds, grass. They started interrogating me straight away, but there wasn't much I could tell them.'

'Then you broke out?'

'I had to, because by then I'd started to remember things. After that, it was just a matter of time before I figured a way out.'

'And then you came looking for me,' said Jeff.

Mitchell smiled softly. 'And then I came looking for you.'

Jeff had hugged himself, as if warding off a chill.

A metal panel, set into Arcorex's main entrance, flashed from red to green as Jeff approached. He half expected alarms to begin blaring the moment he crossed the threshold, but, once again, nothing happened.

Get a grip, he told himself. As far as anyone else was concerned, he was just another member of staff coming in for an all-nighter.

Jeff swiftly crossed an atrium, partly lit by moonlight spilling down through angled panes of glass, and walked past a reception area, where a single security guard sat on a mesh-backed chair. The man flicked his eyes towards the new arrival for a moment, then returned his attention to a bank of screens. Jeff gave him a bare nod and continued across the expanse of polished marble until he arrived at a row of elevators.

As the elevator carried him below ground level, his UP began flashing a standard warning that he was now entering a high-security area. When the doors hissed open, he found himself at one end of a whitewashed corridor that was bleakly illuminated by strip lights. Mitchell had said he remembered seeing the letters B3 painted on one wall, which would mean he had been held in the lowest basement level, where all artefacts from Site 17, and other far-future locations, were analysed under strictly controlled conditions.

He moved further down the corridor, peering in through windows at labs where often incomprehensible alien machinery was X-rayed, chemically tested, blasted with radiation or simply picked apart by teams of engineers. He finally stopped and looked around, feeling frustrated. There was nowhere they could possibly be keeping Mitchell down here. In that case, how could he . . . ?

Of course. How could he have forgotten? Beyond the labs, there was an emergency ward at the very far end of the corridor; but, given Arcorex's excellent safety record, the ward had never been used – at least until now. If they were going to keep Mitchell anywhere, it would be there.

He turned a corner and kept walking, until he reached a door where the corridor ended. Looking in through a window, he spotted four hospital-style beds, all of them vacant, but noticed an airlock at the far end of the ward that clearly led into a separate isolation unit. He entered the room, squeezed inside the tiny airlock, before using a standard staff-access code to unlock the door beyond.

He found the other Mitchell lying there on a single-size cot, various pieces of medical equipment arranged around him and an intravenous tube taped to one wrist. Jeff half expected him to open his eyes and say *Gotcha*. It was exactly the same man he'd left waiting for him outside – but, at the same time, it wasn't.

It was at that moment he decided to think of the man lying on the cot as 'Present-Mitchell'. Working carefully, he pulled the tube loose from Present-Mitchell's wrist. Present-Mitchell moaned and shifted in response.

'Okay, Mitch, got to wake up.' Present-Mitchell grunted and tried to push Jeff away with weak hands, as he tried to persuade him to sit up. The man's eyes flickered open, but failed to focus on Jeff's face. His paper pyjamas crinkled noisily as Jeff finally dragged him upright, and he nearly slid to the floor while being helped off the cot.

'Hey . . .' Present-Mitchell finally mumbled, looking around himself. 'What . . . ?'

'C'mon,' Jeff urged. 'Time to get moving.' He propped Present-Mitchell up against one wall, then slapped him hard on the cheek, desperate to get him to focus. It wouldn't be too long before those security teams he'd seen patrolling the grounds eventually worked their way round to the basement area.

Jeff pulled his hand back to deliver another slap, but Present-Mitchell reached out and grabbed hold of his wrist, spinning him around and locking one arm around his neck like a vice. Jeff was far too startled to resist.

'What . . . ?' Mitchell's voice wavered, but his grip was remarkably strong, despite the drugs '. . . what the *fuck* are you doing with me?'

His grip suddenly loosened, and Jeff pulled free as Present-Mitchell crumpled to the floor, muttering something incomprehensible under his breath.

Jeff stepped around behind him, pulling him up under the shoulders. Present-Mitchell seemed to come awake once more, and feebly reached out in an attempt to steady himself. He didn't resist this time, as Jeff helped him get upright, with one arm flung around Jeff's shoulders.

'Okay,' Jeff gasped, turning them both around until they faced the airlock. 'We're getting out of here. You ready?'

Present-Mitchell shook his head like a man in a trance. 'Jeff,' he mumbled, 'it's you, isn't it? What the fuck are you doing here?'

'Getting you out of here. Weren't you listening?'

'Out?' Mitchell coughed, then sneezed wetly. 'Okay, good. But I need to lie down first . . .'

'No!' Jeff saw Present-Mitchell's eyes start sliding shut again. As he dragged him further, he heard him mumble something else, but by then had managed to manoeuvre him out through the airlock.

Just then, Future-Mitchell contacted him from outside. 'You got him?'

'Yeah, I got him,' Jeff replied. 'You sure all that shit in the back of the van is wired up right?'

'Who are you talking to?' mumbled Present-Mitchell, hearing only Jeff's side of the conversation.

'You,' Jeff replied curtly.

'It's wired up just fine,' Future-Mitchell assured him. 'Do you want me to send the van in now?'

'In a couple of minutes,' Jeff replied, then cut the connection.

'Hey,' Present-Mitchell seemed suddenly more alert, 'what's going on?'

'We're getting you out of here, remember?'

Present-Mitchell grabbed one of Jeff's hands. 'First you tell me where the fuck we are, Jeff. Then you tell me what's going on.'

'I'm here to rescue you, you dumb bucket of shit,' Jeff snapped. 'They brought you here all the way from Site 17 and, unless you do what I say, they're either going to keep you in here for ever or cut you open to try and figure out how you survived. Now, come on.'

This time, Present-Mitchell didn't resist as Jeff dragged him out into the corridor. But an alarm began to wail, the sound of it loud and abrasive, before they were even halfway to the elevator.

Jeff felt his insides turn to ice water. That was it. They were screwed.

'I can walk,' Present-Mitchell slurred, trying to push him away.

'No, you can't,' Jeff snapped. 'But just try and stay awake.'

He hauled him inside the elevator, the sound of the alarm becoming more muted once the doors closed and the car began to rise. He then pushed the semi-comatose man against one wall, holding him upright.

'I'm fine,' Present-Mitchell mumbled. Jeff peered into his eyes and saw that he did, in fact, look a little more awake than just a few moments before. He stepped away and this time Present-Mitchell managed to stay upright without any help.

The doors slid open and Jeff found himself staring down the barrels of three Cobras aimed at their heads. He reached out to hit the close button, but one of the three guards stepped forward, jamming his boot against the door before it could slide all the way shut.

The next minute passed in a blur. One of the guards reached inside and grabbed Jeff by the shoulder, before dragging him out of the elevator and pushing him face-first down against the polished marble floor. As his arms were wrenched behind his back, he was conscious of the alarm still braying discordantly. Jeff glanced

to one side to see another guard securing Present-Mitchell similarly, while the third one kept his Cobra trained on them both.

Light flickered across the polished marble, and Jeff lifted his
head slightly to glance at the glass doors at the main entrance.
He saw Future-Mitchell's van accelerating straight towards them,
flames billowing out of its open windows.

Someone shouted a strangled warning just before the driverless
vehicle rammed through the double doors in a shower of glass,
then continued on across the atrium before ramming into the reception desk. The sound of the impact was loud enough to drown
out even the wail of the alarm.

Jeff felt the intense pressure on his back suddenly relax. The
three guards seemingly had forgotten them, and were firing wildly
at the van, while backing away from it. Clouds of choking black
smoke spilled out of the van's windows and began to fill the entire
atrium. Though several large windows shattered under the impact
of stray bullets, it was a still and windless night, so the smoke lin-
gered, quickly reducing visibility to barely more than a few metres
in any direction.

Jeff scrambled upright, while Present-Mitchell simply stared
around in abject confusion. Whatever they'd been pumping into
his veins, Jeff reckoned, it must have been powerful stuff. He
leaped up, and once again helped the other man to his feet. They
then stumbled out through a shattered floor-to-ceiling window,
and into the cold night air, coughing desperately.

Jeff heard the screech of rubber on tarmac, and turned to see
the sedan that Mitchell had stolen come bumping down the manicured slope separating the Arcorex building from its car park. It
swerved to avoid several bushes, then crashed to a halt at the foot
of the slope. Future-Mitchell leaned out of the driver's window,
gesturing frantically.

While Jeff dragged his half-comatose ward after him, Future-
Mitchell jumped out and took hold of his doppelgänger's other
arm, helping Jeff guide him into the back seat, where he slumped
with a groan. Shouting erupted from behind.

Future-Mitchell slid back behind the wheel and reversed hard, before Jeff had a chance to pull himself fully on to the front passenger seat. The sedan accelerated backwards, at an angle, up the landscaped slope, and Jeff managed to haul himself all the way inside just as the vehicle came crashing down level again at the top of the slope. Gunfire sliced the chill air, and a rear passenger window exploded to his right. Jeff immediately ducked, the side door still swinging open as Future-Mitchell spun the vehicle through a hundred and eighty degrees.

'Keep your fucking heads down!' he screamed, twisting the wheel.

The sedan rammed into something Jeff couldn't see, slewed around, then accelerated away once more. As the door swung back towards Jeff, he managed to grab hold of it, finally pulling it shut as further shots echoed around them. He hunched over, paralysed with fear, as he imagined those bullets tearing into his own soft and vulnerable flesh.

The car screeched to a sudden halt, then accelerated once more. Jeff pulled himself slowly upright, to see they were back on the highway.

'I think we're out of range now,' announced Future-Mitchell, with a look of grim determination. 'How is he?'

A total of three windows had been blown out, and there were also several large holes in the sedan's roof. Jeff squeezed the upper half of his body between the two front seats, the sedan reconfiguring itself, and becoming slightly wider, in order to allow him more room. He glanced back at Present-Mitchell, who still lay sprawled on the rear seat. His eyes were closed, but his lips moved, and Jeff could hear him mumbling incoherently.

'Well?' asked Future-Mitchell, sounding tense. 'Is he okay?'

'Why? Don't you remember?'

Future-Mitchell grunted. 'Point taken.'

Jeff glanced through the shattered rear window to see that Arcorex had already vanished into the distance. 'Can they catch us, do you reckon?'

'I don't know,' Future-Mitchell replied, as he swung the sedan on to a turn-off leading back towards Omaha. 'They'll know who we are as soon as they check the surveillance recordings. What happens after that depends on whether they choose to tell the police or not. Personally, I'm guessing not.' He glanced over his shoulder at his doppelgänger. 'Is he still unconscious?'

'Completely.' Jeff nodded. 'He'll probably sleep for a day before he even begins to wake up again.'

It wasn't long before they arrived back at the motel, where Future-Mitchell helped Jeff haul their unconscious charge up to the room. They dumped him on the bed, and Jeff glanced back and forth between his two companions.

'No matter what you tell me, or how much you try to explain,' said Jeff, gazing down at the prone figure sprawled on the bed, 'this does not get any less weird.'

Future-Mitchell nodded. 'Imagine how *I* feel.'

The man on the bed snorted and his eyes briefly flickered open. He mumbled something, and made motions as if he was about to sit up, but his eyes slowly slid shut again and soon he resumed snoring.

'Okay,' said Jeff, nodding towards the door. 'I guess that's it. Now we go get Olivia, then head for Florida and the Array.'

Something in the look on the other man's face brought him to a halt.

Future-Mitchell shook his head slowly. 'We're not going to the Florida Array. It's like you said yourself, they'll be expecting us to try and make our way there.'

Jeff's expression turned incredulous. 'What, you mean you were *lying* to me?'

'No.' Mitchell shook his head again, 'I wasn't lying. We'll go get Olivia, like I said, and then we'll head for the Moon. But I don't want to try and get there via the Array. I already learned the hard way it's too risky.'

'Mitchell,' said Jeff, his voice cold and flat, 'you'd better tell me right now what the fuck it is you've got in mind.'

'Do you remember when me and Saul did that space-dive? All the way down from near-Earth orbit just in glider-suits? You were the one who put me in touch with the company that runs the flights, I seem to recall.'

'Yeah,' Jeff nodded, 'what about it?'

Mitchell studied him for a moment. 'Something bothering you?'

'Apart from the fact that I have no idea why you're bringing this up, no.'

'Bullshit.' The other man gave him a knowing look. 'It's because I mentioned Saul, right?'

Jeff made a sound of irritation. 'For Christ's sake, Mitchell. The guy had an affair with my wife, is all.'

'Your ex-wife,' Mitchell reminded him. 'And it's still bothering you?'

'Maybe not so much recently,' said Jeff, knowing that it was a lie. 'It was a long time ago but, ever since me and Olivia got back together . . .'

Future-Mitchell nodded like he understood. 'Sure.'

Jeff sucked in air, then expelled it in a rush. 'Anyway, what about the space-dive?'

'Your friends at the company, they also run flights to the Moon for rich idiots, am I right?'

'Sure, on replicas of the original Apollo rockets, that kind of thing, along with the standard VASIMRs.'

'"VASIMRs"?'

'Variable impulse plasma ships,' Jeff explained. 'They can get to the Moon an awful lot faster than . . .' Jeff paused, his eyes widening. 'Fuck me, are you suggesting what I think you are?'

Mitchell nodded. 'You need to get in touch with them right away, find out if they're willing to take us up to Copernicus on board one of their ships.' He stepped over to the door and pulled it open. 'We might not get ourselves to the Moon the same way as most people, but we sure as hell can fly there if we want to.'

EIGHTEEN

By the time Saul's car made its way out of the hopper's belly and joined a networked convoy heading for Florida, the news feeds were running rumours that what people were starting to call 'the Pacific growths' had been imported to Earth through the Array. There were also fresh satellite images of thermal activity on the deep ocean floor, while the hastily recruited oceanographers from Woods Hole, brought in to try and explain it all, soon sounded like they were way out of their depth.

The 'Pacific' prefix became less and less apt as more growths were discovered at further and further removes from the first one. The booming sound produced by that first growth had now been linked to seed-like projectiles fired from its apex, rising on long, curving trajectories that carried them close to the very edge of space before dropping back down at least several hundreds of kilometres distant.

The second growth had been discovered near Vladivostok, quickly followed by two more off the coasts of New Guinea and Malaysia, respectively. Saul happened to see some wobbly footage of the Vladivostok growth pushing out of an austere-looking landscape at what was clearly a phenomenal rate. A camera crew panned up the growth's already considerable height, showing its upper parts rising out of a haze of debris that permanently clouded its base. He watched with a kind of numb dread that he felt deep inside his chest.

The route to the Array, dense with traffic at the best of times, soon became more crowded than Saul remembered ever seeing it. The cars moved along in tight columns, almost bumper-to-bumper, with tailbacks that stretched for several kilometres.

Saul figured, if it was going to take as long as he suspected to get to the Array, he might as well eat something first. He pulled in at a roadside steakhouse, and left his car to graze on compacted biomass. Being part of a popular chain that made a point of using live staff, the steakhouse was packed to the gills.

He managed to find himself a window seat and soon placed his order with a florid-faced waitress with a decidedly harried expression.

'I'm guessing it isn't usually this busy?' he remarked.

'Hell, no,' she laughed. 'This is the busiest it's been since we opened the place, and that was fifteen years ago.'

Saul glanced around, noticing that many of the other customer's faces were tight with worry.

'Looks like they're all headed for the Array,' he observed.

The waitress shrugged. 'Looks like,' she agreed. 'Bunch of idiots all running scared from something they saw on those damn news feeds.'

'You don't think it's anything to worry about?'

She gave him a scornful glance. 'Hell, no, I don't believe a word of it. Some damn fools made it all up, and now they're rolling about on their asses, laughing at us. I stopped believing anything I saw on the news a *long* time ago.'

Saul forced a smile as the waitress left him, and he looked around the diner a second time. Instead of the usual tourists or migrants, on their way to new lives under new suns, everyone he saw here looked like a refugee – like the family of seven huddled together around one small table, their heavy suitcases piled all around them. It wasn't hard to guess what everybody was running away from, and he imagined what would happen once they all showed up, demanding passage, at the Array at the same time. The sense of despair was palpable.

By the time his food arrived, his appetite had vanished. He left most of it untouched and returned to his car, soon rejoining the thousands of other vehicles on the highway.

He found he couldn't stop brooding on Taiwan and the missing shipment. That the growths were alien rather than man-made seemed obvious yet, in all the years since the first interstellar colonies had been founded, no one had found any evidence of intelligent life beyond Earth. Now the more he learned, the more it seemed evident that the ASI had discovered *something* out there amongst the stars – and brought it back. And even though he had no evidence to link them together, he felt increasingly sure there was some connection between the growths and his search for the missing shipment.

It was purest supposition, of course, and entirely baseless, yet the idea stubbornly refused to go away. He felt an urge to find a bar somewhere – anywhere he might get a quick shot of rum on the rocks – but something about the density of traffic and the borderline panic he'd sensed in the steakhouse filled him with a sense of urgency, as if time was running out.

The convoy of traffic his car had joined slowed to a near-crawl. He glanced out of a window and saw to his shock that there were hundreds, quite possibly thousands, of people walking along on foot on either side of the highway. Old women, young women, children, men carrying backpacks; they were all trudging south.

Winding down the window, he thrust his head and shoulders out of the car to see more clearly. Way up ahead, the lines of pedestrians spilled on to the highway, crowds of them picking their way between lines of vehicles that were barely inching forward.

It took another full hour before Saul finally caught sight of the main dome of the Florida Array, glistening under the early afternoon sun. The crowds had by now swelled from a river into a torrent. He was intrigued to see what looked like a real fire-and-brimstone religious service taking place in a lay-by, with dozens of people gathered reverentially outside a marquee tent. Most of them carried handmade signs proclaiming things like: 'JESUS IS COMING TO GETCHA.'

Saul swore in irritation and checked the feeds for the thousandth time that day. Another growth had been sighted, pushing up from the seabed a couple of hundred kilometres west of Hawaii. There were unconfirmed reports of dozens more in locations scattered all around the globe. A giant tsunami had struck Sapporo, Sri Lanka and Karachi, with death tolls estimated in the thousands. Minor quakes had struck Sicily, Bangladesh and the Dominican Republic, amongst other places – all far too diverse to be blamed any more on natural causes.

He looked around in surprise as his car suddenly rolled to a halt.

A message had appeared on the dashboard: *We are dealing with extremely heavy traffic conditions on all approaches to the Florida Array Facility. Please note that, due to prevailing circumstances, all those without a previously booked passage to a major extrasolar destination should now return home. Please . . .*

Something thumped against the side of the car. Saul jerked around, startled, and saw a uniformed ASI cop pushing a middle-aged woman with a hand-painted sign up against a window. Some of the participants in the religious service came running down the shallow embankment towards them, till Saul found himself surrounded by angrily shouting people. Sensing things might turn genuinely ugly, he pushed open the door and clambered out. Someone grabbed hold of him immediately, and Saul stumbled and nearly fell.

He twisted out of his assailant's grasp and simultaneously lashed out with his fist, making contact with something soft amid the press of bodies all around. He ducked away from his car and ran off down the highway, between the rows of stalled vehicles, as he tried to put some distance between himself and what was starting to look like a full-scale riot. Several people stepped out of their cars, pointing beyond him, and he turned to see a phalanx of uniformed cops, wearing face-shields and wielding batons, come pouring down the opposite embankment. Soon he could hear screams, and the sound of batons striking unprotected flesh.

He stopped to catch his breath, and Saul realized that he was almost certainly going to cover the last dozen kilometres to the Array on foot.

He suddenly recalled, with a sense of longing, the tiny wrap of loup-garou still sitting in the coffee jar back home. *Except you swore the damn stuff off*, he reminded himself, seeing in his mind's eye the look of contempt on Donohue's face.

He turned his back on his car and started walking, squeezing between two vehicles and making for the verge. Other people also were abandoning their cars in large numbers. Saul heard a roar, and glanced up just as three jets flashed by overhead. They were flying towards the Array, their silver carapaces glittering in the sunlight.

He started to wonder if Farad Maalouf might be able to tell him a lot more than just where to find Jeff Cairns.

Pulling off his jacket, Saul kept moving through the tens of thousands of others who crowded the stalled highway or made their way along the tops of the neighbouring embankments. After a couple of hours of steady progress, he glanced ahead and saw where the highway divided into filter lanes leading to different sections of the Array. Aerial drones buzzed like mosquitoes overhead in the distance. He moved to higher ground so he could see more clearly which way he should be heading.

Eventually he came to a stop, and gazed down towards the highway in front. From this higher vantage point, he could make out how tangled coils of barbed wire and steel barricades had been placed across the highway a bit closer to the Array. Judging from the sheer number of people marching in that direction, he reckoned they were going to need a lot more than wire and barricades to bring that mob to a halt. The wind carried the sound of voices from the Array itself, sounding loud and abrasive over what appeared to be a tannoy system, but still too distant for the words to be clearly identified.

Just walking straight in clearly wasn't going to work, not if he had to compete with ten thousand frightened fugitives all seeking entry as well. Fortunately, there were other options open to him, since access to the Array would be available to those with the right authorization. He picked up his pace, overtaking people who looked even more tired, hungry and dehydrated than he himself felt. Another day or two, he felt sure, and they'd be hungry and thirsty enough for the soldiers guarding the Array to be forced into using extreme measures to hold them off.

He summoned up a map of the Array, so it floated over to one side of him. Seen from above, it looked not unlike an octopus pinned to the ground, with its tentacles extended. Built of glass, steel and concrete, the central dome contained the wormhole gate linking Earth to the Moon, along with a few secondary gates that connected to other destinations on Mars. Airport-style terminals radiated outwards from the centre, while a twelve-lane ring road girdled the entire complex.

Saul studied the map closely and soon located the entrance nearest to a network of service tunnels that threaded the ground beneath his feet. He would still need to do a fair bit more walking to reach it, however, so he started moving once again, but this time leaving the highway far behind. He finally saw a low concrete bunker in the distance. A final glance to one side revealed at least a dozen tanks with crowd-control turrets rolling up to the makeshift barricades, supported by nearly twice that number of Black Dogs, four-legged multi-terrain weapons platforms laden with riot countermeasures.

He heard a chainsaw-like buzz overhead, and looked up to see a drone moving rapidly towards him. It looked like a metal doughnut, with blades whirring noisily in the centre. Saul shielded his eyes to make sure his UP was active, even as it dropped lower to intercept him.

'I'm with Array Security and Immigration,' he called up to the device. 'I urgently need to get inside the Array.'

'I can see your authorization, sir,' boomed a voice from a hidden microphone. 'I'm sorry, but I thought maybe you were part of that mob.'

'They're frightened people, not a mob,' Saul shouted back. 'What the hell is going on here?'

'I don't know, sir,' the operator's voice replied. 'I just know we're not supposed to let anybody inside.'

'Except me, right? I plan to use one of the bunker entrances.'

'That's fine, but all active personnel have to report in immediately and help protect the Array.'

'Protect it from *what*?' Saul yelled back. But, before the operator could respond, a crackle of gunfire erupted from the direction he'd just come.

He glanced around and saw a crowd of desperate people converging on the barricades. The drone rose into the air and zoomed in their direction without another word from its operator. Saul stared after it, noticing dozens of other drones also converging there. He forced himself to turn away and keep walking until he finally reached the bunker. A single unmarked steel door in its side swung open as he approached.

Once he was inside, a warning light flashed, and a kind of manhole cover in the floor slid aside, revealing a shaft beneath, and a single ladder extending downwards for about six metres.

Before long, Saul was heading along an echoing, empty corridor, in the direction of the central dome.

NINETEEN

Saul continued through stark concrete corridors until he came to a service elevator that carried him back upwards, and into the main Array building. To his shock, it was very nearly deserted, emptier than he had ever known it to be; so the only conclusion he could come to was that gate-travel had been suspended altogether.

Before long, he encountered a small unit of ASI personnel. The three men carrying Cobras were dressed in matte-black armour, and accompanied by a Black Dog whose four thick legs whirred and clanked rhythmically as it trailed after them, its armour-plated torso laden with sonar cannons. The squad was led by a lieutenant named David Murakami, who insisted on checking Saul's credentials.

'Sorry,' Murakami apologized, 'got to check everyone's clearance. And I mean *everyone's.*'

'I was forced to walk here from the highway after the traffic snarled up, and it looks like half of Florida is heading for this place. Any idea what the hell is going on out there?'

Murakami let out a heavy sigh. 'Sir, I've been trying to find someone who can give *me* a straight explanation. You're from Investigations, so I was kind of hoping you'd be the one to set me straight.'

Saul shook his head ruefully. 'Sorry.'

'Yeah, me too,' Murakami replied, clearly far from happy at that reply. 'Between you and me, though, I'd swear on my mother's tits it's all to do with those things out in the ocean.'

'Yeah,' said one of his squad, with a UP tag bearing the name Hall. 'There's people out there on the other side of the barricades who think it's the End Times, except far as I can see they'd all rather run for the colonies than wait around for Jesus to come haul their asses to the big fire.'

Some of the others chuckled. 'Guess they had second thoughts about Jesus being in a forgiving mood,' said one.

Saul turned to Murakami. 'Have they shut off access to Copernicus?'

'Nope.' Murakami shook his head. 'I know it looks empty around here, but there's still a hell of a lot of traffic heading for Luna. Hopper-loads of people have been flying in here twenty-four hours a day for the past couple of days and being sent straight through with no delay.'

Saul frowned. 'Who?'

Murakami shrugged. 'Again, sir, I was hoping you could tell me. Civilians mostly, from what I've seen.'

'It's the government,' said Hall, with an expression of disgust on his face, 'They're getting their own people out and leaving the rest of us here to rot.'

Saul looked over at him. 'You know that for a fact?'

'All I can tell you is there are whole families arriving here, and they're all being escorted by Special Ops types using heavy gear like Fido here.' He nodded towards the Black Dog. 'It's like the lieutenant says. They've been bringing them in to the Florida Array day and night and shipping them through the gates to Copernicus as fast as they can.'

'Special Ops, you said?'

'Hundreds of them,' said the soldier. 'Look to me like they're armed heavily enough to start a war somewhere. And here's the other thing,' he stabbed the air with one finger. 'Nobody, but nobody, is coming back through, the other way. What the hell's that about?'

After he left them, Saul signed into the main security database, downloading anything he could on Farad Maalouf that he hadn't discovered already. At the same time, he continued making his way across one of the huge concourses.

The concourse was eerily silent. Enormous animated advertisements hung in the air, while an electronic display above the immigration checkpoints indicated a variety of off-world destinations. None of the usual civilian staff was visible, and so Saul passed unchallenged through a security gate and entered a transfer station that on any normal day would be processing a couple of hundred passengers at a time on to the shuttle-cars. During peak hours, each transfer station could handle close on three hundred people every seven minutes, both coming and going.

There were further squads of troopers guarding the transfer station, their Black Dogs pounding up and down across the concourse on sturdy steel legs. One swivelled its head towards Saul as he moved towards a shuttle-car, turning away again as soon as its onboard AI registered the newcomer's clearance.

'Hey!'

Saul turned to see a man wearing the uniform of a security commander hurrying towards him. 'Your clearance doesn't allow you through here,' the man told him.

'If it doesn't,' Saul replied, 'that's a first.'

The commander studied Saul's UP clearance for a moment, then rolled his eyes in evident irritation. 'Great, more screw-ups,' he muttered. 'Where exactly are you headed?'

'Newton.'

'Why?'

Saul forced a laugh, deciding the commander didn't really need to know. 'Sorry, sir,' he replied. 'I'm *really* not at liberty to discuss that.'

He watched the other man consider this for a moment, before shaking his head slowly. 'That's not good enough. So long as we're under a state of emergency, you're going to need to get fresh authorization. Maybe—'

'Sir!' A trooper came running up to them just then. 'We've got sixty or more people just broke through a cordon near the secure runway, where we're expecting another hopper to arrive in the next ten minutes. Johnson wants to know what his orders are.'

'Shit,' the commander swore under his breath. 'All right,' he instructed the trooper, 'tell him to use any force necessary to clear the intruders away from the runway. *Any* force, is that understood?'

'Sir.' The trooper nodded, before jogging back the way he'd come.

'As for you,' the commander turned back to Saul, 'I don't have the time for this. Get into a shuttle-car right now before I change my mind.'

Saul stared after the retreating trooper. 'Did I really hear you give that order? You're firing on civilians now?'

The commander's face reddened. 'I already told you I don't have time for this.'

Saul raised both hands in mock surrender, before quickly boarding the nearest shuttle-car. It shuddered as the hydraulic clamps released it and it began to move forward, gradually picking up speed. Saul took a window-seat and watched as the concourse slid out of sight and the shuttle-car was carried into one of several tunnels running parallel to each other, the walls crammed with coolant pipes, radiation feedback buffers and shielding.

Before long he was being transported across the dozen metres of the wormhole itself, as four-fifths of his weight dropped away.

The Lunar Array proved to be just as eerily quiet as its earthbound counterpart, which struck Saul as remarkable, given it was several times larger. Where the Florida Array existed primarily to shuttle people backwards and forwards between Earth and the Moon, its lunar equivalent also provided access to a dozen interstellar destinations. The entire facility sprawled over nearly fifteen square kilometres, challenging even the nearby city in terms of sheer scale.

Saul made it through a series of impromptu checkpoints, with the help of some constructive lying, and soon learned that he was right in guessing that all incoming traffic from the colonies had been suspended, for the duration of an as yet unspecified emergency. But while he waited at one checkpoint in particular, a group of tired and harried-looking travellers were guided past by a phalanx of the Special Ops soldiers Murakami had mentioned earlier. Those they were escorting were clearly civilians, yet no one at the checkpoint attempted to confirm their credentials, or even find out by what authority they were being allowed to pass into areas that even Saul struggled to reach. As they passed close enough, he could see from their tags that every one of them had all-areas clearance. Even the troopers questioning him didn't possess that level of clearance.

Somehow, he got through. Saul jumped on a robot bus empty of passengers, which carried him all the rest of the way to the Copernicus–Newton gate. There he once again found himself forced to do some fast talking in order to continue on his way. His weight increased again, once he had passed through the wormhole, but not to Earth-normal, for Newton was slightly smaller, and less dense. Finally, after yet more clearance checks and terse questioning upon his arrival, Saul looked around to find himself riding on a train passing through the shrouded city of Sophia, beneath an alien sky.

Dense, greenish-black vegetation smothered the valley walls that rose above the tented fabric containing the city's human-breathable atmosphere. As Saul disembarked at the central rail terminus, the air was alive with the scents of sweet tea and roasting chestnuts, and Al-Khiba floated far above, with bands of dark orange and brown girdling its equator. One of the gas giant's other moons was moving with stately grace across the sky, appearing tiny through distance, yet so clear and sharp that Saul almost imagined he could reach up and pluck it out of the air like some fulvous jewel.

It rapidly became clear that many of Newton's public information services had either been reduced in operation or shut down altogether. Saul jumped on to an open-topped maglev bus that smelled of apples and rotting fish, closer to the centre of town, and gazed around as it carried him through the narrow, winding streets. Most of the people he saw wore business suits, or else the same casual clothing people tended to wear almost everywhere throughout the colonies. But the farther out he travelled, the more frequently he saw men wearing keffiyahs or taqiyah caps, some of them accompanied by women in chadors.

According to the scant information he'd been able to scrape out of the ASI's databases, Farad's brother lived in the north-eastern section of Sophia, not too far from where the city's all-covering roof met the upper slopes of the valley. Saul had a distinct feeling, however, that actually finding Farad was going to prove to be a bitch.

It was already getting late, and local businesses were starting to wind down for the night. Saul yawned involuntarily, and realized just how much this long and terrible day had taken out of him. He let his eyelids droop for a moment, but all he saw behind them were scared and hungry people struggling along under a noonday sun, or those echoing concourses populated by nervous troopers following orders they didn't understand.

Disembarking eventually in a part of town where he knew he could find a family-run hotel that he'd used before, he headed past a variety of small coffee shops clustered around one of the massive pillars that supported the city's roof. Choosing a café, he ordered coffee and sweet pastries, and when the coffee arrived it proved so thick and bitter as to be almost undrinkable. But he persevered, and before long the caffeine began to work its magic, filling him with a temporary but nonetheless welcome sense of well-being. By the time he moved on, brushing through softly glowing adverts for baklava or Turkish tea, he was feeling a little more alert.

It didn't take long for Saul to realize he was being followed, even though the streets were still busy with both pedestrians and road traffic. He stopped from time to time, as if to watch the sun slipping behind the gas-giant, and when he glanced back the way he'd come he spotted a couple of faces familiar from the café, but now mingling in with the crowds. He kept his eyes fixed on them, until it became clear they were trying just a bit too hard not to look his way.

Saul started to walk more quickly, while trying to figure out his next move. But before he reached a decision, someone approaching him lunged sideways, propelling him through a dark shop doorway.

He felt hands reach out for him, noticed faces barely distinguishable in the gloom. As he lashed out with his fist, he felt it make satisfying contact with yielding flesh. Someone groaned, but more bodies piled on top of him before he could take another swing.

They were yelling in what might have been Turkish, his contacts struggling to run a translation, but there were too many talking all at once for the software to come up with anything meaningful.

He kicked and struggled, but they had him down, with his face against the floor. One yanked his head back while another thrust a wad of cloth between his jaws, before pulling a bag over his head and securing it tight around his face.

Hands grabbed the back of his coat and dragged him further into the interior of the shop. A boot struck him hard in the ribs and Saul groaned in pain, just before he felt the prick of a needle in his neck. Immediately, dark tendrils of fatigue spread all the way through him, utterly irresistible, dragging him down into a warm and comforting darkness devoid of dreams.

TWENTY

Disappearing turned out to be even easier than either of them might have hoped.

A few days before, Thomas Fowler had procured a set of contacts replete with fake UPs, for both himself and Amanda, from the ASI's own evidence lockers, along with a substantial amount of black-market cash. They took off together one morning for his beach house down in the Keys, the ocean stretching out on either side of the highway, throughout the whole drive down from the airport at Marathon.

They had spent the next few days making love to the sound of the ocean crashing against the wharf near the house, often waking in the early hours when minor tremors sent plates crashing to the kitchen floor. Ashes from the recent eruptions of Soufrière and Mombacho were carried north on the wind, plastering rooftops and lawns, and turning them all a dull, leaden grey.

They often heard cars whipping by on the highway, as local residents fled, and one morning just before dawn they also heard gunshots, followed by the screech of rubber on tarmac. Fowler had got up and walked out on to the veranda, without turning the lights on, peering either way down the long road that ran parallel to the shore, but he saw nothing.

He dreamed of a faceless figure hunting him through the darkened rooms of the beach house, and when he woke knew he wouldn't need a psychiatrist to figure out that he feared Donohue being sent after them. But Fowler had gambled that, with the end so very close, they would be safe – or as safe as it was possible to be, given the end of the world was approaching – so long as they didn't make any attempt to pass through the Array.

The worst of the tremors occurred on their last night in the Keys. The house rocked on its foundations, as if a giant had lifted it up and was shaking it to see if anything might fall out. In the morning they found that dozens of roof shingles had come crashing down on to the patio. Also one of the exterior walls had buckled, sending plaster raining down, while the wind had whipped ashes mixed with salt water through the shattered windows and across the furniture.

They picked their way across broken glass as they packed the few belongings they needed, and climbed into Amanda's car. Fowler didn't look back as they drove away, even though he was leaving the beach house for ever.

There were few signs of life as they drove the short distance north to Key Largo. Palm trees and royal poinciana, whose branches had once blazed red, now bowed under the accumulated weight of volcanic ash. The streets were deserted, making Fowler wonder where his neighbours could possibly have fled. It wasn't like there was anywhere they could possibly go that was safer.

He thought about it a while longer, then decided that the impulse driving the two of them to fly to the Far East wasn't really so very different.

They had barely started out on their journey before they came across a van lying on its side, so that it straddled the divider. An open-topped sports car was parked haphazardly nearby, one of its doors left wide open as if its owner might return at any moment. A recorded voice emerged faintly from the dashboard, warning that the vehicle was low on power.

Amanda guided their own car around and past the second

obstruction. Only once they were past did they see the bodies of a young woman and a man lying side by side, darkening pools of blood staining the tarmac around what was left of their heads.

After that encounter, they drove the rest of the way in silence. The Keys had become suddenly menacing in a way they hadn't been before, even with the constant tremors and volcanic ashes.

In lieu of conversation, Thomas brought a news feed up on the dashboard. There were now up to half a dozen volcanoes reactivated along the spine of South America, all the way from Chile to Nicaragua. Yellowstone, too, was showing ominous signs of seismic activity, while yet more growths had been sighted emerging from the waters off the coast of Ecuador. Thermal-imaging satellites had verified several others, blossoming all along the mid-Atlantic ridge, like a cancer metastasizing throughout a living body.

They dodged several more abandoned cars, and at one point two men stepped out into the middle of the road and tried to flag them down. Having chosen to keep the car on manual, Amanda hit the accelerator and drove straight towards them, until they were finally forced to jump out of the way. Shouted invectives trailed in their wake as they sped on along the highway connecting the chain of islands.

By the time they reached Key Largo, it was clear that plenty of other people had fled north, yet there were still some signs of life continuing the same as ever. Dozens of businesses were tightly shuttered, while others were cheerfully open for business.

Somehow, thought Fowler, this was the strangest thing of all. But, then, there were few people privileged to know just how little time was left to them all.

They drove along the south road, following the natural curve of the key, until they reached the first of several artificial islands floating on platforms just above the waves and supported by spar buoys, each such island linked to the land by a pontoon bridge that extended out into the ocean. The platforms themselves were built from some kind of extremely flexible but tough polymer composite that could survive the worst of the local hurricanes.

The car bumped and juddered as it rolled on to the pontoon bridge leading to Alex Trouillot's flight and fishing business, which extended across an entire platform of its own. Most of the available space was in fact taken up by a landing pad, on which sat two sub-orbital VTOLs that Fowler knew from prior experience could get them to Hong Kong in less than four hours. Next to the platform were moored two antique twin prop float-planes, which Trouillot used for ferrying retired business executives out to sea for deep-water fishing.

They parked alongside a shop front with a grinning plastic swordfish suspended overhead. Fowler hesitated for a moment before getting out. He'd called ahead a few days earlier, explaining what he wanted to do, but, after everything he'd seen in the last few days, there was no reason to assume Alex hadn't fled along with the rest of them. Just then he sighted Trouillot through a window, his feet propped up on a desk as he sat watching a TriView hanging from a nail. Fowler closed his eyes in silent relief and gratitude.

He noted a box of cartridges sitting on Trouillot's desk as they entered, also a shotgun leaning against the wall and within easy reach. The TriView flickered between images of alien growths and volcanoes vomiting ash and smoke high into the stratosphere.

'Mr Fowler,' said Trouillot, rolling easily to his feet, with a glance at Amanda. 'And this must be—'

'Amanda,' Fowler replied, as he shook hands with Trouillot. 'She'll be joining us.'

Amanda's eyes slid towards the shotgun, and then back to Trouillot himself. 'We saw some signs of trouble on the way here. Had any cause to use that thing yet?'

Trouillot shook his head. 'Fortunately, no. But I've seen an awful lot of people heading north up the highway, and I've also heard word of a lot of looters coming the other way.' His gaze flicked over to the TriView, and back. 'I'll have to admit, when you called, Mr Fowler, I got to wondering if you'd found some place safe from all this crap.'

'None that I know of.' Fowler shrugged apologetically. 'I just have some unfinished business out in the Far East, that's all. I'd . . . prefer to pay with paper, if I may.'

Fowler hoped he'd judged Trouillot right. It would be a mistake to automatically assume everyone operating a plane in Florida was involved in smuggling, but that didn't mean a substantial number of them weren't.

Trouillot gave them both an appraising look. 'Like that, is it?'

Fowler waited, saying nothing.

Trouillot sighed and held a hand up. 'Fine. It's not like anyone's much in the mood for fishing these days, anyway. Let's see what kind of notes you've got.'

Fowler reached into a jacket pocket and pulled out a single roll, noticing the way Trouillot's eyes widened when he saw how thick it was. He peeled a number of notes off and handed them over.

Trouillot thumbed through the notes, then his eyes followed the remainder of the roll as Thomas stuffed it back in his pocket. 'That's a hell of a lot of money to be carrying around like that,' he observed.

'Enough for a down-payment on another sub-orb,' replied Fowler. 'But the rest of this is for you, if you can get us to where we want to go.'

Trouillot's eyes flicked back to the screen, his expression becoming troubled. 'Sounds good. Assuming I ever get the chance to spend it, that is.'

They took off less than an hour later, after Trouillot had run a routine systems check on one of the sub-orbs, and primed its engines. The craft shuddered violently, once its primary boosters kicked in at ten thousand metres, the sudden surge of power crushing the three of them back against their seats until Fowler could feel the metal frame of the acceleration couch pressing through its thick padding and into his spine. But just a few seconds later he felt his weight rapidly fall away, signalling that they were close to the apex of a long arc that would carry them halfway around the globe.

Amanda unbuckled herself from her acceleration couch and pushed herself over to the nearest window, while Trouillot, seated forward in the cockpit, continued talking to someone back on the ground. Semi-transparent weather maps and data feeds slid across the windscreen in front of him.

Fowler got up and joined her, and together they gazed down towards the surface of the Earth curving away below them, under the shadows of clouds drifting across the face of the ocean. They could see the water around the Keys, as bright aquamarine shading into vivid azure depths. Ominous clouds of ash drifted across the Gulf of Mexico.

'I know I've said this already,' said Amanda, 'but I'm really glad we're doing this.'

He rested one hand against her back, and reflected on how all the pain and worry and fear that had been keeping him awake for weeks on end had dissipated away the moment he'd decided to follow her to the Marianas. He didn't even have to ask Amanda to know it was the same for her. Her eyes were no longer red-rimmed, and, when she smiled, she looked happier than he ever remembered seeing her.

I just wish we could enjoy it for more than just a few days, he almost said, but didn't, unwilling to spoil the moment. They stayed there for a while longer, watching the world turn beneath them. Florida eventually passed out of sight as their craft boosted itself closer to the edge of space.

'Look,' Amanda said suddenly, her hands pressed against the glass. 'Can you see? There's more of them.'

He looked over to the west of California, now receding into the east, and saw several wide swirls of white cloud out beyond the coastline, about where the deep ocean itself started. Seeing the growths like this awakened something primal within him, as if he were a caveman staring up at a thunderstorm with no comprehension or understanding of the energies about to strike him down.

TWENTY-ONE

Sophia, Newton Colony, 5 February 2235

Saul found his way back to consciousness by small, faltering degrees, at first only dimly aware of a slight greying in the darkness that pressed up close against his face. The floor on which he lay was hard and unyielding and, as he tried to move, he quickly found his hands were securely tied behind his back. The thick cloth of the hood covering his head felt uncomfortably tight, and his chin itched abominably against the rough fabric.

He twisted, wriggling like an eel, until he was lying on his belly rather than his side.

He soon realized, to his considerable relief, that his legs were not similarly bound, so he could stand and even walk. With his tongue he traced the rim of a tiny hole cut into the hood, to prevent him from suffocating. It wasn't nearly large enough.

With a bit of work he shifted himself into a kneeling position. He noticed how the light brightened or dimmed depending on which way he turned his head, which suggested the presence of either a window or a light. He became increasingly aware of background noises, which resolved into the rumble of machinery, and the sound of voices coming from a considerable distance.

He shouted for attention, his dry throat feeling as sore as if he had swallowed a razor. He suddenly felt an urgent need to urinate. Somehow, not being able to see began pushing him close to the edge of outright panic.

He swallowed with some difficulty before making a second attempt at shouting for help. What came out sounded more like the cry of a trapped or wounded animal than anything that belonged in a human throat. He yelled yet again, even though he had already concluded no help would be forthcoming.

Saul froze as he heard the sound of a door opening, then closing again, followed by the sound of rapidly approaching footsteps. He gasped with shock as a pair of hands grabbed him roughly and dragged him to his feet. He kicked out instinctively, and felt something hard slam against the back of his head with sufficient force for his knees to buckle.

Once more, the same hands hauled him upright, and this time he didn't resist. As he was dragged away, the glimmer of light first faded and then intensified, and he was aware, from the echo of his own footsteps, that he was being taken from one room to another. Several doors opened and closed before he was finally shoved against a wall.

A moment later he heard the familiar click of a weapon's safety catch being released, followed by the chill sensation of a gun barrel being pressed up against one side of his head.

'Please,' he managed to mumble, 'you don't need to do this. Just tell me what you want.'

No reply was forthcoming, as a second pair of hands loosened his belt buckle, before yanking his trousers down around his knees. Despite the gun pressed to his temple, Saul tried desperately to twist loose, as sheer panic finally overcame him.

Something hard slammed into his head a second time. A fit of nausea gripped him and he fought the urge to vomit. The two pairs of hands kept him upright, however, then lowered him on to a seat.

Saul became dimly aware of now being seated on a toilet.

'If you need to take a shit,' a heavily accented voice murmured very close to his ear, 'now would be a good time.'

There was something familiar about that voice.

Saul merely nodded, too frightened to say anything more, the air within the bag close and hot, and filled with the smell of his own fear. Groaning with relief, he started to piss.

The two sets of hands held him secure by either shoulder, but the only sound he could hear apart from their breathing was that of his own urine splashing into the pan.

'Finished?' asked the same voice, eventually, and Saul finally recognized it.

Narendra, the information broker. The man who'd told him Lee Hsingyun was legitimate, just before the fiasco on the ice-pharm.

Saul grunted his assent, and he was quickly pulled back upright. As hands refastened his trousers, he felt a trickle of warm urine run down the inside of his thigh.

A door banged open again, and he was led, stumbling, through yet more twists and turns, until a final shove sent him back on to his knees. He heard Narendra begin speaking in Turkish and, when a live translation failed to appear, he realized to his horror that his contacts had been taken from him. And if they had removed his contacts, they had also taken Jeff's encrypted files . . .

A second voice replied, this one deeper and more guttural, its tone angry and dismissive. Saul listened carefully as the two men argued. Finally one pair of footsteps headed towards the door, while a shadowy form kneeled beside him, pressing something against Saul's lips, until it forced him to tip his head back.

Water.

Saul gulped it down, realizing he must have become dangerously dehydrated. Some of it spilled down his neck as he swallowed it greedily, tipping his head ever farther back. Then his unseen benefactor stood up and departed, locking the door securely once more.

Saul slumped back, trying to breathe more evenly, and began to gather up some of his scattered wits. He could still hear the occasional call of distant voices above the rumble of machinery, and came to the conclusion he must be somewhere close by a building site.

Once he felt calmer, he carefully shuffled backwards, on his knees, until he felt the soles of his feet come into contact with a wall. He once again tried to rid himself from whatever was binding his wrists together, but his bonds simply grew tighter the more he struggled. So, in the end, he gave up.

Clumsily staggering upright, he then slid along the wall until he reached a corner of his makeshift cell.

He could feel a faint breeze there, which surely meant an open window. He next slid along the second wall, until he encountered the edge of the windowsill with his fingertips. Cool air ruffled his hair and made him wonder how high up above the ground he was.

Saul continued on his way, shuffling past the window and skirting around the next corner, until he felt a door handle brush against his fingers. He twisted himself around, bending his knees slightly until he could get a grip on it. The handle clicked slightly as he tugged at it, but the door was firmly locked. As he'd expected, really, but there was no reason not to try.

The door suddenly slammed open so that Saul lost his balance, toppling forward to hit the floor hard. He twisted around until he was lying on his back, then felt the air explode out of his lungs as someone drove a fist into his guts. Creasing up, he felt an arm wrap itself firmly around his neck. Something ice-cold touched his throat, and consciousness rapidly slipped away.

Saul woke to blinding light as the bag was ripped from over his head. He sneezed and blinked, before gazing around at four bare plaster walls. To his right, he saw an open door and a half-open window beyond a floor of bare concrete. Plastic crates were stacked in a corner, each stamped with the name of a biotech pharm, probably agricultural supplies or seed stock.

Narendra stood by the window, the cloth bag still clutched in one hand. To one side of him stood a barrel-chested man with a shaven head, gripping a shotgun in both hands. His gaze was dark and entirely lacking in mercy.

'I guessed it was you,' Saul rasped at Narendra. 'My contacts. What did you do with them?'

'They're somewhere safe.' Narendra scratched at his goatee before stepping forward to kneel at Saul's side. 'I'm going to untie you now,' he explained, 'but please don't try anything foolish. Eren here would be delighted to have an excuse to kill you.'

Saul felt his wrists fall loose, and he slowly moved his hands around in front of him. All the while, the barrel-chested man, Eren, watched him with the keen interest of a bird of prey dropping towards a field mouse. Predictably, his wrists were bruised and purple, and on flexing his shoulders, he heard their joints creak in protest.

A third man entered, carrying a tray laden with coffee and what smelled like *kofte ekmek*, rich with spices and onions and wrapped in brightly coloured paper. The man handed the tray to Narendra, then departed without a word. Saul heard his own stomach rumble.

'You can get put away for a long time for kidnapping an ASI agent,' said Saul, trying to ignore the pervasive aroma of the food. 'Just how long have you been keeping me here?'

Narendra assumed a slightly apologetic expression, as if this were nothing more than a terrible misunderstanding. 'Two days,' he explained, placing the tray on the floor next to Saul. 'Eat first, then we can talk.'

Saul laughed weakly. 'What, now you're trying to soften me up before you get to work on me with a pair of pliers? I don't have anything to say to you, or to anyone else.'

'All we want to know is why you're here.' Narendra's gaze flicked towards Eren, then back again. 'I'm sorry about your treatment. If it's any help, it wasn't my decision.'

'I haven't done anything that warrants kidnapping me off the street, believe me,' Saul insisted angrily.

Eren barked some comment at Narendra, then headed over to the door. Narendra followed him abruptly, then paused with one hand on the handle. 'As a gesture of goodwill, we won't put the cuffs back on for the moment,' he said. 'But please think hard about whatever you may want to tell me when I return, or else things may turn out very bad for both of us.'

'It would help if I had the slightest idea what the hell you want from me,' Saul yelled after him.

Narendra quickly locked the door behind him, leaving Saul finally alone with the food. He ate ravenously, his eyes watering from the rich spices flavouring the meatballs.

Once he had finished, Saul made his way over to the window and discovered that he was perhaps thirty storeys above ground level. So far as he could tell, he was confined in one of several residential towers strung along the sloping side of the valley. He could see construction teams, like tiny, multicoloured ants, clambering around the tower that was its nearest neighbour. It stood perhaps a kilometre away, its upper floors presently a tangle of girders. He even thought about shouting for help, but the chances of anyone hearing him were extraordinarily slim.

He stepped back to the door and pressed his ear against it, listening hard. After a moment he was rewarded by the sound of a throat clearing.

Saul passed most of the rest of the morning watching cargo drones drift above the city canopy, obviously on their way to and from other settlements. Without his contacts, he felt desperately isolated, as if he was stranded naked in a jungle with no idea how to get home.

Narendra returned in the early afternoon, again accompanied by Eren. He placed a wooden chair in the centre of the room, while Eren gestured with the barrel of his shotgun, and barked several unintelligible commands indicating that Saul should kneel. Once he had complied, Narendra stepped quickly behind him, binding his wrists once more.

Narendra took a seat on the chair, facing Saul, while Eren moved to stand directly behind him.

Narendra rubbed his palms against his thighs. 'I must ask you again,' his eyes flitted up towards Eren, with more than a touch of nervousness, 'why you came here.'

'None of your damn business,' replied Saul.

Narendra merely nodded, and took out a small pouch. He began to roll himself a cigarette, carefully balancing the paper on one knee as he added a pinch of tobacco. 'I did say earlier that it would be better for both of us,' he remarked, without looking up from his task, 'if you answered.'

There was a faint tremor in Narendra's voice, and Saul noticed the broker's hands were shaking very gently. It wasn't difficult to guess that he was deadly afraid of Eren. *He's out of his depth*, Saul realized.

'Does Eren here know just what you do for a living?' Saul asked suddenly. He could hear the slow in-and-out of Eren's breath, and could picture the shotgun muzzle hovering just centimetres from the back of his skull.

'Yes,' Narendra replied, still focused on his work. 'He is very much aware of it. We are . . . business associates, you might say.'

Saul nodded, as if in understanding. 'So all that information you gave me about Shih Hsiu-Chuan, last time I was here . . . that was all a set-up, am I right?'

Narendra's eyes flicked up to meet his, then lowered. 'Yes. When did you realize?'

Saul shrugged. 'Lee Hsingyun turning up when he did was just too convenient, and he obviously knew a lot more about us than we did about him. Outside of the ASI, you're the only one who knows we had an interest in Hsiu-Chuan.'

'You're not the only person I trade with, Saul. It goes both ways.'

'Yes,' Saul nodded, 'but in return for the information you give us, we allow you to continue trading, just as long as you don't cross us. In all the years we dealt with you, this is the first time you've done that, so why now? What's at stake that suddenly everything's different?'

'You sound,' said Narendra, 'like you already have an idea why.'

'I always realized all that stuff you liked to spout about staying "neutral" was just bullshit, but I could never figure out just where your true loyalties lay. Now I think I do. Your friend Eren's with one of the separatist groups, right?'

Narendra said nothing, lit his cigarette and took a draw, the smoke drifting up pungently.

'Not Fan Pan Zhe,' Saul continued, 'so I figure it's Al Hurr. They're pretty much running Sophia these days.'

Eren muttered something from just behind him, and Narendra nodded in response.

'I asked you a question.' Narendra fixed his gaze on Saul. 'You still haven't answered it.'

Eren pressed the shotgun muzzle up against the back of Saul's neck, forcing his head forward. He then shouted something close to Saul's ear, and Saul closed his eyes, trying not to think about the damage a shotgun cartridge could do at such close range.

'Wait!' he cried out. 'All right, I'm trying to find a man called Farad Maalouf. I believe he has family here.'

Narendra nodded, over his head, at Eren, who withdrew the shotgun. Saul straightened slowly, his heart hammering in his chest.

'So why are you trying to find him?'

'A friend of mine disappeared. I've reason to think Maalouf might be able to help me find him.'

'And this friend's name?'

Saul glared at Narendra. 'Now, that really *isn't* any of your fucking business.'

Narendra gestured to Eren, who rammed Saul in the small of the back hard enough to send him sprawling face-down across the rough-textured concrete. A moment later, Eren straddled him, taking a grip on Saul's bound wrists and twisting his arms up and over his head.

Saul screamed from the sheer pain: it felt as if his arms were being ripped out of their sockets. An eternity seemed to pass before Eren finally let go.

'Jeff Cairns,' Saul gasped, from where he lay helpless. 'I thought Farad could help me find a man called Jeff Cairns.'

'We know who he is,' said Narendra. 'He and Farad once worked together. What do you know about their work?'

'Nothing.' Saul shook his head vigorously, so his cheek rasped against the concrete. 'Something off-world, that's all I know. Might be mineral assessment or something else, I have no fucking idea.'

'But you've been assigned to find both him and Maalouf?'

'No.' Saul twisted his head around so he could finally look up at Narendra. 'I wasn't assigned by anyone. I'm here for personal reasons, that's it.'

'You'll need to give me more than that.'

The last thing Saul wanted to do was tell Narendra about Olivia. 'All I know is that Jeff's in some kind of trouble. That's the sum total of my knowledge.'

Narendra addressed Eren in rapid-fire Turkish. When he looked down at Saul again, his expression was tight-lipped. 'No,' he replied. 'There's some other reason you're here.'

Eren dragged Saul over to the window, fumbling one-handed with the latch and pushing it wide open. Saul tasted air damp from the condensation that gathered under the city canopy, as Eren pushed him up against the frame. He struggled, but Eren seemed to expend little effort in pushing Saul head-first out through the window, a firm grip on his collar the only thing keeping Saul from tumbling to his death. He felt his bowels turn to water as he stared at the void separating him from the ground.

'Eren,' said Narendra, coming to stand by the window, 'thinks we should let you drop, if you have nothing useful to tell us.'

Saul stumbled over his own words in panic, his heart beating so hard it felt like a terrified animal trapped in his chest. 'All I know is Jeff was on to something that the ASI's been trying to cover up, that's it, I swear I have no idea what it is, but they're killing anyone who was involved in any way.'

'And this is the truth?' demanded Narendra.

'Goddammit, *yes*.'

'Are you aware,' asked Narendra, 'that you were followed as soon as you arrived in Sophia?'

'By *your* people, yes.'

Narendra uttered a brief word to Eren, and Saul found himself suddenly pulled back from the window. He collapsed in a heap on the floor, his heart still thundering, and watched Narendra discard the burned-out stub of his cigarette and grind it under his boot. Saul sensed a shift in the atmosphere. Perhaps, he hoped, they were starting to believe him.

'Not *our* people,' Narendra replied. 'Not Al Hurr or any of the other groups.'

'I don't understand.'

'Nor do I. Three men tracked you all the way across town from the Array, all of them ASI agents. At first we assumed they were working in conjunction with you, but then it became clear they were following you without your knowledge.'

'You're saying my own people were following me?'

Narendra nodded. 'There's been a steady influx of government operatives through the Array, over the past couple of weeks. We assumed it was the beginning of another clampdown, particularly when people living here began to disappear or turn up dead. But the military forces pouring in through the Array over the past few days are far greater in number than at any point in the past. Not only that, the news from Earth is full of . . . *things*, indescribable monstrosities growing like weeds. Do you know what they are?'

Military forces? 'No,' said Saul, 'I don't. And I'm not sure anyone does.'

Narendra stared at Saul for what seemed like a long time, then spoke again to his colleague. Eren's reply was angry, but something in the defiant way Narendra replied suggested that he was standing his ground over some issue.

'I'm going to tell you something you don't know,' continued Narendra, turning back to Saul. 'And I want you to know the only reason I'm sharing it with you is because it's clear something very extraordinary is taking place – both here and back on Earth. Farad Maalouf was my brother.'

Saul gaped at him. He recalled the pictures he'd seen of Maalouf and, studying Narendra's face, saw what might be a family resemblance in the eyes and the shape of his jaw.

'You just said he *was* your brother?'

'My half-brother, to be precise,' Narendra continued, quivering with barely suppressed rage. 'He was gunned down like a dog, just a few streets from here.'

'And you think *I* had something to do with it? I only just got here!'

'You are an ASI agent, so it would be foolish of me to take you at your word. We are on different sides of a war.'

Saul groaned. 'What the hell are you talking about? What war?'

Narendra stared at him in disbelief. 'You help to maintain an unjust system, and we oppose it. We should be able to build our own wormhole networks, to find our own star systems to colonize, as and when we please, instead of having to route all our traffic through Copernicus. And now you are sending in your military to crush us without mercy.' He gestured at Eren. '*He* is here in order to carry out your execution. The only reason you're still alive is because I spoke on your behalf.'

Something clicked inside Saul's head. 'That's because you already believed me, isn't it? You know I had nothing to do with your brother's death.'

Narendra's nostrils flared. 'I believe there are reasonable grounds for doubt. But believing you carries a price, because it means placing my trust in you. If that proves to be a mistake on my part, Eren will kill me as soon as he has finished disposing of you.'

'Then, if you don't think I killed Farad, what is it you need from me?'

'I want you to tell me just how you came into possession of the encrypted database we found stored in your contacts.'

Saul's shoulders sagged in defeat. 'I found it when I went looking for Jeff Cairns back on Earth. I figured I might be able to dig up some clue as to where he'd gone, but there was no way to break the encryption on the files.'

'And Jeff Cairns worked with my brother, an expert in such matters. This is another reason you are still alive,' Narendra explained. 'If your intention was to kill him, it makes no sense that you would bring with you the very same information he died helping to steal.'

'And . . . you've cracked the files?'

'We did, yes.' Narendra nodded. 'But what we discovered is . . . troubling.'

Narendra said something to Eren – and Saul gasped as a bag was once more pulled over his head.

'I would rather you didn't see just where we're going,' he heard Narendra say, as Eren lifted Saul back up on to his feet. 'But it's not far.'

Saul stumbled along blindly, one man pushing him from behind while the other led him with a firm grip on his upper arm. When they next came to a stop, Saul felt the floor suddenly lurch beneath him, and guessed they had boarded an elevator. As they emerged once more, he felt a breeze blowing through the narrow slit just above his mouth.

'We're going to put you in the boot of a car,' he heard Narendra say. 'Do not struggle.'

Two pairs of hands bundled him into a cramped space, then he heard the car's boot lock click into place just an inch above his head. A moment later he felt the vehicle accelerate.

No more than ten minutes passed before the car came to an abrupt halt, and soon the boot clicked open once more. Hands reached in and pulled him out, and once more he was led through a series of twists and turns. When they finally tore the bag from his head, Saul blinked under flickering strip lights that illuminated a narrow corridor with peeling, whitewashed walls, and a stairwell at the far end.

They led him to a door, on which Narendra continued rapping until it swung open, revealing a surly-looking man in his early twenties. He wore faded work clothes and held an Agnessa sub-machine gun close to his chest. He nodded to Narendra and Eren, but spared Saul only a brief, contemptuous glare, before leading the three of them into what appeared to be someone's living room. A TriView sat in one corner, while a couch and armchair were positioned on a thick, patterned carpet. The room smelled of a mixture of mint and cigarettes.

'Where are we?' Saul asked.

'This was Farad's apartment,' said Narendra. He gestured to Eren, who merely nodded and collapsed into the armchair, placing the shotgun across his knees.

Narendra beckoned to Saul to follow him into what had clearly been Maalouf's office, where a second TriView was mounted on the wall. Narendra left the door open, and Saul, glancing back towards the living room, saw that Eren could easily keep an eye on them from where he was sitting.

Narendra activated the TriView. 'The database contains many video sequences we are still struggling to comprehend,' he explained as he turned back towards Saul. 'We want to know what they mean.'

'You're buried in shit right up to your neck, I think,' Saul muttered under his breath.

'I am a businessman, not a revolutionary,' Narendra responded *sotto voce*, with a nervous glance towards the living room. 'For all that I would like to see the men responsible for killing Farad pay, I would now prefer to be almost anywhere but here.' He nodded towards the TriView. 'Please, pay attention.'

Saul found himself watching several figures in bulky spacesuits making their way across what appeared to be a bridge that was illuminated by rows of lights. Tinny-sounding voices crackled with static, and a notice flashed up, warning them this recording was classified. To Saul, it all looked very flat and artificial, without the aid of his contacts.

The footage was raw and clearly unedited, and appeared to have been recorded through some kind of suit-mounted camera rather than through anyone's contacts. The view shifted suddenly, as whoever was recording these images glanced up. Saul noticed that the bridge led into a passageway entrance in the side of a building of monumental proportions. An angled wall rose up and up above the bridge, before disappearing into a sky so black and empty that something about it sent a chill all the way through him.

The suited figures began talking amongst each other about low-pressure zones and high-gravity areas, and of Founders and artefacts. At one point, Farad Maalouf's face, pale and nervous-looking, became visible through the smeared glass of a suit helmet.

The scene changed abruptly to what appeared to be the deck of a cruise liner, or a ferry, moving through heavy weather, with dark grey clouds scudding low over a stormy sea. Something huge grew out of the water directly ahead, almost incomprehensibly large – obviously one of the alien growths currently dominating the headlines. Enormous leaves were intermittently visible through the cloud cover.

The view then blurred as whoever was making the record- ing – through contacts, this time – made a sudden movement. There was a brief glimpse of a woman's face and then the scene changed again, as abruptly as before, now showing Copernicus City as it would appear from further along the crater wall.

Something was wrong, however. The entire city was in ruins, as if it had undergone some cataclysmic aerial bombardment. The view slowly panned around to reveal that the upper levels of the city's tallest buildings had been sheared off, and their debris scat- tered for tens of kilometres all around.

Another change of scene, and this time Saul found himself look- ing at what appeared to be satellite footage taken from low-Earth orbit. He saw the surface of the Earth was now dotted with the same flower-like growths, but in far, far greater numbers than they existed currently.

That settled it, then: this footage was obviously faked. Any reasonably skilled graphic artist could generate images like this, impossible to distinguish from reality. But what gave Saul pause to wonder – even to doubt his own sense of disbelief – was the look of utter dread he saw on Narendra's face, as he glanced towards him.

'Farad caused us much consternation,' said Narendra. 'He was given the opportunity to infiltrate a highly secretive research project backed by the ASI. At first we rejoiced, because we now had one of our own deep in the enemy's territory, reporting back to us. It was clear that one of the greatest discoveries ever made in the history of mankind was deliberately being kept hidden from us all. But, within a short period of time, Farad became . . . recalcitrant.'

'What do you mean, "recalcitrant"?'

'At first, he refused to report back on anything he had seen and learned, so he was accused of becoming a turncoat. I tried to speak to him, because I was worried for his life, and finally he admitted to me that he was terrified of telling us what he knew in case we thought he was insane. He swore he was working on assembling the proof we would need in order to believe him.' Narendra shrugged. 'We had no choice but to go along with that explanation.'

Saul pointed to the TriView display. 'And this is the proof he was bringing back?'

'Presumably,' said Narendra. 'Although I would rather it was not the case. Please,' he gestured to the display, 'there's more.'

Saul turned back to the TriView and reeled in shock. The view had shifted back to the figures in pressure suits, except that this time some of them had cracked their helmets open, and were engaged in lifting a naked Mitchell Stone on to a makeshift stretcher. His skin was tinged blue and, as Saul watched, an oxygen mask was placed over his mouth. After that, he was carried down a long corridor with a high, vaulted ceiling, the walls decorated with carefully carved glyphs and shapes so utterly inhuman that they verged on the obscene. Another sudden jump-cut, and Saul watched as Mitchell was lifted out of some kind of cabinet in a sterile-looking room filled with pipes and monitors.

'I can't make sense of any of this,' said Saul. 'What is it supposed to be?'

Narendra regarded him with sad eyes. 'You cannot explain it?'

'It can't be real.' But how, then, to explain that image of Farad

Maalouf peering out of his helmet, surrounded by that impossible landscape?

'That is Eren's assumption,' said Narendra. 'He thinks Farad somehow invented all of this. But this does not explain why someone in the ASI wanted him dead, nor, presumably, why they wanted Jeff Cairns dead as well.'

Saul shook his head and turned back to the TriView, thinking he couldn't possibly experience any greater shocks than he had already received. But what came next was like the final *coup de grâce* in a particularly one-sided boxing match.

He again found himself looking at what he had at first assumed to be a bridge, but which now appeared to be a parapet connecting the monumental structure he had seen earlier to other, identical edifices. Something about them made him think of a cemetery – or, perhaps, a mausoleum. The video had been filmed from the point of view of someone pushing a heavy steel box, mounted on balloon-type wheels, with serial numbers stamped along its side.

Saul recognized it immediately as the hijacked shipment Hanover's squad had been sent to track down.

The suited figure trundling the box came to a halt, whereupon a second figure, which had been walking just ahead, stopped and turned to look back. Saul recognized Jeff's face looking out through the visor, an expression of worried concern on his face as he spoke. This time, however, there was no sound, suggesting he must be communicating over a private link.

'I have studied these video fragments very carefully,' explained Narendra. 'Particularly the ones that were most recently uploaded into the database. There are ways to determine if those images are real or not – certain signs of artifice that cannot be avoided. Yet I have found no such evidence.'

'You can't be serious,' Saul replied stubbornly. 'You're trying to tell me this is all real?'

'You've seen those same *things* on the news feeds. There are hundreds of hours of these recordings, much of it showing what appears to be a ruined and lifeless Earth – lifeless, that is, apart from the growths. Eren may be happy to deny the evidence of his eyes, but I cannot. These are things that have not happened yet – but obviously *will*.'

Something occurred to Saul. 'You said Farad died somewhere near here. Did you recover his contacts?'

'Yes.' Narendra nodded warily. 'Why? Because you think they might have recorded the face of his killer?'

Assassination had become a much harder business once UP-enabled contacts had become a mainstream form of communication, since they were capable of recording their wearer's last moments. 'That crossed my mind, yes,' said Saul. 'If the ASI were really behind the hit, they'd have made recovering the victim's contacts a priority.'

'You're assuming Farad's killer came face to face with him,' Narendra pointed out. 'Or that the killer hadn't disguised himself in some way.'

'That's why Eren thinks I'm here, isn't it?' Saul muttered. 'He thinks I was sent to recover the files Farad stole.'

Narendra's expression told him he'd guessed right. 'We guarded Farad very carefully on his return,' said Narendra, 'but he was killed despite our best attempts.'

'So do *you* know who did it?'

Narendra turned back to the TriView projection and skipped through a series of menus. After a couple of seconds, Saul recognized the streets of Sophia, from the viewpoint, again, of someone wearing contacts.

'You are witnessing the last minutes of my brother's life,' Narendra explained, his expression sour.

From the way the view shifted around, it was clear that Maalouf was casting darting glances all around. He was accompanied by three grim-faced men, Eren amongst them, and it was late at night. The giant struts supporting the city's canopy curved overhead like white bones. The four men crossed a street quickly, all of them shooting glances here and there, as if they were being hunted.

Saul flinched instinctively as the first shots rang out. He saw one of the three men accompanying Maalouf drop to the ground, blood pouring from one side of his head. Maalouf either started to run, or was dragged, in the direction of a doorway. Saul caught a brief glimpse of a van skidding to a halt nearby, its tyres screaming on the tarmac.

Donohue and another man, both armed with Cobras, jumped out of the van and began shooting. Farad's viewpoint spun wildly, then ceased moving, showing nothing but the evening stars and the dark limb of Al-Khiba far overhead. Saul then caught sight of Eren backing into the same doorway, stepping over Maalouf's body before he crouched down to return fire.

Narendra made a gesture and the footage came to an immediate halt. 'Eren was lucky to survive that encounter,' he explained, 'so he would very much like to know the identity of those men who killed Farad.'

Saul figured there had to be at least four in the assassination squad. The shots already fired before the van arrived meant that at least one person other than Donohue and the second gunman had taken part in the hit, while a fourth would have been in control of the van.

'I can't tell you who any of them are,' Saul lied.

Narendra stared at him as if he didn't believe a word.

'The team you say were following me,' Saul asked, 'was it the same lot?'

'Yes, it was.'

At that precise moment, Saul heard a low booming sound, not unlike a thunderclap. At first he thought it had come from the projector, then realized it came from somewhere outside the apartment. Narendra stood and listened, as if frozen, then suddenly broke into action, rushing to the door while directing a flow of dialogue at Eren.

'What's going on?' asked Saul, following, but Narendra reached out a hand to stop him.

'I don't know,' he muttered, then left the room.

Saul watched as the two men conversed in low, urgent tones.

Eren was standing up now, his shotgun gripped ready in both hands. He moved away from the door until he was no longer directly visible to either man, and took the opportunity to push aside one corner of a lowered blind and peer out through the window behind.

He found himself looking directly along the entire length of the valley containing the city, towards the Newton Array at its far end. A dense cloud of grey and black smoke now rose above the Array, and was already beginning to pool under the giant canopy.

For one heart-freezing moment, Saul wondered if the Array had been sabotaged in the same way as the one on Galileo, thus stranding him light-years from home. But then the smoke thinned out a little, and he saw it rose not from the Array but from a tall building immediately next to it. Flames licked out of the building's upper windows.

As he stared in awe, one side of another building, directly opposite the first, exploded into flames and black smoke, sending debris and glass tumbling downwards. A second low booming noise reached him a few seconds later, followed by the distinctive crackle of small-arms fire.

Saul tried to open the window, but found it wouldn't budge. He pressed his forehead against the glass to peer down, and saw he was still a long way above the ground. Jumping out of there would only get him killed.

He stepped away from the window and headed back over to the door. He saw Eren looming over Narendra, his voice turned angry. Narendra backed away, and Eren swung his shotgun at him like a club, battering him across the side of the head. The broker collapsed as if either unconscious or dead.

Saul darted back out of sight, squeezing behind the door into Farad's office. He waited there, gripping the door handle, until he heard Eren's heavy footsteps approaching.

The moment he stepped inside the office, Saul slammed the door into Eren's face. But Eren batted it away with ease before barrelling into the room and levelling the shotgun. Saul lunged forward to try and wrench the shotgun out of his grasp, and for a moment they struggled for control of it.

The young guard who'd been set to watch the entrance came running into the living-room, and instantly brought his weapon to bear on Saul. Without thinking, Saul pulled himself close to Eren, twisting both of them around until Eren's back was facing the guard. The larger man's body jerked violently as the Agnessa's bullets punched through his spine. He slumped forward, lifeless.

Saul grabbed hold of the shotgun and let himself fall back under the weight of Eren's corpse, then heaved it to one side. Aiming the shotgun at the guard, he squeezed the trigger, and a fist-sized hole appeared in the man's chest. The guard fell backwards in an awkward heap, the Agnessa clattering on to the wooden floor beside him.

Saul shuffled backwards until his shoulders were up against the wall beneath the window, his breath emerging in short, rapid gasps. He kept the shotgun trained on the living-room as he listened for the sound of running feet. He waited there for at least another minute, before slowly pushing himself upright and making his way back into the other room.

He kneeled beside Narendra, who lay face-down on the floor, and heaved him over. One side of the man's head was crusted with blood, but he was clearly still breathing.

Narendra moaned, his eyes blinking open.

Saul rifled through Narendra's pockets until he found a slim aluminium case containing a single set of contacts, then glanced back at Narendra in time to see his eyes start rolling up in their sockets.

He shook him fiercely. 'Narendra!' He held the case up where the other man could see it. 'Look at me. Are these my contacts?'

Narendra managed to focus on the case and muttered something Saul couldn't make out, before his eyes slid shut once more. Saul shook him again, slapping the man's face and cursing, but it was clear a response wasn't going to be forthcoming any time soon.

He pinched the contacts out of the aluminium case and dropped them on to his eyes. Relief surged over him like a wave once it became clear that they were his own. He tried first to access the local emergency data sources but found, to his consternation, that they were currently all down. Calling for help clearly wasn't going to be an option any time soon.

Saul swapped the shotgun for the dead guard's Agnessa and made his way back to the elevator. A display informed him that it was currently down at the ground-floor level, which was perhaps a lot better than if it had been shooting back up towards him. He made for the stairwell instead, where he peered cautiously both up and down.

There was no one to be heard, so if any of the neighbours had noticed any sounds of shooting or violence, they were doing the sensible thing and staying well out of sight.

Saul hurried back into the apartment, stepping over Eren's motionless body as he once more entered the office. It took only a moment to locate all of the unencrypted video files on Maalouf's network, before copying everything over to his own contacts.

A quick browse on the spot showed him that there were many, many other files than just the video logs Narendra had already shown him. He noticed documents in their hundreds, all marked for much higher levels of clearance than his own. Technically, his duty was to leave them untouched and hand them over to his immediate superiors.

To hell with that, he decided.

Saul abandoned his blood-spattered jacket, finding another that was a near fit in the bedroom wardrobe. It felt loose around his shoulders – Farad had been a couple of sizes larger – but it was long and roomy enough to conceal the Agnessa within its folds. Lastly he rifled the dead guard's pockets until he found a box of spare ammunition, then headed down the stairwell as fast as he could, pointedly avoiding the elevator.

Once he was back outside, he looked out across the whole of

the canopied city stretching out below. He walked rapidly away from the building he had been held in, sticking to the shadows and keeping an eye out for anyone who might be showing an undue interest in him.

There was another detonation as he moved, and he looked out across the cityscape to see smoke and flames rising from yet another building adjacent to the Array. He glanced up at the overhead canopy and wondered if there was any way of discerning whether or not it had been damaged. If by any chance it had, a very great number of people were going to die.

Picking up his pace, he crossed a street, heading for an elevated transit station a couple kilometres further down the slope. As a shadow flitted past his feet, Saul looked up in time to glimpse an observation drone flying overhead. He watched as it banked right, following the road and ignoring him.

Before long he came to a row of stalls beneath an awning running down the middle of a city block. By the look of things, the owners had left in a considerable hurry, leaving food and fruit scattered all across the street. He passed on down the road and caught sight of an abandoned trike with a kebab cart hooked up to the rear.

He looked around, but whoever owned the trike had clearly gone to ground along with everyone else. He bent down and pulled out the pin to uncouple the cart. As soon as he climbed on, the dashboard sprang to life. He twisted the throttle and guided the trike out on to the street, noting simultaneously that the battery had just about enough juice to get him as far as the Array.

He rode gingerly at first, feeling somewhat less than comfortable on anything with less than four wheels. He saw very few people, though the evidence of ongoing combat echoed loudly through the air. He came to an intersection and guided the trike on to a main thoroughfare, passing several cars and vans shooting at high speed in the opposite direction, away from the city centre.

Saul opened up the throttle, gathering speed and making his way down a second thoroughfare, as he followed the course of an elevated rail line back towards the Array.

The closer he got to the Array, the more ASI drones he saw. One passed him in the opposite direction, broadcasting a message warning people to stay off the streets, but whoever was operating it had failed to spot him hidden beneath the elevated train track. A few minutes later, however, he nearly came flying off the trike when another drone fired on him. He jumped off and dashed for the relative cover of a nearby doorway, then waited and watched till the drone buzzed away over the rooftops.

He glanced across the street and noticed three other men hiding in the open doorway of a shuttered shop. One waved to Saul and beckoned him to come closer. He approached them warily, keeping his borrowed coat pulled tight around him, the Agnessa pressing against his thigh where he'd tucked it into his waistband.

The oldest-looking of the three had a carefully trimmed, greying beard, and he addressed Saul in Arabic. Saul's contacts instantly gave him a rough-and-ready live translation.

'What the hell are you up to?' the old man demanded. 'You'll get yourself killed riding around in the open like that. You don't see anyone else out on the streets, do you?'

'I don't know what's going on here,' Saul replied in English.

From the way the old man squinted at him in confusion, it was clear he wasn't wearing contacts.

'He's not from around here,' one of the younger men informed the old man, before turning to Saul. 'Amid doesn't like technology, but you can speak to me. You're from Earth, right?'

Saul nodded, glad that at least one of them had active translation enabled in his contacts. 'I was at the other end of town, doing some business, and now I'm just trying to find my way to the Array, so I can get back home.'

Amid's younger companion nodded thoughtfully. 'Must have been quite some business to get yourself knocked about like that.' He gestured towards Saul's bruised face. 'You'll have a hard time getting anywhere near the Array, I can tell you. Haven't you heard? We're being invaded.'

'By the Coalition?'

Amid started at mention of the word, then spat out a string of invectives that Saul's contacts struggled to comprehend.

'Their tanks came through just over a day ago,' said one of them. 'Soldiers, too, appearing like ants out of an anthill. They took over the Legislature, and now there's fighting on the streets all around the colonial government building, with Al Hurr taking on Black Dogs and drones.' Maz shook his head. 'A lot of dead people already.'

Sudden shouting from nearby was followed by gunshots, and then an explosion that shook the ground beneath their feet. Several men with scarves or T-shirts covering their faces came running along the street. One of them carried an assault rifle, while another brandished a rusty-looking axe. They soon disappeared around a corner, followed a minute later by a heavily armed drone.

'I'm not hanging around out here any longer,' said one of the men, disappearing back inside the shuttered premises, as smoke started drifting above the rooftops of a neighbouring street. 'You'll all get your heads blown off if you stay out here.'

His companions followed him inside, the old man giving Saul an angry glance, as if he were somehow responsible.

Saul continued in the direction the fighters had emerged from, abandoning the trike now it seemed likely to draw too much attention. He soon came to an intersection, where a truck lay on its side, with broken bodies scattered all around. The rear of the vehicle still smouldered, while every window in the surrounding buildings appeared to have been shattered.

A targeted hit, Saul guessed, almost certainly from the drone that had passed by just a few minutes before. He started moving again, then froze when he heard that familiar buzz-saw rattle from behind. He turned to hear a mechanized voice shouting at him in Arabic.

A drone hovered just a few metres away, its central rotor scattering a blizzard of dust and debris outwards from beneath it. Twin gun turrets were mounted on either side of its primary sensors.

'I'm ASI!' Saul yelled over the din it made, raising his hands slowly. His Agnessa, momentarily forgotten, clattered to the ground at his feet.

'ASI!' Saul screamed again, dropping to his knees.

Dear God, please let it have a human operator, thought Saul, wondering how many seconds he had left before the bullets started ripping into him.

The drone wobbled slightly, light glinting from one of its lenses as a genuinely human voice emerged from it a moment later.

'Hey, you're ASI! I'm picking up on your UP.'

Saul let his breath out in a juddering rush. 'Fine, can I take my hands down now?' he yelled up at the machine.

'Wait a second,' the operator replied, almost certainly speaking from some temporary command post deep inside the Newton Array. 'I need to run further verification on your ID, sir. You could have stolen those contacts, for all I know. Please wait just there.'

There was a click and a hiss of static as the operator went offline, presumably so he could consult with some superior officer. Saul bent down to pick up the Agnessa, keeping his eye on the drone the whole time. He kept the barrel pointing downwards as he waited.

The operator came back. 'Sorry, sir, you check out fine. If you want to rendezvous with a clean-up squad, you can—'

Saul heard the sound of running feet once again, voices calling to each other in Arabic. Ignoring the drone, Saul crawled underneath a bus parked nearby, before turning to look back on to the street.

Two armed men appeared around a corner, and the drone wobbled around to face them. One of the two dropped face-forward as the machine fired several rounds into his body, while the second leaped back around the same corner. Saul heard a subtle change in the sound of the drone's rotors as it moved to follow the fugitive.

A moment later, he heard a sound like a pop followed by a hiss. Something slammed into the drone, as it passed into the next street, engulfing it in flames. It spun wildly, its gyros obviously damaged.

A second rocket struck the drone, shattering it this time, and sent shards of metal spinning across the rubble-strewn roadway. There were shouts of jubilation and, a few moments later, more armed men came running towards Saul along the street.

He crouched low, hoping to stay invisible, but one of the resistance fighters, brandishing a meat cleaver, spotted him and yelled something that Saul's contacts translated as a promise to kill him if he didn't hurry the fuck up out of his hiding place.

Then things got really bad.

First, there was a bright eruption of light, and a deafening bass boom that Saul felt more than heard. The façade of the building opposite came tumbling down, burying most of the men now gathered triumphantly around the remains of the drone.

Saul closed his eyes, his ears still singing from the explosion, and when he opened them once more, the man threatening him had disappeared.

He crawled out from under the bus just as a Black Dog came pounding around the corner, bigger than any other he'd ever seen before, and with heavy cannons mounted between its metallic shoulders. Half a dozen armed Consortium troopers followed on foot, their outlines rendered indistinct by their active chameleon armour.

'Hey, is your name Saul Dumont?' one of them yelled, lowering his weapon to his side, as the rest of the squad moved past Saul towards the other end of the street. 'We got word from one of our operators, so who you with?'

Saul shook his head. 'I'm not with anyone.' He stared down at his torn and filthy jacket, his skin now caked with dust, and realized he had no idea where the Agnessa had disappeared.

'Right.' The trooper looked around, his armour reflecting the smoking rubble, making it hard to focus on him. 'You need transport?'

'I'm trying to get back to Florida,' said Saul, wondering if he was in shock.

The trooper turned around, in an indistinct motion, lines of colour streaking as he looked back in the direction from which he'd appeared. 'Well, we're about to head back that way, because we need to recharge the Dog. Just try not to attract any more attention, will you? I think you just lost us a drone.'

'Right.' Saul nodded, feeling actually sorry.

The trooper turned back to his men, who were recovering the weapons dropped by the insurgents. Saul followed after them, dazed, his head filled with visions of monolithic structures under starless skies.

TWENTY-TWO

Olivia woke with a start.

At first she thought someone must be in the bathroom next door, and had just swept the soap dish and toothbrushes off their shelf and sent them clattering to the floor. But then she saw the window rattle in its casement, the mattress beneath her also trembling slightly.

There was the sound of glass breaking, somewhere outside, followed by the frenzied barking of a dog some way off in the distance. Fingers clenched around the quilt, she waited for the tremor to abate, while adrenalin sent spikes of fear racing up and down her spine.

As the tremors began to abate, Olivia closed her eyes and remained entirely still for a few moments, waiting for her heart to stop beating like a jackhammer. Finally she slid off the bed and peered inside the bathroom; a glass had fallen to the floor and smashed, leaving a pair of cheap plastic toothbrushes among the shards. She grabbed a wad of paper towels and started sweeping it all into a pile.

Suddenly she stopped. What was the point? The owners of this motel had already fled. People were clearly going to ground, or returning to their families, or else rioting in the streets when they failed to get answers from their governments and realized they had been abandoned. She stood up again, leaving the broken glass on the floor. It would be easier to move to another motel room instead.

A few minutes later Olivia stepped out on to the veranda fronting the adjacent room, squinting up into the bright Arizona morning as she continued brushing her teeth. A single car whipped along the highway, doing at least a hundred. They had otherwise seen very little traffic since pulling into the motel, though there were reports on the news feeds of a sharp hike in road banditry and improvised roadblocks along Mexical's disputed border.

Olivia heard voices, and looked down to see Jeff and Mitch standing next to the truck they'd stolen. Jeff smiled up at her and waved.

She waved back, as she thought about their reunion a few nights before, and the things she had learned since. A wave of grief and despair washed over her, and she stepped back from the railing before he could see her tears.

When Jeff had phoned her from out of the blue the day before, it had almost seemed like hearing from a ghost. To her surprise, the first emotion she'd felt was anger that he had left her in the dark for so long without anything like a real explanation. He'd then told her that he was with Mitchell Stone, and asked her to join them both in Arizona.

Arizona? She had been sitting in her kitchen when she received the call, her knuckles white where they gripped the table. 'Why Arizona?'

Jeff's voice had wavered slightly as he replied. 'I'd rather explain in person.'

She caught sight of her own face reflected in the kitchen window, eyes wide and angry. 'Why not just tell me now?'

'It's the kind of thing you really have to hear face-to-face, Olivia.'

She swallowed hard. 'Does this have anything to do with those things growing in the ocean?'

'Well, yeah, as a matter of fact,' he replied, a note of surprise in his voice. 'It has a lot to do with them. You'll be coming, right?'

'I don't know.'

'Jesus, Olivia.' Jeff's tone was quietly persistent. 'You *need* to come. I didn't pick on Arizona for the hell of it. Our lives are in danger and I'm trying to keep us both alive. Can you leave right away?'

'But why Arizona?'

'Remember the Roses?'

She thought for a moment. 'You mean Lester and Amy?'

'Them, yes. We're heading for their space-port.'

'And you're not going to tell me why, is that it?'

'Olivia,' he said, 'we're going to the Moon, on board one of their ships.'

She started to ask why they couldn't just go through the Array, then decided she didn't actually want to know – at least not yet.

'Did you see the news last night?' she asked him instead.

'No. Why?'

'There was a press conference . . . the heads of all three republics, including Mexical. They said there was no way to stop the growths. They said that they didn't know what might happen next.'

She heard the sound of an engine revving, over the link, a voice muttering in the background. *Mitchell*, she guessed.

'They're lying. They know exactly what's going to happen.'

'How could you possibly know that?'

'Well,' she heard him reply, from a thousand kilometres away, 'it's kind of complicated. But you know how the Array allows for a certain kind of time travel?'

Olivia had felt like a passenger inside her own body as she got into a car, less than twenty minutes later. The surrounding streets had been quiet, with hardly any traffic at all. Somehow she hadn't expected that, given the recent news. Most people, she guessed, were just staying at home. Where else, after all, could they go?

The car whisked her out of Jacksonville and on to a highway heading west. Half an hour later it pulled in at a regional airport and she boarded an otherwise empty hopper, spending most of the flight scanning through feeds that were all reporting on exactly the same events – the growths and the million and more people currently camped outside the Florida Array.

Aerial video shots made the Array itself look like a space-age castle under siege. Black Dogs and sonar tanks surrounded the main facility, forcing the crowds back whenever they came too close. Sphere governments were meanwhile demanding the resumption of normal gate services, and once again condemning the Coalition's monopoly of wormhole technology. There were even ominous rumours of war, and unconfirmed reports that some of the growths had already been attacked with nuclear weapons.

She arrived in Phoenix less than two hours later, and soon located the hire car Jeff had sent to pick her up. He had already taken care of booking the hopper flight, with help from the Roses, since it was safer for her not to use her UP any more than necessary.

The car transported Olivia through a busy shopping district, where she saw people going in and out of fab stores, or walking their dogs, while all around them public screens displayed constant images of something enormous and obscenely alien tearing its way through the skin of their world. She realized how people did the only thing they could in the face of such an enormity: they went about their lives the same as always.

In that same moment it occurred to her she had not told Jeff about contacting Saul, and she could all too easily picture his look of hurt betrayal in response.

Olivia rinsed out her mouth and went downstairs, finding Jeff and Mitchell waiting in the motel's foyer.

Jeff jerked a thumb towards the door adjoining the check-in desk. 'I scoped out the kitchen,' he said. 'Found the refrigerator's still running and they're stocked up with eggs and bacon. Who wants to make breakfast?'

A weary-looking Mitchell slapped him on the shoulder. 'I'll make the breakfast,' he said. 'See you both in the restaurant in ten.'

Olivia stared after him as he strode past, the kitchen door swinging shut behind him. She was still struggling to process everything Jeff had told her, after he'd finished apologizing for treating her as he had. Pretty much anything seemed possible now that every day brought further news of growths, earthquakes and tsunamis. Even duplicate Mitchells were no particular surprise.

Jeff laid his hands on her shoulders and gave her a brief kiss on the lips. 'Holding up?'

'I guess.' She nodded towards the kitchen, through which could now be heard the clatter of pots and pans. 'Have you told him yet?'

'You mean what we discussed last night?' He shrugged and smiled. 'I figured we could do that over breakfast. Why? Changed your mind?'

'About Jupiter?' Shaking her head, she reached out to take his hand. 'No, if anything, I'm even more certain that it's the right thing to do.'

Half an hour later, in the motel's otherwise deserted cafeteria, she watched Mitchell devour a second plate of eggs before washing it all down with his fourth cup of coffee.

'Sure, of course I remember Saul,' he responded in reply to her question. 'But it's been a while since I last heard from him.' He put down his knife and fork, and fixed his gaze on them both. 'Why?'

'I got in touch with him a couple of days ago,' she explained, 'when I was worried something bad had happened to Jeff.'

'Where does Saul come into this?'

Olivia glanced sideways at Jeff, and saw he was deliberately not looking her way, his lips set firmly in a thin line.

'I asked him to find Jeff,' she said, turning back to Mitchell.

Mitchell glanced from one to the other, clearly sensing a tension between them. 'And you did this *when*? Before I called you, or after?'

'Just after. When you called me, that's what made me sure something very bad had happened.'

Jeff cleared his throat. 'I still don't see *why* you needed to get in touch with him—'

'For Christ's sake, Jeff,' she snapped, 'we already went over all this stuff last night. There was no one else I could ask for help, so what the hell was I supposed to do? I know you just thought you were protecting me, but I already told you it was the wrong move.'

Jeff raised both his hands as if fending her off. 'Okay, okay, point taken.'

'Just wait one second,' said Mitchell. 'How can we be sure that Saul is on our side?'

Olivia stared at him incredulously. 'Oh, come *on*. You know him as well as we do.'

'It's been a long time since I last saw him,' Mitchell replied tightly. 'You'd be amazed how much people can change.'

She shook her head. 'Sure, but not that much. It took me a lot of effort to even get him to listen to me. When he said he'd help, he was being sincere. I've always been a good judge of character. You must know that.'

Jeff snorted in derision, and Olivia glared at him.

'So he offered to help,' said Mitchell, 'but what exactly did he do?'

'He went up to Montana to find Jeff, but he missed him by a couple of days. When he took a look around, he found the files Jeff told me he'd brought back from Tau Ceti. He didn't know how to break the encryption on them, so I told him he should talk to a man called Farad Maalouf.'

Mitchell nodded. 'I know Farad.'

'He went to Newton to look for Farad, but that was the last I heard from him. I've tried to get in touch, but no luck. I don't know if that means he's gone the same way as Dan Rush and the others, or not.'

Mitchell drummed his fingers on the table top. Olivia guessed they were both thinking the same thing. She tried to pretend to herself that she wasn't responsible for what might have happened to Saul, but the sense of guilt insinuated itself even more tightly around her, regardless.

She decided to change the subject, more to avoid thinking about Saul than anything else. 'I have a question for you: how do you know the ASI won't target your ship before it can land? A rocket landing on the Moon won't exactly be inconspicuous.'

'Lester and Amy Rose have been running sub-orbital flights for nearly half a century,' replied Mitchell. 'And lunar flights for nearly as long. There's no reason for them to be targeted. And, since Jeff used to work for them and still knows them both well, he's been able to swing us a berth.'

'People get hurt,' remarked Olivia. 'There've been accidents.'

Mitchell shook his head and laughed. 'Like we'd be safer staying here?'

She felt her face redden.

'Look,' said Mitchell, pushing his plate aside and leaning towards her, 'the VASIMRs are a proven safe technology. Even the Apollo Saturn replicas they fly are a hundred times safer than the originals. It's not just that this is our best chance of getting away – it's our only chance.'

'And what about the people here? What about the billions we're leaving behind?'

Mitchell shook his head. 'There's nothing you can do for them.'

Olivia felt her muscles tense in horror. 'That's a pretty callous statement, isn't it?'

'Jeff's told you what happened to me, right?' asked Mitchell. 'About how they found me, and how they brought me back here.'

'He said that . . . that there are two of you, and *you're* the one they brought back from the near future.'

'If you look at it from my perspective,' he said, 'all this happened a long time ago. The fact is, you can't mourn what you can't change.'

Olivia fought to control her anger. She glanced at Jeff and saw the warning look on his face, and realized she was obviously close to blowing up.

'Tell him now,' she said to Jeff. 'Tell him what we decided last night.'

Mitchell frowned. 'Tell me what?'

Jeff hesitated, clearly caught off guard, then he reached out and put one hand over hers. She wondered if that meant he'd finally decided to forgive her for getting in touch with Saul.

'I guess this is as good a time as any to tell you,' he said to Mitchell. 'We're not going to the Moon.'

Mitchell sat back and glanced between them. 'Seriously?'

'Just think about it,' Jeff continued. 'Say all three of us went up there together, that only puts us on the surface of the Moon, not even inside Copernicus City or the Lunar Array itself. That means a further trek across the Moon's surface from our landing site to either one or the other, which means we'd still have to figure out some way to get inside. And you've already failed once yourself, which is why you wound up in the cryogenics lab in the first place.'

Mitchell nodded, and Olivia had the uncanny sense he was relieved. She found herself wondering if it was just the strangeness of what had happened to him that made her so uneasy, or if it was something else – something she couldn't put a name to.

'So that's it?' said Mitchell. 'You're going to stay here on Earth, and just wait until the end?'

'No.' Jeff shook his head emphatically. 'You're forgetting about the outer-system research colonies. The older ones have their own dedicated arrays up north, including the Jupiter platform.'

'And that's where you want to go? Back to Jupiter?'

'Even if we managed to get past all the heavy security, all the way through the Lunar Array to the colonies,' said Olivia, 'we've no idea how bad things there are going to be, or how much turmoil there'll be or how long it's all going to last. *Especially* if the same people who've been trying to kill us here end up in charge there. But we can be safe on the Jupiter platform as long as we sever the wormhole link with Earth.' She shrugged. 'Besides, we don't know what things might be like on Earth, or on the Moon, in fifty years or a hundred, or however long it takes for things to get better again – if they ever do. After all, who's to say the Earth won't become habitable again? But, even if it doesn't, we still have a fighting chance at building something new out there.'

'Those platforms aren't set up to be self-sustaining,' Mitchell pointed out. 'They constantly depend on supplies from Earth.'

Jeff shook his head. 'Maybe that was the case when *you* were still running security there, but things have changed a lot. The station's grown enormously. I'm not pretending it's going to be easy, or anywhere near it, but we learned a lot from building large-scale, self-enclosed habitats on Newton as well as the other colonies. We can do the same not just around Jupiter but out at Saturn as well. We have seed banks available, and the means to gene-alter any-thing we need to. That means we can farm oxygen and water from the Jovian moons and asteroids.'

Mitchell sat back. 'What about the people already there – the station staff? Have you been in touch with them?'

'I already talked to Jacob Morello this morning,' said Jeff. 'He was working in groundside admin when I was stationed on the platform, but he spends most of his time out there now, and he says they can use both of us. Besides, both me and Olivia know the station inside out, so we know what it's capable of.'

'And don't forget the Inuvik–Jupiter gate is a lot more isolated than the one in Florida,' said Olivia. 'They won't be dealing with the kind of mobs Florida's been getting – not all the way up in Alaska.'

Mitchell gazed at Olivia, his pupils deep and blue and seemingly infinite. 'What about me?' he asked. 'Are the Roses still going to take me on board, without you there to back me up?'

'Of course they are,' said Jeff. 'We'll all go to the space-port first, and help arrange everything. Besides, they're expecting us. They confirmed they had room for three, so they'll definitely have room for just one.'

'And you're both absolutely set on this?' asked Mitchell, looking back and forth between the two of them.

'More so than anything else for a long time,' Olivia replied, clutching Jeff's hand more tightly.

Mitchell sighed and stood up. 'Then you'll have to figure out how to get north. Remember, most of the flights to Inuvik are run by the ASI.'

'Already thought of that,' said Jeff. 'Bob Esquivaz runs mission control for the Roses, and they have a sub-orb that can fly us out there.'

Mitchell looked impressed. 'Sounds like you've really thought this through.'

Jeff stood up as well and nodded towards the door. 'But, for the moment, we're all still heading for the space-port. I'll go pack our stuff in the car. Olivia?'

'In a minute,' she said. 'There's one other thing I want to ask you first, Mitchell. Jeff told me two of you were caught in those pits. What happened to . . .' She waved one hand, momentarily unable to recall the other man's name.

'Erich Vogel,' Jeff finished for her, stepping back from the doors and gazing at Mitchell. 'I already asked you about Vogel, but you never gave me a straight answer.'

One corner of Mitchell's mouth twitched. 'He's not dead, if that's what you mean.'

'Then where is he?' asked Olivia.

'He went ahead.'

Olivia frowned. 'Ahead to where?'

The corner of Mitchell's mouth curled again, into an almost apologetic smile. 'To the very end of time.'

Olivia stared at Jeff, then back at Mitchell. 'What?'

'Look,' said Mitchell, 'the exploration teams went a long, *long* way into the future, but there are routes through the Founder Network that can take you much farther still – so far ahead in time that I don't even know how to describe it. Except that it's long after the universe, as we know it, has effectively ceased to exist.'

'You believe this?' she asked, looking at Jeff.

Jeff shrugged helplessly. 'After what I've seen during the past couple of weeks, I think I'll believe pretty much anything.'

'The Founder Network zigzags across the whole universe,' Mitchell went on. 'Jeff told you about it, surely?'

She nodded, and Mitchell reached up to tap the side of his head. 'The pools – the learning pools, I call them – they put a road map of the whole thing here inside my head.'

'What about Erich?' asked Jeff. 'How could you have spoken to him? There was no sign of him at all when we found you.'

'I can't tell you exactly how I know, but some time between losing consciousness and when you found me, I talked to him.'

'Talked? How?'

'I just know that, before you found me, Erich and I'd . . . *communicated* in some way. He said he was going up ahead, to find the Founders and the civilization they created close to the end of everything. When I woke up, I was all alone.'

'Why didn't you go with him?' asked Olivia.

Mitchell paused, as if he was being careful to find the right words. 'There were things I had to do first.'

'What things?'

'I had to remember certain things,' he answered after a pause.

Olivia could feel herself getting angry, again, at what struck her as deliberate obfuscation. '*What* things?'

'Everything . . .' said Mitchell. 'Like taking a snapshot of everything living on Earth, and preserving it with all its thoughts intact, and carrying it through to the far future. "Remember" isn't really the right word . . . but the memories will live and breathe and think, put it that way.'

Olivia stared at him, suddenly frightened. 'And you can do that?'

'In a sense,' he replied eventually, his expression almost reverential as he continued. 'All this would make more sense if you'd seen what those learning pools showed me. Death has no real meaning to the Founders. It's not a concept they really understand, because they vanquished it so very long ago.'

Olivia stared at the strange half-smile on his face and shivered.

A fresh tremor caused the table to rattle. The three of them waited, ready to bolt outside if it grew worse, but it faded after a few seconds.

'Time to get moving,' said Jeff, heading towards the exit. 'We've probably wasted too much time already.'

TWENTY-THREE

It took Saul nearly sixteen hours to make his way back through the gate to Copernicus. Measured in light-years, the distance he had to cross was impossible for a human mind to contemplate, but measured through the wormhole it was a little under three and a half kilometres – three kilometres to the Sophia Array in the company of a squad of ASI troopers, then three hundred and fifty metres from the outer security perimeter to the transfer station, and a final stretch of one hundred and fifty metres, including that short, anticlimactic trip through the wormhole itself. And yet every step involved hours of interminable waiting, as he passed through security cordons that hadn't even been in place when he'd been heading the other way.

If anything, Narendra had underestimated the scale of the military operation taking place. Sophia's public UP networks had remained out of action, while the remaining communications bandwidth had been commandeered by military networks to which Saul soon found he was not permitted access. He felt overwhelmed by the sheer quantity of equipment and personnel pouring through from Florida: even once he had passed through the final checkpoint within the Sophia Array, he was then obliged to wait for another three hours while battlefield-equipped Black Dogs and their human operators were shipped through to Newton. Saul sat on a bench in a warehouse area, eating from a ration pack, as he watched dozens of the four-legged machines being unpacked from crates by engineers who then ran them through software checks, before sending them out on to the streets of Sophia.

He passed time by playing back the decrypted video fragments or else browsing through a selection of the hundreds of classified documents that accompanied them, hoping they might help make some sense of what he had witnessed so far, but the more he read, the more an almost physical dread overwhelmed him. Some of the documents focused solely on the growths, including speculations on their origin, while the majority detailed the exploration of something called the Founder Network. Saul read on, numbed by what he now learned. No wonder Donohue had worked so hard to suppress it all.

One report detailed an incident on a world so far in the future that – assuming he interpreted what he read correctly, although he was far from sure he did – the last remaining stars had long since burned to cinders. The main part of the report explicitly referenced Mitchell, appearing to suggest that he had somehow died and then come back to life – a claim no less extraordinary than any other Saul had so far encountered.

He closed his eyes and leaned forward to rest his head on his folded arms, inhaling deeply just to counteract a sudden rush of nausea. He couldn't imagine what it must have been like for Jeff Cairns to know so much and never be able to talk about it. If it had been Saul himself, he'd have cracked up long ago. And, if some of the personnel psych-eval reports he'd glanced through were anything to go by, a lot of people had done precisely that.

No wonder Narendra had been so eager to show him this footage. That hadn't just been because he wanted Saul to explain it; he'd been unable to sustain the horror of knowing everything – on Earth, at any rate – was shortly coming to an end.

Saul stretched out on the bench and dozed for a few hours amidst the roar and whirr of machinery being assembled. He woke up to find that the last of the Dogs had departed, his UP flashing a message to inform him that he could now board a shuttle-car.

As he disembarked in the Lunar Array, twenty minutes later, he saw several hundred troopers in chameleon armour preparing to head the other way, their outlines blurring as they jostled like some nightmare assemblage of ghosts. Saul made his way directly to the Copernicus–Florida gate, still trying to process all the information he had absorbed, not least the destruction of everything he had ever known.

He boarded an elevator and slumped back against cool steel, closing his eyes as it whisked him twenty floors up to the Florida ASI's command centre. The air was full of a distant rumble, like static; the massed voices of however many millions of refugees that had by now arrived at the perimeter. He thought of the crowds he'd already passed through, and wondered with a chill how many of them had since died.

Stepping out into a wide corridor, he made his way straight over to a window and stared out, with appalled fascination, at a sea of human flesh pressing up against a security cordon that had clearly undergone heavy reinforcement since he'd last seen it. A blaze of red on the horizon heralded the coming dawn, and he could make out hundreds of bodies, scattered across a no man's land separating the mob from a nearly unbroken phalanx of sonar tanks and illuminated by powerful arc lights. Black Dogs roamed this no man's land, while armoured drones buzzed through the air like a swarm of mechanical locusts.

There must be at least two million . . . no, he decided, more like three million people gathered all around the Array. Maybe even more. The land itself had disappeared beneath their swarming mass.

He managed to pull himself away from this appalling sight and headed for his locker, pulling out a duffel bag already containing a change of clothes. He then headed for the gym and emptied the bag on to a bench. Something fell out and clattered on the tiles.

It was an inhaler, he realized. He picked it up and stared at it for a moment, then opened it up to find it was loaded with half a dozen cellophane-wrapped balls of loup-garou. He stared at the device with a peculiar hunger and licked his lips. He should throw it away – indeed, he wanted to – but some instinct made him shove it back in the bag, instead.

He took a shower, standing under a blast of hot water for a good twenty minutes until the heat had permeated through his skin and into his bones. He then put on a change of clothes, grabbed a coffee and sandwich and found a random workstation in the main operations room that registered his clearance as he approached, projecting custom pre-sets on to the dark panels on either side. He first checked his latest messages, all of them internal memos detailing personnel's duties under the current crisis. Saul deleted them all in disgust.

Not for the first time, it occurred to him that there were very likely people working in the offices all around him who would not hesitate to have him killed simply because of what he now knew. And, if what Narendra had told him about his being trailed by an ASI team was true, it was conceivable that such an order had already been given.

He slunk lower in his chair, brooding, but looked up in time to see Donohue pass by.

A glass partition separated him from the corridor along which Donohue was striding, in an obvious hurry. If he'd so much as glanced to one side, he'd have noticed Saul staring back at him. But the Public Standards agent continued with brisk purpose, his gaze focused directly ahead.

Saul slipped out of his seat, intending to follow him, then paused as he remembered the inhaler still in his duffel-bag. He retrieved it before hurrying out into the corridor.

Trailing Donohue at a discreet distance, he watched as the man proceeded into an executive suite, leaving the door fractionally ajar.

Saul quietly stepped up to the door, with a quick glance back the way he'd come. The command centre was very nearly deserted, much more so than he had ever seen it. Only a very few individuals were either still working at their desks or conferring quietly behind semi-transparent partitions. Luckily none of them paid him any attention, as he peeked through the open door to see Donohue leaning over a desk, with his back to him, staring at information on a screen that only he could see.

Saul ducked away from the door, and made his way to another vacant workstation nearby. He waited there, one hand up to conceal the side of his head, leaning forward as if to concentrate on some piece of scrolling information. He was watching discreetly when Donohue emerged from the executive suite a few minutes later, hurrying back towards the elevators.

Saul followed him, rigid with tension, aware that stumbling across Donohue like this was sheer luck. He kept a discreet distance, hovering around a corner while Donohue boarded an elevator. As soon as its doors closed, Saul quickly boarded the one adjoining, punching the button for the basement car park. He couldn't be sure that was where Donohue was heading, but the chances were pretty good.

Adrenalin chased away all the aches and pains that still plagued him as the elevator dropped, but it wasn't enough to overcome the fatigue. *I need this*, he thought, fumbling for the inhaler. Just one more shot to give him a little bit of killer instinct. Maybe things had gone badly that time on Kepler, but the real mistake had been taking too much, too fast.

Just enough, and no more. That was all he needed.

He pressed the device against his lips, hitting the activator and inhaling deeply. He gasped as the loup-garou exploded into his lungs, reeling back against the wall of the elevator as the drug punched its way into his bloodstream and began racing towards his brain's chemoreceptors. His fingers twitched slightly as he pushed the inhaler back into his pocket.

After the doors slid open, Saul stepped out into an enormous, dimly lit space that normally would be filled with maintenance trucks and Agency vehicles. Instead, more than a dozen battle-scarred Dogs, surrounded by yelling repair crews, dominated most of the available space, while nearly as many sonar tanks stood waiting next to an impromptu repair station. Half a dozen engineers were crowded around the display panel of an industrial robot that whirred and vibrated while applying the bright flame of a plasma torch to the treads of one tank.

Saul stared around wildly, desperate at the thought that he'd managed to lose Donohue.

There! Saul recognized Donohue's ID tag bobbing along past a cluster of troopers, almost unnoticeable amongst their vari-coloured UP icons. He hurried past a pair of Black Dogs carrying sonar cannons on their backs, their batteries blaring noisily as the ear-muffed operators ran test checks across the ceiling.

He noticed Donohue was making his way towards a row of cars parked along one wall and hurried after him, closing the distance while casting a quick glance over his shoulder to make sure no one was looking their way.

Saul slammed into Donohue from behind, just as he was pulling the door of a car open. The man grunted under the force of the impact, which sent him flying forward across the driver's seat. He recovered quickly, however, ramming his left elbow back into Saul's ribs, while struggling to pull his gun from its shoulder holster.

Saul brought a knee up hard between the man's thighs, and Donohue slumped forward, wheezing noisily. Saul leaned further inside the car and locked an arm around Donohue's neck, while groping with his other hand until he found the holster, and pressed Donohue's standard-issue Agnessa up against the back of the man's head.

'Slide over, and keep your hands visible,' Saul commanded.

Donohue nodded wordlessly, and moved himself over to the passenger seat. His eyes widened in shock as he turned to face his assailant.

'You son of a bitch,' Donohue hissed. 'If you ever had a chance of getting out of this alive, you just lost it.'

A tide of white-hot anger obscuring his thinking, Saul flicked the gun around to grasp it by the muzzle, then whipped the handle viciously across Donohue's head.

Donohue reeled back in shock, then reached up one trembling hand to feel the blood seeping from his forehead. 'What the *fuck* do you want?' he screeched.

'Shut the fuck up,' Saul snapped, pressing the Agnessa between Donohue's eyes. He groped at the dashboard, opaquing the windows as far as they would go, so as to hide them both from outside scrutiny.

'Why were you following me when I arrived in Sophia?' Saul demanded. 'Were you intending to kill me, like you did Farad Maalouf?'

'You have no idea what you're involved in,' Donohue snarled. 'I told you to get the fuck off Earth, and you ignored me. You got yourself caught up in something you shouldn't have had any part in.'

'Tell me, about Mitchell Stone,' Saul demanded through clenched teeth. 'You told me he was dead, but that's not what I've been hearing. Why bother lying to me?'

'So it's true what I heard,' Donohue snapped back. 'You *did* get your hands on the Tau Ceti files. We'd never have figured that out if you hadn't sent them to your girlfriend over a public network.'

'How the hell can you know about that?'

'You don't have high enough clearance even to ask me that fucking question,' Donohue replied angrily.

'Before you sent me after Hanover, you told me I had a chance of finding out who blew the Galileo link – and that whoever did it was linked to Hsiu-Chuan. Or was all of that just so much bullshit?'

A Black Dog clumped past them, followed by two sonar tanks, only blurrily visible through the opaqued glass. The car trembled under the impact of their passing.

Donohue pulled himself more upright, one corner of his mouth twitching up into the same sneer Saul remembered from Hong

Kong. 'I don't have to tell you,' he said, enunciating the words carefully, 'One. Fucking. Thing.'

Saul shot him in the thigh, taking a chance that the din of surrounding machinery would drown out the sound of the gun firing. Donohue screamed and jerked back against the door, his face turning alabaster white as he grabbed at his wounded leg. He seemed to grow suddenly smaller, his breath hissing in and out in small, tight gasps between his clenched teeth.

Saul leaned in closer, his gun now angled towards Donohue's crotch. 'I just want you to understand exactly how I'm feeling,' he said coldly. 'I've been waiting ten long, *miserable* fucking years just so I can find out if my wife and daughter are even alive. I want to know who did this thing – what person is responsible for putting my life on hold for all this time. So I want *you*, Agent Donohue, to tell me every last fucking thing you know. I've been arrested, held prisoner, tortured, had guns pointed at me, you name it – and if there's one person around here who seems to have a better grasp of whatever the fuck is really going on, it's you.'

'Or what?' Donohue gasped. 'Or you'll kill me?'

Saul shook his head. 'No, I'm a *lot* more imaginative than that. First I'll blow your right arm off.' He gestured with the gun. 'Then the left. Then I'll drill a hole through your balls. Then—'

'All right,' said Donohue. 'All right. Jesus, I'll tell you.'

Saul leaned back and waited, the loup-garou making him feel superhuman, invulnerable.

'It was never really about Galileo,' said Donohue. 'When we sent you after Hanover, I mean. It was just about the shipment.'

'The artefacts from the far future? What exactly were they carrying in that shipment?'

Donohue laughed weakly and rolled his eyes. 'What the hell do you *think* was in that shipment? It was something that triggered the growths, left behind by whatever it was that built the Founder Network. But we got careless.' He winced in pain and shifted slightly. 'Turns out that shipment went to the bottom of the Pacific before it even managed to reach Taiwan.'

'And that's the cause of all this?'

'Looks like it,' said Donohue. His skin had by now taken on a pale and waxen appearance.

'And Galileo?'

'We figured you needed an added incentive to find that shipment.'

Saul fought the urge to place the gun between Donohue's eyes and pull the trigger. 'And Hsiu-Chuan? Where does he come into it?'

'No.' Donohue shook his head, and looked back at Saul with wide, frightened eyes.

Saul pushed the gun barrel against Donohue's uninjured leg. 'Five seconds.'

Panicked, Donohue put out a hand. 'Wait! Okay, all right.' He cleared his throat. 'Hsiu-Chuan was just one link in a very long chain of Sphere politicos that wanted the shipment hijacked.'

'Why did they want it so badly? Because of whatever triggered the growths?'

'No, we didn't have any idea what the artefacts were or what they could do. The Sphere couldn't have known either.'

'But there has to be some reason they wanted that particular shipment. They wouldn't have planned things that carefully just for the hell of it.'

'They got wind of the fact that we had discovered wormhole generators the size of your fist.' Donohue coughed. 'They were right, but they didn't realize it was an alien technology. Maybe they suspected it . . . all I know is, they wound up grabbing the wrong shipment.' Donohue groaned, clutching at his injured leg. 'For Christ's sake, let me go. I need to see a doctor.'

Saul shook his head in astonishment. 'I can't believe this. Billions of people are going to die, all because you people fucked up. Did you ever think it might have been better just to let the Sphere have their own damn wormholes?'

Donohue grunted, baring his teeth from the onslaught of the pain. 'You really think technology like that would have been better in the hands of men like Hsiu-Chuan? Then you're a fucking idiot.'

'Tell me what you know about Hanover. Where does he come into it?'

'We found out that he was taking bribes from organized smuggling gangs on Kepler. We kept him in business on the understanding that he could stay out of jail as long as he funnelled information back to us, but it backfired.'

'Backfired? How?'

'Hsiu-Chuan's people found out he was playing both sides, and threatened to kill his entire family in front of him if he didn't give them what they wanted. That meant access codes, times and places, delivery dates and security hacks. Everything they needed to send a team into Florida, and walk right back out with the shipment.'

'Jesus.' Saul had a mental picture of Donohue running up and down a leaking dam, trying to plug up hundreds of ever-widening cracks. 'You really made a mess of this, didn't you?'

'Listen to me,' rasped Donohue, his voice growing weaker. 'About Mitchell Stone.'

'He's still alive, isn't he?'

'Yes, he is, and whatever you do with me, you need to help us find him. And stop him.'

'Why? What's he got to do with this?'

'We interrogated him. Put him under, and asked him questions. The things he told us, he's . . . he's not even goddamn *human* any more.'

'What?'

'That shipment we sent you to look for?' Donohue coughed. 'There's no reason why the Sphere drone carrying it should have gone out of control the way it did. Those things are near as damn fail-proof. Then we found out that the Sphere lost contact with it at *exactly* the same instant Stone—'

The shot came from nowhere, blowing out the car's front windscreen. Saul ducked instinctively, slamming the accelerator down, without pause for thought. The car surged forward.

More shots followed, and Saul grabbed hold of the steering wheel as it emerged from the dashboard. Donohue scrabbled at him with claw-like fingers, attempting to wrest the wheel from his grasp.

Somewhere amid the din and fury, Saul realized the terrible mistake he had made in not forcing Donohue to remove his contacts. The whole time they'd been talking, rescue had already been on the way.

Troopers scattered as the car hurtled towards them, their outlines shimmering. Donohue wrenched at the wheel and the car side-swiped a Black Dog, ripping the passenger-side door away. Donohue screamed and held on tight, as Saul managed to accelerate away again. Saul let go of the wheel just long enough to raise one leg and boot Donohue hard enough to send him tumbling out of the car.

He then grabbed hold of the wheel again, glancing in the rear-view mirror to see Donohue rolling to a halt behind him. Saul nailed the accelerator to the floor, gunning the vehicle for a ramp down which daylight filtered from above. He twisted the wheel wildly, skirting another Black Dog making its way down the same ramp, and cursing as troopers darted out of his way with only centimetres to spare.

Suddenly, miraculously, he was outside, the early morning sun pale and wan behind clouds. A cordon of tanks and Dogs surrounded the Array directly ahead of him. He kept his foot on the accelerator, swerving past several vehicles heading towards the ramp from the direction of a hopper, then past the armoured cordon and on into the no man's land separating it from the crowds. The car ploughed through a dense tangle of barbed wire before jarring to a sudden halt.

He stumbled out of the vehicle and saw that spiked steel balls, scattered all around, had blown the tires. The crowds of refugees were just metres away, hidden behind a cordon of cars that had been pushed over on to their sides, mirroring the ASI's own defences.

Shots came from there, aimed at the cordon of tanks. Hunching over, Saul ran forward, hoping to lose himself in the mass of people surrounding the Array. The sonar tanks let out an ear-splitting blast and he dropped to his knees, hands clasped to his ears.

Somehow he managed to get up again and keep running, half blinded with pain and unable to hear a damn thing. He squeezed between two torched cars, and seconds later was caught up in a great mob of people desperate to get away from the tanks.

Another sonar blast rolled over him, and he collapsed on to churned black mud and vomited noisily. Barely avoiding getting trampled, he balled himself up, his breath emerging in shuddering gasps as people thronged past him.

It had started to rain, a gentle pattering of it cool against his skin and washing away the blood and sweat. Saul stood up and staggered away, the world so silent in his deafness that it felt as if he were in a dream, yet pushing and stumbling past an endless mass of humanity. Passing a burned-out shopping mall, its windows shattered and its shelves stripped bare, he kept moving until the muted sound of fighting faded with distance.

The rain became torrential, thunder booming out across the Array and its surroundings, so he sought shelter under the corner of a vast tarpaulin that roofed an impromptu chapel, where several hundred worshippers kneeled on the grass to listen to a preacher deliver a sermon from the rear of a flat-bed truck. As he slumped down to the ground, the air was filled with hosannahs, at which point he realized he could hear again.

He waited until he'd recovered his breath, then put in a call to Olivia.

TWENTY-FOUR

Florida Array, 8 February 2235

'Saul? What the hell happened to you? Are you okay?'

'I'm still alive, if that's what you mean,' Saul replied over the link. He had to clamp his hands over his ears to be able to hear Olivia's voice. 'Can't say it wasn't a close call a couple of times.'

'Jesus, Saul, I really thought . . .'

The preacher's voice grew to a roar, full of the promise of damnation. Saul ducked back outside from under the tarpaulin, deciding he'd rather take his chances with the rain, after all.

'I know what you thought. Listen, those files I found at Jeff's cabin? I cracked them. I know what they are now.'

'Saul . . . I'm in Arizona, with Jeff.' She paused. 'And Mitchell.'

He stopped dead in his progress. 'You're fucking kidding me? Do you have any idea what he was hiding round the back of that damn cabin?'

Her words came in a nervous rush. 'Yes, he told me everything. About the growths, Mitchell, the Founders – all that, and a million and one other things. But he doesn't have a copy of the files himself. He's going to need them. We all are.'

Saul started moving again. 'I've seen classified videos,' he said, aware of the hysteria lurking at the bottom of his throat, 'and I've read documents all telling me how the world is coming to an end. I'm even scared to let myself think about it too much, in case I go crazy.'

'Are you *sure* you're okay?'

'I don't know, Olivia. How the hell *should* I be?'

'I don't know either,' she replied, her voice choking on tears. 'I wish I did.'

Goddamn her. A part of him still wanted to hold her in his arms. He thought of Jeff, and felt a simmering resentment that he thought he'd outgrown long ago.

'Look, I can send a copy of the files over to you right now.'

'No, *don't* do that. I found out they've got routines built into them that give away your location if they're transmitted over any kind of network.'

Saul groaned, remembering that Donohue had told him much the same thing. 'I sent them to you,' Saul reminded her, 'when they were still encrypted.'

'Then it's a good thing I didn't stay at home, where I could be found.'

'Fine, so what exactly does Jeff want to do with the files?'

'Broadcast them,' she replied. 'People need to know what's really going on, especially out there in the colonies. By the time the news starts spreading, we'll be on our way to somewhere safe, and then it won't matter if those people who tried to kill Jeff figure out where we are.'

'Why Arizona?'

'We're at the Launch Pad facility,' she said. 'With the same people that took you and Mitchell up on your sub-orbital jump, remember?'

He had a sudden mental flash of sleek black VASIMRs extending in ranks across the desert sands. 'Like I could ever forget. But why are you there?'

'Because they also run flights to the Moon, old-style Moon launches for people rich enough to afford it. It takes about three days to Copernicus City, the hard way – especially if you want to avoid passing through the Florida Array, for any reason.'

He realized, with a start, what she was telling him. 'You're seriously telling me you're going to *fly* to the Moon?'

'Strictly speaking, it's only Mitchell that's flying there.'

The rain started to ease off. 'But what about you and Jeff? How are *you* getting there?'

He heard her sigh. 'I'm not going to the Moon,' she explained, 'and neither is Jeff.'

'I don't understand.'

Saul listened as Olivia told him their plans to head for the Jupiter orbital platform.

'You're crazy,' he said, once she had finished. 'The research platforms weren't designed to sustain independent populations. They need constant gate contact with Earth to function, as it is. And even if you could find some way to survive indefinitely, you'd be cut off from everything you've ever known.'

'And, out in the colonies, we wouldn't be?'

At least on some of the colonies you'd have open air to breathe, he thought.

Saul's feet were getting numb from all the walking. He came across an army truck, with trampled bodies scattered all around, and pressed both hands over his mouth and nose, to avoid inhaling the dreadful stench of decomposition. He next made towards a maintenance shed, in hopes of finding a car that hadn't been trashed or burned out.

'What about Galileo?' he asked, once he'd left the foul-smelling truck behind. 'There's nothing to stop you and Jeff both going there, and Mitchell too.'

'The new wormhole gate won't reach orbit around Galileo for months.'

'Doesn't matter. There are enough emergency supplies on board that starship carrying the gate to keep several people alive for months, maybe longer.'

'No,' her voice was adamant, 'I've talked this over with Jeff. I know you think we're crazy, but we spent a good chunk of our lives on the Jupiter station, and the people there need us.'

'I . . . guess I understand.'

'For you it's easy. You can just head through to the Lunar Array and make your way to the Galileo gate.'

He laughed bitterly. 'Not any more. There are people out looking for me here.'

'What happened?'

'It's a long story, but if they find me or if I try and get back inside the Array, I'm a dead man. But if I can reach the Lunar Array some other way, I have a fighting chance of getting through.'

'Then that's it. You need to come to Arizona, and ride up with Mitchell.'

'That's doable, is it?'

'Christ, Saul, of *course* it is.'

'That's great,' he said, feeling enormously relieved. No, more than relieved; it was a real chance at survival. 'But before we talk about getting those files to you, or anything else, there's something important we need to talk about – something seriously fucking important. One of Jeff's video files showed Copernicus City in ruins, sometime in the future. The entire city was devastated, like a meteor had hit it. That *must* have been caused by whatever it is that's caused the growths back down here.'

'I guess,' said Olivia, hesitantly.

'But how could it – whatever *it* is – get there except through the Array? And if it can come through the wormhole gate all the way from Florida, then who's to say it couldn't spread through the rest of the gates, to the colonies as well?'

'But . . . surely the gates will all have been shut down before that can happen?'

'Which is exactly what I assumed,' Saul replied. 'But then I got to wondering why they hadn't closed down the Florida gate *before* Copernicus was destroyed? If the footage I saw is anything to go by, the Lunar Array is going to be reduced to a ruin – but there's no way of telling whether the gates themselves will be shut down before it's too late.'

'You think it's possible they won't be?'

'What I think is that, if they're going to shut anything down at all, it would have to be the Florida gate. That way they can still save Copernicus City and keep a foothold not just on the Moon, but also our solar system. But since we know they won't manage to shut it down, that tells me something went wrong – and maybe they didn't manage to shut down *any* of the Copernicus gates. Whatever happens to us,' he said, 'nothing is more important than making sure the worst scenario doesn't happen. If it does, the colonies are finished, and the human race along with them.'

'So what exactly is it you want to do?'

Saul looked around, suddenly and irrationally worried that someone nearby might overhear what he was about to say, and cry out in accusation.

'I'm saying we ourselves need to destroy the gates at the soonest opportunity. Right now, if possible.'

He waited for what felt like a long time before she finally replied.

'You can't be serious,' she said finally.

'I'm entirely serious. Just think about the tens of millions out in the colonies who'll wind up dead if we don't do this. We're talking survival of the species here, Olivia.'

'We could still save some people—'

'No.' He shook his head violently. 'At most you'd save a few thousand, if even that. There are billions more who are going to wind up dead, either way.'

When she spoke again, her voice sounded neutral, carefully controlled. 'And how exactly do you intend to do this?'

'We can use the Emergency Destruct Protocols to collapse the wormholes.'

'Wouldn't work,' she replied immediately.

'Why not?'

'You need a minimum of two people, to activate the codes simultaneously, or it won't work, and it's not like they hand those codes out to just anyone who asks for them. You'd need special clearance from an executive committee, and I don't think that's going to happen any time soon.'

Saul thought for a moment. 'Fair point. In that case, who does possess that kind of clearance?'

'Not many people, for a start,' she replied. 'I'd guess a few dozen at most.'

'Then maybe we need to try and find some of them. We need to track them down.'

'Jesus.' She laughed. 'You really think it's going to be that easy?'

'No, I don't,' he replied. 'That's the one thing I don't think. But I don't know what else I can do.'

'I'm not sure I should even consider helping you do this,' she said, with a touch of outrage in her voice.

Saul punched the air in frustration, barely able to contain his anger. '*Listen* to me, goddammit. I've been through hell ever since you came asking me for help, so unless there's some genuine flaw in my logic, some reason *why* we shouldn't do exactly what I just described, I can't see why the hell you wouldn't want to help me.'

'All those people—'

'Are never going to make it into the Array alive,' he said. 'Believe me, I'm here right in the thick of it, and nobody's going in who isn't being allowed in. The whole place is surrounded by soldiers, tanks and drones, and I've already seen more dead bodies than most people get to see in a lifetime. It's a war zone, Olivia. No other word for it.'

Another trumpet-like blast from the sonar tanks a way off in the distance briefly drowned out the clamour of the crowds.

'Do you realize what I'd have to do to find out who has that kind of clearance?' she said. 'You're asking me to hack into the ASI's own databases.'

'To which,' he reminded her, 'you have privileged access as an ASI employee yourself.'

'That makes no difference. It'd set off a trail of security alerts leading straight back to me.'

'I think we're long past the point where we need to worry about stuff like that. There are much more important things to consider than what happens to either of us, Olivia.'

'Okay, okay,' she said, sounding defeated. 'But I don't know how long it's going to take me to locate that kind of information, even assuming that I *can* find it.'

'All I'm asking is that you try.'

'You really do sound like a callous son of a bitch, you know that? Between you and Mitchell, I don't know which one of you has changed the most.'

Saul stiffened as he remembered Donohue's unfinished warning. 'What about Mitchell? How has *he* changed?'

She made an exasperated sound. 'Why?'

'Just humour me.'

'Nothing I can really put a finger on, okay?'

'Please,' he said, 'just try.'

'There's just something about the look on his face that sends chills through me. I don't know how else to describe it. Maybe that's because I know what happened to him. Anyway, why? Is it important?'

'I don't know,' Saul replied. 'Go and find out what you can, and get back to me straight away. We can talk about Mitchell later.'

They spoke for another minute or two, but there was a new brittle quality to Olivia's voice, as if she no longer quite trusted him. The rain eased off as their call ended, the sun finally breaking through the clouds. Thousands of faces were now turned upwards, while Saul himself leaned, exhausted and weary, against a roadside bollard.

People, he'd already noticed, were giving him a wide berth. He could imagine what he must look like, drenched in blood, mud and sweat. What would they all think, he wondered, if they realized he was trying to take away the one shred of hope they were all desperately clinging to?

Don't think about that, he urged himself, all too aware of just how easy it would be to sink into a bottomless feeling of malaise. He had to keep moving, figure the rest out as he went along. He was never going to get to Arizona without putting serious distance between himself and the Array, and that meant a lot more walking unless he could find some form of transport. At the very least that would keep him busy while he waited to hear back from Olivia.

Hauling himself upright, he started walking again, wondering where the hell he was going to lay hands on some food. He was still running on adrenalin after his encounter with Donohue, but at some point soon he was going to have to eat.

As it turned out, he waited only a few minutes before Olivia got back to him.

'Send me your coordinates,' she told him briskly. 'I need to know exactly where you are right now.'

Saul did as requested. 'It's going to be a lot harder than I thought to get out of here,' he told her. 'Every car I come across is either burned out or a total wreck. But I can see what looks like a medical drop zone just south of here, with manned choppers landing and taking off. There might be some chance of swinging a flight back to Orlando, or to somewhere else I can get to Arizona from.'

'Stay put for now,' she advised. 'I've got hold of the names of some senior staff who're cleared to carry EDP codes.'

'I'm impressed,' he remarked sincerely.

'What can I say, I'm resourceful. But under any other circumstances I'd be facing about six life sentences right now. Is that impressive enough for you?'

'I guess it is. So, who's on your list?'

'Turns out one of the people you want is holed up in a hotel near the Array. Place called the Dorican. You know it?'

Saul stared over at a row of hotels a couple of kilometres beyond the medical drop zone. 'I see it. What's his name?'

'Constantin Hanover.'

Saul laughed. 'You're shitting me.'

'You know him?'

'You could say that. I wonder what he's doing there?'

'Go ask him yourself. Maybe he's waiting to be evacuated. Saul, just to be clear on one thing. I don't know that he actually has the codes you need, only that he's authorized to carry them. And, even then, I don't know how the hell you're going to persuade him to reveal them to you.'

'I guess I'll have to rely on my natural charm and powers of persuasion.'

'Now I really feel sorry for him. How long before you can make it here to Arizona, do you think?'

'No idea.' Saul stared at the drop zone with longing. 'But it's going to have to wait until I've spoken to Hanover.'

'Fine.' He heard her sigh. 'They're going to try and hold off one of the launches until you get here, but there's only so long they'll be prepared to wait.'

'I understand.'

'Good luck, Saul. But, before you go, I want to ask you something.'

'Fire away.'

'What made you ask about Mitchell?'

Saul started walking towards the group of hotels. 'A man named Donohue was trying to tell me something about him.'

'Tell you what?'

'That's the thing, I don't know. We got interrupted before he could finish.'

'This isn't making a great deal of sense,' she said.

'Right before you tracked me down at Harry's, I was helping to track down an ASI shipment hijacked out of Florida. According to Donohue, it was loaded with Founder artefacts, but it wound up sinking to the bottom of the Pacific at the exact same location the first of the growths appeared.'

'I remember hearing about a hijack on the news, but I'd no idea they were in any way connected.'

'Nobody did, at least not then. But I think Donohue was trying to tell me that the plane going down, when it did, was connected with Mitchell in some way. What that connection might be, I can't even begin to guess.'

'But you think there's something in that?'

'After the past couple of days, Olivia, I'm prepared to believe pretty much anything.' He hesitated. 'This means I'm going to need to ask you for at least one thing more.'

'What exactly?'

'That's kind of hard to define,' he admitted. 'I thought if there was anything significant, then maybe it would be buried in the ASI's own databases.'

'You're asking me to break into their records *again*?'

'If you can.'

'I could end up attracting a lot of unwanted attention if I keep doing things like this, you know that, right?'

'Even if they realize what you're up to, they're not going to come after you, not this late in the day. All their resources seem to be going towards protecting the Array.'

'I hope to hell you're right,' she grumbled. 'There's nothing else you can give me to go on before I go looking?'

'I'm afraid not. I don't know the exact time the shipment disappeared off the radar, or the precise coordinates, but I'm hoping that it might not be restricted data. Maybe you won't risk setting off so many alarms this time.'

'You were lucky this man Hanover turned out to be so close at hand,' she said. 'But I don't even know what I'm supposed to be looking for this time.' She paused. 'Unless you think I should just go find Mitchell and *ask* him?'

Saul thought of that video footage he'd seen of Mitchell's suit disintegrating in some vast alien vault, then of him being lifted naked on to a stretcher. He remembered the medical reports he'd read suggesting that Mitchell had died and come back to life.

'No,' he said firmly. 'Don't do that. Just see what you can find out, if anything.'

He stared over towards the Dorican, wondering if he might be better off not knowing just what it was Donohue had been trying to tell him earlier.

TWENTY-FIVE

Off the coast of Guam, 8 February 2235

By sheer good fortune, their ferry departed Tumon Bay on the afternoon of the 6th, just hours before a bad storm struck the west coast of Guam, setting the sky above the island ablaze with a lightning storm the likes of which Thomas Fowler had never seen. There was something about the sight that inspired a near-religious terror in his heart, as if he were witnessing the retribution of an angry god. He stood at the starboard rail alongside Amanda and the rest of the passengers, watching this eerie display until the coast faded to a thin smear of green sandwiched between ocean and sky. He overheard someone saying that the same lightning was now wreaking havoc on Yona and Mangilao on the island's east coast, both setting towns ablaze and killing dozens unlucky enough to be caught outside when it struck.

As she pressed closer against him, he slid one hand around Amanda's waist. 'Have you seen the rust on the hydrofoils?' she asked, gesturing over the rail towards the foaming waters below. 'And the hull's so patched-up, it doesn't look like it could survive a squall, let alone a thunderstorm.'

'It'll make it,' he said confidently, glancing back at the brightly lit windows of the restaurant deck, as rain began to patter down. Above the restaurant entrance, some of the crew had strung a banner that read 'END OF THE WORLD CRUISE', the letters hand-painted in bright rainbow colours. 'Maybe we should head inside.'

They found the restaurant mostly deserted but for a small group of men and women huddled around a lengthy table, playing cards. These were the geophysicists from Tokyo University, whom they'd met on arriving in Guam, and one of them now waved at them to come over.

'Jason,' remarked Fowler, approaching the table, 'you're up pretty late.'

'Never too late for gambling,' replied Jason, tapping a spread of cards lying face down on the table before him. 'Care to join us?'

'Thanks, but not this time.' Fowler took a seat along with Amanda. 'We won't be sticking around for long. It's been a long enough night as it is.'

Jason turned towards him, resting one elbow on the back of Fowler's chair, the Minnesota University t-shirt stretched taut over his not inconsiderable belly. 'Some show, huh? Tesla would have been proud of it.'

'Tesla?' asked Amanda.

'He means Tesla's earthquake machine,' said an older Japanese man, his accent by way of Southern California. 'Resonant frequency, that kind of thing. He reckons those growths are going to shake the world to bits, and that tonight's lightning storm is the prelude.'

Some of the others around the table chuckled at this suggestion, then carried on with their own separate conversations.

'Just because it sounds crazy doesn't mean it can't be true,' Jason huffed.

'I heard someone say the growths were disrupting the normal flow of magma deep beneath the crust,' said Fowler, recalling one pet theory that had circulated amongst his own scientific staff. 'Something like that would be more than enough to trigger the kind of seismic activity we've been seeing.'

A middle-aged man, with dark features, laid down his cards and sighed. 'I will tell you exactly what is happening,' he said. 'The slate is being wiped clean.'

'Then you're a bigger nut than Jase is, Nick,' someone else pointed out.

'If anyone – or any*thing* – really wanted to destroy our world,' Nick continued, 'there are far, far easier ways to go about it. Like triggering a solar flare, or dropping a black hole into the Earth's core.' He gestured towards the north-west, in the same direction they were sailing. 'It seems to me that whatever created those things out in the ocean, their intention was clearly *not* to destroy our world.'

'Then what do they want?' asked Amanda, clearly fascinated.

The man called Nick smiled, placing his cards face-down on the table. 'I can only hazard a guess, I fear. Perhaps the growths are a means of sterilizing this world in preparation for implanting an entirely alien flora and fauna for the benefit of forthcoming invaders. Or perhaps the reason is something entirely alien and unimaginable to us. What is clear, however,' he continued, fixing his gaze on Fowler, 'is that they could only have found their way here through the Array.'

Fowler felt Amanda's hand reach out to take hold of his own under the table. 'That's hardly an original observation,' he replied.

Nick smiled. 'Imagine, if you would, that out there amongst the stars, we found something that we did not understand. Perhaps we would study it carefully, even bring it back here to Earth for closer scrutiny. Does that not seem like a reasonable conjecture?'

'Sure, if you subscribe to the kind of news feed that runs items about two-headed babies and biblical visions,' Fowler replied, doing his best to ignore the fear clutching at his heart. All the same, his comment elicited a few smiles from the rest of the table.

'Oh man, conspiracy theories,' said Jason. 'I *love* conspiracy theories.'

'What is irrefutable, to my mind,' Nick continued, a glint of malice now evident in his gaze, 'is that we are currently witness to the greatest act of murder in history. I mean the murder of an entire planet and its civilization.'

Amanda's grip on Fowler's hand became so tight that it hurt.

'You really think someone *caused* all this?' Fowler replied.

'An act of negligence, perhaps, if not outright murder, but the result is the same.'

'I think Jason was right,' said Fowler. 'I've heard a hundred conspiracy theories just like that one in the past week.'

The table had by now become quite silent.

'Perhaps,' said Nick, conceding the other man's point. 'And yet I have found myself encountering the most remarkable people on this voyage. Some, I suspect, are far better informed than one might reasonably expect.'

'I'm sorry,' said Amanda, 'but I didn't catch your last name.'

'That is because I did not offer it,' Nick replied evenly.

'If you'll excuse us, we have to go,' she said, suddenly standing up and tugging at Fowler's arm. 'Like we said, it's been a long night for all of us.'

'Of course,' said Nick, his smile tightening across his teeth. 'I wish you a good night.'

'He recognized you,' she whispered as they hurried back to their cabin. 'I don't know who he is, but he sure as hell knows who *you* are.'

'Can you place him? Was he working anywhere on the Tau Ceti station?'

'I really don't think so. There's very few of the staff we didn't account for during the clean-up process, and he's not one of them. But the way he was looking at us . . .' She shuddered despite the tropical heat. 'He knows, Thomas, I feel sure of it.'

'It's not like it takes a great leap of logic to figure out that the growths might be the result of some error of human judgement. It's unlikely he was making any *personal* reference to either of us.'

'No,' she said, 'stop trying to rationalize this! I could see it in his face, the way he was looking at you. It's not just that he knows about the Founders: he also knows who you are.'

They came to the door of their cabin, and Fowler put a reassuring hand on her shoulder. 'Even if that turned out to be the case, it's much too late to worry about it now. We already know what's in our future.'

'But how sure are you, really, that it's set in stone?'

He hesitated, but only for a moment. 'Sure enough to believe that what I saw in that video is bound to come to pass, whatever else happens in the meantime.'

They were woken during the night by angry shouting, followed by gunfire. Fowler pressed his ear to the cabin door, unwilling to risk stepping out into the corridor and wishing he had thought to arm himself. When first light came, he summoned up the courage to venture out on his own and learned, from a member of the crew, that a few of the more belligerent passengers, who had apparently come on board armed with sports rifles, had demanded the ferry make a detour towards a pod of whales sighted several kilometres to the east. The captain's blank refusal had led to an argument, and the argument – largely fuelled by alcohol – had led to a violent altercation, leaving two of the passengers dead and another seriously injured. Their sleep after that was restless, and Fowler dreamed of bone-white flowers growing from blood-red seas.

The Pacific growth – the first one of all to come into existence – became visible on the horizon the following afternoon. It looked to Fowler like something that Magritte might have imagined: a silver and gold behemoth resembling a flower only in the most abstract terms, and self-constructed on a scale that defied all logic. The senses rebelled at the sight of it when seen directly, and he felt the same tight knot of primitive terror deep in his chest that he'd experienced on first seeing the news footage of this same growth.

Once again they gathered by the rail with the rest of the passengers, steadying themselves cautiously as the ferry rose and dipped with the waves. The growth was still sufficiently distant for the lowest part of its base to be hidden below the curve of the horizon, and yet the complex structures sprouting from its massive stem, like tangled nests of leaves, were clearly visible even at so great a distance. So was a haze of barely discernible black dots and curious twists of light that clouded its upper half.

'Do you think he was right?' Fowler asked, tasting salt as waves broke against the hull. 'That man last night, I mean – in what he said about the slate being wiped clean.'

Amanda laughed and shook her head. 'Nick? I think he's watched too many bad TriView shows. No, it's probably something much more prosaic than that.'

'Like what?'

'A construction tool,' she suggested. 'An earth-digging machine that a bunch of ants accidentally figured out how to switch on, and now it's rolling over their own anthill. That would be about the size of it.'

'He was right about one thing: there are easier ways to wipe us out.'

'What you said about the earthquakes. Do we know if that's the case?'

'Think about the amount of energy the growths must need to reach such an enormous size in so little time.' A big wave smashed into the ferry, and they staggered slightly as the deck tilted first one way, then the other. 'The leaves are for gathering solar energy, but I reckon that wouldn't give them a fraction of the total power they'd need. Geothermal power is a fast way to get the rest of that energy, so they drill deep into the crust, or maybe even further.'

'And the atmospheric phenomena we're seeing? What about that?'

'I don't know,' he admitted. 'But I don't think Tesla's got much to do with it.'

'I'm still glad we came here, you know,' she said. 'Somehow seeing it like this – actually *being* here – makes all the difference.'

'You think we're getting what we deserve by being here?'

She looked at him. 'Don't you?'

He shook his head. 'I think we were just unlucky. Curiosity defines us. It's what makes us human. There's no way you could explore something like the Founder Network and not expect to get your fingers burned.' He pulled her closer and nodded up at the sky. 'Out there, we'll survive . . . or other people will, at any rate.'

A message was broadcast over the ferry's tannoy system before Amanda could form a reply. The captain proposed taking a vote on whether to sail the ferry to within a kilometre of the growth's base, and the result of the vote would be announced the following morning.

Fowler felt overcome by a mixture of excitement and terror as he listened. That single glimpse, in a fragmentary video, of Amanda standing on the deck of this very same ferry, had given him the sense of fulfilling some kind of personal destiny just by being here. The end was close, but at least it was an end they had chosen together, and of their own free will. From this point on, there could be no surprises.

Quite soon they retired once more for the night, waking frequently to the sounds of shattering glass or loud music emanating from the deck, then later to screams and moans coming from the cabins adjacent to their own. They both woke early, to find the sun still boiling its way up over the horizon, and stepping over snoring bodies and the remains of smashed wine bottles as they made their way to the restaurant deck. It proved to be deserted, except for the man called Nick, who stood by the railing, looking out to sea. He turned and nodded to them as they approached, almost as if he'd been waiting for them.

'Mr Fowler,' he said. 'I've been up all night thinking about you.'

Fowler managed to hide his shock. They'd used false identities this far, after all. He glanced sideways at Amanda and saw the look of silent fury on her face. But, instead of feeling angry or afraid, he himself felt only a sense of calm inevitability.

'I wondered if you recognized me,' he said, stepping outside again to join him.

The man called Nick leaned once more against the railing, this time with his back to the sea. He shrugged. 'At first I wasn't sure, but then I did a little research in the feed archives, to be certain. So . . . are you here with us to save the day? Or is that just too much to hope for?'

'Would that I were. Do the rest of your friends know who I am?'

'Why?' The scientist laughed. 'Are you afraid of what they might think of you?'

'I wasn't aware I had committed any crime,' Fowler replied levelly.

'Merely a crime of hubris, perhaps,' said Nick. 'I know about the Founder Network, Mr Fowler. I even have a good idea how all of this came about.'

Amanda caught Thomas's eye as she stepped up beside him, glancing pointedly first at the rail against which the scientist leaned, and then at the empty restaurant behind them. He guessed what she was thinking: there would be no witnesses if they could manage to tip the man over the railing.

He squeezed her hand and shook his head fractionally. What was the point of killing this man, when their own lives were now numbered merely in days, if not hours?

'We don't know who *you* are,' she then said to the scientist, her voice low and almost menacing. 'Did you follow us here? Is that why you're on this ferry?'

He shook his head. 'Not at all; serendipity, nothing more. This trip was my one chance to see direct evidence of the things that took my brother away from me. After I recognized you at the airfield in Guam, I managed to persuade my colleagues that we should board this same ferry. I needed to be sure, you see.'

Fowler frowned. 'Your brother?'

'My name is Nicolas Rodriguez,' he said. 'My brother's name was David.'

Fowler saw Amanda's eyes widen, her complexion turning even paler than usual.

'You know that name, David Rodriguez?' Fowler asked her. There was something familiar about it.

She nodded. 'One of the early casualties from Site 17. He got caught in a . . . in a temporal anomaly, I guess you'd call it.'

Fowler nodded, something cold and indigestible settling into the pit of his stomach as he finally remembered the unpleasant details of the incident.

'I'm sorry about your brother,' he told Nick. 'I wish there was something we could have done for him.'

Nicolas Rodriguez shook his head like he was disappointed. 'It took a long time, and a fortune in bribes, to learn the truth. I envy him for the things he must have seen. But you told us lies about him, and our mother died believing he was killed in some routine laboratory accident. Imagine how I felt when I discovered he was caught up in some miserable form of limbo between life and death. I clung to the hope that my informants were wrong, and I had been fed just some ridiculous fantasy.'

He glanced over his shoulder towards the growth, which was now towering overhead. 'Then I began to understand that I had not, after all, wasted my family's fortune on bribes. I kept digging for more information. I learned that you were one of those responsible for the research programme of which my brother was part. Now, it seems, we are all to be exterminated like cockroaches scuttling in a drain.'

'So now you know who we are,' said Fowler, 'but there's no reason to blame us for what happened to your brother.'

'On the contrary,' Rodriguez replied, staring directly at Amanda. 'What happened to him was no accident, was it? And I recognized you in particular, Miss Boruzov.'

Fowler glanced between them in puzzlement. 'What are you talking about?' he demanded.

'I suppose it doesn't matter now,' said Amanda, her eyes fixed firmly on Rodriguez. 'His brother was smuggling high-security data back home. We . . . decided to arrange an accident to neutralize him.'

'And is that how you choose to deal with your brightest and best?' demanded Rodriguez. 'Better that you'd simply put a bullet in his brain than allow him to suffer this . . . this living death.'

'He has no idea that he's caught in a temporal field,' Amanda insisted. 'His subjective experience of time ensures he isn't even aware that anything's wrong. You could hardly call it a "living death".'

'Perhaps,' Rodriguez replied grimly, 'that is something we should leave for others to decide.'

'Others?' echoed Amanda.

'My colleagues,' Rodriguez explained. 'I eventually told them of my suspicions last night. Then we went to the captain, who will give you more of a chance than you allowed my brother. We will select a jury, and let them decide what should be done with you.'

Amanda burst out laughing. 'That's absolutely ridiculous! We're all going to be dead in a few days anyway. What difference can it possibly make?'

'So it's true?' Rodriguez countered. 'Those things sprouting everywhere from our planet *will* destroy us?'

Amanda opened and closed her mouth, then turned away to stare fixedly out to sea.

Rodriguez eyed her for a moment, then turned back to Fowler with a look of satisfaction. 'We seek closure, you see. I, for one, desire closure. I want to see you made an example of – in front of God, if no one else.'

Amanda swung back round, her face twisted in fury. 'This is insane,' she spat. 'We're not responsible for that . . . thing out there. We did everything we could to stop it.'

'No,' intervened Fowler, putting a restraining hand on her shoulder. 'Listen to me, Nick. We came here ourselves because we know we share at least some responsibility for what's happening. We're not running away, like so many others, and you *must* take that into account.'

'Then let us find out the truth.'

Fowler now became aware they were no longer alone. He looked to one side and saw three of Rodriguez's colleagues had joined them on the restaurant deck, in the company of two crew members who were conspicuously armed. He noted, with an unpleasant churning in his stomach, that one of the latter had a length of rope slung over one arm.

'Wait,' said Amanda. 'Please, before anything else, there's something we have to do.'

'What?' asked Rodriguez impatiently.

Fowler saw Amanda swallow hard. 'We need to make a recording. I swear it won't take long.'

Rodriguez's eyes narrowed with suspicion.

'Please,' Fowler beseeched him. 'Think of it as a last request, if you prefer.'

Rodriguez's nostrils flared briefly, then nodded assent with a brief jerk of his head.

Fowler stepped away from the rail, and set his contacts to record and upload the proceedings to a secure server he'd long since prepared. The video would then be stored, along with a cache of other files, in half a dozen separate orbital satellites that would remain untouched by the growths.

He panned up the entire height of the original growth, looming nearby, to where it disappeared into the clouds. The memory of previously watching these same images now collided with the experience of creating them for the first time, every action and thought so thoroughly locked in place that even the desire to break free of the cycle of predetermination was, he saw now, predetermined.

He panned back down, until he had Amanda encompassed in his gaze, her pale and beautiful features marred by worry and fear of what the next few hours held. But before he could do anything more than grab a fleeting recording of her, rough hands grabbed him from behind, dragging him towards the bridge and a fate that seemed as certain as anything else that had come tumbling down from the future into the present.

TWENTY-SIX

By the time Saul reached the Dorican, it was clear that the hotel had been caught at the centre of a riot. A fire truck had been rammed through the polished glass and plate steel of the hotel's entrance, and what at first appeared to be bundles of rags turned out to be huddled corpses afloat on a sea of debris and torn-up carpeting.

He headed across the lobby, his stomach reduced to a tight knot of hunger and his feet a spider-web of painful blisters. He wondered if he was foolhardy to hope that Hanover might still be there, but just then he spotted the man himself sitting on a sofa at the far side of the lobby. He was facing away from Saul, towards a pair of sliding glass doors through which the Array was clearly visible in the distance.

Hanover looked up with a start as Saul approached him, glass crunching under his feet, then nodded almost as if he'd been expecting him. There was a raincoat draped across his lap, as if in readiness to go somewhere.

'I suppose you've come to finish the job,' he said, as Saul halted before him.

'You mean kill you? Why would I do that?'

'Good question,' Hanover replied. 'Because it would be pretty pointless under present circumstances, don't you think?'

'Why are you still here?' Saul nodded towards the Array. 'I'd have thought you'd have fled with all the rest of them by now.'

'Hardly.' Hanover laughed. 'Who sent you? Donohue? Or did Fowler decide to get his hands dirty for once?'

Saul shook his head. 'Neither. I think it's fair to say I don't work for the ASI any more.'

'Really?' Hanover regarded him with mild surprise. 'So what did *you* do to piss them off?'

Saul thought about it for a moment. 'I asked too many questions.'

Hanover nodded. 'Never a good career move. So if you're not here to kill me, what in God's name are you doing here?'

'I've learned quite a few things since Taiwan. I've seen video footage of Copernicus City recorded from a few years into the future, and it offers pretty conclusive evidence that whatever's going to wipe out life here on Earth is going to do the same up there. And the only way it could have got there that I know of is through the Florida Array.'

Hanover nodded. 'That's the general consensus. So what's your point?'

'If it can reach the Moon from here, what's to stop it getting all the way to the colonies as well? The only way to stop that happening is to shut down the entire Lunar Array. I might just have a chance of doing that, if I can get hold of a set of EDP codes.'

'What makes you think just such an eventuality hasn't already been carefully planned for?'

'Has it?'

'Of course it has,' Hanover barked irritably.

'Then what the hell happened to Copernicus City, in those videos from the future?' Saul demanded. 'If they couldn't shut down the Florida–Copernicus gate in time, how can you be sure they'll manage to shut down any of the rest?'

Hanover let the raincoat slide off his lap, revealing the Agnessa concealed beneath. His fingers were already gripping the trigger mechanism.

'Tell me,' asked Hanover, 'why do *you* feel you have to be the one to do this?'

Saul took a step back, his eyes fixed on the gun. 'Because somebody has to.'

'You're talking about an act of gross terrorism. Do you really want to be responsible for something as serious as that?'

Saul ran his tongue around a dehydrated mouth. 'I've thought this through, every which way. I've explained my reasoning to you. What would *you* do?'

Hanover shook his head. 'What would *I* do? I don't exactly have a golden track record for making the correct decisions, son, so if you really want advice, you're better off getting it from someone else.'

Saul tried a different tack. 'If I don't do this, the colonies are finished – and the whole human race along with them. Surely you can understand the logic in what I'm saying?'

Hanover nodded fractionally, his eyes turning down towards the gun in his hand. 'I suppose I can,' he replied, so faintly that Saul struggled to hear him.

'So you'll give me the codes?'

Hanover aimed the Agnessa towards Saul. 'I know a few things about you, Dumont. I've read your psych-eval, and you're loaded to the gills with resentment and self-pity, not to mention a barrel-load of self-destructive tendencies. If it were up to me, you'd have been kicked out of the ASI a long time ago. Maybe you've gotten it into your head that you can become a big hero, and kick your former employers in the balls at the same time.'

Saul felt his face grow hot. 'You're saying my motivation is suspect. Fine, shoot me then. Put me out of my fucking misery. What the hell do *you* owe them, anyway?'

Hanover stared at him silently for a good twenty seconds, then lowered the gun back towards his lap.

'Fuck it,' he said, 'maybe you're right. Besides, I don't have enough bullets in this gun for you as well, even if I did decide to shoot you.'

Saul frowned. 'I don't understand.'

Hanover raised his eyes towards the ceiling. 'My family are

upstairs. Cassie and both the kids, that makes four of us. There isn't a fifth bullet for you.'

Saul felt a hollow sensation in his gut. 'You're going to kill them?'

Hanover smiled bitterly. 'They're not allowed passage through the Array. *I* am, but not them. That's my punishment, apparently. If they'd killed me, or ordered me to stay behind, I could have accepted that after everything that's happened, but . . .' He shook his head and began to weep. 'But this is cruel.'

'I'm sorry,' said Saul. Somehow the words seemed far from adequate.

'I don't know how long it's going to take – if it's going to be sudden or slow, painful or just like going to sleep. Do you understand me?'

Saul shook his head. 'Not really.'

'We don't know what's going to happen,' Hanover rasped. 'All we know is that everything's going to end. The *means* aren't clear.'

The Agnessa slipped from Hanover's grasp, and clattered to the floor next to him.

'Here,' he said, and a moment later, Saul's contacts flagged him regarding the arrival of a string of letters and numbers.

'What's this?' he demanded.

'An access code,' replied Hanover. 'You need to head straight for the ASI offices up in the Lunar Array. Soon as you're in range of the localized security network, activate it. It'll log you into a restricted network, and guide you to where you can get a keycard that'll trigger the entire process.'

'And that's it?'

'More or less. There's a terminal room from where you can use the keycards to then trigger a manual shutdown. Its exact location's kept secret from everyone but the director of the ASI, but assuming the restricted network accepts your authorization, it'll guide you there as well.'

'And then?'

'And then, assuming you're operating under normal circumstances, there'll need to be two of you, with separate authorization and one keycard each, before the system will respond. You have to activate two separate terminals at exactly the same time, or nothing will happen.'

'There's no way to trigger the process remotely?'

'Of course not. The security risk would be preposterous.'

'Then just the one access code isn't any use, unless I'm sure of someone being there to help me. Is there any way I can get hold of another?'

'I said "under normal circumstances",' Hanover replied. 'There are measures, however, in case only the one person is available.'

'What kind of measures?'

Hanover leaned forward. 'Both ends of the Copernicus–Florida gate are linked to shielded servers that maintain constant radio contact with each other. If the servers at either end of a wormhole gate stop transmitting, for any reason, it triggers a major security alert.'

He sat back. 'Now say, for whatever reason, there's only one person in a position to respond to that alert; maybe because there's been an attack, or – and this is why they set things up this way in the first place – because something alien and vicious, something completely unknown, has come through one of the colony gates. That puts all the rest of the gates in equal danger. What they don't tell you is that it's possible to simultaneously shut down not just one wormhole gate – but *all* of them.'

'Why have I never heard about this before?'

'Because it's such very dangerous knowledge,' Hanover replied. 'It's the kind of thing you really don't want your enemies knowing. Or most of our friends, for that matter. If there isn't an immediate response to the security alert – within, say, half an hour – the two-man rule is automatically rescinded and just the one person can trigger a gate shutdown. Are you following me?'

'That's what happened to the Galileo gate, isn't it?' asked Saul. 'You were in charge of the investigation, and you were the one who dismissed the idea that EDPs had played a part in causing the wormhole to collapse. But Donohue told me you'd been playing both sides, that you gave the separatists everything they needed to cut Galileo out of the network. Did you tell the separatists the same thing you're now telling me?'

'Let's just say,' said Hanover, 'that I wasn't given a great deal of choice in the matter.'

Saul stared at him, momentarily speechless. All these years, and the man responsible for so much pain and anguish had been right there, working for the same people as he did. But instead of anger he felt only a curious emptiness, as if a cavity had been dug out of the core of him.

Hanover regarded him with evident amusement. 'Are you really sure you're up to this, then?'

'No, but I don't feel like I have any choice either.'

Hanover nodded wearily and bent over the side of his chair to retrieve the Agnessa. 'You should probably go now.' He stood up stiffly, inspecting the gun before heading towards a bank of elevators, without so much as another glance at Saul.

'Wait,' Saul called after him.

Hanover paused, without turning. 'Please don't try and stop me, son. Especially since I'm armed. I hope you manage to pull this off, I really do. But to be frank with you, I'm glad I won't be around to find out, either way.'

Saul watched Hanover step inside an elevator, and the doors closed behind him. He then turned and walked back out the lobby entrance and into the warm, moist air, and realized his hands were shaking.

He received an incoming call from Olivia, as he was putting distance between himself and the Dorican. 'Did you get what you were looking for yet?' she asked.

'I did. Have you explained to the others what I'm planning to do?'

'Mitchell didn't say much, at first. Jeff was pretty shocked, but he seems to be on your side.' There was a bitter tone in her voice as she revealed this. 'Mitchell offered to fly out there and pick you up.'

'Really?'

'Yep. Insisted on flying out all on his own to fetch you, but Lester vetoed that. Said he wanted one of his own pilots on board.'

'Who's Lester?'

'Lester Rose. He runs Launch Pad with his wife, don't you remember?'

'Christ.' Saul felt the warm patter of rain on his skin. 'I do, now.' Lester had been a cantankerous old fellow even back in those days, and Saul was surprised to learn he was still alive.

'How is Mitchell getting here?'

'He's borrowed a tourist hopper. Try and see if you can find somewhere flat and even for it to land in the meantime.'

Saul moved further away from the Dorican until he spotted a deserted car park around the far side of the hotel building. 'I think I've found somewhere, and I'll send you the coordinates in a minute. How long before he gets here?'

'Two hours maximum. Think you can hold out that long?'

'Sure I can.' Saul paused before his next question. 'How long before you and Jeff set out for Inuvik?'

'I . . . Saul, we're already on the way there. We boarded a sub-orbital just a few minutes ago. We'll be landing in the North-west Territories in another hour or so.'

Saul felt something lurch deep inside him. He pictured the sub-orbital arcing high over the northern wastes of Canada, before dipping down towards a settlement spread out along the shores of an Alaskan lake. It was a journey he'd made many times before, for the Inuvik Array had been one of the first of its kind, located in the remote north when the technology had still been experimental. It was still the only way to get to the Jupiter Research Platform.

'About that enquiry you asked me to make,' she continued. 'I'm still not sure just what it is I'm supposed to be looking for, but I've set up a couple of automated queries. Assuming they aren't discovered, they'll return any correlations between Mitchell and the shipment. I don't know how I'll get anything back to you, once we're out there, but if there's a way, I'll find it.'

Saul felt his throat tighten. 'Thanks.'

'One other thing,' she added. 'Once you're on your way to the Moon with Mitchell, we want you to send the contents of the Tau Ceti database to this network location.' Saul received a string of data even as she spoke. 'We'll share those files with any survivors on Mars and the other research platforms, see what we can find out. After that, it's up to you to get your own copy through to at least one of the colonies.'

'I'll miss you,' he said.

He could hear the catch in her throat as she replied. 'Goodbye, Saul – from both of us. Take care.'

And with that she was gone.

He sat down hard in the dirt and dust, suddenly light-headed. After a minute he heard something like gunfire from the direction of the hotel. Three shots in rapid succession, then, after a brief pause, one last shot that affected him like a hammer blow.

TWENTY-SEVEN

Florida Array, 8 February 2235

The hopper dropped from the sky later that afternoon, a bright fleck of silver resolving gradually into a brightly coloured tourist bus, descending on VTOL jets. Random detritus erupted from the car park as Saul watched from a short distance away. The bus rotated a few times before folding its wings away and landing, its turbines diminishing from a high-pitched whine to a low rumble.

He then jogged forward and climbed through the hatch as soon as it opened. He spotted Mitchell sitting in a cramped acceleration chair – just behind the pilot, who raised one hand in greeting before reaching back for his controls.

'Saul.' Mitchell smiled a greeting hesitantly, almost shyly. 'It's been a while.'

Saul stared back at him, his mind full of all the things he'd learned about Mitchell.

'For Christ's sake, man, at least sit down.' Mitchell then glanced at the pilot. 'Hey Sam? I think we can—'

The aircraft lurched immediately with an escalating howl, and Saul stumbled as he quickly pulled himself into the seat next to Mitchell's. A light blinked on, and a computerized voice urged him to strap in.

'Sorry,' Sam called over one shoulder. 'Figured it was best not to stick around here. We got shot at during our approach.'

While Saul strapped himself in, the sun went sliding past the window, as the hopper rotated in mid-air.

'Olivia told me you were aiming to head for the Moon,' he began.

Mitchell nodded. 'And she explained what you're planning to do. I mean about shutting down the whole Array.'

'What else did she say?'

'That you'd done a pretty good job of digging up a lot of classified information.'

'I know about the Founder Network and the recovered artefacts, if that's what you mean. And I also know what happened to *you*.'

The hopper quivered as its wings realigned themselves in preparation for boosting it into the high atmosphere. Somewhere beneath their feet, the engines built up to a noisy rumble, and Saul gripped his armrests as the acceleration pushed them back deep into their seats.

'What gave you the idea of using the EDP codes?' Mitchell yelled over the roar.

'It was the obvious thing to do,' Saul yelled back. 'I mean, Jesus, think about what will happen if we don't shut those gates down.'

'That depends,' said Mitchell, 'on what you think really is happening.'

Saul frowned at him. 'What?'

Mitchell waved a hand dismissively. 'Forget it.'

'Mitchell, I've argued this through with two other people, one of them Olivia. In the end, they both decided to help me. So if you want to know how I'm sure it's the right course of action, then know that I am very, *very* damn sure.'

'Even if it means having the blood of countless innocents on your hands, once you slam the door shut on all of them?'

Saul felt his face grow hot. 'I know what the goddamned consequences are. But doing nothing would be a hell of a lot worse, don't you think?'

Somehow, that had seemed to be the end of any further discussion for the remainder of their journey. Once their craft had levelled out, Saul found himself some quick-heating food in a crew locker and devoured it. He then fell asleep for a while, and dreamed he was back in that car, with Donohue shouting warnings about Mitchell, and woke only when the hopper began its final approach to the Roses' private spaceport, his body racked by a bone-deep ache.

Little about the spaceport had changed over the years since Saul had last seen it. Two lengthy roads cut their way through scrubby desert, while a hangar complex, looking like yesterday's vision of the future of space flight, sat next to the point where they converged. He saw several huge VASIMRs mounted on the backs of trucks, while an airstrip ran parallel to one of the roads. A small hotel and several other buildings of much more recent vintage were strung along the side of it. Rail tracks extended towards a launch pad consisting of a strip of blackened concrete, several kilometres distant from the hangar complex. A massive gantry stood in the centre of the launch pad, supporting a full-sized working replica of an ancient Apollo Saturn multi-stage rocket that towered over the landscape. The gantry had been empty the last time Saul had seen it, several years earlier, waiting for the Roses to finish a round of fund-raising with a consortium of billionaire adrenalin-junkies, so that the pair of them could build more rockets.

He gestured past Mitchell and out the window. 'I never understood the appeal of going up in one of those things.'

'Adventure,' said Mitchell. 'Doesn't get much simpler than that.'

'What's wrong with VASIMRs, then?'

Mitchell chuckled. 'Where's the adventure in that?'

'You sound like Jeff.' Saul turned away from the window and let his head drop back against his seat. 'Did I mention that I never forgave you for talking me into that sub-orbital jump?'

'I didn't talk you into it,' Mitchell reminded him. 'You just took pity on me after my brother died.'

'You told me the experience would reaffirm my enthusiasm for life.'

Mitchell shrugged. 'You sounded pretty enthusiastic to me, at the time. You were screaming all the way down.'

'Yeah, well, I'm just glad it's someone else who'll be flying in that thing, instead of us.'

He glanced sideways at Mitchell and felt a frisson of alarm on seeing the look on his face.

'We're going up in a VASIMR, right?'

The corner of Mitchell's mouth twitched. 'We would be, except all the seats are taken.'

'Who by?'

'The ground control crew and their families. There are maybe a hundred of them, altogether, not including relations – all those responsible for the engineering, fuel supply, onboard systems and general maintenance. The ones that haven't taken off already are going up as soon as we head up on board the Saturn.'

Before Saul could say anything more, a landing warning flashed, and the hopper began to decelerate hard. He watched buildings hurtle by, and a stretch of black tarmac blurring past, before the hopper's engines came to a halt and it dropped down, with a gentle thump, next to what looked like some kind of administration building. Sam stood up and pushed open the hatch, letting sunlight spill into the aircraft's interior.

The air outside tasted gritty, dry and furnace-hot. Saul shielded his eyes with one hand and glanced past the VASIMRs towards the Saturn rocket, clouds of steam now drifting down its sides. Centuries before, men had flown craft just like it all the way to the Moon and back, but the development of the wormhole technology had put paid to almost all of that.

'Car's on its way,' announced the pilot, indicating an open-top vehicle approaching from the administration building.

'You're going up in one of those?' Saul gestured towards the VASIMRs.

Sam nodded. 'Soon as we get lock-in from the orbital powersats, yeah.'

'I rode in one once before,' said Saul. 'It was a pretty bumpy ride.'

Sam shrugged. 'Sometimes that's down to the weather conditions. They've been taking off from here round the clock, over the past couple of days. The ones parked over there'll be the last to go up. You know the Saturn's going to be much, much bumpier, right?'

'No,' Saul sighed, as the empty car stopped beside them, 'I didn't know that.'

The car wasn't much more than a glorified golf cart. It carried them past a lone billboard advertising lunar flights, and then a prospective, VASIMR-powered tourist flight to Mars that was now clearly never going to happen. Saul saw a gaggle of men and women in hard hats standing by a VASIMR mounted on the back of an enormous truck that was parked next to one hangar. Their car came to a halt nearby, and one of the men came over, his dark and weather-beaten skin scored with deep wrinkles.

'Mr Dumont,' said the man, as they all climbed out, 'I'm Lester Rose. I believe we met some years ago?'

'Briefly,' said Saul, shaking Lester's hand as he was offered it.

Lester nodded. 'Well, we're going to get plenty reacquainted before long, because I'm gonna be one half of your flight crew.'

'I'm sorry?' said Saul, not quite able to hide his disbelief.

The old man chuckled. 'Don't look so worried. I'm an old hand at this game. Matter of fact, I was one half of the flight-crew on our last three launches, as well.' He paused, then continued, 'Jeff told me a lot about you. You two worked together, right?'

'Yeah,' Saul nodded, 'although it was a long time ago.'

Lester's expression became serious. 'Jeff's told me a lot of things, since he got in touch. I know what I heard on the news feeds, but' – he glanced at the landscape around them, and shook his head slowly – 'I'll be honest with you, if it wasn't for what I've seen on the news I'd have a hard time believing one damn word he told me. But Jeff's a good man, so I know he ain't going to lie to me.'

'So if you're one half of the flight crew,' asked Saul, 'who's the other half?'

'That'd be my wife, Amy,' Lester replied. 'She's an engineer and pilot, and a good one, too, knows every ship we own inside and out.' He turned to the hopper pilot. 'Sam, you should get over to Bay Fifteen, give Arkady a hand. There's something fishy going on with the fuel-gauge readings on bird number five.'

'Sure thing.' Sam headed over to the truck and began talking to one of the men standing nearby.

'In case I don't get the chance later,' Mitchell said to Lester, 'I want to thank you for holding the launch back for us. It means a lot to me.'

Lester shook his head. 'Way I see it, we might all owe Jeff our lives. So if he wants us to give you a ride up, we'll give you a ride up.' His expression became uncertain. 'It's really going to be as bad as he says?'

'Yes,' said Saul, 'it's really going to be that bad.'

'Right.' Lester sniffed, staring out towards the horizon for a moment. 'You know, a couple of generations back, a girl in my family went off to live on a mountain for a year with some people who all reckoned the end of the world was coming. Shaved her head, got herself pregnant, then a solar eclipse came and went, and she returned back down the mountain and found the world was still there. Everyone pretended it never happened, so she went on and got a regular job and never did anything crazy ever again. I can't imagine how foolish she must have felt, but there's a tiny part of me thinks maybe this is all the same kind of situation, and we're all going to fly up there and find the world isn't going away, and we're all going to come home again feeling foolish. Do you know what I mean?'

'If I thought shaving my head and going to live on a mountain might help things to come out any other way,' said Saul, 'I'd be reaching for the razor right now.'

Lester nodded with a look of inexpressible sadness. 'Come on,' he said, and led them through the hangar towards a side-office. 'I'll introduce you to Amy.'

Amy Rose proved to be an equally leather-skinned old person in her eighties, who had once worked on the early construction of

Kepler's biomes, and even helped carry out course adjustments on board one of the CTC-gate-carrying starships. When she wasn't reminding Saul and Mitchell that she was too busy to retire, she was airing her political convictions.

'We fucked 'em over every which way for no good reason,' she said, when Saul described the invasion of Sophia he'd witnessed. 'The colonies, that is. Should'a shared the technology with the Sphere nations a long time ago.'

'Amy,' intervened Lester, a note of warning in his voice, but this only earned him a scowl from his wife.

'No, *Lester*,' she continued, scowling, 'long as they could control all the gate traffic, they reckoned they could keep the colonies under their thumb. The human race could have expanded a lot further out into the galaxy by now, if it weren't for that kind of shortsighted thinking. That's how they've maintained the same historical imbalance between rich and poor, even over light-years. Enough to make you sick.' She shook her head with evident disgust.

'When are we going up?' asked Saul.

'First thing tomorrow morning,' replied Amy.

Ice trickled through Saul's veins. 'That soon?'

'That soon,' Amy echoed. 'In the meantime, you look like you could use a night's sleep.'

They put Saul up in a hotel next to the runway, where he woke early the next morning, still feeling bruised and sore and tired. Mitchell had already departed the room he'd taken next door to Saul's own, and so Saul ate alone in the hotel's tiny restaurant, staring out across the desert landscape towards the Saturn rocket a few kilometres distant.

Lester picked him up just before eight, driving him to another building nearby that turned out to contain a suite of changing rooms, the walls lined with sportswear-model spacesuits. He found Mitchell there, following Amy's detailed instructions and by that time already halfway into donning his own suit.

Amy waved Saul over to join them, ordering him to strip down before showing him how to put on a pair of rubber-lined long johns studded with flexible microscopic monitors. Following that, he clambered inside one of the racked spacesuits, which proved to be a one-piece garment entered through a diagonal zip running from the crotch all the way up to one shoulder. A how-to, uploaded to his contacts, described the function of each piece of equipment his suit contained in interminable detail, before guiding him through a full systems check that required him to put on a helmet and pressurize the suit to check for potential leaks or any other problems. Once he had the helmet on, icons appeared along the bottom of its curved interior surface, each bearing a name: Saul, Amy, Mitchell and Lester.

'Jesus,' exclaimed Amy, when she noticed Saul struggling to remove his helmet a few minutes later. 'Trust an amateur.' With a sorrowful look, she helped him unlock it from his suit's neck ring.

'How does the suit feel?' she asked.

'Itchy,' Saul replied. 'Not very easy to move.'

'Believe me, it'll be harder once we get to the lunar surface, but we'll be there to guide you along the way.' She turned and snapped her fingers at Mitchell, until she had his attention, too. 'Didn't you say Saul's been up in space before?'

'Just a sub-orb jump,' Mitchell replied, still adjusting the fabric hood he had pulled over his head.

'Right,' Amy turned back to Saul, 'well, this time it's going to be a little different. We're launching way ahead of schedule as it is, which means you need to be ready for anything.'

'Like what?'

She patted his shoulder. 'I wouldn't want to worry your pretty little head with the grisly details. You've got your rubber underwear on, that's the main thing.'

Mitchell glanced across at him. 'Like when we jumped,' he explained. 'You have to pee inside your suit, remember?'

'Somehow I'd managed to wipe that detail from my mind,' Saul grumbled. 'What about, uh, everything else?'

'There's a hose attachment for that,' said Lester, helpfully.

'Just remind me,' said Saul, now flexing his arms and knees. 'There are people who actually pay for this experience?'

Lester started to reply just as a mild tremor rolled through the ground under their feet, lasting several seconds in all.

'I'd better go check on things,' Amy said quickly.

Saul watched her hurry away. 'How much trouble could a tremor like that cause?' he asked Lester.

'Hard to say.' Lester shrugged, as he finished climbing into his own suit. 'Doesn't take much more than a cracked exhaust pipe or fuel line to cause more trouble than you'd believe. We've been very lucky we weren't forced to postpone the launch a few days more, but the faster we can get up now, safety permitting, the better chance we have of avoiding any trouble.' He waved a beckoning hand to the both of them. 'All right, we're about done here. Keep your suits on and come with me.'

Saul picked up his helmet and trailed after Mitchell and Lester, down a narrow passageway decorated with images of vintage space-craft from centuries past. Every step he took in the heavy boots felt as exaggerated and forced as if he were fleeing some nameless dread in a nightmare.

The flight control room adjoined to the rear of the hangar, and consisted of little more than a low-lit booth with several wall-mounted screens, each showing a different view of the Saturn, either from close up or some considerable distance. Several personnel were crammed into this small space, all of whom greeted Lester by his first name before returning to their tasks. Saul listened to them quietly mutter to each other about liquid fuel ratios and payloads, their eyes fixed on one display or another.

'This is it?' Saul asked Lester. 'I thought there'd be more to it.'

'Technically speaking, we don't even need this room,' replied Lester. 'We could run the whole thing through our contacts, if we wanted.'

'Except you need at least a dozen people working together on something this complex,' said one of the technicians, a narrow-faced woman with blonde hair. 'And they need to talk to each other constantly. There's too much that could go wrong, and just slip right by you, if you're not careful. So run it from your contacts, my ass, Lester.'

'Ginny,' Lester retorted, in a tone of mocking disapproval.

She turned round in her seat to face Saul and Mitchell. 'We'll be here for the first part of your launch,' she explained. 'There are too many variables and things that need to be monitored for us not all to be keeping an eye on things. But as soon as you're out of orbit and well on your way, we're heading up ourselves.'

Saul stared up at the image of the Saturn. 'And there's really no room for us on one of the VASIMRs?'

Ginny just looked at him like he was crazy.

It took another hour for the launch technicians to run the final safety checks, before it was safe for them to board. Amy returned from her other duties looking hot and tired. She appeared to be even older than Lester, but it was clear they enjoyed tremendous loyalty from their staff. Saul thought he understood why, for there was something about them that seemed as permanent and unchanging as the desert outside. He watched as the Roses took turns in hugging each of their staff in turn, talking over their plans to reunite once they had all reached Copernicus.

He leaned in towards Mitchell, who sat next to him on a bench at the rear of the booth. 'They know not to stop once they get to the Lunar Array, right?' he asked, under his breath. 'They can't risk stopping until they reach one of the colonies.'

Mitchell shook his head. 'Jeff told them not to stick around Copernicus, put it that way. Listen, while we're on the subject, I've been thinking about your plan to shut down the Array. I'm not sure you've thought it through as thoroughly as you could have.'

'How so?'

'How many EDP codes did you get hold of?'

'Just the one,' Saul admitted.

'Maybe you don't know this, but you'll need at least two people before you can trigger a wormhole collapse. It's not something you can do without help.'

'That depends. Why, are you going to help me?'

'Of course I am,' Mitchell replied. 'but how the hell do you propose to do it with only one EDP code?'

'I don't *need* more than one EDP code, not if one end of the Florida–Copernicus gate falls out of contact with the other. When that happens, everything changes, and the system will accept just the one code for *all* the colony gates.'

A look of anger flickered across Mitchell's face, just for a second, before he repressed it. 'Are you sure of that?' he asked.

'It's the one scrap of hope I have left to hang on to,' Saul replied, remembering the things Olivia had said about Mitchell and knowing, in that moment, exactly what she had meant.

A little while later, Saul and Mitchell, accompanied by Lester, Amy and a couple of their technicians, boarded a small bus that carried them towards the Saturn rocket, standing tall and glorious in its gantry. The sky above was a perfect vivid blue, and Saul had the sudden terrible realization that this was the last time he would ever see it. He felt like a man on the way to his own execution.

The Saturn grew larger, the closer they approached, until Saul realized how immense the thing really was. He vaguely recalled archival footage of the earliest days of the space race: images of eerily similar gantries populated by hard-hatted technicians, and rooms filled with scientists and engineers working with impossibly primitive technology.

'I'm not sure I really believe this thing is anywhere near as authentic as they say,' Saul muttered quietly to Mitchell.

'Gotta make some concessions,' said Lester from up front, having obviously overheard everything he'd said. 'Plus, nobody really wants to get blown up on the pad because of a valve that's faulty simply because it doesn't use up-to-date specifications.'

'So . . .'

'So the onboard computer systems are modern, all other appearances notwithstanding, and the whole thing's built from similar composites to what they use in VASIMRs.' He gazed over his shoulder at Saul, elbow resting on the back of a seat. 'Plus, the original birds only carried three people, not five. The experience is the important thing. It just has to feel authentic, regardless of whether it really *is* authentic.'

And it's the last of its kind, thought Saul. He wondered how the Roses managed to cope; the way they were acting you'd almost think it was any other day, but maybe that was just what they had to do to keep it all together.

Saul heard a rumble echoing from somewhere behind him, and turned to see one of the VASIMRs taking off at a terrifyingly steep angle. He craned his head to watch as it rose higher and higher, and caught sight of the Moon floating serenely above the top of the gantry.

As the bus came to a stop by the base of the gantry, they all climbed out, Lester and Amy leading them over to an open elevator platform. A cluster of UP-compatible icons appeared around the elevator as Saul approached, mostly tourist stuff offering him the chance to view interactive information about the launch. Saul decided he'd like that just fine, since pretty much anything that took his mind off what he was about to do seemed like a good thing. Tiny, primary-coloured animations demonstrated the flow of fuel within the tanks, and also their expected trajectory in the seconds and minutes following take-off.

The elevator swiftly carried the six of them up, before clanging to a halt near the gantry's peak. Saul looked down through a window towards the ground and swayed slightly, one hand on the rail. It felt as if the land below were pulling him back towards it with something more than mere gravity.

Grief overwhelmed him at that moment with a nearly physical

force, as if he were understanding for the first time just how much they were losing. It was as if it fell out of the sky, unexpected as a lightning bolt on a calm spring day, before wrapping itself around his chest and squeezing until he could no longer breathe.

'Easy there,' he heard Mitchell say to him, as if from very far away.

'I can't . . .' Saul gasped.

Mitchell leaned in close to him. 'What's happening out there,' he whispered, casting his gaze around the bowl of the sky, 'isn't what you think it is.'

What the hell does that mean? Saul wondered. But, before he had the chance to ask, Lester was beckoning him towards the open hatch in the side of the spacecraft, which was reached by a short bridge connecting the gantry to the rocket.

'Get your helmet on and go first,' said Lester, with a sympathetic expression. 'Just take your time, and be careful as you go inside.'

Saul nodded and clicked his helmet into place, then waited a few moments while one of the two technicians, a young woman named Sandy, double-checked its seal. Then she and the other technician, an older man named Frank, guided him across the bridge, before helping him climb in through the hatch feet-first.

Saul carefully manoeuvred himself inside, and felt a surge of claustrophobia as he looked around the dark and cramped interior of the capsule. It looked considerably more primitive than he'd feared.

A great deal of shuffling and manoeuvring was required as Lester, then Amy, and lastly Mitchell took turns to climb through the hatch. Amy directed Saul to get into one of five reclining acceleration seats – two up front and three behind, each mounted on shock-absorbers. When Frank climbed inside as well, the capsule became almost comically crowded. After a bit more shuffling, Frank carefully strapped first Saul and then Mitchell into two of the three rear couches before hooking them each up to the air supply.

Saul looked around with a growing sense of dismay as Lester collapsed into one of the two front seats, studying a battered manual held in one hand while he began flipping toggle switches on an instrument panel with the other. Everything here was hard-edged and intensely physical, a direct contrast to the soft, rounded edges of most technology he had encountered throughout his life.

After a moment Saul's UP locked into the capsule's data network, and a series of softly glowing displays, rendered in three dimensions, materialized around both the pilot and the co-pilot seats. He felt himself relax a little, realizing it was like Lester had said – it might look primitive, but appearances could be deceptive.

He noticed Amy watching him. 'It looks basic, but only on the surface,' she said, tapping at a check-list floating in the air before her. 'It's like Lester said, a lot of what you see here is just for show.'

Saul nodded in appreciation, working hard not to let her see just how scared he really was. His mouth felt paper-dry, his heart hammering so hard in his chest he wondered if he was in danger of having a stroke.

Frank finished strapping Lester into the co-pilot's seat, then performed the same task for Amy before finally exiting the capsule and securing the hatch behind him. A moment later Saul heard Ginny speaking to Lester over a shared A/V link.

'All electrical systems look fine,' he heard her say, 'but we should have run a proper pre-launch check on the engines. Shit like that can get you killed.'

Amy cackled. 'Any problems with those and I'll be too busy decorating the desert to worry about them. Just set us a countdown, and we'll be on our way.'

'Yeah, roger that,' said Ginny, her voice tense. 'You're go for launch in one hour. And . . . good luck. We'll see you there in a couple of day's time.'

'That we will, sweetheart,' Saul heard Lester say with undisguised fondness. 'Good luck to all of you as well.'

Amy and Lester spent the better part of the next hour going over a series of interminable system checks. They talked about heat exchangers, fuel mixes, control valves and power assemblies. If Saul had really wanted to know what they were referring to, he could have checked with the how-to, but instead he stared up at the capsule's ceiling, waiting for it to all be over.

Once the countdown fell below ten minutes, Saul's helmet began showing him the last seconds ticking away prior to lift-off. Thirty seconds before the display indicated zero, the capsule lurched very softly, while a crescendo-ing roar grew to such a volume that further thought became almost impossible. The countdown passed zero and they began to climb and, before very long, an invisible block of iron began to press down on Saul. Powerful vibrations shook his couch with such force that his vision blurred.

'Hey, Dumont,' Amy called over the shared comms, 'any history of heart problems? Anything like that?'

Saul struggled to form a coherent answer in the face of what he felt certain was his imminent death. 'No,' he finally managed. 'Not that I know of.'

'Good answer,' she replied. 'Because, under normal circumstances, no way in hell we'd have let you get on this boat without six months of medical check-ups and a daily work-out in the gym.'

'He got checked out just fine before we went on our jump,' Saul heard Mitchell announce.

That was ten years ago, Saul wanted to say, but his throat refused to form any words.

Finding he could access a ground-based video feed of their launch through his contacts, he was shocked to see how far the Saturn had already climbed. A pillar of flame billowed out from its engines, nearly overloading the filters of the cameras as they angled upwards to follow their progress.

The whole craft meanwhile shook with an insane violence. All Saul could do was stare fixedly at the back of Amy's and Lester's heads, visible through the clear polycarbonate shells of their helmets, while they continued to throw technicalities at each other with enthusiastic abandon.

After another minute, a loud metallic boom jerked him hard against his restraints. His heart nearly stopped from sheer fright.

'That's first-stage separation,' explained Lester. 'Second stage kicking in now. And a nice even burn, if I may say so,' he added with clear approval. 'We're doing good, folks. On any other day, I'd be popping champagne corks for a flight this smooth. So just hang in there.'

The shuddering began to diminish, and the intense pressure slowly began to abate. Lester had the grace to at least warn him of what was coming next, when the module shook with even more furious force.

'What the hell is going on?' Saul yelled.

'We're dumping our second stage now,' Lester explained. 'They're so much dead weight once you've used the fuel they contain, so down they go. Check your how-to and you'll see a live feed of it falling behind us. Only the best for our customers, right, sweetheart?'

'Except he ain't payin',' said Amy. 'Nothing less than the end of the world's going to get you a free ride in this firework.'

Saul distracted himself once more with the how-to, which showed him a cylindrical section of the craft falling behind them, spinning away as it receded. The Earth was falling behind as well, a storm front fast spreading along the North-west Seaboard.

The roar had now faded, but the air was filled instead with the sound of pinging metal and creaking bulkheads. Saul felt his weight slipping away. His stomach lurched as he remembered his long drop to the ground, years before, and he fought a surge of panic, clenching and unclenching his fists until it passed.

'Not much of a head for heights, has he?' he heard Amy remark.

'Yeah, well,' said Mitchell, 'that's probably my fault.'

Before long they were unstrapping themselves and changing out of their spacesuits into loose-fitting overalls handed out by Amy. Lester and his wife kept them both busy after that, occupying their minds with small, routine maintenance tasks; but only those, Saul suspected, unlikely to result in any life-threatening failures.

Over those first several hours of their journey, he came to know the three of them better than he'd ever really wanted to know any other human being. The cabin was too cramped and space too valuable for anything resembling privacy to be remotely possible, although, when they ate, the food proved to be distinctly more palatable than he might have reasonably expected. It was far from being high cuisine, mostly consisting of reconstituted dried food meant to reflect the diet of the original Apollo astronauts but, for all that, Saul felt considerably calmer after finishing his first meal in zero gravity.

They climbed back into their seats while Lester first separated the lunar lander, then spun the command and service modules together through a hundred and eighty degrees to rejoin with the lander via the docking hatch. Once the air pressure had balanced, he opened up the docking tunnel to the lander and pulled himself through, returning a few minutes later.

'Once we're in lunar orbit, we'll separate the lander again and it'll take us all down to the surface of the Moon,' he explained to Saul and Mitchell. 'Any time you want to rest, or need the extra elbow space, you can head through to the lander. There are some sleeping bags there you can hook up to the bulkheads.'

'I've decided,' announced Saul, 'that if I live through the next couple of days, I'm never wearing clothes again. Wearing that damn suit put me off them for life.'

He floated at a ninety-degree angle to Mitchell inside the lander, his brain tissues liberally soaked in barbiturates Amy had provided him with from her medical kit. Their pilot and co-pilot were still in the command module, talking with the crew of the last VASIMR to lift off. Almost every surface in the lander was covered in banks of toggle switches and dials, leaving Saul terrified of bumping into any of them.

'It's not so bad, really,' said Mitchell. 'At least not when you think about what explorers had to cope with in previous centuries, like starvation, scurvy, dehydration. At least Armstrong didn't have to worry about getting a spear through his chest when he landed on the Moon.'

'I guess,' Saul conceded, then peered back through into the command module, where he could just see the top of Amy's and Lester's heads. 'Do we know what's happening back home?'

'The feed reports are getting pretty confused.' Mitchell glanced towards Lester and Amy, and dropped his voice. 'You ought to know, one of the VASIMRs didn't make it into orbit.'

'What happened?'

'Fuel-line break. Might be due to the tremors, or maybe because everything was so rushed. Ginny was on board, so Lester and Amy are having a hard time of it. You see, Ginny was their niece.'

'Shit.'

'Not that you could really tell. They're so good at keeping things buttoned up.'

'Well, thanks, I guess, for letting me know.'

'Lester also grabbed some public feeds from back home, and . . . well,' he shrugged. 'I guess you'd better see for yourself.'

Most of what Saul then received from Mitchell, a moment later, consisted of amateur footage recorded either on witnesses' contacts or handheld video recorders. All featured bright twists of light that danced through city streets, reducing them to dust within seconds. The view from hovering camera-drones showed the same twists of light roaming across suburbs and crowded cities, leaving nothing in their path but dense choking clouds of dust rising above a grey and featureless landscape. Dense conurbations, filled with people and traffic and homes, disappeared in an instant. Other video segments showed the same disaster happening to forests, grassy mountain slopes and equatorial jungles, the soil turned to lifeless grey ash that billowed up to blot out the sun. Yet another segment showed the same twists of light dancing around a growth, like so many glowing snowflakes.

The next time he looked at Mitchell, Saul felt like he'd aged another decade. 'I don't know if I really believed what was happening, until now.'

'You wouldn't have any trouble believing it if you were still stuck down below there,' remarked Mitchell.

'Look . . .' Saul let out a sigh. 'We're not going to get too many chances like this to talk about what we're actually intending to do once we reach Copernicus or the Lunar Array. Getting past whatever security operation is still running up there is going to be one of our biggest priorities.'

'Agreed,' said Mitchell.

'But the *real* priority is triggering an Array-wide shutdown. And for that I still need your help.'

Mitchell threw him an appraising look. 'I got the impression earlier that you didn't need anyone else.'

'I can trigger a shutdown on my own, sure, but *only* once the Lunar Array's security systems fall out of contact with Florida. I don't know how much time that's going to leave either one of us to set the shutdown in motion. For all I know, it might not be anywhere near long enough. But if we had a second code, it might make all the difference.'

'Except,' said Mitchell, 'you don't *have* a second code.'

'No, but we need to head for the Lunar ASI offices before any code at all can be activated. While we're there, it might be worth scanning through the servers to see if we can find any kind of information that might help us.'

'That's a seriously long shot,' said Mitchell, looking unconvinced.

'Better than no shot,' Saul replied. 'A little while ago,' he said, 'I had the feeling that maybe you weren't so keen on helping me with this.'

Mitchell hesitated. 'The only thing that makes me hesitate is knowing I'd be complicit in something that would make people revile the pair of us for a thousand years, if they ever learned what we'd done.'

'You think I don't know that?' Saul snapped. 'Or that it hasn't been on my mind every single second since it first occurred to me? If you know a better way to stop the rest of the human race from extinction, I'm fucking desperate to hear it. Really, truly *desperate*. If there was any other way—'

'Saul,' Mitchell put up a hand, 'I get it. I understand.'

'Just so I know I can count on you.'

'Absolutely,' said Mitchell, flashing him a grin full of bright, sharp teeth.

TWENTY-EIGHT

Translunar Space, 10 February 2235

Saul climbed into one of the sleeping bags in the lander, and blacked out more than just fell asleep. He woke several hours later, groggy and bedevilled by a thousand aches and pains, his sleeping bag twisted slightly where it had been Velcroed to a bulkhead. He saw Mitchell, snoring loudly, wrapped in another sleeping bag across the lander.

Saul swallowed to get rid of the dry, gummy taste in his mouth, and spent the next few minutes figuring out how to unzip himself from the bag and its Velcro straps. He then kicked himself through to the command module, finding Lester and Amy still at their stations.

'Still alive?' asked Amy, glancing up at him.

'Barely,' Saul mumbled. 'What's the latest?'

'See for yourself,' suggested Lester, without turning.

A second or two later, Saul found himself watching live satellite feeds of Europe and Africa. He could just make out the coasts of Morocco and South Africa, and saw that both landmasses had become almost entirely hidden under an impenetrable grey haze. Occasional streaks of light chased each other through the ashen murk, come and gone so quickly that they almost didn't register.

Saul scanned through more feeds and saw that, although the same haze had not yet crossed the Atlantic to North America's eastern seaboard, it could nonetheless be seen approaching from the other direction, spreading across the Bering Straits, and reaching as far as the northern tip of Alaska.

He inhaled loudly through his nose, fighting off a surge of bile that rose into the back of his throat. A billion years of evolution, and millennia of human history, all wiped out of existence in the course of just a few days. It defied comprehension. Olivia and Jeff came to mind in that moment, and he prayed they had managed to shut down the Inuvik gate in time.

'Try not to throw up, son,' said Lester. 'It's more dangerous than you think.'

'I won't,' Saul gasped, tasting sour phlegm. He floated, eyes shut, with one hand gripping the back of Lester's seat.

'He'll be fine,' Amy muttered. 'Barbiturates'll keep him from puking too bad.'

'Saul, did you notice anything weird?' asked Lester. 'About the distribution of those clouds, I mean.'

Saul forced himself to open his eyes again, despite a rush of dizziness. 'Weird in what way?'

'I ran a comparison between the spread of the clouds and some speculative climate simulations designed to predict the effect of nuclear winter and major eruptions – that kind of thing. From what I can tell, they're not acting like clouds are supposed to act. They're moving *against* the prevailing winds, for a start, except for where there's a storm system in the Indian Ocean.' He shook his head. 'I can't even begin to tell you how much that scares me. It's like those clouds are *alive*.'

'Worst thing,' Amy muttered, 'is not even knowing what started it all.'

'How much did Jeff tell you about the growths?' asked Saul.

'Well.' Lester squinted, as if uncomfortable with the subject, 'more than we wanted to hear, to be honest. Mainly he talked about some whole big network of CTC gates leading all over the galaxy. He talked about so much stuff it was kind of hard to take a lot of it on board.'

'Did he tell you about stealing confidential files from a secret research platform out at Tau Ceti?'

'He did, yes.' Lester nodded. 'But what you just said there is about the sum of what he told us.'

'We only got the essential details,' Amy added. 'But Olivia did say you had copies of the files. Did you bring them with you?'

'I did. They're all the proof you need. Here they are.'

Their expressions glazed over for several seconds, as they each received their own copies of the stolen files.

'There's a lot of stuff there,' Saul warned them. 'It took me a good few hours just to skim through the document abstracts. Jeff wanted to broadcast it all to the world, but it looks like he ended up on the run instead.'

'Not that there's much of a world left to broadcast it to,' Amy said quietly.

'A couple of days ago I was on Newton,' said Saul. 'The military have been moving their people through, and staging an armed take-over of the colonies. They're desperate to suppress any evidence that the growths reaching Earth was the result of human error.'

'Then why are you giving this to us?' asked Lester, refocusing his gaze on Saul.

'Oh, for God's sake, Lester,' said Amy, her tone sharply admonishing, 'they want the colonists to know what happened. That's what Olivia said, remember? And damn right, too.'

'You can carry the files in your contacts through to whichever colony you head for,' said Saul. 'Same for the rest of your people on the VASIMRs. Do you have secure links you can use to forward those files to the rest of your people?'

'Sure do,' said Amy. 'Matter of fact, I'm doing it right now.'

'We're getting news back from some of the others who've already got to the Lunar Array,' said Lester. 'They got detained at first, but then they were allowed through to Da Vinci, along with almost everyone from Copernicus City. From what we're hearing, it looks like most of whoever they want to bring through from Earth is already through.' His expression became troubled. 'But

I can't stop thinking about those millions of refugees back in Florida. It makes no damn sense, just leaving them there to die like that. Couldn't they at least save some of them?'

'I don't know,' Saul admitted.

'Oh, it makes sense, all right,' said Amy, 'in a twisted, callous kind of way. The colonies haven't been around all that long, and most of them can only sustain small populations, as it is – especially places like Newton, with the sealed biomes. They'd be hard pushed to cope with even a small increase in their populations.'

'You're sure of that?' Saul asked.

'Think about it,' she said, her tone flat. 'It's what they call a cold equation. There just isn't enough food, water and air to go round. It's the logic of the lifeboat: if you've got a lifeboat big enough for six people but seven hundred are drowning all around you, there's no way you can get more than a tiny fraction of that number into the lifeboat without sinking it and drowning everyone.'

She reached over the back of her chair to touch Saul's arm. 'You did a good thing getting those files here, son. There's nothing we can do for those people back there, much as it makes me sick to admit it, but that doesn't mean we can't do our damnedest to make sure the ones responsible for all this will pay for what they've done.'

Saul came to a decision and pulled himself into the seat directly behind Amy's. 'There's something I need to tell you both. When we get to the Moon, I'm going to try and shut the Array down – collapse every one of the wormholes.'

'Shut it *down*?' said Lester, a confused look on his face. 'Is that even possible?'

'Maybe Lester and Amy have got enough on their plates right now,' interrupted Mitchell, pulling himself through from the lander.

Saul jerked his head around in surprise. 'You're awake.'

'No,' insisted Amy, 'I want to hear what Saul has to say.'

Saul turned back to her. 'Take a look at the files I just sent you. Particularly the video sequences listed under "Copernicus".'

Amy stared sideways at a bulkhead, as Mitchell floated down to join them, with a look of disapproval on his face. 'Okay, I've got it.' She frowned. 'Hey, it looks like—'

'Like something's completely devastated the entire city. Is that what you're seeing?'

She stared in silence at the bulkhead for several more seconds. 'Shit,' she said at length. 'That's just about right.'

'Whatever's about to happen on Earth is going to happen to Copernicus as well, and it's going to be soon. So I need to shut the gates down before the same thing can happen to the colonies. I'm telling you this so you'll understand why you can't hang around once we get up there. You have to find your way through a gate as soon as possible, or you'll be stranded.'

'How sure are you that you need to do this?' Lester demanded.

'All I know,' Saul said truthfully, 'is that I've seen what's going to happen to the Moon, and the only way it could have got there is via the Array.'

'Not necessarily,' said Lester. 'It had to have come through the Array on the way to Earth, right? Maybe they had more of those artefacts stored up there in Copernicus, somewhere. Maybe they caused it?'

'He's got a point,' said Mitchell. 'You can't deny it's a possibility.'

'Jesus, Mitch,' Saul rounded on him, 'don't you think you're clutching at straws?'

'But it's at least a possibility,' said Lester, his expression pained.

Amy reached out and touched her husband's shoulder. 'No, Lester, what Saul's saying makes sense. We can't put our hope on a distant possibility. We have to think for the rest of the human race.'

'Not all of our people have made a landing yet,' Lester insisted, suddenly looking all of his years. 'We already lost Ginny. What if the rest of them couldn't get through in time?'

'I've seen what's happening back home – just like you have,' she said, her voice gentle now. 'Way I see it, we have a moral obligation to do everything we can to help Saul. I just wish we had a name for the thing causing all of this. Otherwise everything feels so . . .' She shrugged '. . . so *random*.'

Saul glanced at Mitchell in time to see him shake his head, and push himself back up towards the tunnel leading into the lander.

'If no more people are being allowed through the Array,' said Saul, 'then maybe you're right, Amy. There's too many of them for the colonies.'

Amy looked at him with old eyes. 'Just tell me you don't *want* to be the one to have to do this.'

'I don't want to be the one to have to do this,' affirmed Saul, with all the feeling he could muster.

Saul made his way through to the lander, where he found Mitchell waiting.

'What the hell was all that about?' Saul demanded. 'They've got every right to know what we're intending to do.'

'I just thought they'd been through enough,' Mitchell replied mildly. 'You didn't really need to tell them you were planning on triggering a shutdown.'

'They got us this far, they *deserve* to know.'

'I don't know, Saul. Sounded to me more like you were making a confession.'

There was just enough truth in what Mitchell had said to hit home. 'Listen,' Saul was angry now, 'something happened to you that I can't even begin to understand. I saw the footage of you falling into that pit, then being pulled out of it. I read reports that said you'd died and come back. How is that even *possible*?'

'It depends,' said Mitchell, 'on your definition of life and death.'

'Is all of that why you're acting so different? You said, just before we launched, that none of this was going to be as bad as I might think. What the hell did that mean?'

Mitchell shook his head and sighed. 'I shouldn't have said it.'

'Give me,' Saul insisted, 'an explanation.'

'Look, when they pulled me out of that pit, I was changed. That's true. I . . . I knew things. Things about the Founder races, about how the network came into existence, where they went to after they disappeared.'

Saul could hardly believe what he was hearing. 'How?'

'I don't know how. I just woke up and it was all there, swirling around inside my head. But when I said what I said back then, I was trying to tell you something for which I seriously doubt there are words – something so far outside of my own experience or that of any other human being that I'm still struggling to comprehend it. Once I do, assuming I ever do, I'll try and choose my words more carefully. I'm sorry.'

Saul hesitated. After all, his worries stemmed from a single unfinished statement from Donohue, hardly a man he felt he could trust at the best of times. But, then again, something had put Olivia on edge as well.

'There's still something you're not telling me,' said Saul. 'I don't know what, but I've been in my job long enough to know when someone's not being straight with me.'

'I'm sorry you don't trust me,' said Mitchell, 'but what happened to me isn't my fault.'

Saul stared at him, feeling even more frightened than he cared to admit to himself.

Saul had already found that time on board the spacecraft became strangely elastic in the absence of any clear evidence of day or night. Amy and Lester appeared to have run out of minor maintenance checks for either himself or Mitchell to perform and, although he had little else to do, he didn't have the stomach to keep watching the slow march of death as it continued to spread across the face of the planet. He dozed intermittently, but both module and lander were filled with constant creaks and rattles that did little to soothe his nerves. At one point he awoke to find Mitchell zipped into a sleeping bag across the lander from him, apparently asleep. Yet Saul could see, from the way the other man's eyes moved under their closed lids, that he was watching or reading something via his contacts.

When Saul awoke a few hours later, he unzipped himself from his bag and ventured back through to the command module. He sat down next to Amy while her husband was sleeping, securely strapped across the three rear passenger seats and apparently oblivious to the tormented rattle of metal under stress, or even to his wife's description of endless technical details about fuel mixes and delta vees. All that she said meant little to Saul, but was oddly comforting when delivered with that effortless confidence with which she was imbued. Finally, he let his head sink back and closed his eyes, linking once more into one of the few satellite-feeds still transmitting out of Earth orbit.

Much of Brazil had already slid beneath those flickering clouds and disappeared forever. *Goodbye, São Paolo,* thought Saul with infinite sadness; *goodbye Rio de Janeiro, rain forests and macaws.* All places and things he'd never set eyes on, but now found himself missing with bottomless remorse.

He discovered a few static-ridden broadcasts still coming out from other parts of the South American continent, and listened to people who knew death was approaching them. He saw a jerky handheld video shot in Venezuela, taken within the hour, that showed black clouds like thunderheads slowly spreading outwards to choke out the sunlight, those familiar twists of light dancing high in the stratosphere.

One by one, the voices faded into the hissing static, never to be heard again, until all that was left was a single audio transmission of a man alternately praying in Spanish and weeping. Saul listened for a few moments before cutting the link, unable to bear any more of it. There was, by contrast, no news coming out of Copernicus whatsoever, and Saul remembered Amy telling him that most if not all of Copernicus' population had already been evacuated.

'That's us officially past the halfway point,' Amy informed him when Saul opened his eyes again. 'Less than two days before we touch down.'

'What about the VASIMRs?'

'The last of them already touched down. They've got a far more efficient burn ratio than an old-style bird like this.' She glanced round towards him. 'You know, if you'd told us about your plan to shut down the gates back there before we took off, we might have tried to get you on board one of the VASIMRs instead.'

'Sorry,' said Saul. 'I guess I wasn't sure if you'd want to take me up, if I told you that first.'

She barked a laugh. 'You thought maybe we'd just leave you behind? Can't say the thought mightn't have crossed my mind, if I thought you were crazy. But I don't, more's the pity.'

He squeezed his eyes shut for a moment, feeling momentarily dizzy.

Amy's face had creased in a frown, when he opened his eyes once more. 'When was the last time you ate?' she asked.

'Why?'

'Amateurs,' she sighed. 'You need to eat at regular intervals.' She placed her hands on the steel bars on either side of her acceleration couch, and levered herself upwards until she floated free. 'Zero gee screws up your body's internal signals, makes you think you ain't hungry when you are. Here.' She pulled a tinfoil-wrapped package out of a cupboard and pushed it into a microwave oven bolted to one of the bulkheads. It dinged after a couple of seconds, and she retrieved it.

'I'm not hungry,' Saul protested, and it was true.

'Bullshit.' She unwrapped the tinfoil and pushed the tray of steaming hot food at him. 'Chicken Surprise.'

Saul sniffed at it. 'What happened to all that dried food?'

She shrugged. 'Strictly speaking, that's for the tourists. Can't feel like they're being authentic if they're eating the decent stuff.'

'It smells okay,' he said, regarding the contents doubtfully. 'Doesn't look anything like any chicken I've ever seen, though.'

'That's the surprise,' she said. 'Now eat. Can't save the universe without eating.'

'I guess.'

Saul felt suddenly ravenous, as if a switch had been thrown some-where inside of him. He wolfed the contents down, Amy watching him the whole time, a vacuum tube held ready in her hand, but Saul didn't spill even a drop.

'Hey, check the board,' said Lester, loosening his restraints and hauling himself upright, before yawning loudly. 'We've got incom-ing. Transceiver Two.'

'You're kidding,' said Amy, her eyes becoming unfocused. 'Hot damn, it's that girl Olivia.'

Saul stared at them both in shock.

'All the way from the Jupiter platform?' said Lester. 'How the hell did she manage that?'

'Data looks like it's been routed through a couple of surviving satellite networks, from what I can see,' said Amy. 'Bob's VASIMR relayed it back to us.'

'Clever girl,' said Lester, in a tone of appreciation.

'It's addressed to you,' said Amy, turning to Saul. 'And it's marked private,' she added, raising an eyebrow. 'Want me to patch it through?'

'Please,' Saul replied, and a *message received* icon appeared before him a few seconds later. 'Excuse me,' he added, handing the empty tray back to Amy.

His heart beat wildly inside his chest as he pulled himself back through to the lander. Mitchell looked like he was genuinely asleep, eyes closed and mouth hanging half open in the dimmed light.

Olivia's message turned out to be a pre-recorded video file. He noticed her eyes were red with fatigue, as she sat at a terminal in what looked like a busy operations room, men and women he didn't recognize hurrying past or talking together in tight groups behind her.

'Saul,' she began, 'I hope you made it okay. It took me a lot longer than I'd have liked to figure out how to route this to you, so here's hoping you still get to see it.'

He watched her take a moment to gather herself. 'Before any-thing else, I want you to know we're all fine here. We shut down the Inuvik–Jupiter gate without any major problems, except there just wasn't enough room for everyone wanting to come through. So we . . .' She paused for a moment '. . . We drew straws, basically. And some of those who stayed behind helped to make sure the wormhole collapsed.'

Saul studied the lines in her face: she looked like she'd aged ten years since he'd last seen her. Then he wondered how he would look to her, if she were able to see him. Just as bad, probably.

'You asked me to find out anything I could about Mitchell,' she continued. 'And I'm going to have to tell you now I don't think it's good news – assuming you even believe what I'm about to say.'

Here it comes, he thought. His fingers tightened around the hand-grip secured to a bulkhead.

'You know how I already said you didn't exactly give me much to go on, except that there's some link between Mitchell and that shipment? I talked to the others here, Bob Esquivaz and the rest, and told them everything I know. I guess it's no surprise that there are other people here who've had some knowledge of the Founder Network. Some of them have higher clearance than I ever did, which means they can get deeper inside the ASI's security records than I could. That made things a lot easier than they would have been otherwise.'

She licked her lips, her expression nervous. 'Assuming the records are correct, we now know the precise time Mitchell recov-ered consciousness after they brought him back to Earth from Tau Ceti. It's the *exact* same moment the plane carrying your missing shipment fell off the radar.'

Saul felt a chill spread through his bones, as he listened intently.

'Now I don't know what the hell that means,' Olivia continued. 'I can speculate certainly, say that somehow Mitchell's waking trig-gered the artefacts inside that shipment into becoming the growths, or maybe it was the other way round and something inside that ship-ment caused *him* to wake up.' She sighed. 'But if you asked me to go with my gut, after seeing how much he's changed and knowing what happened to him . . . then I can't help wondering if that really *is* him, no matter how much it looks or acts or sounds like him.'

She then went on, Saul listening but not really hearing as she told him their plans for the future. There were three hundred of them on board the Jupiter platform, with stockpiles enough to survive for decades yet, and perhaps even centuries, if their agricultural programme took off.

Saul felt that same bottomless sadness he'd experienced when he'd last spoken to her directly, knowing that if he survived this day then this would be his one remaining memory of her, sitting bleary-eyed and haggard in front of a terminal, while all those strangers hurried past.

She started to finish up, but he stopped the file, unwilling to hear her say goodbye a second time. He saw Mitchell peering at him across the lander, and once again Saul felt a familiar chill settle beneath his skin.

'I heard the three of you talking through there in the command module,' he said. 'You've heard from Olivia?'

'Yeah.'

'And?'

'And she's alive,' Saul replied. 'They all are.'

Mitchell nodded. 'I'm glad to hear that. Can I see it? The message?'

Saul felt his throat tighten. 'I'd rather not.'

'Any reason why?'

'It's . . . personal.'

He frowned. 'Can't be that personal, surely? I—' A look of enlightenment crossed his face, and he nodded. 'Do you know, I actually forgot, for a moment there, about you and Olivia.'

'You were out of the loop for a couple of years back there. It's understandable.'

'You two . . .' Mitchell traced a loop in the air with the forefinger of one hand. 'I know you met up while Jeff was still on the run. Did you . . . ?'

'No, all that was over a long time ago,' Saul replied, unable to hide a hint of regret.

'Right,' Mitchell nodded, 'if it's private, it's private.'

'Thanks for understanding.'

Saul tried not to show his relief that Mitchell was not being more insistent.

More time passed, the seconds ticking by interminably slowly, and Saul drifted into a kind of reverie. It was a half-awake, half-dreaming state, aided greatly by his feeling of weightlessness. Sometimes he slept, or scanned more of the records from the Tau Ceti base. Instead of feeling bored, his mind was occupied by a kind of unrelenting nervous tension. At one point, Saul re-entered the command module and noticed, through one of the tiny angular windows, how the Moon had expanded enormously. He gazed down on its craters and billion-year-old lava plains.

Lester was now in charge again, while Amy lay curled up on the rear three seats with a pair of large black ear-muffs strapped over her head. She yawned, her eyes flickering open, as Saul floated past her and landed gently in the seat next to Lester.

'What's the latest?' asked Saul.

'No news.' Lester shook his head. 'I've been scanning regularly for live feeds, and can't find a damn one.'

'You mean everything's gone?' Saul felt a spasm of shock. 'Have the clouds reached Florida yet?'

'Not yet,' Lester reassured him. 'There's still some patches left untouched, but those damn clouds are scrambling signals all over the place, is my guess. Even if there's any people left to talk down there, we won't be able to hear them.'

'How long before we touch down?'

Lester blinked at the empty air for a couple of seconds. 'Another four or five hours. I'm calling that a personal best.'

Saul couldn't contain his surprise. 'I thought we had at least maybe a day to go?'

'Depends on how much fuel you burn,' said Lester, 'particularly during your initial acceleration. Faster you take off, the faster your escape velocity is, the faster you get to your destination. I forgot to mention that we used most of the fuel we'd normally use for the return trip on take-off, for that added velocity.' He nodded towards the lander, keeping his voice low. 'Is Mitchell okay?'

'Why?'

'Well, he's keeping to himself a lot, through there.'

'Is that a problem?'

'No, not necessarily. But stress affects all kinds of people in all kinds of ways.'

Saul shook his head. 'I'm not sure what you mean.'

'My point is, if anyone becomes unbalanced or has some kind of breakdown out here, there isn't anyone we can turn to for help, and we've all got more than enough reasons to lose it right now. I'm not suggesting that's what's happening with Mitchell, but when somebody starts hiding away that much, it's not necessarily a good sign.'

'No, he's not crazy,' Saul replied. 'At least, no more than I am.'

'Les?' interrupted Amy, sitting up and pulling the muffs off. 'This might not be a good time for you to chat. We've got deceleration coming up. I want you and the boys to get yourselves strapped in.'

Lester nodded to her, then returned his attention to Saul, throwing him one last leery glance. 'Then I hope to hell you're right,' he said. 'Now, get yourself suited up, and I'll go fetch Mitchell.'

'Is it absolutely necessary to get suited up?' Saul protested. 'We're not even on the surface yet.'

'I swear, you're worse than my damn kids ever were,' said Lester with a grin. 'It's something our insurers have always insisted on.'

'Not exactly something you need to worry about out here, Lester.'

'No, but it keeps Amy happy, since you never know what damn thing's going to go wrong. So suit up and strap yourself in.'

Saul conceded defeat, pulling his suit out from where it was stowed, along with the long johns that helped keep his body temperature regulated. Lester meanwhile pushed his way through the tunnel leading from the command module to the lander, returning a minute later with Mitchell in tow. Mitchell immediately got into his own suit before returning to the seat directly behind Lester, without comment.

Lester and Amy helped each other put on their suits before conducting more interminable checks on the engines and computer systems. After half an hour, Amy fired the engines. The craft instantly slammed them forward in their seats, as the deceleration burn kicked in, slowing them in their headlong flight, and putting them on target for a lunar insertion. The burn only lasted for thirty seconds but, when it ended, Saul's lungs ached as he exhaled.

Amy raised one gloved hand up above her head in a thumbs-up, and Saul closed his eyes, listening to the sound of his own breathing, so strangely close and claustrophobic inside his helmet.

The Moon gradually began to fill all of the ports over the next few hours, and Saul spent quite some time peering out at the lunar surface from a vantage point he never thought he'd get the chance to experience. His contacts dropped labels over the Mare Imbrium's ancient lava flows, similarly highlighting the Copernicus crater lying close by the equator.

Dense ashen clouds had by now covered Canada and much of the Pacific, and had also spread across Washington State like grasping fingers. The Hawaiian Islands had long since disappeared beneath the murk, but a storm front running down the West Coast towards Mexical appeared to be holding the clouds back in the south. Florida remained unaffected, but Saul knew, with grim certainty, that wouldn't be the case for much longer. More clouds were meanwhile spreading north across the Gulf of Mexico.

'We're going to all move through to the lander now,' Amy announced, 'Then we'll separate the modules before all heading down to the surface in the lander. We'll be doing a fair bit of walking across the lunar surface once we land, so I want you all to run more checks on your suits. Access your how-tos and follow the instructions.'

'Speaking of which,' said Lester, 'separation due in fifteen minutes, and counting.'

They moved through into the lander, one by one, securing themselves into the padded chairs there as Lester sealed off the hatch. He then made a series of further checks, along with Amy, flipping rows of toggles before strapping in with just a few seconds to go.

Thirty seconds passed, and the lander jerked violently. At the same moment, Saul heard a dull thump, like an executioner's blade biting into wood.

'And that, lady and gentlemen,' declared Lester, 'is what we call a separation.'

'What now?' asked Saul, his skin already coated with cold sweat.

'What's now is that we land,' replied Amy in a distracted tone. 'So try not to interrupt your flight crew, okay?'

Saul mumbled an apology, and noticed Mitchell's eyes were closed under the curved plastic of his helmet. Behind their lids, his pupils darted constantly here and there, his lips twitching.

Saul used his contacts to watch the lunar surface slip by beneath them. Before long it became clear that they were dropping lower and lower, the craft oriented so it was flying upside-down in respect to the surface. More time passed until the nearest edge of Copernicus itself crept into sight, growing wider and deeper as they descended towards the low hills beyond the crater's rim.

'Tight,' muttered Amy. 'Look at that. Not much flat ground round here. Shoulda stuck to our usual designated landing zone.'

'Doing fine, hon,' said Lester, his tone calm and reassuring. 'Just guide her in best you can.'

The craft twisted around in its flight until it was oriented the right way. They dropped yet lower over the next several minutes, until thick plumes of grey dust billowed up around the lander, obscuring the view through the external cameras. Almost before he realized it, the lander had touched down with a gentle thump.

Saul let out a shaky breath. *I'm alive*, he thought.

'That was a sweet landing, honey,' said Lester, turning to her with a look of approval. 'Why, I—'

Saul saw the back of Lester's helmet shatter under a blow from the wrench gripped in one of Mitchell's gloved hands. Lester exhaled sharply and reached out with one hand to the control panel before him. Another blow followed immediately, smashing through the ruins of his helmet to strike the back of his skull with sickening force.

Saul scrabbled at his restraints, then raised one arm in a feeble attempt at defending himself, just as Mitchell aimed the next blow at him. Saul's helmet fractured under the impact, but still held together.

Mitchell leaned over him, his face filled with a snarl. Out of the corner of his eye, Saul could see Amy unbuckling herself, before bending forward to reach under her seat.

Mitchell pulled the wrench back for a second swing, but the module was too cramped and the weapon slammed into a control panel behind him, tumbling from his grasp. Saul tore frantically at his restraints while, swearing under his breath, Mitchell crouched down to find the wrench.

Amy stood up from her seat just as Saul managed to fight loose of his restraints. She gripped a weapon of her own in both hands. At first glance it looked like a regular shotgun, but with a peculiarly home-made appearance, as if it had been assembled from random pieces of junk.

Before Saul had time to wonder what the Roses were doing with a shotgun hidden on the lander, Amy fired it at Mitchell from point-blank range.

It took some moments for Saul to register what happened next. Mitchell had shifted to one side with startling, inhuman speed, the bullet smacking into a computer mounted on the bulkhead behind him. It was as if someone had inserted a jump-cut into reality: first Mitchell had been *here*, but now he was *there*.

Saul already knew from the how-tos how easily the bullet could have punctured the lander's thin walls.

Amy swore and tried to take aim a second time, and Saul noticed how the trigger mechanism was roomy enough for a spacesuit-gloved finger to fit around it.

Mitchell leaned over Lester's prone form to snatch the weapon away from her, moving once again with that shocking fluid velocity.

Saul then remembered what Donohue had said. *He's not even human*.

He grabbed hold of Mitchell from the side, only for the man to swing Amy's rifle around like a club, slamming the stock into Saul's ribs and sending him stumbling backwards. By the time Saul had struggled half upright again, Mitchell was swinging the rifle back and forth between him and Amy. The lander felt more intensely cramped and claustrophobic than ever.

'I don't want either of you getting in the way,' Mitchell shouted. 'Amy, I—'

The interior of the lander was so tiny that, when Mitchell glanced towards Amy, it was easy for Saul to reach out with one gloved fist and knock the rifle barrel upward, so that it smacked into a control panel mounted on the ceiling. Saul pushed his advantage by grabbing hold of the barrel, struggling desperately to pull it from Mitchell's grasp. Mitchell was sweating inside his suit, with an expression suggesting he was in considerable discomfort. As his eyes became unfocused, Saul felt the man's grip on the weapon begin to loosen.

'Now you listen, you piece of shit,' Saul barked, 'you're going to—'

A sound like a hammer blow filled the tiny cabin, and a nearly irresistible force almost lifted Saul into the air.

He slammed shoulder-first into one of the forward control panels, hard enough to leave him feeling dazed. He caught a glimpse of lunar regolith, down between the lander's legs, then realized the forward hatch had somehow been blown, the air inside the craft explosively decompressing. Mitchell pushed Amy out of the way and literally dived head-first through the narrow hatch, before landing between the lander's legs, in a great cloud of dust.

'Don't move,' he heard Amy warning him over the A/V. 'Your helmet's cracked. I need to resecure that hatch before we can do anything else.'

'What the hell just happened?'

Amy reached down for a handle attached to one side of the hatch. 'Give me a hand here,' she ordered.

Saul took hold of the handle on the opposite side, and held it in place, following her clipped directions as she reset the locking mechanism. He had to lean over Lester to do so, and noticed his unmoving eyes staring off through one of the lander's triangular windows.

'I don't know how he figured out how to do that,' Amy muttered tightly, 'but he triggered the emergency release.'

Saul remembered studying Mitchell when he had assumed he might be asleep, and seeing the man's eyes dart back and forth under their lids, no doubt planning and preparing, while searching out flaws in the lander's UP-linked control systems.

'I think I might know,' he admitted.

Once Amy had finished resecuring the hatch, she reached out and flipped a couple of switches on a control panel, then did the same with a virtual panel floating to one side. A distant hiss quickly built to a roar as the cabin filled up with air once more, from an emergency tank.

'How he did it doesn't matter right now,' said Amy. 'Well, that's us repressurized. Now we've got to help Lester.'

'Amy . . .'

She ignored him, pulling open a steel cabinet and withdrawing a large white plastic box. 'Medical kit,' she explained. 'We'll need to dress that wound.'

Saul gazed down at Lester's slumped form, with a feeling of hopelessness, as Amy hurriedly pulled off her helmet and dropped it to one side.

Saul pulled off his own damaged helmet too, then helped her remove Lester's. Tears trickled down her cheeks, as she murmured Lester's name over and over again, like a litany. Lester's head rolled to one side, his jaw slack and his eyes vacant.

'Amy, please, listen to me.'

She began weeping in earnest. 'We can get him to a hospital in Copernicus,' she insisted. 'Someone might still be there, someone who can . . .'

Saul stared down at Lester's lifeless features. 'It's too late for that.'

Amy sniffed and reached up to pinch away the tears gathering around her eyes. She stood up abruptly, the medical kit slipping from her grasp. 'I don't understand . . . why did he do this? He tried to kill you, too.'

'I don't know,' Saul replied, reaching out with two gloved fingers to close Lester's eyes.

Amy kneeled on her seat, her face twisted in anguish, as she stared down at her husband. 'Listen to me, Saul,' she said eventually, her voice hoarse. 'There are some auxiliary suits.'

'There are?' Saul felt a sudden stab of hope.

Amy nodded listlessly and touched one gloved hand to Lester's cheek. 'You can get yourself another helmet belonging to one of them.' She took a deep, shuddering breath, and then stood up as straight as possible. Her eyes, blazing with anger, met Saul's. 'I want you to kill him, do you hear me?'

'Amy . . .'

'No, dammit, I want him dead.'

Saul tried to think of something to say. 'I need to find out why he did this, and if I kill him, I can't do that.'

Her gloved fists clenched themselves by her sides. She might be an old woman now, but Saul suddenly saw just how very formidable she must have been in her youth.

'Then make damn sure he never gets as far as the colonies,' she hissed in a half-whisper.

The spare suits were located in a locker hidden beneath a floor panel at the rear. Amy helped him pull out a new helmet.

'Now listen up,' she said. 'We've landed a couple of klicks

south-east of the Lunar Array. Any normal day, we'd wind up in jail for flying anywhere near this close to it.' She retrieved the rifle from where she'd propped it against a bulkhead. 'Here, you're going to need this thing when you go after Mitchell.'

Saul searched her eyes as he took it from her. 'Why in God's name would you need something like this on board a tourist craft?' he asked. 'You could have blown a hole in the lander and killed all of us, not just Mitchell.'

'It's an insurance policy.'

'Insurance against what?'

An uncomfortable look crossed her face. 'Against getting caught.'

'You were smuggling, is that it?'

'Not necessarily in this bird. In the VASIMRs, mostly. Things got tight a few years back, and we were on the verge of going under. This way, we can slip all kinds of stuff past customs and fly it straight back home without going anywhere near Florida. People, sometimes, too.' She shrugged. 'I guess telling you this doesn't matter now.'

'So what were you planning on doing, if you got caught? Have a shoot-out with the ASI?'

Amy made a sound of irritation. 'Officials we can pay off, but we had competitors – sometimes very vicious ones. We thought they might plant someone on board, a ringer of some kind, so . . .' She gestured at the rifle. 'You should realize that thing's designed to work in a vacuum.'

Saul nodded. He rather suspected that the rifle, when disassembled, might look, to the casual eye, like nothing more than random components of normal onboard equipment.

She squinted at him. 'You'd figured this out already, hadn't you?'

'I had a feeling, yes.' He lifted up the helmet and paused before sliding it on. 'You'd better put on your own helmet, if we're going.'

She laughed. 'You're kidding, right? I'd only slow you down.'

'You need to get to the city, Amy. Your friends will be waiting for you.'

She nodded slowly, with a look of desperate sadness in her eyes that Saul recognized. It was the same way he himself had looked on the day the Galileo wormhole had collapsed.

'Not yet,' she said. 'I need to stay here with Lester. Just for a little while longer.'

'Amy . . .'

'No.' Her expression was stony. 'Go find him now, before he gets away.'

TWENTY-NINE

Saul pocketed some extra ammunition that Amy gave him, her mouth pursed all the while in a thin line. By the time she had depressurized the lander again, Mitchell had already gained half an hour's head-start.

'You're better equipped than he is,' Amy pointed out, over the A/V, after he mentioned this. 'Remember, you're carrying a full air supply in your backpack, while he jumped out with just his suit's inbuilt emergency supply. He's not going to waste time doing anything but heading straight for the Array. Besides,' she added, her voice crackling slightly, 'it's not like you're going to have too much trouble following his trail.'

Saul pulled himself through the tiny hatch and then down a narrow ladder, a plume of dust rising around his weighted boots as he touched down. He looked back up at the lander, shocked at how tiny, frail and primitive-looking it seemed, and gave Amy a wave just as she swung the hatch shut again.

He looked around and saw that the lander stood on a wide shelf of rock, only a few kilometres from the edge of Copernicus Crater. Hills ringed the crater's rim, and he could spot part of the city, where it lay further around the crater in the narrow gap between two peaks. The city itself spilled down the wide, terrace-like steps of the crater's inner wall, its tallest buildings reaching upwards like pale spears that had been thrust into the regolith. The snaking lines of pylons that carried trains back and forth between the city and the Array were as yet invisible from Saul's vantage.

Mitchell's footprints stood out clear and sharp in the dust, and Saul followed them along the lunar surface, in long strides that would have been impossible back on Earth. He looked ahead and saw that they led straight to the rim of hills, a few kilometres away. He breathed evenly as he ran, pacing himself and keeping his eye out for any loose rocks that might trip him. He recalled reading somewhere that the close proximity of the lunar horizon made it hard to judge distances.

'Mitchell!' he yelled over the A/V. 'Can you hear me? Mitchell!' No answer.

The most economical way to run on the Moon, he knew from previous visits to Copernicus, was a kind of lope that fell just shy of skipping. It exhausted him all the same, so that when he came to a halt, about halfway towards the hills, the inside of his suit already reeked of stale sweat. The terrain had meanwhile taken on a different texture, the regolith giving way to ripples of ancient lava and boulders left over from the time when part of the crater wall had collapsed, aeons before. This made it a lot harder to pick out Mitchell's footsteps.

'I just want to know what the hell's going on,' Saul shouted again over the A/V. 'You owe me that much.'

'Do I?' came the unexpected reply.

Saul straightened up, still panting from his exertions, and stared over towards the hills. If Mitchell was there somewhere, he couldn't see him. He tried zooming in with his contacts, but there was so much debris scattered everywhere, it would be easy for Mitchell to hide himself amongst it.

'I know there's some connection between you and those arte-facts,' Saul gasped. 'Olivia found the proof: this all started when they brought you back from Site 17.'

'What's happening now,' said Mitchell, 'is too important to let you, or anyone else, interfere.'

Saul could tell from the sound of the man's breathing that

he had also been running. So he started moving again and, after another few minutes of steady progress, he spotted movement amongst the deep shadows cast over the base of one of the hills. He squinted intently, till one of those shadows resolved itself into a tunnel mouth cut into the side of a hill. Saul stopped, exhausted, and sucked water through a straw located inside his helmet.

He looked around and saw he had come to the edge of an old construction road. Rubble was piled into mounds by the roadside, while several abandoned-looking construction vehicles and a broken-down mobile foundry stood nearby, stark and black against the stars. He started running again, gradually picking up his pace.

'You were never actually going to help me shut down the Array, were you?'

'I should have killed you first, instead of Lester,' Mitchell replied. 'I can see that now: my stupid mistake. I had to find some way to stop you interfering. But I couldn't take a chance on Lester and Amy sending out a distress signal, if I went for you first. But I screwed up, didn't I?'

'What's too important for me to interfere in?'

Mitchell just laughed. 'You wouldn't understand.'

'Try me.'

'Would it make you turn back? See things my way?'

There had developed a subtle change in the tone of Mitchell's voice. There was a touch of echo to it, as if he were no longer wearing his helmet. Saul searched for local networks, and came across a public map of the area that included the locations of several emergency access entrances just inside the mouth of that tunnel. It now yawned ahead of him, just a hundred metres or so away.

'I said try me.'

'I'm trying to save the human race,' replied Mitchell. 'Is that good enough?'

Saul nearly stopped dead in his tracks. 'What?'

'Some of the Founder species wanted to destroy the network, because they came to realize that, once they'd created a wormhole leading into the very far future, as a result time between the two mouths became fixed, immutable. Do you understand?'

Saul saw he was now very nearly at the tunnel entrance. He'd hoped that, if he could just keep Mitchell talking, he had a better chance of catching up. But his muscles were starting to protest, and Mitchell meanwhile sounded like he hadn't done anything more strenuous than take a short jog.

'That doesn't make one damn bit of sense to me,' Saul gasped.

'You've heard of the observer effect in physics, right? Once you observe an event, an infinite range of possible outcomes collapses to just one. It's the same with time. Whenever you create a wormhole, and move one mouth through space at relativistic speeds, you create a path into the future – but the objective time that passes *outside* the wormhole becomes fixed into a single, unchangeable destiny. Do you see? It's the death of free will. That's why the Founders fought each other for control of the networks. Some of the artefacts we found had been weapons in that war.'

Saul finally reached the mouth of the tunnel, his lungs burning from overexertion. He knew he had to keep going but, in truth, he wasn't sure he could. He glanced back the way he'd come, but by now the lander was lost amidst the boulders and dust.

'The growths?' he panted, his back resting against the tunnel wall. 'They were one of those weapons?'

Mitchell laughed. 'You've got it all wrong. The growths aren't trying to kill us,' he said. 'They're *saving* us.'

Saul pushed himself away from the wall, and headed further into the tunnel until he came to a door. 'Tell me how the growths are saving us,' he asked, still stalling for time.

'You think they're killing people,' said Mitchell, 'but they're not. They're preserving them.'

A UP-enabled menu sprang up in front of the door, just as Saul stepped closer. The interface was primitive, a set of simple textual menus displayed in lines of bright-green text hovering in the blackness before him.

'*Preserving* them?'

A light blinked on above the same door, and it swung slowly open. Saul took a step back, suddenly afraid of Mitchell lunging out at him – but there was no one there. He stepped inside and found himself standing by the top of a ladder set into an unpressurized shaft that fell away into darkness. He lowered himself over the edge and began to descend, his suit's shallow lights illuminating the shaft walls around him. It felt too much like descending into some bottomless pit.

'Our lives are meaningless without free will,' Mitchell continued. 'The wormholes' very existence reduces us to automatons following predestined paths. The growths are incredible, Saul; they copy everything, all the way down to the superposition of every particle in the bodies of every living organism on Earth. Every living human being is going to wake up as if nothing happened – but way, way up the time-stream. They'll find themselves in a place that looks just like Earth, but they'll be truly free for the first time in their lives. It would be wrong not to let the growths preserve everyone, Saul. I mean *everyone*.'

'You want the same thing to happen to the colonies?'

'Of course,' Mitchell replied, sounding surprised as if the answer were self-evident. 'The pools showed me everything: a grand strategy, to recover sentient life from all through the period of the universe fixed by the wormhole networks, and rebirth it in the deep, deep future, at a point when the wormholes no longer exist. They showed me glimpses of it, Saul. It's beautiful – and we can all be a part of it. But if you shut the Array down, you're dooming the colonies to a living death. That's why I had to stop you any way I could, because I knew you would never understand. Not if you hadn't seen what I've seen.'

Saul paused, letting his helmet rest gently against a rung. He felt like he couldn't move an inch further, but he had no idea just how far down the shaft went. He forced himself to start moving again, tightly clenching his jaw, and stopped only when a black wave of dizziness threatened to suck him into unconsciousness. He then thrust his elbows through the bars of the ladder to support him, and waited until it passed.

He finally reached the bottom a few minutes later, his suit lights showing polished rock walls. Saul slumped down on the floor and waited for the agony in his muscles to pass. A new menu appeared, listing the location of emergency air supplies.

'Mitchell? Whatever those pools told you, did it ever occur to you that maybe they were feeding you lies? How can you know that any of what they told you is really true?'

Silence.

Saul staggered back upright and headed, as quickly as he was capable, down a long, low-ceilinged corridor that forced him to hunch over. He soon left the shaft behind, whereupon his universe shrank to encompass only the bubble of light projected by his suit and the sound of his own laboured breathing. The muscles in his legs threatened to cramp up once more and, when he sucked at the water pipe inside his helmet, a warning flashed up that he'd already used up most of it.

Just when Saul started seriously considering turning back, he noticed a certain greying of the surrounding darkness.

He pushed on and a dim light grew until he could see where the corridor ended at another ladder, extending downwards into brightness. He halted there and peered down, noting that this second shaft was nowhere near as deep as the previous one. He could just make out a door no more than thirty metres down, and he descended quickly towards it.

It proved to be part of an airlock complex, which he stepped through, cycling the atmosphere and pulling his helmet off once the pressure had equalized. The air tasted cool, and sweeter than it had any right to.

He thought of Amy, almost certainly still grieving for Lester, back there in the lander.

Got to move. He stripped his suit off, abandoning it on the floor of the airlock. He next pulled his own clothes out of a backpack slung beneath his air supply, and changed into them quickly.

He had emerged from the airlock to find himself at one end of a curving corridor located in a service and maintenance area close to the southern tip of the Lunar Array. Hanover had told him he needed to get to the ASI offices, but he guessed they were still at least thirty minutes away on foot, or less if he could find transport. As he started walking, he again hailed Mitchell, but the man had fallen silent once more. The only thing Saul could feel sure of was that he hadn't seen the last of him.

Saul eventually came to the first of thirteen enclosed concourses, each of which accessed a different wormhole gate. The place was eerily silent and clearly abandoned. Heavily reinforced windows at one end of it looked out towards the far lip of Copernicus Crater, a hundred kilometres away. The bright lights of the city were clearly visible closer to hand, and only a little further around the inner rim of the crater wall. Escalators at the concourse's opposite end led to a higher level not far below the roof, where shuttle-cars that normally carried passengers through the wormhole gate to the Clarke colony waited in silent ranks.

He walked past empty shop fronts and flickering UP-ads, until he discovered a small service car abandoned next to an information booth. He grunted with satisfaction on finding it to be fully charged.

The concourses were all linked to each other by a wide lane that ran through the whole Array, along its inner edge and just below the windows. Automated transport vehicles used for shifting heavy goods had been abandoned all up and down this route. Saul boarded the service vehicle and guided it along the lane, the vaulted space all around him so still and quiet he could almost believe the entire facility had been abandoned for a century, not just a few hours.

He drove steadily, though the car's top speed wasn't much more than a few kilometres per hour, till he passed through an archway and into the next concourse, which proved to be equally abandoned. As he passed through the one after that, he had to guide his vehicle around the still-smoking ruins of a Black Dog, dark smoke spiralling upwards to the curved ceiling far overhead.

He came across further evidence of fighting when he reached the Kepler–Copernicus gate. Half a dozen armoured personnel carriers stood parked close together below the embarkation area, all of them showing the signs of having come under heavy fire. One still burned fitfully.

Saul drove closer, constantly ready to hit the accelerator if he ran into trouble. The bodies of troopers were scattered all around the APCs, and the air reeked of cooked meat. He stepped out of the car to retrieve a Cobra from the outstretched hand of one of the troopers, seeing from the weapon's readout that it was fully loaded with concussion shells. He adjusted the strap and slung it over his shoulder, feeling more confidence in it than in Amy's home-brew concoction, which he now abandoned in the rear seat.

He noticed two APCs standing about twenty metres away from the huddle of vehicles surrounded by corpses. They had suffered less damage, but had clearly also come under fire at some point. He moved closer and saw a body slumped in the driving seat of one of them, while another corpse rested against a wheel, with a Cobra cradled in his hands.

Something in the way these bodies were positioned, and the fact that this one group of APCs stood apart from the rest, made Saul sure there had been infighting here of some kind. He wondered if some of the troopers had countermanded their orders and been executed for their trouble. Perhaps they had families back home, and hadn't wanted to be forced to leave them behind.

He finally climbed inside the less badly damaged APC, trusting it to get him further faster, and to afford him a much greater degree of protection at the same time. Saul placed a hand on the dashboard and waited until it blinked, accepting his authorization, the wheel unfolding to become rigid enough for him to take a grip on it. He drove it straight back on to the transport lane leading to the Copernicus–Florida gate, from where he could take an elevator down to the ASI's main operations room.

*

Saul smelled smoke not long before he passed through the archway leading into the Copernicus–Florida concourse.

At one end of the open area stood all that remained of a terminal station for passengers arriving from Copernicus City. Much of it had been reduced to rubble, and a cool swift breeze told Saul that the Array's atmospheric integrity had been compromised. Several Black Dogs stood motionless at the foot of the escalators leading up to the station itself, their weapons systems clearly active still.

Saul glanced the other way, towards the departure area, accessible by another bank of escalators. He could see shuttle-cars standing at the top of them in silent and empty rows. No Dogs had been set to guard them, although there were numerous crowd-control steel barricades arranged in rows at the bottom.

One of the Dogs turned itself in a half-circle as Saul drove towards the middle of the concourse, tracking his progress with an eyeless gaze. Saul watched with deep trepidation as the weapons systems mounted between its shoulders whined and shifted. He slowed the vehicle to a crawl and eased the driver's-side door open in case he had to make a run for it, but the machine merely continued to track him without taking any further action.

He got out of the car, eased the Cobra off his shoulder and stared around. There were the corpses of yet more troopers by the barricades, so clearly fighting had occurred here as well. The only sound he could hear now was the occasional click-whir of the Black Dogs echoing across the concourse.

At the centre of the concourse was a recreation and dining area, consisting of several low buildings and open-air restaurants surrounding a paved courtyard, where a small fountain stood in the middle, surrounded by shrubs. Saul looked around, but there was still no sign of life. If Mitchell was really determined to prevent him from shutting down the gates, he was certainly taking his time about it.

Saul made his way towards an elevator set into a recess beneath a plaque reading 'ARRAY SECURITY AND IMMIGRATION'.

His shoes squeaked slightly on the polished floor of the silent concourse, sounding unnaturally loud to his ears.

Something suddenly clattered to the ground at an indeterminate distance away. Glancing immediately towards the row of Black Dogs, Saul noticed that the same one that had tracked him earlier was now turning to face the other way, as if something on the far side of the recreation area had drawn its attention meanwhile.

Something, or someone?

It had to be Mitchell. He was obviously hiding somewhere close, and Saul wondered what he was waiting for. He took a firmer grip on the Cobra, ignoring the rapid tattoo that his heart was beating against the inside of his chest, and tapped on the weapon's screen so that it integrated with his contacts. Targeting information instantly superimposed itself over everything he saw.

He scurried towards the elevators, crouching low, passed through a cordon that would normally be manned. Recognizing his UP, one of the elevators opened at his approach. Saul stepped inside, pressing his back against the interior wall, while aiming the Cobra back in the direction he had come.

Just before the doors closed, he caught sight of movement somewhere by the fountain. Mitchell, he decided: it couldn't possibly be anyone else.

THIRTY

Saul logged into the Array's localized security network. As he stepped into the lobby of the operations room, he saw personal belongings scattered on desks and jackets hooked over the backs of chairs, as if the staff here had simply got up in the middle of their work and departed en masse. Perhaps, he thought, that was exactly what they had done, and he wondered just how much warning they'd received. If that was the case, had they chosen to flee, or simply gone back home to be with their loved ones?

He slung the Cobra back over his shoulder, its targeting data fading the moment his fingers released the barrel. Moving on quickly, past the empty desks and workstations, he began activating the code given him by Hanover. A further layer of information appeared on top of his usual UP overlay, guiding him towards the single elevator that serviced the executive suites assigned to the members of the ASI's directorate. It carried him yet further below the lunar surface, depositing him in a carpeted corridor, where he headed past conference rooms and numerous locked doors until he was guided to the suite of offices belonging to Thomas Fowler, the Director of the ASI himself.

The door was locked, and there didn't appear to be an option in the EDP overlay that would allow him to bypass it. He swore softly under his breath, then unslung the Cobra and fired a short burst directly into the door. It swung inwards as if it had been kicked.

Saul entered to see an enormous oak desk to one side, a couch and several leather armchairs on the other, along with a wall-sized display of a beach at sunset.

The EDP overlay drew him towards Fowler's desk. As he sat down in the chair, the surface of the desk automatically came to life, with sets of icons floating above its surface. He followed the overlay's instructions, reaching out to one icon in particular and once again entering Hanover's code.

Hearing a click from somewhere next to his knee, Saul pushed the chair back to find one of the desk drawers had slid open. He dipped a hand inside and withdrew a single unmarked keycard.

He stared at it dry-mouthed. It looked so innocuous for something that could change the fate of the human race. That caused a momentary flicker of doubt, and he wondered if perhaps Hanover had tricked him deliberately, and the keycard served some other purpose.

Only one way to find out.

He stood up, letting the overlay guide him to a single unmarked door at the far end. The door was locked but a single slot, at waist height, was just about the right size to accommodate the keycard. Saul inserted it and the door swung open with ease.

Saul retrieved the keycard and let the door swing shut behind him. He found himself standing in a functional-looking space that was almost as large as the office itself. Apart from a couple of terminals facing each other from opposite walls, the room was entirely bare.

This, then, was the secret terminal room that Hanover had told him of.

Security menus appeared as Saul walked further into the room. He waved them to one side, while the overlay directed him towards the terminal set against the right-hand wall. He stepped right up to it, more menus appearing around him. He scanned them quickly, then reached out to touch one in particular. Following its instructions, he then re-entered the access code.

With one trembling hand, he placed the keycard into a slot and waited to see what happened next.

Nothing.

Of course. He'd almost forgotten Hanover's warning that the two-man rule was only rescinded when one of the pair of security servers fell out of contact with the other.

Maybe, he surmised, that was the reason the Copernicus–Florida gate had never been shut down. Maybe the paired servers had stayed in contact with each other until it was much too late, and the force devastating the Earth had done the same to Copernicus.

If that was the case, maybe he was going to need someone else's help after all. He slammed a fist against the wall next to the terminal in fury, nearly weeping with frustration.

At that moment, he heard the sound of movement through the door leading back into Fowler's office.

Saul gripped the Cobra close to his chest, remembering the speed with which Mitchell had moved inside the lander.

He stepped cautiously back out into the main office, swinging the barrel of his weapon from side to side.

Nothing to be seen.

He licked his lips and moved on past the desk, and towards the ruined door.

From of the corner of his eye, he saw part of the image in the wall-display move, the beach-front houses rippling. The scene looked like it might be somewhere in the Florida Keys.

Too late, he realized it was a trooper with his chameleon circuitry activated. Saul caught a brief flash of an angry face before something slammed into his skull with terrible force, plunging him into darkness.

Saul woke to the smell of smoke and an intensely bright light shining into one eye.

'He checks out,' said a voice from somewhere close by. 'Minor concussion, but that's it.'

346

'Fine,' said a second voice, as the light receded.

Someone kicked Saul in the shin. 'Get the hell up,' ordered the second voice.

With a groan, Saul heaved himself upright. He looked around to see he was back on the concourse that served the Copernicus–Florida gate. Six troopers – four men and two women – stood in a semicircle gazing down at him, where he had been propped against the wheel of an APC. Their faces streaked with grime, their eyes uniformly bloodshot, they looked more like the walking wounded than anything else.

'Where the hell did you come from?' asked Saul, rubbing at the back of his neck. He noticed that the owner of the second voice was a man in his late thirties, his sandy hair cropped short above frightened eyes. The UP ident floating next to his head identified him as a Colonel Bailey.

Bailey responded by dragging Saul to his feet, then slamming him hard up against the APC. 'How about you tell me what you were doing here in a restricted area?'

Saul glanced to one side, at the open back of the APC, and saw that it was loaded with several crates. The top of one had been ripped open, revealing a load of flat, grey bricks that stirred up a mote of recognition. He knew that he should know what they were, but somehow he couldn't seem to recall.

'For Christ's sake,' replied Saul. 'You can see my UP, can't you? I have clearance.'

'Yeah – and, according to the last update we got before everything went quiet back home, you're currently wanted for attempted murder, sabotage and terrorism.'

'Listen to me, will you? There's a man here planning to kill us all. We've got to stop him.'

'Answer my question, Mr Dumont.'

'I'm trying to prevent whatever's happening back home from happening to the colonies as well.'

'Well, shit,' said one of the women, 'that's exactly what *we're* here to do. We got sent back through from Clarke, and—'

'Shut up, Peggy,' snapped Bailey, before returning his attention to Saul. 'Prevent it how?'

'Emergency destruct protocols,' said Saul. 'You know what that means?'

'I do – and so do you, clearly.' Bailey pulled out Saul's keycard to the terminal room and held it up. 'Mind telling me who gave you the access code?'

'I got it from Constantin Hanover. He's a task-force leader. I was about to shut down the whole Array, when you smacked me over the head.'

'The *whole* Array?' Bailey frowned. 'The only gate you need to shut down is the one leading back to Florida. Why the hell would anyone want to cut off the colonies from each other?'

'Maybe he's working for the separatists,' suggested one of the others. 'Maybe he's one of them. Maybe that's the real reason he was there.'

'That's not how it is,' protested Saul, feeling a surge of panic.

'But that is what the separatists want, isn't it?' Bailey demanded.

The flat grey bricks, Saul suddenly realized, were explosives. Being knocked unconscious had made it hard for him to think clearly. Things were starting to come back to him now, little recollections and fragments from over the last several days, but some if it was still disconnected, as if all the thoughts and memories gathered in his head had been knocked out of synch and were now struggling to reconnect with each other in the right order.

'For Christ's sake,' said Saul, 'if you reckon all you need to do is close down the Florida gate, ask yourself why Copernicus City was evacuated! Why even bother doing that, if anyone thought the Moon was going to be safe? Shutting down the Florida gate isn't going to work.'

'What the hell makes you so sure?' said Bailey, his expression still disbelieving.

Saul started to form a reply, then he stopped. *I'm sure because I've seen into the future*, he thought, and realized there was no answer he could offer Bailey that they might accept. He had Jeff's stolen files, of course, but there wasn't nearly enough time now to go over all of that.

Bailey nodded, as if Saul's silence were an admission of guilt. 'I'm going to need you to give me whatever access code you have, and wherever the hell you got it from.'

'Is that why you were sent here?' asked Saul. 'To shut the Florida gate down?'

'No, the man we were escorting here was supposed to shut it down, except now he's dead. We've only got one of the pair of codes we need. So give me,' Bailey snarled through gritted teeth, 'your fucking *code*.'

'I will if you'll tell me why your truck here is filled with explosives.'

'We were going to try and blow up this end of the Florida gate with HMX,' Peggy butted in. 'With our guy dead, we figured that was the only—'

Bailey turned to glare at her. 'Peggy, what part of shut-the-fuck-up do you not *understand*?'

He turned back to Saul, and slid his Cobra off his shoulder, taking aim at the prisoner's head. 'I won't bother counting to five. Just give me your fucking access code or—'

'Okay!' said Saul, raising his hands in a gesture of surrender. 'Okay, I'm sending it now.'

The colonel lowered his weapon as he received the code, then turned to one of the other soldiers. 'Isnard, check it out, will you?'

A trooper with a shock of red fuzz standing straight up from his scalp nodded, staring off into the distance as he scanned the information now arriving on his contacts.

'They wouldn't have sent only the six of you,' remarked Saul. 'Where's the rest of your squad?'

'We're all that's left,' said the other woman, apart from Peggy, her expression grim.

'The code's legit,' said Isnard. 'But his authorization doesn't square with his ID.'

'So it's stolen?' asked Bailey.

Isnard made a face. 'Guess so.'

Bailey grimaced and turned back to Saul. 'Don't even think about trying to talk your way out of this one.'

Bailey turned to the surviving members of his squad and started giving orders. 'Isnard, Jessup, take up positions over at the courtyard. Keep an eye out there. I don't want to get caught out like last time, and lose anyone else. Merrill, take Dallas with you and get to work placing the rest of the HMX. Peggy, you're with me.'

'Before you do anything else, you need to listen to me,' said Saul, his voice sounding ragged. 'There's a man named Mitchell Stone . . . he's going to try and stop you from destroying the gate. When you grabbed me upstairs in the executive suites, I thought you were him, coming to try and stop me.'

'He wouldn't be the first to try stopping us, Mr Dumont, but we're more than ready for trouble.'

'That's not going to be enough,' Saul insisted, watching the others head off, which left him alone with just Bailey and Peggy. 'This isn't any ordinary human being you're dealing with.'

'Unless he's driving a tank, I'm not worried,' Bailey replied dismissively. 'Right now we're going to go head down to that terminal suite and shut the Florida gate down.' He turned aside. 'Peggy!'

Peggy moved up beside Saul and pushed him back in the direction of the elevators, while Bailey took the lead, striding fast.

At that moment a deep and almost subsonic rumble came from the direction of the Florida gate. *It's coming*, Saul realized, breaking into a cold sweat.

Bailey stopped, staring towards the gate, his face several shades paler than just a moment before.

He turned back towards them. 'Get moving,' he barked, '*now*.'

Peggy shoved Saul forward again, and this time they broke into a run.

Bailey suddenly made an *oof* sound, after they'd covered a couple of dozen metres, before collapsing to his hands and knees. At first Saul assumed he'd tripped over something, but then the colonel slid to one side, his jaw slackening. Blood began pooling under his chest, and quickly spread out across the tiles.

Peggy gaped down at him, her eyes round and wide. *He's been shot*, thought Saul, realizing he had heard a sound like a wet cough from somewhere far away across the concourse, just before Bailey had collapsed.

Peggy swung her Cobra all around, but there was nothing for her to aim at. If the attacker was Mitchell, he was thoroughly hidden.

'We need to keep moving,' hissed Saul, and began backing towards the elevators. 'We're too exposed. He can pick us off easily while we're out in the open.'

'No!' she yelled, spinning around until the Cobra was directly trained on him. 'Stay right where you are.'

Saul glanced towards the barricades, fifty or so metres away, and saw Mitchell materialize next to Merrill, with alarming suddenness. He drew a knife across Merrill's throat and the trooper collapsed, blood spurting out from his neck in a gruesome arc.

There was no sign of Jessup. Already dead, Saul guessed.

Peggy must have seen Mitchell too, for she fired off her Cobra, explosive rounds digging cavities in the tiled floor at the precise spot he had been standing. But Mitchell was already gone, speeding back towards the central courtyard and the deserted restaurants surrounding it.

'Isnard,' Peggy yelled across the concourse, her face twisting in panic, 'where the fuck *are* you?'

Saul heard more gunfire, followed by screams.

'Peggy,' Saul tried again, 'if you want to stay alive, we need to get to those elevators now.'

She glanced at him blankly, as if she'd forgotten he was there. 'Okay,' she said, 'let's go.'

They started running again, Peggy sprinting ahead of him. That subsonic rumble had intensified, he thought: it was definitely a little louder. He prayed that didn't mean it was already too late.

The door of one of the elevators slid open at their approach, and Saul allowed himself to hope that his lifespan might still be measured in more than just seconds. Then a shadow flew past him, slamming Peggy against the wall adjoining the elevator, and he then realized it was already much, much too late.

Mitchell had one arm tight around Peggy's neck. She uttered a small cry, like a bird, in the moment before Mitchell snapped her spine. As she dropped in a lifeless heap at his feet, he stepped back, his chest heaving from exertion. There was a Cobra slung over one shoulder.

'So you gonna thank me for saving your life?' Mitchell panted, wiping a forearm across his brow.

Saul forced himself to meet Mitchell's calm blue gaze. 'What are you waiting for?' he demanded. 'Aren't you going to finish the job now?'

'Saul,' Mitchell's voice was almost gentle, 'they were going to *kill* you, is what it looked like to me.' He nodded towards the departure area. 'Didn't you listen to one damn thing I said? We'll be *transformed*, and so will the colonies. Then we can live for ever. I just wish Jeff and Olivia could have been here to share in it.'

'You're out of your fucking mind,' Saul shouted. 'Back there you said you wanted to kill me.'

Mitchell laughed. 'That was when I thought you posed a significant threat, but now you're unarmed and defenceless. Look,' he said, gesturing towards the departure area, with a radiant smile on his face.

Saul looked, and saw a heat-haze like shimmer make the air tremble at the top of the escalators. The low rumble had given way to a kind of ululation, like the wordless moan of a million massed voices, and growing incrementally louder by the second.

'If you're not going to kill me, that means you'll let me go?'

'No, I want you right here with me, because I can't take any chances on you doing something stupid, not now. Come on.'

Mitchell stepped closer and took a grip on Saul's upper arm. Saul tried to break loose and Mitchell yanked him closer still, twisting his arm behind his back, and then putting a stranglehold on him before pushing his face up against the wall.

'Saul,' he hissed in his ear, 'be reasonable. I know you don't believe me, but I'm genuinely trying to help you.'

The ululation had begun to infiltrate Saul's brain, like a score of icy needles working their way into his skull. He was finding it harder to concentrate, to even think.

He realized that an icon was blinking in one corner of his eye. How long had it been there without him noticing?

Seeing it was from Amy Rose, he activated the link.

'Let's go,' said Mitchell, stepping back while dragging Saul along with him, his other arm tight around Saul's neck.

Barely able to breathe, Saul tried to break loose, but the slightest movement sent shards of agony shooting through his shoulder. Mitchell was meanwhile dragging him towards the escalators, closer to the strangely shimmering air.

'Saul?' he heard Amy say inside his head. 'Give me a sign that you can hear me. I can see you, but where is he taking you?'

I'm not sure, Saul tried to reply, but Mitchell's grip around his neck was too tight.

Mitchell came to a halt. 'You're talking to someone.'

'No,' Saul managed to croak. How the hell could he have known?

'Bullshit, you think I can't tell?'

He let go of Saul, shoving him down on to the tiles, where he sprawled helplessly, his right arm completely numb.

'I can see you,' Amy muttered inside his head. 'I'm some way back, next to a fountain in a courtyard. I could take him out from here.'

Mitchell checked the readout on his Cobra, then gazed intently across the concourse towards the courtyard. Had he, Saul wondered, somehow *heard* Amy over all that distance?

If Mitchell had any idea where Amy was, she wouldn't even see him coming.

'Mitchell,' Saul croaked, 'there's something I have to tell you.'

Mitchell spared him only a brief glance. 'Whatever it is, I don't have the time,' he muttered.

'It's about your brother, Danny.'

Saul licked his lips and struggled to avoid looking at the courtyard. He wondered if Amy had picked up one of the Cobras; there had been plenty of them scattered about. Of course, she was getting old, but the Cobra targeting systems were designed to do most of the work for their users.

'Jesus, Saul,' said Mitchell, his expression almost pitying. 'I don't know what you're up to, but this is low.'

'I never told you the truth about him,' Saul persevered. 'He wasn't dead when I found him. He was still alive.'

Mitchell blinked and shook his head. 'What?'

'You asked me to try and find him.' Saul remembered telling Olivia the same story back in Orlando, but with one vital difference. 'Well, that much I did manage. I tracked him down, all right.'

It felt like lancing a festering wound, with all the old poison spilling out in a rush. 'He'd been left there to guard the place and, when I turned up, I tried to talk him into leaving with me. I told him I could keep him safe, make sure that no one ever knew he'd been involved. Instead, he tried to kill me.'

'No.' Mitchell shook his head. 'That's not possible. Danny would never—'

'He was in very, very deep, Mitch. He shot at me, but he didn't know how to use the gun properly. All I got was a flesh wound.'

'You told me you'd been in an accident,' said Mitchell, his tone numb. He had turned his back towards the courtyard, the Cobra dangling forgotten from one hand.

'I killed him. To save my own life, I had to. I never told you that because I didn't think you could handle knowing what really happened.'

'You're lying!' Mitchell screamed. 'You miserable son of a bitch, you're making this shit up!'

He lunged at Saul, enraged, locking both hands tight around his throat.

Do it now, thought Saul, desperately pushing the heel of one hand against Mitchell's jaw, to try and force his head back. The shimmering haze had spread, tiny specks of light like fireflies dancing everywhere under the high ceiling of the concourse.

Saul heard a damp cough, much like the one he'd heard before Colonel Bailey had died, and Mitchell jerked forward. He stared down at Saul, his mouth hanging open with shock, and a look of utter disbelief in his eyes. He staggered upright, with evident difficulty.

'You don't know what you've done,' he gasped at Saul, then sat down hard on the tiles. There was a dark circle of blood in the middle of his chest, growing wider.

Saul pushed himself upright and grabbed hold of the Cobra that Mitchell had dropped. 'I'm sorry,' he wheezed, meaning it.

'True?' asked Mitchell. 'About Danny?'

Saul nodded. 'Yes. I'm sorry.'

Saul peered across the concourse, and spotted Amy crouching to one side of the fountain.

Mitchell nodded. 'I wish . . . I wish things had been different.'

Saul realized his own cheeks were damp as he levelled the Cobra between Mitchell's eyes. 'That makes two of us,' he said, and squeezed the trigger.

THIRTY-ONE

Saul let the Cobra rifle slip out of his fingers and tried to make sense of the emotions warring inside him. There was anger, but also regret and sorrow, in equal measures.

He turned away from Mitchell's lifeless body and saw Amy Rose come jogging towards him. She was still wearing her spacesuit, minus the helmet, her grey hair tangled into knots. She bent over, once she reached him, hands resting on knees and gasping for breath.

'Wait here,' said Saul, and quickly made his way back to where Bailey's body lay. He dug through the dead man's pockets until he found the same keycard Bailey had deprived him of.

'You okay?' she asked, standing up straight again as he came back.

'You saved my life,' he said. 'Thank you.'

'It was a pleasure. Have you done it yet? Shut the gates down, I mean.'

'No, but it shouldn't take long.'

'Good.' She glanced uneasily towards the gate itself. 'Do you need any help from me?'

Bailey had mentioned that he had a second code, which they might have been able to use to shut the gates down together, but now that code had died with him, and they were back down to just the one code again. Saul could only hope it would prove enough this time.

'No,' he told her, 'I can take care of it on my own.'

Amy nodded, and sat down on the floor, with her arms resting on her knees. 'If you don't mind, I'll wait here,' she said. 'I'm pretty winded after all that running around.'

'When I left you in the lander,' said Saul, 'I felt sure you were going to stay there.'

'No, that was never my plan. I just . . . I just needed time to say goodbye.' Her eyes glistened as she drew in a sharp breath. 'Then I suited myself up and got out of there.'

'Amy . . .'

She made a shooing gesture. 'Go,' she said. 'Do what you have to do to fix things. I'll still be here when you get back.'

Saul nodded and stepped inside an elevator, watching her disappear from sight as he was carried downwards once more.

Saul sprinted past workstations and conference booths, feeling the seconds weighing heavy on him as he raced for the second elevator that would carry him even deeper beneath the Array. The EDP information overlay slid back into place as he stepped inside, and a minute later he was running along the hallway towards Fowler's office and the terminal room there.

Once inside, he pushed the keycard back into the same slot he'd used before, and again entered the access code, quickly navigating through the menus.

A message appeared, telling him there had been a remote-server malfunction. Saul interpreted this to mean that the Florida communications server had finally failed.

'CONFIRM TO RESCIND TWO-PERSON ACTIVATION PROTOCOL,' advised another message.

Yes, Saul confirmed, working his way through several more menus until he found what he was looking for. He reached out with a trembling hand, and ordered the ASI's computer systems to close down every last wormhole within the Array.

'EMERGENCY SHUTDOWN PROTOCOL INITIATED,'

read a new message. 'TERMINAL WORMHOLE FAILURE IN 1800 SECONDS.'

1800 seconds: just thirty minutes from now.

He thought about the flickers of light he'd seen dancing beneath the concourse ceiling, and wondered if even only thirty minutes was too long. An alarm began to sound, low and urgent, and he turned to run back through the main office and down the hallway to the elevator.

Saul found Amy waiting for him when he stepped out of the elevator and into the main operations room.

'What happened?' he demanded. 'I thought you were going to wait for me up on the concourse.'

She shook her head. 'Couldn't think straight up there. Whatever's happening up there, it's getting worse. Is it done yet?'

He nodded briefly, leading her back towards the elevator that would take them back up into the Array. 'It's done. We've got thirty minutes to get ourselves through a gate. Whichever way you look at it, we're going to be cutting it close.'

Saul kept willing the elevator to move faster as it carried them back up. The strange noise penetrated the walls of the elevator car more clearly the higher they ascended, drilling into his thoughts. He glanced at Amy and saw she wasn't having any easier a time of it.

The entire concourse shook as they emerged, the air now so thick and fluid it almost felt like being underwater. That dreadful ululation seemed to vibrate right through the atoms in Saul's body. He looked up at the twists of light that now crowded the concourse ceiling. Something about them made his eyes hurt, so that he couldn't look at them for more than a second or two.

'Thirty minutes won't be enough time, will it?' Amy yelled to him over the din. 'Whatever's driving those clouds is going to get through before that. No telling what might happen then.'

Saul remembered something. 'The HMX,' he shouted.

'The what?'

'Explosives,' Saul yelled. 'Those troopers Mitchell killed had an APC filled with HMX explosives. They were wiring the Florida gate so they could blow it up.'

'Would that work?'

He shook his head. 'I don't know. Maybe it might delay the clouds, but that's about it.'

'Better than nothing,' she yelled back.

He nodded, and they made their way quickly over to the APC. Saul took the lead, but Amy struggled to keep up, so he put one arm around her waist and half carried her. She didn't protest or try to push him away, which only showed how exhausted she was. In truth, he was running on little more than adrenalin himself.

All they had to do was keep going just a little longer.

'I'm getting a bit too old for this,' panted Amy. 'Seriously.'

They now came to the barricades, where the bodies of Merrill and Dallas still lay alongside a crate filled with bricks of HMX. Amy picked one up and studied it for a moment.

'Demolition charges,' she said, glancing towards him, then slumped against one of the barricades, looking pale and ill. 'By the looks of it, the detonators are already in place.'

'I didn't know you were some kind of demolitions expert?'

'We used HMX when we were building biomes out on Newton. Good for excavating land real fast.'

Something about the ululation made Saul's skin itch like it was burning. 'The question is, how were they going to set off the detonation?'

'Remote trigger?' she replied. 'That's my guess, anyway.'

'You mean through their contacts?'

'No.' She shook her head. 'That way there's too big a risk that somebody might hack your contacts and then trigger an explosion from a long way off. They'd have planned to use a dedicated device of some sort.' She nodded towards Merrill's butchered corpse. 'Check him out. Maybe he's got something on him.'

Saul grimaced as he bent over Merrill's body, pushing his hand inside pockets soaked with the dead man's blood. When he found nothing, he moved over to Dallas, and soon found a slim device sporting several inlaid buttons.

'That's it,' Amy said, as he showed it to her. 'Same as what we used ourselves. Nothing like having a nice fat button to press when you're blowing shit up.'

'Then we can blow the HMX remotely, before we head through the Galileo gate? The starship gets there in a couple of months, and we'll be able to survive until—'

'Wait a minute,' interrupted Amy. She stood up and glanced towards the APC parked nearby, with the rest of the crates of explosive still piled in the back. 'That's what they used to transport the HMX here, right? So how many of those bricks do you think they managed to place already?'

Saul studied the APC, still mostly filled with unopened crates. 'I don't know,' he said, 'but I reckon not that many.'

Amy nodded. 'That's what I thought too. Looks like they barely got started before Mitchell killed them.'

'Then there's nothing we can do,' Saul said grimly.

Amy rubbed her mouth pensively. 'No, I think we've got one other option.' She glanced towards the escalators that led up to the departure area. 'Is there any way to get that APC up to where the actual wormhole gate is?'

'Why? What are you thinking?'

'I'm thinking,' she said, 'that if someone could get all that HMX up there and close to the gate, it could do an awful lot of damage.'

'No way,' said Saul. 'You'd never have enough time to get back out before it was too late.'

'Whether or not I get out doesn't really matter, Mr Dumont.' She reached out a hand. 'I'd appreciate it if you'd let me have the detonator device.'

'Just look around you,' he yelled. 'I don't know if the explosives would make any difference at all. They built the machinery maintaining the wormholes to sustain an awful lot of damage.'

'You said yourself that we could at least slow it all down,' she yelled back. The noise and the shimmering light were intensifying. 'We've got less than twenty minutes, so there isn't time to argue over this.'

'You'll kill yourself.'

'Yeah, like I hadn't figured that out. Go now,' she said. 'I can take care of this.'

'No, wait, maybe I should—'

'I don't have time for this bullshit!' she shouted, snatching the detonator from his grasp. She then picked up some of the bricks of HMX, clutching them close to her chest. 'All my life I had Lester, and now he's gone. You still have family on Galileo, right? Now tell me how the hell to get this APC up to that level.'

'There's a passageway running up behind the centre pair of escalators, over there,' Saul pointed. 'It leads to some cargo elevators big enough to take even the APC up.'

'Fine.' She nodded curtly. 'Don't say anything more now. No goodbyes or sentimental crap or anything like that, okay? Grab one of those other vehicles over by the courtyard and get yourself the hell through a gate already, will you?'

Saul nodded wordlessly, then turned and ran.

He pulled himself inside an empty APC, reversing it in a half-circle before taking one last glance back at Amy. He watched her get inside the one packed with HMX, and drive it away towards the tunnel accessing the service elevators.

Saul turned away and gunned his own vehicle towards the main transport lane linking all the concourses. Warnings flashed at him as he pushed the vehicle to its limit, whipping the wheel around and accelerating hard. He figured he had at best fifteen minutes to make it all the way to the Galileo concourse, which lay at the farthest end of the Array; that left him barely enough time to get on board a shuttle-car that would transport him to the starship carrying the far end of the new wormhole gate, before the wormhole collapsed.

If he was lucky, he might even manage it with a few minutes to spare.

The constant noise and shimmering faded as he put distance between himself and the Florida gate, and soon it felt as if a heavy fog had lifted from his thoughts. He guided the APC through a series of concourses in turn, each as eerily silent as the last. Everywhere he noticed more abandoned APCs and barricades, and more corpses, but of civilians this time.

A powerful roar surged along the lane far behind him. Saul glanced back, but a gentle curve to the route now made it impossible to see all the way back to the Florida concourse itself.

It's worked, he thought, his hands still clamped tightly around the wheel. He steered around a truck slanting across the lane ahead, and shot through another concourse, feeling the seconds tick away.

As he passed through another concourse, and then another, it occurred to him that he might very well be the last living person on the Moon, until he remembered that there was another Mitchell Stone somewhere out there, not so very far from the Array itself, even now beginning his decade-long slumber.

Saul finally reached the last concourse, separated off from the rest of the Array complex by a tall temporary barrier that had stood in place ever since the original Galileo gate had been sabotaged. A single security entrance was set into the high barrier, and it was clearly far too narrow for his APC to squeeze through.

He abandoned the vehicle and sprinted through the security door into the concourse beyond. It was as devoid of life as the rest, yet lacked the evidence of violent conflict such as he had observed in most of the others. There were small open trucks parked here and there of the type used by maintenance crews, along with evidence of recent preparations for the reopening of contact with Galileo. Before the growths had appeared, the news feeds had been full of speculation about the reception that might be expected from whoever turned out to be currently in charge of the colony, and whether the Coalition governments might attempt an invasion.

A second great roaring sound set the ground beneath him shaking. Saul stumbled and then stared around him. *That wasn't the HMX*, he thought wildly.

He climbed a stairway to a platform raised several metres above the concourse, from where he could get a clear view through the windows. He glanced halfway along the curving length of the Lunar Array to where the Florida gate was located. Thick smoke, like ashes, billowed out across the lunar landscape from a rent in the wall. Light danced inside that smoke, like something alive.

Saul backed away, dry-mouthed, realizing Amy's sacrifice hadn't been entirely in vain. But, then again, it didn't look like it had done more than gain him a few minutes of a head-start.

He turned to run back down the steps and across the concourse, fatigue already clouding his thoughts. He climbed inside a maintenance cart, then cursed as it began trundling towards the elevated departure area with not nearly enough speed. There he jumped off, throwing himself up on to a stationary escalator and stopping at the top just long enough to momentarily recover his breath.

The ground beneath his feet was shaking, and the air further along the Array howling as it vented on to the lunar surface. A wind picked up, growing stronger within seconds, until Saul was forced to claw his way forward, past abandoned security cordons, and towards the waiting shuttle-cars.

He pulled himself into the first one he came to and collapsed on to a seat, his lungs screaming with pain as the doors slid shut. The shuttle-car jerked slightly, then began to slowly move towards the gate's entrance.

Saul pulled himself upright and staggered to the front of the vehicle, watching the heavy steel doors slide apart at the car's approach. Beyond lay a wide tunnel ringed with steel and dense clumps of instrumentation.

Almost there.

He touched the curving glass of the car's window and felt it vibrate – the tremors increasing and decreasing in a way that reminded him of the throbbing that had filled the Florida concourse.

A second set of doors slid open, and the shuttle-car glided inside the body of a starship light-years across the galaxy. His weary muscles protested as Saul came under the influence of the ship's deceleration-induced gravity.

As his UP connected with the shipboard network, he squeezed through the shuttle's doors almost before they'd had a chance to open fully. The network then surrounded him with frantically blinking alerts to warn of terminal wormhole failure.

Only seconds left, he realized with desperate alarm. Really, he had no time left at all.

Saul hurtled out of the shuttle bay just as the ship shook with such terrifying violence that he was thrown to the floor of the service corridor beyond. He hooked his fingers through the black-painted metal grid comprising the floor, and held on tight. Meanwhile the ship was struggling to correct the spin resulting from the sudden collapse of the wormhole, its emergency thrusters firing as the one tenuous thread linking it back to Copernicus vanished in a blaze of dissipating exotic particles.

Panting furiously, Saul crouched in that same spot for what felt like a very long time, while the ship continued to shudder all around him. Slowly, one by one, most of the alerts faded away. He let himself close his eyes, just for a moment . . .

He woke up again some indeterminate amount of time later, his fingers still hooked through the gaps in the metal grid. Saul stood up uneasily, wincing at the sharp pain in his muscles.

After that, he wandered through the silent starship until he found the emergency bay, kitted out with freeze-dried food supplies and tanks of water, enough to keep him alive for a long time if need be. He drank until he'd slaked a raging thirst, then wandered through the ship until he found an observation bay, its overhead display revealing a sprinkling of stars.

One star in particular was far brighter than all the rest. He collapsed on to a couch and stared up at it. 94 Aquarii, more than a hundred light-years from Earth – home to the Galileo colony.

FINAL DAYS

Saul stared up at it for a long, long time, knowing that the rest of his life lay somewhere in that single bright point of light.

Over, he thought, in the last moments before consciousness deserted him and he passed out once more.

It was over.

THIRTY-TWO

Galileo Colony, 94 Aquarii System, Four Months Later

'This way, please.'

Erkrnwald, polite as ever, indicated a series of steps, cut into the cliff face, which descended towards a shoreline of pale-grey sand far below.

Saul glanced back at the transport and saw it reverse away from the cliff edge, before turning and heading back, presumably, in search of the nearest charging port. Further inland, he could see rows of agricultural buildings stretching into the distance, each surrounded by fields of experimental crops specially designed for the Galilean soil and atmosphere.

He turned back to Erkrnwald and nodded, the young political officer's expression politely bland as he placed one hand on the railing that guarded the steps down. White-capped waves thick with yellowish-blue algae crashed constantly against the shore, beyond which dozens of drilling platforms were visible, stretching out to the horizon. A motorized launch waited for them below, rising and dipping with the tide.

'Is there a reason we couldn't just fly out there?' he asked.

'Not at this time of year.' Erkrnwald shook his head. 'We're coming up to drift-spore season, so too much risk of getting our engines clogged.'

Saul nodded and they began to descend the steps. The air away from town smelled different, lacking that particular odour all of

Galileo's larger settlements seemed to share. It wasn't quite the smell of the sea back home on Earth, but close enough. He tasted salt on his lips as the wind carried a thin spray of sea water up towards the cliff top.

A few dozen metres out from the shore, a submarine whale's single eye pushed up from the water on its rubbery stalk, glancing briefly around in a typically comical fashion before once more sliding beneath the waves.

The launch was a one-piece fab job, low and sleek, its lines distinctly organic. Another man, older than Erkrnwald, waited on the shore close by.

'I'm Representative Kayes,' he said, stepping forward to greet them. He glanced at Erkrnwald the same way Saul had seen most people here do, with a mixture of cautious respect and unease. 'And you must be Mr Dumont,' he said, addressing Saul. 'I've been following you on the news ever since they brought you down from orbit last month.'

'To be honest, if heading out to the platforms means I can get away from all the press attention, that's enough reason to be here, all on its own. And, please, call me Saul.'

Kayes chuckled in sympathy. 'Still, it can't have been easy for you. You were stuck on that starship for Lord knows how many weeks before it reached Galileo.'

Saul smiled wanly. 'It could have been worse.'

'When they first contacted you, I was glued to the feeds,' said Kayes. 'I know there's still people don't believe your story, but I believe it. I listened to every word you said during the interviews. If I could have been there when they brought you down from orbit, I would've been.'

'About the girl,' said Erkrnwald, an impatient tone to his voice, 'does she know?'

'Yes.' Kayes nodded, turning back to the officer. 'There was still some uncertainty over her identity until this morning. We've asked her to take the afternoon off from her duties.' He glanced at Saul.

'She . . . she doesn't know you're coming, though she should by the time we get there.'

'You're absolutely certain it's her?' asked Saul. 'Definitely her?'

'You must understand it took quite some time to sort through the Revolutionary Council's records,' Kayes explained. 'So many government records were destroyed in the early days, before the fighting ended.'

'I've been thoroughly informed of the political changes since the first gate failed,' Saul replied drily.

'Then I'm sure you understand why it took quite so long to be sure,' Kayes continued. 'But we are now *quite* sure.'

Saul felt momentarily dizzy. He stepped over to the launch that had been pulled up on to the beach and placed a hand on its hull. It felt very slightly slick to the touch. 'You're *absolutely* sure?'

Kayes nodded. 'It's your daughter, Mr Dumont. There's no doubt.'

To his consternation, Saul found that by the time he had arrived on Galileo he was already something of a cause célèbre. Once the Revolutionary Council had realized an invasion force was never going to come pouring through the starship, they had allowed Saul greater freedom, although he was accompanied always by Erkrnwald and other men who served the Revolutionary Council.

He quickly discovered that the Council had been working hard all those long years at reverse-engineering the technology within the defunct Galileo Array, so that they might learn how to create their own paired wormholes. Once they had heard Saul's story, the Galileans began talking excitedly about reconnecting with the other surviving colonies, all now stranded from each other with the destruction of the Lunar Array.

Sometimes, on those rare occasions he had a moment to himself, Saul would look up at the night sky and wonder if Olivia and Jeff were still alive. Even though he had no way of knowing, he felt somehow sure the answer was yes.

Sometimes, he thought, the one thing keeping him sane in the face of all that he had witnessed was the single goal remaining to him, coming ever closer as they crossed the choppy waters towards the nearest of the platforms.

They moored amid the tangle of rusty girders, conduits and concrete posts supporting the platform. The Galilean sun was like a pale spectre as it shone through a dense freezing mist that still clung to the surface of the ocean. They ascended in a steel cage that rattled and jerked as it was drawn upwards. Erkrnwald clapped his hands together, his breath frosting, a heavy coat wrapped tightly around his shoulders. Kayes, clearly of a hardier nature, eyed the political officer with a touch of disdain whenever Erkrnwald wasn't looking his way.

They'd awoken her that morning without explanation, it turned out, at just about the same time that Erkrnwald had also roused Saul from a sleepless night. He wondered how Gwen was taking it. He kept trying to picture how she must look now: she'd be sixteen, very nearly a full-grown woman. But, when he tried to picture her as an adult, he kept getting her mixed up with his last memories of Deanna. In his mind she was still the same little girl he remembered from ten years before, frozen in time like a snapshot, barely much more than a baby back then.

Kayes led them up a series of ladders to a walkway lined by doors with rusting latches, the air thick with the odour of burning petroleum. Kayes stopped at one of the doors and began to push it open.

'No,' said Erkrnwald, stepping up next to Kayes. 'I should speak to the girl's foster parents first. If you don't mind, Mr Kayes, we won't be needing you any longer.'

'That's all right,' said Kayes, flashing Erkrnwald a tight smile. 'I was looking forward to a chance to chat with our famous friend here. It'll pass the time while you *talk* to them.' Saul didn't miss the emphasis in Kaye's tone.

Something glinted in the political officer's expression. 'I'm sure Mr Dumont would rather gather his thoughts, given the circumstances. And I'm sure you have other duties to attend to.'

'Do you mind us talking, Saul?' asked Kayes, eyeing him with an innocent expression.

Saul tried not to smile at the look on Erkrnwald's face. 'I'd be happy to, Mr Kayes.'

'Jackson, please,' Kayes replied.

'Jackson.' Saul nodded.

Erkrnwald's face turned red with impotent fury and, for a second, Saul thought he might have pushed the man too far. But, after a moment, Erkrnwald pushed on past the door without a further word, letting it shut loudly behind him.

'Not tired yet of him trailing after you everywhere you go?' asked Kayes.

Saul let out a sigh. 'He spends half his time telling me who I can and can't talk to. It gets old fast.'

'That's the Revolutionary Council for you. They're turning out worse than the people they replaced. You know he's scared that your daughter or her foster parents will try and brainwash you into joining us out here, right?'

'Seriously?' Saul laughed out loud, though shivering in the cold air. 'Brainwash me how?'

A grin spread over Jackson's face. 'By offering you the chance to get away from people like Erkrnwald. See, he's talking to the wrong people. *I'm* the one who's going to try and brainwash you.'

A little while later they ushered Saul inside, where he met Gwen's foster parents in an anteroom. It was clear Gwen's foster mother had been crying, the father clearly agitated and jumpy. Saul assured them he had no intention of taking their daughter away from them and, in truth, he knew it had been long enough for Gwen's memories of him to perhaps have faded. Ten years was a long time, after all.

Even so, nothing felt more important to him than getting the chance to see her face-to-face, even if it was just the once. Saul caught Kayes' eye and nodded, before following Erkrnwald through to what appeared to be a staff cafeteria, with only a young girl sitting alone at a chipped plastic table, a mug clutched nervously in both hands.

She looked, thought Saul, just like her mother. He picked up a chair and sat down across the table from her, waiting until Erkrnwald had exited the room, and realized suddenly that he didn't know what to say. He sat there searching for something, for any suitable words at all.

'I know this can't be easy for you,' he finally managed to blurt out.

'You're . . . my father?' she asked tentatively. 'They . . .'

'Yes?' he asked.

'They told me you were dead.'

She wore a long overcoat, much like his own, and had pulled the sleeves down over her knuckles so that most of her hands were hidden except for the fingers holding on to the mug. She then put the mug down and started playing with the hems of her sleeves. Like her mother she had a wide, round face, and even wore her hair in much the same way, parted down the middle into thick braids and tied back in a bun. Her skin was a light chocolate colour, not quite as dark as his own. Beneath the overcoat, he could see she wore the overalls of a platform worker.

'No,' Saul shook his head, 'very much alive.' He looked around. 'You're . . . working here? And living here?'

She nodded, then glanced past him towards the same door he'd just come through. 'That man said I shouldn't talk to you about anything I do here. Not about my work or any of it.'

'Erkrnwald?' Saul grimaced. 'Ignore him.'

She nodded and smiled, a little less tentatively this time. 'Dad is . . . I mean, my foster father's a geologist. I'm at school, but I work too. Everyone here has to chip in.'

'While I was waiting outside, Jackson Kayes told me a bunch of stuff. He claimed the Revolutionary Council don't have much influence out here on the platforms. Is that true?'

Her eyes darted constantly between Saul and the fabric clutched between her knotted fingers. 'Dad . . . Gregory wanted to come out here once the platforms declared themselves an independent republic. I was a lot younger back then, but everyone on the platforms votes on everything. We all get involved in the major decisions.'

'Tell me,' he said, 'about your mother.'

Her face grew red and she swallowed. 'I . . . have trouble remembering. I was really small when it all happened. I think I just remember when you went away that last time, when we were living in Main Settlement, and I thought you weren't going to come back.' Her eyes glistened under the strip lights. 'And then you didn't . . . come back, that is. I'd almost forgotten about it, but then they told me you were the one on that ship out in orbit, and you'd been looking for me and . . .'

She did remember him, he realized.

He stood up, walked around the table and put his arms around her shoulders where she sat. She half-turned in her chair and pressed her face into his overcoat, breathing deeply. 'There's something you need to know about Mum,' she said, her voice muffled.

'It's okay. I already know.' Erkrnwald had already told him how the fighting had gone on for weeks following the collapse of the first wormhole – before the ASI forces trapped on Galileo by the collapse had been suppressed. A lot of people, it seemed, had got caught in the crossfire, and when they found Gwen, she'd been left all alone in their old apartment in Main Settlement for most of a week. Deanna had apparently gone out hoping to try and find food for them both, but she had never come back.

Gwen pulled back a little, her eyes darting up to his, and then down again. 'Are you . . . staying here?'

Saul fought to hold back the great swell of emotion that threatened to swallow him up. Kayes had already offered him a chance at a better life than anything Main Settlement could possibly offer him, and he had accepted the offer. Erkrnwald would wail and protest, but that would make no difference. He would be returning to the mainland alone, and damn the Revolutionary Council.

'Yes,' said Saul. 'For good, this time.'